THE
FLIGHT
GIRLS

THE FLIGHT GIRLS

NOELLE SALAZAR

mira

mira

Recycling programs for this product may not exist in your area.

ISBN-13: 978-0-7783-6922-6
ISBN-13: 978-0-7783-0916-1 (Library Exclusive Edition)

The Flight Girls

Copyright © 2019 by Noelle Salazar

Eleanor Roosevelt's quote from "My Day," September 1, 1942, appears courtesy of the estate of Eleanor Roosevelt.

For questions and comments about the quality of this book, please contact us at CustomerService@Harlequin.com.

BookClubbish.com

Printed in U.S.A.

For Harry and Allene

THE
FLIGHT
GIRLS

This is not a time when women should be patient. We are in a war and we need to fight it with all our ability and every weapon possible. Women pilots, in this particular case, are a weapon waiting to be used.

—Eleanor Roosevelt

My father once said, when my mother was pregnant with me, it felt like I was fluttering inside. "Like a tiny bird, trapped in its egg, straining to be free." And as soon as I could walk I was running, arms outstretched like little wings.

He always said I was more bird than girl, flitting about, leaping without looking, never afraid of the fall.

Trusting my wings would carry me…

PART ONE

OCTOBER 1941

CHAPTER ONE

Oahu

The surf swirled and frothed around my ankles as the sweet Hawaiian trade winds whispered through palm trees, carrying the scent of coconut oil across the sand to where I stood staring at the skyline.

"Audrey!"

I glanced over my shoulder to the three women sitting on a large blanket whisked from someone's bed this morning as we hurried out the door, hoping to arrive at Sunset Beach early enough to find a parking spot. The impending winter waves were bringing more and more surfers out, crowding my favorite beach and making it impossible to have a moment of solitude. As we'd feared, the lot was near capacity with army jeeps, woodie station wagons and Ford Coupes teeming with boards in every color and other assorted beach gear.

"Yes?" I shouted back.

Ruby, Catherine and Jean lay in different levels of repose, their skin gleaming in the late morning sun.

"You planning on standing there all day?" Ruby asked, adjusting the top of the new fire-engine red two-piece bathing suit Catherine had accused her of purchasing a size too small, the top straining to cover her bosom.

"Maybe."

"Well then, move this way a tick. I could use a little shade."

"Her wisp of a shadow ain't gonna help you much," Jean said, pulling off a wide-brim straw hat and fanning her face while fluffing the thick blond curls matted to her scalp with her other hand.

Catherine, resplendent in a white halter-style suit with a ruffle at the hem, flipped from her front to her back and sat up. "I've an entire lake between my breasts," she said, making two men strolling by take pause. She bestowed a coquettish grin on them and ran a manicured hand up and down one long leg. The kitten, always grooming, fussing, touching.

As I turned back to the water, I paused, my gaze hesitating on a man lying on his side thirty yards away. He looked up from his book and our eyes met.

Lieutenant Hart.

I sucked in a breath and turned away. For reasons I couldn't ascertain, the commanding officer of airmen recruits at Wheeler Army Airfield, and my boss's superior, unsettled me. Not in a fearful way. No, it was something else. Something quieter. Compelling. A fluttering that had nestled low in my belly the first morning we'd met on the tarmac four months ago and wouldn't settle. Try as I might, thoughts of him permeated my mind even when I wasn't training new pilots with him right under my nose. That he was often where we were on our days off didn't help.

The roar of the waves drowned out the sound of my heartbeat as they swelled, crashed and lapped onto the shore around me, calming my nerves and bringing me back to my reason for standing there.

Per the calendar tacked to the wall outside the break room of

the training hangar, I'd seen that a couple planes were scheduled to be parked at Haleiwa airstrip fifteen minutes south of
where we were and, knowing their route would take them up
through the middle of the island before looping around and
down, I wanted a front-row seat as they flew past.

"What time is it?" I called over my shoulder.

"Eleven thirty-six," Jean said. "Maybe they ain't coming after
all."

I peered north, listening for the sound of an incoming motor,
but nothing could be heard over the chatter of beachgoers, the
thud of a ball being hit in a game of volleyball nearby and Jimmy
Dorsey's "Green Eyes" playing on the radio of a car.

I sighed and raised a hand to shield my eyes from the sun,
scanning the horizon to the north. Something bumped my leg
and I glanced down at a vacant white-and-blue surfboard.

"Sorry about that, cutie," a male voice said, pulling the board
out of the water with ease and tucking it under his arm.

"It's fine," I murmured, waving my hand as though shoo-
ing a fly.

"What's so interesting out there that's got a sweet thing like
you so fascinated?" he asked, moving in, his arm brushing mine.

I straightened all of my five feet six inches, crossed my arms
over my chest and took a step away before looking up at Mr.
All-American. His blond hair still had the tracks from the comb
he'd pushed through it, and his well-built chest puffed with self-
importance. His audacity to both crowd and touch me without
approval attested he was everything I couldn't stand about the
male species. Most of them anyway.

My eyes flicked to the lieutenant and saw he was on his feet,
the book in his hand forgotten as he peered at the Adonis beside me.

I looked back up at the blond and he winked and grinned. The
sun glinted off his teeth as he unabashedly took in everything

from my wet hair to my modest navy one-piece. I blanched and
took another step back.

"You bothering my friend, Eddie?"

Ruby stood behind us, hands on her hips, the sun lighting up
her auburn hair like fire.

"Well, Miss Ruby Carmichael." He turned his gleaming smile
on my roommate. "How are you this fine afternoon? You still
spending time with that man Travis?"

Ruby giggled and I sighed. She had the worst taste in men.
They were always oversize in ego and undersized in brain.

"Oh, that was ages ago," she said. "I can't believe you even
remember."

"How can I forget when the sweetest gal I've ever had the
pleasure of meeting is seeing someone who isn't me?" he asked,
his eyes glued to her chest. "But no more, you say?"

"No more," she said in a breathy voice.

"Well then, can I interest you in a walk on the beach?"

"Don't mind if I do."

Had I been interested, I'd have been offended at how I'd
been not only ignored, but completely forgotten. As it was, I
was relieved.

I looked over at the lieutenant, who held my gaze for a moment before giving me a small smile and shaking his head. He
tossed his book onto his towel, waded into the water and dove
out of sight. He surfaced several feet away and began swimming,
his strong, measured strokes pushing him out to sea.

"Was Eddie giving you a hard time?"

I jumped as Jean materialized beside me. She stared down
the beach, narrowing her brown eyes behind the peach-framed
sunglasses that sat perched on the end of her upturned nose.

"I think he was going to try, but then he got distracted," I
said.

Jean snorted.

"That Eddie is doll dizzy," came another voice. I turned to

see Jean's friend Claire, a nurse we'd met our second day on the island, when Ruby thought she'd broken her wrist. Her eyes followed Ruby and Eddie, her pale lips pursed in disapproval, her frumpy pink sundress damp with perspiration.

"Ruby can handle him," Jean said. "She goes through men like Catherine does false lashes. She dumped poor Travis yesterday after only seeing him for two weeks."

"If that," I said.

"Sounds like a match made in heaven then," Claire said.

"Well," Jean said, nudging me with her elbow, "you may have lost out on Eddie, but you sure have our dear lieutenant's attention. He looked ready to defend your honor."

"Oh, he did not," I said, shaking my head.

"Mmm-hmm." She grinned and Claire nodded.

"Couldn't take his eyes off you," she said.

"I'm sure he was just concerned for the safety of one of his employees."

"Right." Jean smirked. "I'm sure that was it. Doesn't explain all the other times we've caught him staring at you though."

The two women tittered as I turned back to the horizon once more.

"He swam that way." Jean pointed and I pulled her hand down.

"I am not looking for the lieutenant," I said, my voice stern. "I'm looking for those damn planes that were supposed to fly in today."

"You girls and your planes," Claire said. "I don't understand it. They're so—"

"Shh!" I waved for her to stop talking.

The sound was faint, like static, but growing quickly into a hum.

My body tingled with anticipation. The air began to rumble with the vibration of the incoming engines and people on the beach stopped what they were doing, sitting up, the game of volleyball halting, surfers sitting on their boards, all eyes rising to the sky.

I grabbed Jean's hand as two Curtiss P-40 Warhawks roared toward us, the noses of their fuselages painted like shark faces, their wicked white teeth flashing as they flew past.

"Woo!" Jean shouted, waving at them.

"Gorgeous," I whispered.

"Too loud!" Claire yelled, her hands over her ears as she cowered behind us. "Golly, you gals are nuts for flying those things. How can you stand the noise?"

I glanced at Jean who feigned confusion. "Noise?" she said. "What noise?"

"My ears are gonna be ringing for the rest of the day," Claire said.

Jean put an arm around her friend's shoulders. "Come on. Let's go for a swim. Audrey? You coming?"

I searched the sky for a moment more, but the water beckoned, bumping up against my shins like a small, insistent child wanting to play. With a last look north for more planes, I eased in up to my waist and pushed off the soft ocean floor, taking long, lazy strokes parallel to the beach and keeping an eye out for incoming surfers.

I rolled onto my back. The waves undulated beneath me as I stared up at the bright blue sky and sighed, luxuriating in the feeling of freedom. It was all I'd ever craved, and coming to Hawaii had finally brought it to me. Far from my mother's all-seeing eyes. From who I was expected to be. From the responsibilities that came with being born into privilege—always having to attend the party, host the brunch and dress the part of the dutiful daughter of the Coltrane fortune. My father's accomplishments represented by the brand names on my clothing. But my mother came from old money, which added to the show. Diamond stud earrings, a tasteful gold signet ring, a string of pearls like a collar around my neck. A collar I'd strained against for twenty-two years until my father had mercifully cut me free.

At least for now. This island was my chance to prove to my mother, and myself, that I could support myself and earn the money it would cost me to buy the only thing I'd ever wanted to own—an airfield. It had been my goal ever since I'd grown sensible enough to dream it. Ever since I'd sat at one of my mother's many soirees and watched the women gossip over sparkling drinks while keeping their eyes on their husbands, prepared to tend to their every need, as the men talked and laughed over amber-colored drinks, never once giving mind to their wives. I didn't want to be like the women I was being bred to emulate— I wanted to be who *I* was.

My father could see it, and he encouraged it. When the opportunity arose to come to Oahu and instruct airmen recruits and earn a good wage doing it, my father not only insisted I go, but also bought my ticket, citing it a reward for my accomplishments at university.

"She deserves a little fun before settling down, don't you think, Gennie?" he'd asked my mother while I stood out of sight, straining to hear. "She's worked so hard."

"But a year?" she'd said.

"I seem to recall your own father sending you to Paris after you finished your schooling."

I'd had to bite my lip to keep from snickering. My father was always prepared for an argument. My mother often said he should have been a lawyer. But a lawyer didn't make half as much as an oilman.

"It's different and you know it, Christian. I have family there. And Paris is full of culture. Hawaii is full of…beach bums. Slovenly sorts all oiled up and barely making a living."

"Sounds divine," he'd said. "Sign me up."

She'd harrumphed and he'd laughed in response.

"That is hardly the case," he'd continued. "It is a vacation destination. George and Millie went last year and had a marvelous time. Don't be such a snob. Hawaii has plenty of culture, and it would allow our Audrey to earn a living doing the thing she loves best."

In the end she'd given in, all her efforts to convince, sway and bribe me to stay thwarted by the one thing she couldn't promise—freedom.

A surfer went down a few yards away and I kicked my legs to put some distance between us, accidentally striking a passing swimmer.

Not just any swimmer.

"Lieutenant Hart," I gasped, tucking in my knees and swimming backward as heat flooded my face. "I'm so sorry."

"It's fine, Miss Coltrane." His voice was low and deep, the surface of the water carrying it and making it sound as though he were closer, creating an air of intimacy in the midst of the dozen or so people frolicking nearby.

Little rivulets of water streamed down his neck from the dark hair slicked back on his head, giving me a clear view of his eyes, which—with the sun reflecting off them—were the color of the glass 7UP bottles Ruby was always leaving around the house.

He looked as though he might say more but then nodded and began to move away.

"Good day," he said, his voice once again landing softly in the shell of my ear.

"Good day," I whispered.

With a sigh, I swam back to shore.

A few hours later we packed up our belongings along with the other beachgoers, preparing to head home.

"Come on, girls," I said, slinging my bag over my shoulder. "Let's go. I'm starving and I only have a couple hours until my father calls."

Every Sunday evening like clockwork he called. He caught me up on the news at home: what society events Mother was planning, what fella my younger sister, Evie, was torturing, and I entertained him with stories of life on the island. He particularly liked my tales about Ruby. She was like a character in a book. "What's that Ruby up to now?" he'd ask.

After my father and I were through talking, my mother would get on the phone, her tone unrelenting in its disapproval. She would reiterate everything my father had told me, adding in all the minute details I couldn't care less about. If Evie was home she'd hop on after my mother, talking a mile a minute about this boy or that one. It could be exhausting, but I wouldn't miss the phone call for the world.

Jean, Catherine and Ruby—who'd returned from her walk with Eddie—threw their belongings into the trunk of the baby blue 1936 Ford convertible we'd all chipped in to buy when we'd arrived on the island, and then piled into the car.

I shoved my bag in next to the others, closed the trunk and climbed into the back seat.

"Looks like someone has an audience," Jean murmured as she backed out of our parking spot.

I turned to see Lieutenant Hart standing next to his car across the dirt lot, his eyes on me.

I chewed my lip and sank down in my seat, trying to ignore my quickened heartbeat and resisting the urge to let my own gaze linger. This was not the time in my life to get distracted by a man. Even if the man was Lieutenant Hart.

CHAPTER TWO

The wind whipped past my head as my warplane cut across the sky. Above me, streaks of pink and orange stretched from one end of the horizon to the other. Below, the Pacific Ocean sparkled with light and the shadow of my aircraft.

From the corner of my eye, I watched the silver plane keeping pace with me. I turned my attention to the array of gauges in front of me, checking each one in quick succession.

"Ready?" I asked the blue-and-yellow Fairchild PT-19.

She'd been sitting in the back corner of the training hangar for months, damaged during a training session last year. Bill, the old crew chief, had been fixing her up on his own time and I'd fallen in love with her at first sight. He'd let me take her up as soon as she was ready and I'd named her Roxy for her fiery attitude in the sky. Originally she'd been white with navy stripes down the sides of the fuselage, but Bill had let me pick new colors to paint her. Remembering Jenny, the little sunshine-colored plane I'd learned in so many years ago, I asked him to paint Roxy yellow with blue tips and stabilizers, and he'd delivered. She was recognizable everywhere for her bright colors, which had gotten me into a bit of trouble when Bill learned I'd been flat-hatting all over the island on my off hours. After getting grounded for a week, I stopped doing it as often. But it was hard to resist.

The silver plane moved closer and I grinned, biding my time. The AT-6 Texan may have been the faster plane, but the PT-19's smaller engine had its own benefits.

It wasn't about the plane though. It was about the pilot. And the pilot of the Texan was as green as the five-dollar bill Ruby was going to owe me when I beat her trainee in this race across the Hawaiian sky.

We sped toward the northern tip of the island, the goal to swing around, race back and touch down at the base first. The AT-6, as expected, hit the northern tip first, flying past it, going too fast and blowing his turn.

I laughed. Male pilots were all the same, their arrogance getting the best of them. And the trainees were sometimes the worst of all.

As he tried to correct, making a wide arc around, I pulled the throttle back toward my stomach.

The little plane slowed for a moment above Oahu's beauty before I gave it full throttle, using the rudder to roll as fast as possible. I idled and applied full opposite rudder to stop the roll as we dove, my heartbeat quickening as the nose dropped and sent me hurtling into a steep dive. I watched the gauges in front of me and held my breath, counting in my head before pulling the stick hard once more to complete the maneuver and level out, speeding now in the opposite direction and ahead of the AT-6.

"Winner!" Jean yelled as I climbed down from the landed plane a few minutes later with a grin.

There was a small commotion near the AT-6 and we glanced around the Fairchild to see Ruby's airman recruit jumping to the ground and running outside, his hand over his mouth. The Texan was notorious for making its pilots sick.

"Good job, Parker!" she yelled after him and then shook her head at us. "Damn kid just cost me five dollars." She linked her arm through mine. "Nice work."

"Thank you."

We hauled our gear to the supply room, discussing our dinner options as we hung our parachutes and stored our helmets and goggles.

"Ladies."

We stopped and nearly stood at attention, our gazes steady on our boss who had entered the tiny supply room behind us on silent feet.

Mae Burton would've been a soldier had they let her. Tall with gray hair pulled back tight, a daunting stare and the rigid stance of someone ready to give or take orders. She'd hired each of us after we'd answered the same call—an advertisement we'd all seen promoting the need for flight instructors on the island of Oahu.

The flyers had hung in airfields and airports around the nation, but you had to have a certain number of flight hours logged and your pilot license to apply. The four of us arrived within hours of each other that summer.

Jean hailed from St. Louis, where she'd earned her hours as a crop duster in the early mornings before working at her family's restaurant during the day. Ruby came from Kansas, disembarking her flight with lips the color of her name. Catherine, from Wisconsin—where the only ocean she'd ever seen was the green of the fields she'd flown above doing deliveries for the postal service—arrived with more bags than the rest of us combined. And I'd flown in from Dallas on the ticket from my father, a month after graduating college with a teaching degree, and a week after refusing an offer to take on a third-grade class at my old elementary school. Teaching, in my mind, had always been a backup plan. The real goal was to buy the airfield. Much to my mother's dismay.

Genevieve Elizabeth Rose O'Hare Coltrane was a force in pale pink Chanel, pecking out orders for my life, my future and the happiness she thought I was assured if she was at the helm.

It was quite funny to me, this vision my mother had of my life, so different from what I imagined—from what I wanted. She would never understand me, and I knew the real fight to live the life I wanted hadn't yet begun. And as much as I dreaded the confrontation, the hysterics and threats…I would not be shoved into this archaic mold she'd made for me.

"Reports?" Mae said and we handed over our reports for all the men we'd trained that day. "How'd they do?" she asked without looking at the paperwork.

"Fine, ma'am."

"Swell, ma'am."

"Could use some work on maneuvers, ma'am."

"Good. Good. Fine," Mae said, glancing at the report on top. "And who won the race?"

We glanced at one another, trying to keep the grins from our faces. I slowly raised my hand.

"Again, Dallas?" We were all a city or state to her. She never called us by name.

"Yes, ma'am," I said.

"Y'all need to work on your skills. Dallas is flying circles around you," she said, raising her eyebrows at the others before leaving us to finish stowing our gear. "Just don't let ol' chrome dome catch you racing in his precious planes."

Ruby and Catherine snickered as we glanced at Bill, who stood rubbing his bald head and swearing under his breath while staring at the engine of a half-gutted plane.

"Yes, ma'am."

"Good night, ma'am."

Jean snorted a laugh as soon as we were alone.

"God, that woman scares me," Catherine said, sinking onto a bench. "I thought we were about to get in trouble. And how does she know about the racing?"

"One of the boys probably told her," Ruby said. "I'll twist a few arms and find out who."

"Oh, leave them alone," Jean said. "If you terrorize those boys, you'll just confuse them, and they're already confused enough having to do what a bunch of women tell them to do all day long."

"Poor little pilots," I said as I backed out the door—and straight into Lieutenant Hart.

I cursed myself as I pictured him on the beach and felt my face heat. "My apologies, sir."

He nodded at the three women who'd exited behind me before meeting my gaze. "Miss Coltrane," he said. "I was looking for you."

"You were?" Ruby sidled up next to me. "For an after-work rendezvous perhaps?"

His cheeks turned as red as I feared mine were.

"Mae informed me of your…shall we call it…spirited teaching method?" he said.

I heard Jean swear quietly behind me.

"It's fine," he said, his lips curving up in a small smile. "I'm in favor, actually. I find a little friendly competition beneficial. Makes one think on their feet, so to speak. As long as everyone keeps to regulation and is safe, of course."

"Oh, we are, sir," Ruby said. "Always. I assure you."

"Wonderful," he said, his eyes locking on mine again. "I am wondering though about the maneuver I hear you've been doing in the Fairchild. Mae says you've been performing a low altitude split-S in it and I'm a little concerned. It's a daring and slightly reckless move, being performed with one of my men in it."

I bit my lip, my gaze lowering.

"It's been a while since I've flown a PT-19," he said. "I'd like you to take me through it so I can see it performed for myself."

"She'd love to," Catherine said, discreetly pinching me on the behind.

"Of course, sir," I murmured, my heart sinking. "I'd be happy to."

"Tomorrow morning then?" he asked. "Say at zero five thirty?"

"Yes, sir."

"Wonderful. Thank you, Miss Coltrane." He nodded at the four of us and walked away.

"Shit," I said under my breath as we headed to our car.

But the girls were excited, talking of nothing else all the way to Skip's, our favorite spot for burgers, fries and milk shakes.

"Did you see the way he focused on Audrey?" Ruby asked, resting her cheek on her palm dreamily during dinner. "He barely even noticed we were there. No man ever looks at me like that."

"Men look at you all the time," I said, dragging a fry through my vanilla shake. "He was only focused on me because he was angry."

"I don't think so," Jean said. "Concerned maybe, but not angry."

"I think he likes you," Catherine said. "Did you see the way he blushed when Ruby asked if he wanted to take you out?"

"She embarrassed him," I said, shooting Ruby a look.

"I think Catherine's right," Jean said. "I saw the way he was watching you on the beach the other day."

I sighed and pushed my plate away. "You gals done?" I asked.

"Why the hurry to get home?" Ruby asked. "Anxious to get a good night's sleep so you're fresh for your date tomorrow?"

I threw my napkin at her.

"Ruby," Jean said. "Don't you have a date tonight?"

"Oh shoot!" She stood and gestured for us to follow. "Shake a leg, ladies."

CHAPTER THREE

I woke before the other girls and tiptoed around Ruby's and my room, careful not to wake her as I tripped over her piles of clothes on the floor and dug through our closet for my last clean flight suit.

I dressed in the one tiny bathroom we all shared, shoving my legs into the suit and pulling it up over my shoulders, banging my elbow against the door as I zipped it.

After styling my hair in a Gibson Roll—*neat and tidy* were the army's requirements for our appearance—I splashed my face with cool water and patted it dry, brushed my teeth and swiped on a pink lipstick one shade darker than my natural color, hearing my mother's voice in my head. *You have no color, Audrey. Put on some lipstick. You'll scare people.*

Not that it mattered. I wasn't trying to impress anyone. Certainly not Lieutenant Hart.

I sighed. That wasn't exactly true.

There had been moments. Moments I'd replayed in my mind dozens of times after the lights had gone out and Ruby snored softly beneath her pink satin sheets in her twin bed across from mine. Moments I'd never admit to the girls, not even Jean who would understand and keep the conversation private.

At first I'd thought I was imagining it, the furtive looks he shot my way. The glances around planes. The reddened cheeks when we accidentally brushed up against one another as we passed through a doorway—or when our hands touched exchanging a clipboard. But it had happened so often, I knew I couldn't be dreaming it. I also knew I would have never noticed if I hadn't been looking too.

The fact that he'd piqued my interest at once infuriated me, embarrassed me and created an increasing curiosity. What was it that made me notice him? I'd gone all my life not giving a second thought to a man. Why this one?

I told myself he looked at me only because he thought me strange. It wouldn't have been the first time. Most men thought me odd. Pretty, smart, but odd. Intelligent, witty, beautiful even. But always also odd. And it wasn't just men who thought this. Women did too.

I grabbed an apple from the bowl on the kitchen counter and leaned against the sink, my eyes on the red clock on the wall. It was a sunny little kitchen with yellow walls, white countertops, a beige linoleum floor, and Catherine's jadeite bowls and canisters lining the counters and shelves.

The house was small and cozy, with furniture that barely fit more than one person at a time. The green sofa was hardly bigger than an armchair, and the dining table was meant for two, but we'd crammed four mismatching chairs around it regardless, our knees touching whenever we all sat down together.

In the center of the sitting room was a large soft rug with pale blue stripes, and on one of the walls was a large lauhala mat our neighbor and landlord, Erma, had made us when we'd moved in. Erma and her husband, Ken, lived at the other end of our little cul-de-sac with their four children. Ken often came by to make small repairs on the house. A creaky shutter here, a leaky pipe there. I never noticed any noise, but he swore the last time he'd been there, he had made a ruckus. I suspected Erma sent him though, because every time he left he invited me to lunch or dinner or some small gathering they were having. I had a feeling Erma had noticed I didn't go out as often as the other girls and thought I was lonely. Regardless of the reason, I was honored to be brought into the fold of their little family. I enjoyed learning their Hawaiian customs and tasting the cuisine.

I grabbed the keys of our shared car and slipped out the front door. The sky was a deep periwinkle as it waited for the sun to rise, and I took in a breath, smelling the plumeria that wafted from the yards of our little neighborhood, scenting the air with its sweet perfume.

"Good morning," I said to the guards at the security booth as I stopped to show them my badge.

"You're here awfully early, Miss Coltrane," Wes, a stocky young man with a shock of black hair, said.

"I am," I said, covering my mouth as I yawned.

He waved me through and I quickly parked and hurried to the training hangar, the humidity of the day already rising off the asphalt.

"Good morning, Bill," I said to the old crew chief who was limping around the hangar.

He grumbled. "You the reason I had to come in at this hour and pull out that little plane you love so much?"

I glanced at the Fairchild sitting proudly on the tarmac, her yellow nose raised and gleaming.

"You didn't give Roxy a hard time, did you now?" I said, my hands on my hips. "She's sensitive, you know."

"How do you know it's a girl?" he asked, wiping his face on a grease-stained rag.

"I'm no prude, Bill. I looked under her tail of course."

The bark of his laughter echoed off the metal walls of the hangar.

"So that's how you determine a plane's gender," a voice said from behind me. "I was absent that day of training."

My breath caught in my throat.

"Morning, Lieutenant," Bill said.

"Good morning, Bill," the lieutenant said. "Miss Coltrane."

I turned. "Good morning, sir," I said, my voice low as I allowed my gaze to rise and meet his.

He stared intensely for a moment and then looked at the plane.

"Shall we?" he asked.

"Yes, sir."

The blue began to lighten on the horizon as I flew us east across the Hawaiian sky, trying to ignore the lieutenant's presence in front of me in the trainee's seat he'd insisted on sitting in.

"You take the reins," he'd said. "You're the boss this morning."

I did a slow barrel roll over Diamond Head into one high-reversing Immelmann and then another. Each maneuver eased the tension in my shoulders a little bit more, the sight of the lieutenant's head inches from mine weighing heavily on me.

I breathed in the cool air, watching as a streak of tangerine seared the sky.

"I could look at that all day." Lieutenant Hart startled me as he spoke through the intercom system Bill had rigged in the little Fairchild.

Unlike the bombers and fighter planes, trainers didn't have radios. But after a near accident when a trainee didn't understand his trainer's signals to hand the controls over the week before we girls arrived on the island, Bill had mounted a microphone in each cockpit and wired two helmets with headphones. I'd only been shocked twice so far.

I stared at the back of the lieutenant's head. Was I to answer him? Was he commenting or making conversation?

I heard my mother's voice in my head, admonishing me. *Audrey, dear, it's impolite not to respond.*

While I struggled to find the right words, he spoke again.

"How long have you been flying?" he asked, turning his head slightly and giving me a view of his chiseled profile.

I sighed. This was easier. A direct question. I could answer a direct question.

"I began flying for the army on June fourth, sir," I said.

"And before that?"

"Oh!" I said, my cheeks coloring. "You meant— Twelve. I was twelve, sir."

"You've got me beat," he said. "I didn't start until I was fourteen. I grew up in a town with only a couple hundred people so finding someone to teach me wasn't easy. My mother ended up paying the crop duster two farms over to do it, much to my father's horror. Who taught you?"

"My father," I said. "And old Hal Hudson. He owns the little airfield I learned at."

"Your father, huh? He didn't worry about you flying?"

"He always wanted a boy so he was thrilled when I took interest."

"Is he a professional pilot then? Is that what he does for work?"

"No. Flying is a hobby," I said. "He works in oil."

My father *was* oil. Big oil. Texas oil. But I didn't talk about that here. Back home everyone knew I was the firstborn daughter of Christian and Genevieve Coltrane, and lived in the elegant farmhouse-style mansion in Preston Hollow. Here, I was just a girl who loved to fly. Which was the simple truth of me.

"And your mother? What does she think about you flying?" he asked.

"My mother would like my feet on the ground, preferably surrounded by several pairs of other little feet."

"Ah. I know this argument well," he said with a chuckle. "So how did you get her to let you come here?"

"I didn't," I said. "He did."

We zipped along Maui's northern coastline, passing Paia and glimpsing waterfalls in the deep-forested hills before rounding the northeastern tip to where the rugged shoreline of Hāna hid.

We flew across the southern part of the island toward Molokini. Below us the Pacific sparkled around the little crescent piece of land as though the sky had rained diamonds overnight. The yellow halo of the sun began to make its appearance, pulling the blue from the skyline as she prepared to make her grand entrance without competition.

I did another Immelmann and then dropped us lower for the split-S, my heart sinking. If I didn't do this well, I had a feeling I'd never be allowed to do it again.

I flexed my fingers and squeezed my eyes shut for a brief moment before pulling the throttle back.

I performed the maneuver as I always had, with precision and meticulous attention to my surroundings. The Fairchild, as she always did, glided effortlessly through the thick Hawaiian sky as I finessed her around and down, slicing through the air and then leveling out.

"Again," the lieutenant said.

I went through the maneuver three more times and then he took the controls and tried it for himself.

"Effortless," he said, giving the controls back to me.

"That's why she's my favorite," I said and steered us back toward Wheeler.

"She suits you."

I smiled in the island wind.

"What will you do after you tire of all this beauty?" he asked. "Will you find another base to teach at? Or maybe a flight school?"

No man had ever asked me that before. As though I had plans, a vision for my life other than what had come to be expected of a woman. As though I were more than just a creature whose mere existence was solely dependent on serving men.

"I'm going to buy an airfield," I said and held my breath.

But if I was expecting him to balk at my idea, I had another think coming.

"Do you have one in mind?" he asked.

I blinked. "I do," I said. "Hudson Airfield, where I learned. Hal wants to retire in a few years. I've let him know it is my intention to purchase it."

"Would you run it and hire others to do the flying for you?" he asked. "Or would you fly as well?"

"I have to fly," I said. "At least part-time. The place needs a lot of work. It's old and some of the hangars are leaning. There's a little café and general store I'd love to fix up."

"Is there a hotel nearby?"

"No, why?" I asked as I flew us west over the north shore of Oahu.

"If you had a small hotel, just a dozen or so rooms, then anyone flying in for the night could stay there instead of heading into town. Especially if it's a late flight in. Or an early one out for that matter. Might make you a few extra dollars."

My mind reeled. I knew just where it could go. There was a stretch of bare land where Hal had contemplated putting in another runway, but the airfield was so small, it really wasn't needed. A hotel though...

"That's a great idea," I said. "Thank you."

"You're welcome."

"Well, what about you?" I asked, mustering up the courage to ask some questions of my own. "Is flying a hobby or your life? Are there other things you'd like to do for the army?"

"If you can believe it—flying for the army is all I've ever wanted to do. Since I was five, maybe six. I saw a picture of my grandfather in uniform and knew it was for me. My plan is to keep rising in the ranks and then retire somewhere warm one day. Maybe here. Maybe elsewhere."

"And a wife? Kids?" I was glad he couldn't see my face as I blushed furiously at my own question.

"Maybe. But neither is high on my list of priorities."

"Oh," I said. "So you don't have... You're not..."

"Married? No!" he said and then threw back his head as he laughed. "Sorry. Did that sound terrible? I'm not against the idea. Not entirely anyway. I'm just not sure it's for me. I want to travel the world. You know, fly off for a weekend at a moment's notice. I don't know if that would be possible if I had a family. Did you think I was married?"

"I just thought... I often see you eating alone. And you go to the beach by yourself. I assumed you had someone back home. A wife. A fiancée. Something."

"I've noticed you spend a lot of time alone as well," he said. "Are you married?"

"No!" I said.

"You sound about as interested in the institution as I do."

"What gave me away?" I asked.

He chuckled low and deep in my ears.

"I know people think it's odd," I said. "It makes my mother crazy. She doesn't understand at all. But it's never been a goal of mine. I've dated, of course...mostly to keep her happy, but every man I've ever gone out with expressed, in no uncertain terms, that they thought it was nifty I like to fly, but no woman of theirs would continue to do so if she were to become their wife."

"Sounds like you were going out with the wrong men," he said.

"I don't think there's a right man for me," I said. "And that's okay. I like my freedom."

"I've encountered a bit of the same," he said. "The women I've taken out expect me to come down from the clouds once marriage is on the table and get a nice desk job. But I don't like wearing a suit and tie. So, as you can imagine, marriage never makes it to the table."

"And rightly so," I said.

"I have to say, you are a breath of fresh air, Miss Coltrane."

"And you have given me faith in the male species, Lieutenant Hart. Limited faith, but still, it's more than I had before we took off."

We bumped down onto the runway a few minutes later.

"That was spectacular," Lieutenant Hart said. "She handles better than I remembered."

"She's a good little plane."

"Her pilot isn't so bad either. I'll be your copilot anytime, Miss Coltrane."

But the moment we disembarked the lightness between us disappeared as we stood fidgeting with our goggles in the early morning sunlight, our eyes glancing off one another.

"Well, thank you for coming in early." He gave Roxy a pat. "And for reminding me what a great plane this is."

"You're welcome, sir."

He gave me that one-sided grin of his and raked a hand through his dark hair.

"Can I—"

"Sorry. I don't mean to interrupt," I said, checking my watch. "But I have to go. There's only one car between the four of us girls and I have it. I need to retrieve them before our shift starts or Mae will have our hides."

I swung the parachute from my back and pulled my helmet off, my updo not holding, blond strands tumbling around my face. I tucked them behind my ear and frowned as he held out his hand.

"I didn't know about the car," he said, his brow furrowed. "I'm sorry to inconvenience you. Let me take your things. I'll let Mae know it's my fault if you're late."

"Oh, you don't have to do that. Truly. I—"

"Your good manners are going to make you even later, Miss Coltrane."

"Right. Thank you, Lieutenant."

I ran for the car. There was no way we'd make it back in time. Mae would be furious, no matter what Lieutenant Hart said and even though he was her superior.

"Hurry, hurry, hurry," I muttered under my breath, waiting for the guards to wave me out.

We were six minutes late, ducking in and sprinting to the supply room to grab our gear.

"Nice of you all to show up," Mae said as we rushed back to the hangar, clipboards in hand. "Your assignments." She handed us each a small stack of paper.

I glanced down at the first name on my list. Corporal Harper was a favorite among us instructors. Somehow the arrogance gene so many male pilots boasted had skipped him, leaving a kind and intelligent young man who loved to fly and didn't care if his instructors were female. He was talkative, curious and always up for one of our shift-ending races.

Lieutenant Hart was already talking to the recruits, running them through the day's maneuvers, reminding them of their responsibilities as pilots for the army, and their manners.

The men dispersed at lunchtime and Ruby and Catherine went to the car to take a nap while Jean and I ate lunch in the break room with Mae.

"You girls give any more thought to that ferrying program I told you about?" Mae asked from behind the newspaper she was reading. "I hear Ms. Love ain't allowed to recruit anyone yet, but perhaps you should send her a letter if you're interested. I'm happy to write you a recommendation—not that I want to lose the two of you, but it might be a good opportunity."

Nancy Harkness Love. A pioneer for women in aviation. She'd participated in air races, performed as a test pilot and had even ferried a plane overseas. And now, Mae had heard she was trying to put a group of female pilots together for some sort of ferrying program for the military.

"I have," Jean said. "I just don't know if Joe will allow it. It was hard enough getting him to agree to this job. If it weren't for a wedding to pay for, he'd have said no. And I don't want to have to commit to a time period. We're supposed to get married next summer. Who knows how they'll be about time off. I can't get stuck halfway across the country from my fiancé when I'm supposed to be saying I do at the altar."

"What about you, Dallas?"

"I've given it some thought," I said, shoving my hands in the pockets of my flight suit. "I might be interested, depending on the timing."

"You'd get to travel all over the country instead of just doing circles around these islands."

"I like doing circles around these islands."

"That feeling will wear off," she said.

But there would be rules and uniforms in Ms. Love's program. More so, it sounded, than here. And having escaped my mother's strict regime only months before, I wasn't too keen on jumping back into a situation where I was being regulated. My job under Mae as a subcontracted pilot for the army was a dream. I flew during the day and went to the beach in the evenings, or just curled up on a blanket beneath the lemon tree in our backyard reading a book. And I was on my own here. Truly on my own, for the first time ever. No mother to poke her nose into my business. No father to lean on when things got stressful. No kid sister to complain to. It was just me, making it on my own. Making something of myself.

"Well, something to keep in mind," she said. "Shoot, if this war keeps on like it has been, they may ask all of us to give a hand ferrying those planes, here and overseas. And if the war comes here, they may even ask us to fight. I'd happily pick up a gun and fight those Nazi bastards."

She left the little room then and I picked up the newspaper she'd left on the table. USS *Kearny* Torpedoed Off Iceland, the headline read. My heart sank. The war was getting closer.

Being on the island, surrounded by officers whose lives were dedicated to the protection of their country, rather than at home where the war was barely spoken of in most circles, made me feel a part of the wider world. In Dallas they called it Europe's war. A clear distinction. It was not ours. It was spoken of in passing mostly. Comments about a news report read or heard, but many had no interest in getting involved. It was "their" problem.

Here on Oahu, talk of the war was more commonplace. There was still debate over whether the United States should enter or not, but the officers were trained for war—and many were keen to get in it.

Even in our home the opinion was split. Catherine and Ruby thought it not our place to enter.

"It's none of our business," Ruby had said one day.

"People are dying just for being who they are," Jean argued. "For being born!"

"I just don't think it's up to us to save the people of another country. Their own people should stand up and do it."

Jean had sighed and thrown her hands up in exasperation. "She just doesn't want any of her playmates taken from her," she'd said to me later. "God forbid there be one less oversize dimwit for her to kiss."

I'd nodded in agreement.

Jean and I, two women who above all else loved the freedoms we'd fought to attain and that life had rewarded us, believed that as a country we should rise up and wield our power for the good of those being tormented and killed. Would lives be lost? Yes. Would fathers, brothers and sons once again be sent overseas to give their lives for a war that wasn't theirs? Yes. But by doing so, lives would be saved, countries salvaged, the world would be stronger for it, and freedom would be a right afforded to every man, woman and child.

"We're just two girls whose opinions only began to matter twenty years ago—and even then we've got a long way to go. We're not even allowed to join the military."

I chewed my lip as I read the end of the article about the USS *Kearny*. Eleven men had been killed, a couple dozen more injured. I sighed and folded the paper in half and set it on the table. Targeting our ships could only mean one thing. Our inclusion was imminent, and the outcome of our country joining would change us all.

CHAPTER FOUR

The grim news from overseas continued to permeate our daily lives. But we carried on as if we didn't have a care in the world, playing in the Hawaiian sunshine and going about our simple lives.

And when we did have moments of fear, the men Ruby and Catherine hung around with were quick to assure us that America was too strong to be worried about being attacked—and too smart to get involved in other people's business.

Their ideals left me feeling uneasy and slightly sickened.

"They can't touch us," Don said as he reclined on our little sofa, Ruby at his feet, one Saturday evening in November. "They wouldn't even dare. Have you seen those battleships out there?" He waved in the direction of the harbor. "They'd have no chance. And right next to the ships is a fleet of planes! Planes with guns! I will admit I'm a little disappointed though. I'd love to get a piece of this war. Get in the action. Show those Nazi bastards where the real power is."

He flexed a bicep and Ruby swooned.

I eased out of my seat at the dining table where I'd been reading and walked down the hall to my bedroom. I hated the way
he spoke, arrogant and foolish. I didn't know how Ruby could
stand him.

I pulled a navy sweater from the closet and slid on a pair of
shabby sandals I'd bought when I'd first arrived on the island in
lieu of the several pairs of heels my mother had insisted I pack.
Grabbing my handbag from the hook on the wall, I glanced in
the full-length mirror on the back of the closet door. My hair
hung in loose waves around my shoulders and my cheeks were
pink from the anger I'd been holding back listening to Ruby's
beau speak.

After brushing the tube of pink across my lips, I returned
to the sitting room. "Anyone mind if I take the car?" I asked.

"Where are you going?" Jean asked.

"I'm not sure yet, but I won't be late." I fixed Don with a stare.
"You can drive them if they want to go out, can't you, Don?"

He swept his arms wide. "Wherever you ladies desire, Don
will take you."

I kept myself from rolling my eyes and grabbed the keys, waving as I hurried out the front door.

I drove into Honolulu, unsure of where I was going as I
cruised down the main strip. Dozens of people roamed about,
laughing and spilling into the streets, entering and exiting clubs,
enjoying the warm Saturday night. Just a bunch of carefree
Americans. If I'd wanted peace and quiet, I'd come to the wrong
place.

I parked and got out of the car, stood on the sidewalk and
looked up and down the street. A block up was the Varsity Theater. A movie would be dark, quiet, and there was popcorn. Perfect. I hadn't eaten dinner and I was famished.

How Green Was My Valley was still playing. Last Weekend!
the sign on the ticket window said. I bought a ticket, a soda and
popcorn and found a seat near the back in an almost empty row.

The newsreel before the picture was filled with disturbing images of smoking planes spiraling out of control, buildings in flames and crumbling, and towns that had become nothing but rubble. Soldiers sat injured and bleeding. Hitler gave yet another speech. And the Jews kept walking, walking, walking… One would think we'd become numb to it by now, but I nearly abandoned my soda and popcorn and left the theater, sickened by the despair and destruction and inexplicable loss of life.

But this is what I had wanted to see, even if I hadn't realized it. I'd wanted to be reminded of what was happening after that horrible man back at my house had spoken. That man—so full of himself, so proud and bloated with his own self-importance— he didn't know what he was talking about. We were Britain's ally. If they needed us, surely we would go eventually. If not… what would that say about us as a country?

Movement to my right caught my attention and I glanced across the empty seats to find Lieutenant Hart sitting alone, watching the screen. I looked away, turning my attention back to the screen, my heart quickening as I wondered if he'd seen me too.

"Miss Coltrane."

I gasped and looked up. Lieutenant Hart stood an arm's reach away from me, a small, hesitant smile on his face, which, in the dim lighting of the theater, felt intimate and made my insides tighten.

"Lieutenant," I said in a soft voice.

"Are you alone?" he asked, pointing to the seat beside me where my sweater and handbag resided, as though trying to determine if I was saving it for a friend.

"I am," I said.

"May I?"

Had he been any other man I'd likely have told him I didn't own the theater and he could sit where he liked. But this was Lieutenant Hart.

"Yes. Of course."

He nodded and lowered himself into the seat. "M&M?" He reached across the seat between us, a box of the colorful candy in his hand.

My breath was stolen from me as I met his gaze in the darkness. He smiled again, this time less cautious than before.

I held out my hand. "Just a few," I said. "Thank you."

The movie began and in silent agreement, we passed the popcorn and candy back and forth, every so often brushing against one another, buttery fingertips grazing sweet candy-scented ones.

When the lights came up over an hour later, I stood and gathered my things, preparing to hurry out.

"You wouldn't be interested in getting a bite to eat, would you?" Lieutenant Hart asked, holding up the empty box of candy. "This and your popcorn really don't constitute dinner. I'm famished. Have you eaten, Miss Coltrane?"

"I haven't but…" What if someone saw us?

"Have you been to Kemo'o Farms?" he asked.

"I've not, though I've heard it's wonderful. I'm just not sure… If people saw us they might think…" My face grew hot and I was glad to still be standing in the dim theater.

He frowned. "Oh. Right. I see. Well, I'm not opposed to setting anyone straight who might have untoward thoughts about us if that helps sway your decision? And I promise I have no other intentions. It would just be an opportunity to have good food. Nothing more. Except possibly some mediocre conversation."

"Mediocre conversation?" I couldn't help grinning. "Well now, that does sound enticing, Lieutenant."

"I'm an excellent salesman when it comes to my own virtues."

"I can see that," I said. "Well, it's hard to pass up a bad discussion so, yes. That sounds swell. Thank you for the invitation, sir."

He held up a hand.

"One condition. No 'sir,'" he said. "No 'Lieutenant Hart'

either. We are not on base, Miss Coltrane. Mae is nowhere in sight. Please—call me James."

"Then I'm Audrey," I said, my voice soft. "No 'Miss Coltrane.' And definitely no 'ma'am.'"

"Done," he said and escorted me out of the theater.

We exited right into the center of what looked like a sailor convention, the sea of white seemingly unending.

"Whoa!" Lieutenant Hart said, pulling me out of the way of a young man who was clearly inebriated and weaving in and out of the crowd and straight into us. "Watch it, swabbie."

As he shooed one away, another appeared.

"Hi, cutie!" A round, freckled face materialized inches in front of mine. "You rationed?"

"Yes," Lieutenant Hart said, stepping between us, his hand on my arm. "She is."

The man wandered down the sidewalk to the next young lady.

"Sorry," he muttered and ushered me across the street, still holding my arm. "Better to say yes than give him an opportunity to persist."

The warmth of his hand caused goose bumps to rise on my skin and I inhaled and pulled away, rubbing the spot where he had touched as our eyes met.

"Thank you for defending my honor," I said.

"It is my duty to serve, Miss," he said, tipping an imaginary cap.

A laugh escaped me as I pictured the man's freckled face. "He was so drunk, I honestly don't think he knew the difference between me and a lamppost."

The lieutenant laughed in response and then sobered, his green eyes serious as he stared down at me.

"Oh he knew," he said, his voice soft and low.

He took me in a borrowed army jeep to Kemo'o Farms. The Home of the Sizzling Steaks, the sign out front read. We were led through a main dining area with walls of rich dark wood, gold-framed paintings of the islands displayed here and there, and tables covered in dark green tablecloths, presumably to hide any grease stains from the famous steaks. We were seated at a small table for two on the patio, with a pretty pink arrangement of flowers in a jar in the middle, and a good view of the band that was about to start playing beneath a string of white lights with a backdrop of palm trees, orchids and moonflowers.

"Do you come here a lot?" I asked from behind the safety of my menu.

"Usually only on weekdays when it's less crowded," he said.

We ordered beers and, as the alcohol took effect, began to loosen up, the conversation becoming easier to navigate and less inhibited. The steaks were some of the best I'd tasted and we swapped stories as we ate. James grew up on a small farm in Iowa with a banker father and a mother who was a nurse. He had a younger sister, Ava, who sounded a lot like my own sister, Evie, and his best pals, four boys from the same town, had all enlisted the same day he did.

"All but Cal," James said. "He had an accident that took half of one of his legs during our sophomore year of high school. When we left for basic training, he threatened to steal all our girlfriends."

"That's awful," I said. "Poor Cal."

His bark of laughter surprised and pleased me.

"Poor Cal nothing," he said. "He gets more action than most of these sailors."

"In Iowa?"

"In Iowa," he said. "He has no shame in using that leg for leveraging a woman's indecision."

He was easy to talk to, and halfway through dinner I found I wasn't overthinking everything I said, worried he might take it as an invitation as so many had before him.

"Thank you for bringing me here," I said, dabbing the corners of my mouth with my napkin and sitting back in my chair. "This was lovely."

"Thank you for letting me," he said. "Look at us—getting along."

"Did we not get along before?"

"I just meant—I've always been hesitant to strike up a conversation. And you never seemed particularly inclined… Of course, now I know why. But here we are, dare I say enjoying one another's company and not feeling the least bit awkward about it?" He rubbed his jaw and grinned. "Well, maybe a little awkward."

"But only a little," I said with a shy smile.

He chuckled and then his expression turned serious as he nodded to someone behind me. I turned to see a formidable man with a gray mustache taking a seat at a table with an equally stern-looking blond woman who was undoubtedly his wife. Military wives, I'd found, were in a class all their own. And this one, with her steely eyes and hawkish nose, looked as though she could lead her own brigade.

"Who's that?" I asked in a low voice.

"The commanding general at Schofield Army Base and his wife."

Seeing the austere man brought up feelings I hadn't let myself ponder since my first days on the little island. It had been exciting flying to a new place and my heartbeat seemed to do double-time as we flew over the vast Pacific. And then it would begin to pound, a thin layer of sweat rising on my face and under my arms.

Of course I knew how far Oahu was from the US mainland. Of course, as a pilot, I'd pored over my favorite, well-worn map, plotting a course as if I were to be the one flying the plane. But never once did I imagine how seeing so much blue beneath me would make me feel.

Excitement would wane as fear began to take its place. Compared to Texas, Oahu was tiny. And in the middle of an ocean.

Leaving it vulnerable to many things—like another larger island farther west.

We all knew America's relationship with Japan was strained. And who was to say the Germans wouldn't make a strategic move to attack us? It must be a thought in somebody's head. I couldn't be the only one. And, while the Territory of Hawaii wasn't technically one of the United States, we had millions of dollars in military personnel and equipment here.

It had taken days of Ruby's nonstop chatter, Jean's inquisitive questions and Catherine's constant grooming for me to quiet the quaking inside my body in those early days. But still, in the silence of the night, when everyone slept and I lay awake staring at the ceiling, I thought back to those ships and this tiny island—so vulnerable despite the massive weaponry. So exposed.

I took a sip of my water, wondering if it would be inappropriate to ask, and finding I didn't really care. I needed to know.

I leaned forward, ignoring the voice of my mother in my head reminding me of no elbows on the table.

"Can I ask you something?" I said in a hushed voice.

James gave me a small smile and leaned toward me. "Anything."

"Should we be worried? We're sitting in the middle of the ocean and…I know we have those great big ships in the harbor, men on the ground, planes, but…are we in danger? Is Hawaii in danger?"

He sat back, his eyes taking in every inch of my face, before he leaned in again, a frank look on his face.

"I honestly don't know," he said. "I haven't heard anything, if that's what you're asking—not that I could say if I had…" He glanced at the table where the general sat and then back at me and shook his head before saying the words I'd only felt but hadn't spoken aloud. "But I'll tell you—while being out here in the middle of the Pacific on this beautiful island is idyllic—I can't help but feel vulnerable. Exposed."

"Even with all those battleships in the harbor?"

"Maybe even because of them."

He drove us back to the city and parked three cars down from mine on University Avenue, turning off the ignition. The effects of the beer had worn off and we'd both returned to feeling awkward, not knowing where to look, words evading us.

Outside the car, the city pulsed around us, sailors yelling across the street to women who shouted back, music and laughter muted by the glass and metal of the vehicle encasing us.

"Thank you for dinner," I said. "I enjoyed it."

"You sound surprised," he said and I blushed. "I wish you would've let me pay."

I shook my head. "It wasn't a date."

"I know, but I feel like a lout regardless. My father would be mortified." He furrowed his brow and raised a finger. "'A man always pays for a lady, James.'"

I laughed. "I hear my mother's voice in my head constantly. 'Elbows off the table, Audrey.' 'You're not leaving the house in that, are you, Audrey?' 'Audrey Fitzgerald! Cross your ankles, for goodness' sake! Are you trying to give it away?'"

James rested his head against the headrest and laughed.

"How is it they never leave us?" he asked. "No matter how old we are?"

"I've no idea," I said. "It would be endearing if it weren't so infuriating."

He glanced over at me with that crooked grin of his and I held my breath, waiting for him to say something.

"Audrey Fitzgerald?" he asked.

"My middle name." I blushed. "My father is a fan of F. Scott."

"I like it."

"Thank you," I said.

"Can we do this again sometime?" James asked.

I opened my mouth and shut it, turning to stare blindly out the windshield as several emotions swirled around my typical reflex to this sort of question. By nature I felt I should say no, it was not a good idea. He was a distraction. But instinct told me I had nothing to fear from this man. He understood me, and my reasons for not engaging in romantic relationships. He had his own reasons for doing the same. But was it a ruse? Surely not. He'd had more than one opportunity to approach me before and he never had. It was only upon happy coincidence that we ended up at that movie. Having dinner had been an almost natural progression for two professionals needing a meal.

"My feelings won't be hurt if you say n—"

"Yes," I said, before I could think about it anymore.

"Yeah?" A little sigh escaped his lips as my heart pounded. Our eyes didn't seem to know where to focus, bouncing off every surface of the car before finally landing on one another.

"Well," I said, grabbing the door handle. "I suppose I'll see you Monday."

"You will. May I walk you to your car?"

"No, thank you, Lieutenant. Have a nice night."

"And you, Miss Coltrane."

I glanced back once before getting into my car. Lieutenant Hart sat behind the wheel of the jeep watching me. I smiled and he waved, and then I got in and drove home.

CHAPTER FIVE

Thanksgiving came two weeks later. The girls and I hosted a casual buffet-style meal for our neighbors and several of our friends who had no family on the island. Which included James, invited by me, red-faced, at the insistence, whining and constant badgering of my roommates.

"Happy Thanksgiving, Miss—Audrey," he said, holding out a bottle of wine when I opened the door. "Thank you for the invitation."

"I'm glad you could join us. Please come in." I stood aside and let him in. "Everyone is in the backyard. Please make yourself at home."

I pointed to the back door, open off the kitchen, and he made his way through the house, smiling and looking around at the typical friendly Hawaiian decor provided by Erma and Ken, and sprinkled with items indicating our different personalities. My stacks of books, Catherine's vanity case in the corner, one of Ruby's silk scarves over a lampshade and Jean's ever-present bottle of red nail polish on the windowsill.

"Can I help you ladies with anything?" he stopped to ask Jean and Ruby in the kitchen.

"Oh!" Jean said. "Lieutenant Hart. Aren't you a peach to ask? But don't even think about it. Just enjoy yourself."

"James," he said. "Please."

"Happy Thanksgiving, James," Ruby said with a little wag of her hips, making her burgundy pleated skirt swish around her knees. "There are drinks and hors d'oeuvres outside. Help yourself."

"Thank you," he said and exited into the yard.

I watched out the kitchen window as James grabbed a beer and struck up a conversation with Marty, the bartender from Skip's. As soon as he'd stepped outside everyone had turned to look at him, even little Annie, Erma and Ken's five-year-old daughter who had been clinging to her mother's leg. It was the way it was with him. People stopped whatever they were doing so they could observe him, hear what he was saying, look at what he was wearing—which was a pair of tan slacks and a navy short-sleeved button-down that somehow made his eyes seem greener than they were.

"He's sort of spectacular, isn't he?" Jean asked, standing beside me so that our shoulders touched.

"Look how everyone stops to stare at him," I said. "It must be irritating."

Jean chuckled. "I don't think he's aware."

"How could he not be?" I asked. "Look at them."

"Do you notice?" she asked, leaning her slender hip on the counter and taking a bite of one of the celery sticks she'd been cutting.

"Do I notice what?"

"People have the exact same reaction to you."

I frowned. "They do not."

"See?" she said, picking up the tray of vegetables. "Oblivious."

She slipped out the back door and I glared at the space she'd just vacated.

"Well, that's not true," I said.

"Talking to yourself, hon?" Ruby asked. "Ooh! Did James bring that?" She pointed to the bottle of wine still in my hands. "Pour me some, will you?"

I poured us both a glass and then grabbed mine with one hand and a dish of corn with the other before joining the party outside.

I did my best impersonation of my mother, flitting from one group to the next, making sure glasses were full, and dirty plates and unsightly napkins were taken away.

But no matter how busy I kept myself or what conversation I contributed to, every time I looked up, James was right there. Even when I went inside to grab a tray of cookies, there he was, sitting on the sofa in the living room commenting on the new construction in downtown Honolulu with Erma's husband, Ken, and playing hide-and-seek with Annie.

"Audrey!" Annie said, wrapping her sticky brown arms around my legs.

"Hello, bunny," I said, kneeling down and handing her a cookie off the tray I was holding. "You having fun?"

She nodded and held up the little stuffed dog she was never without. I kissed his nose.

"How is Flower?" I asked.

"Flower naughty. She eat my turkey."

"Mmm-hmm." I glanced up at Ken who smiled and shook his head. "Is that what you told your mama?"

The little girl nodded, her shiny dark hair swaying back and forth.

"Well, you must be starving then. You should probably have two cookies."

Her dark eyes widened. "Yes!"

I handed her another cookie and she scampered out the back door.

"You're good with her," James said as Ken followed his daughter outside.

"It's all about bribery," I said. "Cookie?"

He peered at me and then the cookies. "Consider me bribed." He chose a chocolate-dipped shortbread cookie and took a bite.

"How is it?"

"Delicious."

"Good. I made them."

"You should go into business."

"Right after I buy my airfield."

"You could put them on the pillows of your new hotel."

"In the shape of little airplanes!" I said.

As the sun began to set, our guests took their leave, gathering their belongings, thanking us for a lovely time and hugging us goodbye.

As I pulled a tablecloth off a picnic table, James took hold of one end and brought it to me, our fingers brushing ever so slightly as he let go and I grabbed on to the flimsy fabric.

"Word is we're getting a new crop of recruits in a couple weeks," he said. "Would you girls be interested in some extra hours?"

"I would," I said. Anything for my airfield. "What day?"

"They come in the sixth and the boss wants them logging hours early the next day."

"That's a Sunday?"

"It is."

I finished folding the tablecloth and draped it over my arm as I peered at Catherine and Ruby, who stood nearby with Marcus, the man Catherine had been dating for the past month, and Francis, a musician Ruby had invited. Both men were tall with dark hair and could've been brothers, much to Jean's and my amusement and Ruby's and Catherine's delight. They'd oft said they should find a pair of twins to date, as they seemed to like the same boys. Thankfully, Don had been left off the guest list.

"I'm not sure the others will be up for it," I said. "Catherine and Ruby are throwing a little beach party that Saturday night. I can ask, but it's doubtful they'll say yes. Jean might be up for it though."

"Well, let me know," he said.

"I will." I smoothed the fabric on my arm, my gaze on the grass as I struggled to speak. "You're welcome to come to the party."

"At the beach?"

I nodded, unable to meet his eyes.

"I'd like that. Thank you." Now it was his turn to stare at the lawn. "Would you— Could I interest you in going out for a drink?"

"Now?"

"Or, in a few minutes from now. It doesn't have to be this second."

I glanced at Catherine and Ruby, who were grabbing sweaters and moving toward the house with Marcus and Francis.

"It looks like Catherine and Ruby are about to leave and there's so much to clean up still. I'd hate to leave Jean alone with the mess. Plus, I'd have to tell them I was going and..."

"Would it really be that bad, their knowing we enjoy one another's company?"

"You don't know the half of it. They're insufferable. I'd have to find a new place to live."

He laughed as Jean stepped outside. "Claire called," she said. "Her shift at the hospital just ended so I'm going to meet her at the Royal for a few drinks. Wanna come?"

I glanced at James, who had picked up a newspaper someone had left behind and was pretending to read.

"I think I'll just stay here and clean up."

She looked around and wrinkled her nose. "It can wait until tomorrow. Come with me!"

"I'm tired. Really. Tell Claire hi for me."

"Okay. Fine," she said and turned her attention to James. "I'm so glad you could come, Lieutenant."

"I'm grateful for the invitation," he said. "Thank you again."

I stood looking around the backyard as the last of the guests left and then it was just James and me, alone in the yard, the little twinkle lights Ruby had hung shining against the navy sky.

"So?" he said, his voice soft. "How about that drink?"

The hairs on my arms rose as something deep and low in my body tightened.

"Maybe just one," I murmured.

"Where are we?" I asked, getting out of the jeep after he'd pulled into a nondescript parking lot just off the main road.

"Haleiwa Airfield," he said, his voice muffled as he grabbed something from the back seat. "You were watching planes fly into it a few weeks ago from Sunset Beach."

"I remember," I said.

"Come on," he said, gesturing to me to follow him.

There was a path that led from the parking area through the trees to a patch of beach just north of where the airfield started. James put down the towel he'd brought and placed a paper bag in the center.

"Beer or wine?" he asked, taking a seat.

"Beer."

He pulled two from the bag, opened both and handed one to me. We each took a sip and then he reached into the bag again.

"I stole these," he said, pulling out something wrapped in a napkin.

"Isn't that one of our napkins?" I asked.

"I only borrowed that."

He peeled back the napkin to reveal four chocolate-dipped shortbread cookies.

"So that's where they all went," I said with a laugh.

"If I couldn't get you to come for a drink, I was going to have to be satisfied with eating these in bed later."

I took a cookie and we ate in silence, sipping our beers, listening to the waves crash on the shore.

He rubbed a hand over the stubble on his chin. The sound reminded me of my father and a wave of sadness washed over me. This was the first holiday I hadn't spent with my family. I'd felt it when I'd woken that morning, the strangeness of not being with them, the loneliness of getting dressed without Evie banging in and out of my room, pilfering my nylons, my rouge, my shoes…

My mother always had nearly identical dresses made for us. I wondered what color they would've been this year. What different details they would've had. Would I have worn pearls with mine? Or perhaps the sapphire pendant I'd gotten for my eighteenth birthday that sat in an ornate ceramic box on top of the white bureau that had been my mother's when she was a girl.

"If I tell you something," James said, "do you promise not to get angry?"

Pricks of anticipation made their way up my spine. "That's a hard promise to make when I don't know what you're going to say."

He chuckled. "Fair enough." He turned to look at me, his gaze meeting mine over the paper bag between us.

"What is it?" I asked.

"I like you," he said.

The words hung between us.

"I wish I didn't," he continued, turning so that he was facing the beach once more. "It doesn't change anything about how I intend to live my life. But I needed to tell you. I needed to say it. In case I never have another chance."

I dropped my head, tears welling in my eyes.

"You're mad," he said. "I'm sorry, Audrey. I shouldn't have—"

"I thought you were going to say you're leaving," I said, my voice catching. "I thought you'd received a new post and...I'm not ready to say goodbye yet."

"Why not?"

I closed my eyes and lifted my head, desperately not wanting to be having this conversation but, like him, also wanting him to know.

"Because I like you too," I said, my voice soft. "But, James—" I turned to face him. "It's not enough. For me. You understand that, right?"

"I do. Because I feel the same way. If I were different—if *we* were different—you would be the one I'd want to spend my time with. You are witty and intelligent and kindhearted. And I hope we will always stay in touch. No matter how much time goes by. I will always be curious what you're doing. What books you're reading. What planes you're flying. If you've built the hotel I suggested. Maybe one day I'll even fly into your little airfield and you can give me a tour of Dallas."

"That'll cost extra," I said.

"And I will pay it happily."

The trade winds carried the sweet scent of flowers over us and I breathed it in and rested my chin on my knee, staring out at the horizon.

"I almost can't imagine going back to Dallas," I said. "I love it here."

"It will be hard. But if we stay, we'll never get where we're both trying to go."

He raised his bottle. "A toast," he said.

"What are we toasting?" I asked, raising my own bottle.

"Our dreams. And our friendship. No matter the distance or how much time passes, may we always remain friends."

"I'll toast to that," I said.

I don't know how it happened and, if asked, I don't think he would either. One moment our bottles had clinked together, the next his lips were on mine.

His fingertips traced the lines of my face as I ran my palm along the scratchy surface of his jaw, thrilling as the stubble bit into my skin. His lips were soft, gentle, almost hesitant as I leaned into him, overwhelmed by a passion I'd never felt before. But as soon as his arms slid around me, pulling me closer, I gasped and pulled away.

We didn't say anything for a long moment, our gazes averted as we caught our breath.

"I'm sorry," he finally said, his voice hoarse.

"I don't know why I did that," I whispered.

I peeked at him. One side of his mouth rose in a crooked grin and I chuckled and looked away.

"Still friends?" He held out a hand.

"Still friends." I reached out to shake it.

Electricity sparked off our skin and we yanked our arms back.

"Maybe no physical contact though," he said. "To be on the safe side. Deal, friend?"

"Deal."

CHAPTER SIX

At least three-dozen people came to the party on the beach. We sat in small clusters around a bonfire, sharing food and drinks, and enjoying one another's company as the sun slowly made her way to the horizon, turning the sky into a brilliant pink-and-orange masterpiece.

Ruby, ever the perfect hostess, flitted from group to group, effervescent in a pale green romper, her auburn hair swept off her face in two victory rolls. Catherine too took her duties as hostess seriously, looking lovelier than ever in a white sundress, her hair held back by a pale pink scarf. But after making the initial circle to greet everyone, she sat beside Marcus and looked content to stay there for the remainder of the night.

Jean had camped out on a huge blanket with Claire and two other women I recognized but had only spoken to a couple of times since moving to the island. She wore a sundress with ties at her shoulders that perfectly matched her forever red-painted fingernails.

As the sun dipped below the ocean, two of the men pulled out guitars and began playing.

"This reminds me of being back home," James said, sitting beside me on a blanket he'd pulled from the back seat of the jeep. "We used to go down to Clear Lake on hot summer nights. Couple of guys would bring guitars. Another one or two would sneak beer from their folks..." He grinned in the dimming light. "It was a good time. What about you? You ever do anything like this in Dallas with just your girlfriends?"

"Lake Grapevine," I said as a warm breeze ruffled my hair and pulled a tendril loose from the yellow scarf holding it back.

I'd worn it down for once, letting the pale strands rest against my shoulder blades. It was longer than most women's hair these days, and devoid of the large curls they were always wearing. I could never bring myself to sleep in curlers.

"We went mostly in high school," I continued. "But sometimes during my summers home from college some of us would meet up there. No guitars though."

"What else did you do during your summers home?" he asked.

"Fly." I sighed, remembering the hot, miserable summers, made bearable only by my days in the sky and my mother's iced tea.

"Like a little bird." He reached out and brushed the lock of hair from my face.

"That's what my father calls me," I said, smiling.

"It's what you remind me of. Slender but strong, perceptive, protective...and cautious. I find myself trying not to move too fast, in case you flitter away from me."

"It's hard not to," I said. "Flitter, I mean. I'm so used to it now. Anytime someone tries to make me something I'm not, or do something I don't want to do, I run. I flitter away."

"I will never ask you to do something you don't want to, little bird. I promise."

I met his gaze and for once held it, unafraid. "I believe you," I said.

He smiled. "Walk with me?" he asked.

I nodded and got to my feet.

I glanced over my shoulder as we walked away from the party. Ruby sat on Francis's lap, giggling as he whispered something in her ear. Catherine and Marcus were still side by side, her head on his shoulder, grinning dreamily, her dark hair hiding one brown eye. Jean and her little party had gotten to their feet and were dancing and twirling one another to the music. I took in face after face, smiling, laughing, kissing in the warm Hawaiian air.

We strolled along the shore, the waves lapping at our ankles. James opened up about his parents' death, how he'd been torn apart by their loss and how he'd almost given up his dream of flying for the army to do as his father had wanted, and go back home to Iowa to become a banker. But his sister, Ava, hadn't let him.

"She knew it would kill me," he said. "That it would change me and make me miserable. My father had loved it. He'd lived for it. But I couldn't fathom it. Ava was right."

"What was your mother like?" I asked, wondering about the woman who had borne such a kind and intelligent son.

"Beautiful. Every girl in school wanted to look like my mother. They tried too. Two girls in high school even colored their hair to be as dark as hers—but something went wrong and they both ended up with a strange sort of purple hue." He grinned. "She was funny too. She told the best jokes. And highly intelligent. My father always said that's what he liked about her most. She challenged him. You couldn't get anything past her." He looked at me. "You remind me a lot of her, actually."

"I'm flattered you think so," I said. "She sounds like she was magnificent."

"She was a great mom. I miss her every day. Him too—but she and I were the closest. Like you with your dad."

I nodded. "You actually remind me of him."

"Yeah?"

"Except he's handsome and smart."

I didn't see the spray of water until it was too late.

I chased him down the beach until we were both breathless and laughing and soaking wet.

I finally stopped, raising my arms in the air. "I surrender," I shouted. "No more!"

James emerged from the ocean where he'd been standing knee deep, ready to send another spray of water at me.

"Truce?" he asked.

"Truce."

We walked back to the party, taking turns wiping our limbs dry with the one towel he'd brought.

"What happened to you two?" Jean called, walking toward us, her camera hanging from a strap.

"Water fight," I said.

"Who won?"

"No one."

"Clearly," she said. "Stand together. I want a picture."

"Jean—"

"It's a party! I want photos. Come on. Don't be so argumentative all the time."

"I'm not— Fine," I said.

I looked up at James, who had a smirk playing about his mouth, and rolled my eyes.

He wrapped his arm around my shoulders tightly, playing with me still, and I hesitated a second before placing mine around his waist.

"Okay, you two," Jean said. "Smile."

The camera clicked and I dropped my arm. James held on a moment more and then released me with a last squeeze of his hand on my arm.

"I'm gonna go dancing with Claire and some of the other

girls," Jean said. "I'll be home late, but I promise to be there in time for you to take the car in the morning."

"You're not taking the extra shift tomorrow?"

"Depends on what time I get in." She glanced at James and gave a little shrug. "Sorry, Lieutenant."

"It's James," he said. "And not to worry. I completely understand."

She leaned over and gave me a sloppy kiss on my cheek that I then wiped off before waving goodbye to them.

"You want to get out of here?" James asked.

"Yeah." I yawned.

We pulled into the little cul-de-sac and he parked at the curb and turned off the ignition.

"May I walk you to your door?" he asked.

"What?" I said. "You're not going to carry me?"

I regretted saying it the moment it came out of my mouth. He ran around the front of the car, swung my door open and pulled me into his arms so fast, I barely had time to protest. Which I then did by yelping in surprise and kicking my legs.

"I'm going to drop you if you don't stop." He laughed and delivered me onto the woven doormat.

We stood face-to-face, breathless and laughing, the quiet of the neighborhood enveloping us until we too grew silent.

We were drawn together like magnets, wrapping our arms around one another, our mouths seeking each other's in the dark. We stayed that way for a long time, beneath the eave of my little cottage, holding on to something we didn't truly understand but weren't ready to lose.

CHAPTER SEVEN

Jean roused me in the middle of the night.

"Wake me up in the morning so I can go with you," she slurred, breathing alcohol in my face.

The early morning light poured through the window between Ruby's and my beds a few hours later. Yawning, I swung my legs over the side and stood, heading for the door and tripping over the piles of clothes Ruby had left everywhere in her search to find the perfect beach party outfit.

"Good morning," I said from Jean's bedroom doorway. "Time to get up, sleepyhead. We have twenty minutes before we have to leave."

She mumbled something unintelligible.

I pulled the covers from her head and lifted the pillow she was sleeping beneath.

"Jeanie," I sing-songed, poking her in the ribs. "Time to get up."

"I'm not going," she said, her voice muffled. "Too tired. Head hurts."

"Are you sure? It's extra wedding money."

"Audrey, I love you. But if you don't stop talking, I will punch your nose. When I can see one of you, instead of two."

"Fine," I said, chuckling quietly. "I'll see you tonight."

I hurried back to my room and pulled on a thin, long-sleeved shirt over my brassiere before sliding into my flight suit with a groan. Most days I could do without the extra layer, but early mornings and high altitudes called for a bit more clothing than usual. I'd be sweating until we were airborne though.

Buzzing with an excitement I didn't want to acknowledge, I stared at my reflection in the bathroom mirror, wondering if what I felt could be seen as well. But the woman in the mirror looked no different than usual.

I put on my boots, clomped to the kitchen to grab an apple, grinning at the four stockings and the tiny fake tree we'd put up the weekend before, and took the car keys from the little bowl on the counter.

A wave of memory hit me as I applied lipstick before leaving the house, thinking of James's lips on mine. It was strange how natural it felt to be in his arms, when I'd only ever felt awkward and claustrophobic with other men. How fun he was to be with. How easy. I'd read a book once where the heroine said she felt lost whenever she was with the handsome hero. But I didn't feel lost with James.

I felt found.

His acceptance of me as I was—undone hair, no makeup, no gravity-defying brassieres or skintight dresses, gave me something I'd never experienced outside of a plane before. Self-confidence. He made me realize what I'd always hoped to be true—I wasn't defective. I was whole, just as I was. I wasn't missing any parts. There wasn't an absence of emotion or a malfunction in my brain. Everything was where it was supposed to be. I had just made a conscious choice not to have certain things. And I was okay with that.

★ ★ ★

James stood outside the hangar flipping through the papers on his clipboard when I pulled up and parked at Wheeler.

"Good morning," he said with a sheepish grin as I got out of the car.

"Good morning," I said, praying desperately I wouldn't blush and failing in spectacular fashion.

"No Jean?" he asked.

"No," I said. "She tried. But when I attempted to wake her this morning, she threatened bodily harm."

His eyebrows rose and he laughed. "Good thing you left her home then. It's going to be a long day and nursing a hangover while training new recruits would be a miserable way to spend it. By the way, you are not obligated to stay all day. Just say the word when you want to leave."

"As long as I'm in the air, I'll be happy," I said, moving toward the door.

"Audrey..." His voice was so low I almost didn't hear him. Had he not put his hand on my arm, I might have walked right past.

"Yes?" I said, tipping my head up to look into his eyes.

"Thank you for coming today. I like working with you."

The last time my heart had felt this full was when I'd taken Roxy up for the first time after her new paint job.

"I like working with you too, Ja—Lieutenant."

He grinned a lopsided smile at my near mistake.

"See you in the sky," he said.

"See you up there," I said and slipped inside.

"Couldn't get any of the others to come in?" Mae asked from behind her paper as I entered the break room.

"There was a party on the beach last night."

"Isn't there always a party on some beach?" she asked.

"Usually."

My first trainee of the day was a nineteen-year-old by the

name of Hurst who conducted preflight inspection while grumbling under his breath about having to fly with a female instructor. I made notes as I watched him scrutinize Roxy and tried to keep from laughing. When he was done, I handed him a helmet fitted with headphones and ran him through the intercom system.

As the wheels left the tarmac I sighed, smiling into the sweet layer of Hawaiian air before we rose above it into an atmosphere crisper and cleaner than any I'd smelled before. I snuggled into the extra layers I'd put on that had felt too hot on the ground, but up here were nearly too little, and stared out over the island as Hurst took us south toward Ewa, then east to where he'd eventually loop around over Diamond Head before heading to the other side of the island doing a variety of exercises.

I loved to be at the helm of a plane, but there was something to leaving it to someone else at times and just staring out at the view. Flying was flying—and I was meant to be among the clouds, the early morning sun rising, and the blue-green water winking up at me as though, in all its vastness, it understood me just as well as the sky.

As we made our turn over Diamond Head and began our route west, I sat up straighter in my seat, preparing to shout out the first of a list of instructions to the young airman. Keeping my eyes on the gauges in front of me, I told him the first maneuver and then talked him through it as he rolled us slowly to our left, upside down, and back up.

"Excellent," I said into the intercom. "Moving on."

We completed the first set of maneuvers and I breathed, pleased with Hurst's command of the little plane. As we got closer to Mā'ili and Mākaha Beaches, lush green Hawaiian land climbed upward, forming the jagged peaks of Makua Kea'au Forest up to Mount Ka'ala.

I noticed a plane ahead of us and recognized it as the B-17 Lieutenant Hart had taken up with nine of the trainees. They flew lower than us to practice bombing maneuvers in the larger plane, and slower too. My fingers itched to take the controls. Had it been one of the girls, this is when we'd begin a game of cat and mouse. I found that often the trainees learned quicker if they could test out their training, rather than moseying through the motions. Also, it was more fun. But since it hadn't been discussed before takeoff, I decided it would be better not to and we flew past them and prepared for our next series of maneuvers.

"Ma'am?" Hurst said.

"Yes?"

"What's that approaching us?"

I frowned at a large squadron flying toward us like a swarm of bees, their buzz growing louder the closer they got.

"One of the other airfields must be getting a new crop of planes," I said. "Are you ready to begin your next set of drills?"

"Yes, ma'am."

As he pulled up I kept my eyes on the planes. One of them dipped down, breaking formation and coming almost level with us.

A strange whistling sound passed close by my ear followed by a ping behind me. Startled, I spun as best I could in my seat to the back end of the aircraft, where a small gray mark tarnished the tip of Roxy's blue tail. I frowned. I knew every inch of this plane and she hadn't had a mark like that when we took off.

Thwip thwip thwip.

The plane vibrated violently and Airman Hurst sat up in his seat as several more marks appeared in the fuselage between us. A shadow from above darkened the little plane and I looked up, ice pricking my spine as I saw the red circle on the underside of each wing of the fighter flying over us. I knew that symbol. It had been in the newsreel the last time I'd gone to the theater.

The Rising Sun—the symbol of the Japanese flag.

My breath caught as thunder rolled across the sky above us in a dark swarm.

"Oh God," I whispered, then yelled, "I'm taking over!"

I flipped the switch and pushed the throttle forward, heading for the western tip of the island and in the opposite direction of the enemy planes, the wind screaming past our heads. I dropped us lower, scanning the sky for James's B-17 and hoping the Japanese plane that shot at ours was done with us.

I found the heavy gray bomber flying low over the mountain range, smoke spilling from the cockpit and one of its wings. Behind it was the Japanese fighter.

"What are you doing?" Hurst screamed as I banked right and pushed the Fairchild even faster.

I ignored him and concentrated on the planes in front of me. I had no guns—no way to defend the bomber or us. But I couldn't stop pushing the little plane, hoping I could at least deter the fighter so James could get out of the air.

I took stock of my options. Wheeler was about thirteen miles away, Hickam even farther. We had to get out of the air but I didn't know where to go.

I scanned the range below us. Perhaps if James took the bomber lower, the other plane would follow. The trees camouflaging dangerously protruding ridges were perfect for taking a wing off. Maybe James could lead the Japanese plane toward the ridges and make it crash in the unfamiliar territory.

I ducked at the sudden sound of gunfire, knocking the intercom to the floor.

"Get down!" I yelled to Hurst, looking behind us for our attacker.

We hadn't been hit and the plane that was pursuing us now veered off to join its squadron. I looked for the B-17 again, finding it heading north, the fighter still behind it.

"Dammit," I whispered.

Dropping the Fairchild even lower, I focused on closing in on the fighter. It was faster and more nimble, but if I could get its attention and have it follow me instead—

A loud boom shook the air around us and I gasped and held tighter to the throttle, looking frantically for the source. Orange flames shot up from the harbor like a geyser, a plume of black smoke bigger than I'd ever seen billowing above it.

"Miss Coltrane!"

I glanced behind me and spotted the fighter plane on our tail again. As the guns discharged, I tipped us sideways into a barrel roll.

Rat-tat-tat! The little plane reverberated as bullets found their mark, a small wisp of smoke rising from somewhere near the tail.

"You okay?" I shouted as we leveled out.

No response.

"Hurst!"

"I'm okay!" he shouted, waving a hand and then tucking it back into the cockpit as he lowered in his seat.

The fighter flew past us, so close the wash from it knocked us sideways. My palms sweating as I steadied us, I kept my eye on the enemy plane as he banked left and came back around. I tensed, waiting for the bullets to strike again, but this time he flew past.

The fighter was still on the B-17's tail. Every move the larger plane made, the smaller one mimicked in an evil game of follow-the-leader. It was only a matter of time before the pilot tired of his chase and shot them down. I realized though that since he was flying so slow, I could catch him.

"Hang on!" I yelled.

I pushed the Fairchild harder than I ever had before, passing over the top of the fighter and dropping down between it and the B-17.

The B-17 dropped even lower and we flew over it. As I'd hoped, the fighter took to following me instead.

I sped along the range, flying low over the valley between the mountains of Mokulē'ia Forest, waiting for the right moment.

The guns of the Japanese plane discharged. *Rat-tat-tat!* I barrel-rolled us to the left, gasping as we once again were hit.

I grabbed at the intercom, pulling it to my lips.

"You still with me?" I shouted to Hurst as I pulled us upright.

"Yes," he croaked back.

My heart pounded in my chest. I'd never done this maneuver this close to the ground. Inhaling, I shoved the yoke forward.

Hurst screamed as we dove, but the Japanese plane screeched past us, unable to turn fast enough to catch us. The earth came up and I yanked the yoke back as the fighter banked left and finally gave up, flying off to rejoin his squadron.

The Fairchild evened out and I allowed myself a single big breath. And then the engine sputtered and died.

"No no no," I said, trying to get it started again.

Smoke rose from the yellow fuselage, a sad sputtering sound coming from the engine. But it started.

"Hold on!" I yelled, looking ahead for somewhere to land before the engine failed for good.

My eyes widened. Haleiwa, with its tiny unpaved airstrip, was only about a mile out.

"Come on, Roxy," I murmured. "You can make it."

The engine died right before we hit ground, throwing us forward hard against our harnesses. We bounced once, twice, before grinding to a halt as Roxy's wheels dug into the thick sandy soil just past the tree line.

I jumped down, Hurst right beside me, and looked up, searching for the B-17.

I heard a crack and looked south.

The larger plane was headed for the airstrip, coming in low, no landing gear to be seen.

"Go!" I yelled, pushing Hurst ahead of me as it cleared the trees and hurtled toward us.

We sprinted out of the way and I spun as I heard the plane land. It careened through the dirt, kicking up dust, its wing nicking Roxy's as it plowed down the strip and spun in a ground loop that sent dirt and sand spraying in a brilliant arc into the air before finally stopping, the tail half of the plane resting in the water.

"James!" I yelled and ran toward the plane.

Several other people appeared on the airstrip, everyone hurrying to the bomber.

The navigator's hatch opened and two of the trainees came out, both bleeding and wild-eyed, one cradling his hand with his other arm, blood dripping to the dirt.

"Here," Hurst said, helping him take a seat on the ground.

My eyes were glued to the hatch. Another pair of legs and another unfamiliar face appeared. And then another. After another two trainees exited I started to panic.

"Lieutenant Hart," I choked out, looking from one face to the next. "Is he…"

"Audrey."

I spun.

"James!" I said, ripping off my goggles and hurling myself at him, not caring who saw.

"Hi there, little bird," he said, wrapping his arms around me. "Thank God you're okay. I was so worried when that fighter went after you."

A loud boom shook the beach.

"We need to get out of here," he said.

"Where?" I asked, stepping back and peeling off my goggles as I looked up at him. "James, you're hurt."

Blood clotted a wound on his temple and soaked one arm of his flight suit. There was another small trickle going down his neck behind his ear, darkening the collar of his white T-shirt.

"They blew out the radio," he said, wincing and raising a bloodstained hand to his head. "Killed the navigator and bombardier." His voice dropped, the look in his eyes anguished.

"The landing gear wouldn't come down and the ball turret was jammed. The gunner—" His voice broke and he closed his eyes.

I glanced over at the plane, not understanding at first—but then I knew. The gunner in the ball turret couldn't escape. He was still inside, beneath the plane, buried in the sand.

"James," I whispered.

"We need to go," he said.

He looked around, assessing the situation around us and then looking to the sky. Another blast shook the air.

Save for Hurst and two others, most of the trainees were injured and being tended to by the guards who had run to help when we'd all crash-landed. One of the men had lost a couple of fingers, another looked to have broken an arm. All of them, like James, had been hit by shrapnel when bullets had splintered the metal of the B-17 and sent it flying at them, embedding it in their skin.

"You men get fixed up and then find a way to the base. Audrey, come with me."

"What about me, sir?" Airman Hurst asked.

"You're in charge of the others. Make sure all injuries are tended to before heading back."

"Yes, sir."

I ran, keeping up with James as he limped along, our feet pounding the dirt beneath us.

"There," he shouted, pointing to a jeep at the edge of the airfield. He bent over, his hand on his knees as he tried to catch his breath. "Get in. I'll find keys."

"You get in," I said. "I'll find the keys."

Before he could argue, I ran to the guard booth. I pulled the keys off a hook and raced back.

"Get in," I said, pointing to the passenger seat.

"You're not driving," James said.

"The hell I'm not," I said. "You're in no shape. Get in or we're not going anywhere."

He did as he was told without further argument and I ran around to the driver's side and jumped in, my eyes on the sky.

"Where to?" I asked.

He pointed and my gaze followed his finger. Black smoke rose from what looked like the center of the island.

"Hang on," I said and threw the jeep into gear.

The closer we got to Wheeler Army Base, the thicker and higher the smoke rose.

I tore down the highway, swerving around the few cars on the road and throwing James into the door more than once, causing him to shout out in shock and pain and grab his right knee.

"Did you get hit in the leg?" I yelled through the wind. I hadn't noticed any blood, but maybe I'd missed it.

"I got out of my seat when the navigator was hit," he shouted, grabbing on to the rail above his head as the jeep bounced over the uneven pavement. "The boys were all shouting and panicking. We got hit again while I was up and I fell. It's fine. Just a bruise."

As we rounded a corner and Wheeler Army Base came into full view I slowed, my lips parting in horror at the scene.

"Jesus," he said.

I sped to the gate but the guard was running toward us, shaking his head and waving his arms.

"What's he saying?" I asked, trying to read his lips.

"Go," James murmured.

"What?"

"Go, Audrey! Go!"

That's when I heard them.

I screamed as James pushed me down, covering my head with his arms as the Japanese planes strafed the base, bullets flying, pummeling the asphalt beside us, explosions blasting into the sky.

"Go!" James yelled, pulling me upright. I hit the gas.

We screamed down the highway. Ahead of us more smoke

curling into the sky, turning it black, acrid fumes filling the air. I glanced at James but his eyes were closed, his head leaned back against the headrest. His wound had started weeping again and I wiped a trickle of blood from his cheek with my hand.

"We'll get you patched up," I said and he nodded.

Pearl City was ahead of us and the sight beyond it unbelievable. The entire harbor looked like it was on fire, orange fingers reaching toward the sky, explosions like fireworks, cracking and booming, and smoke…so much smoke.

A blast so loud it sounded like it had happened right next to us sent another plume into the air—but I kept going, praying as I drove that we didn't get hit so I could get James to Tripler Hospital before he passed out from blood loss. As we neared the town of Aiea I noticed it too was smoldering.

"James," I said, shaking his leg. "I have to stop at my house. I have to get Jean. James?"

"I'm okay," he said, opening his eyes. "Head hurts. Go get Jean."

I sped through the winding streets to our neighborhood and our little house, coughing as smoke billowed into my face the closer I got. I hit the brakes, realizing I'd passed our cul-de-sac and threw the jeep in Reverse.

"Hold on," I said.

I stopped again and was gripping the stick shift to throw it back in first when I saw it.

"What's going on?" James asked, sitting up. "Audrey?"

I didn't say a word as I grasped the door handle and slid from the vehicle.

"Audrey!" James shouted. "What— Oh God. Audrey, stop!"

But I couldn't. I couldn't stop moving toward it, my breath coming in short puffs, my eyes burning from the smoke rising from the massive hole that sat where my house once had.

CHAPTER EIGHT

We sat side by side on Erma and Ken's floral sofa. James had a bandage on his head and he and Ken were speaking but I didn't hear a word they said. Annie had clamped on to my leg and I absentmindedly stroked her silky black hair with one hand while Erma spread ointment on my other one and applied a bandage.

"There you go," she murmured, patting my knee.

I nodded and placed my hand in my lap, my mind spinning. My house was gone and Jean...

I'd cut my hand pulling away the remains of our home, searching for her and hoping she'd gotten out before the shell of the Japanese bomb had fallen. But my hopes were dashed. I groaned at the memory of her slender arm, her forever red-painted nails covered in dust beneath the headboard of the bed I'd shoved out of the way. James hurried to me, wrapping his arms around my waist, physically hoisting me out of the remnants of my sweet island life.

"It's quiet," I murmured now, tilting my head.

Everyone stopped talking. James and Ken went to the windows.

"You should get your family out of here," James said in a low voice.

I glanced down at Annie. She clung to her little stuffed dog, her tiny face streaked with tears. "How are you doing, sweetheart?" I asked her.

"Bad men." She pointed to the sky.

"I know, little love." I looked at Erma. "Where are the other kids?"

She pointed down the hall to the bedrooms. "Under their beds."

"James is right," I said in a hollow voice. "You should get out of here. They might be back. You're too close to the harbor here." My voice caught. We were closer than we'd ever realized.

"Where are Ruby and Catherine?" she asked.

I shook my head, my gut filled with dread. I had no idea. I didn't know where they stayed when they didn't come home.

Erma's sister, Constance, lived on the eastern side of the island in Kaneohe. James and I distracted the kids while Erma and Ken rushed around the house, packing necessities—change of clothing for each family member in one bag, food in another. Ken and James loaded everything into the trunk of their car and I hugged each of them tight and promised we'd talk soon before watching them drive out of the cul-de-sac.

As the now-familiar buzz of planes filled the sky once more, James and I climbed into the jeep. I pulled the keys from my pocket and handed them to him.

"Where are we going?" I asked, gasping as we skidded out of the neighborhood and holding on to the door.

"I don't know. Hickam maybe. If they'll let us in."

The assault had already begun again as we neared the base, the smoke here even heavier, marring our view so much we missed a stop sign and nearly crashed into a car speeding by.

"That's Claire!" I shouted, pointing at Jean's friend.

We flew past the guard booth, following behind Claire to

the base hospital, screeching to a halt and jumping out. Japanese planes dropped in above us, raining bullets on the hangars, planes and ground nearby. James pulled me down and lay on top of me as the ground shook beneath us.

"You okay?" he asked, rolling off and pulling me to my feet.

I nodded, dazed, my gaze moving to the airfield just beyond. There wasn't much left of Hickam Field. Warplanes stood, their noses pointed to the sky as if waiting for their turn to go up, their wings and tails burned and broken and lying on the pavement around them. Some were completely gutted, others still on fire. The buildings, barracks and hangars were riddled with bullet holes, except for the ones hit by bombs and barely standing.

My throat stung from the fumes of burning fuel, oil and bits of soot. I unzipped my flight suit and pulled my shirt, damp with sweat, over my nose and mouth and ran with James to the entrance.

The front steps were splattered with blood, the hallways crowded with men lying on the floors. We carefully hurried through, trying to find someone to ask what we could do to help.

The doors flung open behind us and bleeding men carrying bloodied men on gurneys rushed in.

"What can we do?" James asked a medic rifling through a bag.

"Who are you?"

"She's civilian. I'm army. We're from Wheeler. How can we help?"

"Gurneys."

"What?"

"Grab a gurney and help bring the patients in. Haul the empty gurneys back to the trucks—get more patients."

"You got it."

The stream of bodies was unending, and after carrying a dozen inside, my arms ached. After two dozen they were numb. But I kept going, following James in and out of the hospital and delivering them wherever there was room, which was quickly becoming nowhere.

Each patient was given a color: black for morgue, red for needs immediate care or green for non-severe. It didn't matter how many trips we made to the makeshift morgue in what had been the cafeteria, I felt sick every time. But the injuries needing immediate care were even worse. The disfiguring burns, the smell of scorched flesh, the wild eyes of shock, young men calling out for their mothers... If I never saw another drop of blood in my life, it would be too soon.

We were on our way back out to the trucks when I noticed the silence. The door to the hospital had closed behind us and the stillness in the air that had just been buzzing with the engines of dozens of planes was unnerving.

"What is it?" James said, a few steps ahead of me.

"It's quiet," I said for the second time that morning.

A couple of soldiers kneeling over a patient in an ambulance glanced out.

"Is it over?" someone said.

"I don't know," James said. "Let's not stand around waiting to find out though."

We helped a young man with a patch over one eye out of a truck, the tag on his uniform marked green, and then laid out the gurney for the next patient.

The steady stream turned into a trickle and soon James and I found ourselves standing out of the way in a corner, unsure of what to do next.

"Audrey?"

I turned to see Claire, her face and uniform streaked with blood and other fluids I didn't care to know about.

"Claire," I whispered. "I'm so glad you're okay."

"You too." She looked around. "Is Jean with you?"

James gently squeezed my fingers.

"The house…" I said, my eyes filling with tears as I shook my head.

"Oh," Claire whispered. "Dammit." She dropped her head, her shoulders shaking. I reached out to her and we clung to one another, grieving the loss of our dear friend. "What about Ruby and Catherine?" she asked when she pulled away, swiping the back of her hand across her face to dash away the tears.

"I haven't seen them since last night on the beach. Do you know where they went? Or with who?"

"We all went dancing at the Hollywood. The last I saw of Catherine she was wandering off with that soldier she's so smitten with. Marcus, right? I'm pretty sure he has officer's quarters on Makalapa. And Ruby was still on the dance floor when Jean and I left. Her beau couldn't stay. So maybe they're safe."

"Maybe."

"Do you have somewhere to stay?"

I hadn't even thought about that. I was homeless. And James—what was left at Wheeler for him?

"I don't," I said, taking a deep breath as reality sank in. I was stranded. Everything I owned here had been in that house. Except for my little blue handbag that was in my car at Wheeler. And who knew what condition that was in.

"You're welcome to stay with me," Claire offered. "You both are more than welcome. You can have the bed and I'll take the couch."

"Oh," I said, shaking my head and looking to James. "We're not— It's…"

"I'll take you both to Claire's," James put in. "I need to get back to Wheeler to see what the conditions are and what I can do to help. If my barracks are still standing, I'll stay there. Do you have a phone?" he asked Claire and she nodded. "I'll call if I need to take you up on a bit of floor to sleep on."

Exhausted, we walked to the jeep. Claire's eyes were at half-mast and James's limp had grown worse. I took the keys gently from his hand and he smiled, grateful.

"Thank you," he whispered and squeezed my fingers.

I helped the two of them in and then slid into the driver's seat and turned the key. But as I put it in gear, rather than head for the main gate, I turned toward the harbor.

"Where are you going?" James asked. I looked at him, my eyes filled with anguish, and he sighed and nodded. He needed to see too.

Nothing could have prepared me for my first view of the harbor. Fires blazed from the decks of the mammoth battleships, enormous black billows blotting out the sky.

And the smell...

Death hung in the air where only hours before the sweet scent of flowers and salt water had. Smoke mixed with sweat, burning fuel with charred bodies, tears with blood.

The scene on the docks was unfathomable, and as I stared at men lying on rows of cots or on the ground, bandaged, bleeding and burned, my mind went numb with despair. The once blue-green water was dark with blood and lapping at the harbor as though looking for more victims to drag into its depths. Fires rocked the enormous ships that were shrouded in smoke and in some cases sinking. Some men jumped into the blackened ocean, while still more lined up on the underside of a sunken ship, trying desperately to cut holes in the metal in hopes of freeing those inside.

I felt sick and moved toward a building whose windows had been blown out. Bracing my hands on my knees, I took several deep breaths.

"Audrey," James said, his hand making slow circles on my back. "You okay?"

I nodded, but I wasn't. I felt hollowed. Unable to wrap my mind around the enormity of the destruction and loss of life. Everything I thought I'd known about the world before this

morning had been obliterated. The feeling of safety was gone.
I began to shake.

Small motorboats towed something toward the pier and Claire
grabbed on to my hand. The ropes were wrapped around ankles.
Dozens of ankles—attached to drowned soldiers.

A large truck backed up to the docks and the doors swung
open to reveal wooden coffins.

"Let's go," James murmured, herding us to where I'd parked
the jeep.

He took the wheel this time, driving us through debris litter-
ing the streets to Claire's apartment. Not one inch of the harbor had gone untouched. A little grocery store's front had been
completely blown off and comic books, children's beach pails,
Christmas cards and decorations lay scattered across the sidewalk.

"I stop here every morning," Claire said, peering out of the
jeep. "At least, I used to."

I stared back over my shoulder at the buckets strewn about,
cracked and burned on the pavement. I closed my eyes and
prayed no child had been hurt.

Claire lived off base in an apartment on the northern side of
Pearl City. James and I followed her up a wooden staircase to
her second floor unit and she swung the door open and ushered
us in with a yawn.

The sitting room was small and cozy, with a large friendly
picture window adorned with tiered pale green curtains, a floral sofa with matching embroidered throw pillows and an end
table with a lamp and radio. One wall nearest us was covered
in wood paneling where nine framed photos of different views
of the island hung above a forest green armchair holding a third
embroidered pillow. And in the center of the room atop a pink-
and-green oval hook rug was a dark wood coffee table with a
small vase filled with flowers.

The kitchen had white cupboards and countertops and pale
green walls. A white eyelet valance hung above the window

and there was a pale yellow table with two matching chairs in the tiny room's one open corner. Matching ceramic canisters labeled Flour, Sugar and Coffee sat aligned on one small counter, while the other boasted a large cutting board.

"It's lovely," I said, taking care not to move farther in than the entryway, aware my clothing was covered in filth.

James too seemed to be doing his best not to dirty his surroundings, crossing his arms over his chest and glancing around to make sure he wasn't touching the wall behind him.

"Come in," Claire said, slipping off her bloodstained shoes and padding into the kitchen. "Don't worry about the mess. I'll clean up later. Let me feed you before you go back, James. Please. Sit. Both of you." She pointed to the kitchen chairs.

We slipped out of our boots and James raised his hands in front of him.

"Where can we wash up?" he asked.

Claire pointed. "The bathroom is at the end of the hall."

"After you," James said to me.

I made my way to the bathroom, where I turned on the faucet, catching sight of my reflection in the mirror. Splatters of blood and soot were smeared across my face, neck and collarbones. I ran my tongue over my gritty teeth and dry lips and then grabbed the bar of lavender-scented soap and went to work. When I returned, James and Claire were hanging blankets over the windows.

"It was recommended by several of the police officers," James said. "Just in case."

I glanced at Claire, who had a little crease of worry between her brows. James had said *recommended*. He meant required. I picked up another blanket from the chair they were stacked on.

"Let me help," I said.

After James washed up, the three of us sat around the kitchen table, James refusing the second chair and instead perching on a wooden step stool. We ate sandwiches thick with ham and cheese, no words shared, just the sound of us chewing and breathing and drinking. We gulped water as though we hadn't had any in ages and finished every last bite of our food.

"Thank you," James said, standing. "I should go though. If my barracks are no longer standing, is it okay to come back?" He looked from me to Claire and back again.

"Of course," Claire said. "No matter how late."

I went to him, wrapping my arms around his waist.

"Call, okay?" I said. "Don't forget?"

"How could I forget to call you, little bird?"

He squeezed me once tight, kissed the top of my head and waved at Claire.

"Be safe," he said and then disappeared out the front door.

"Well." Claire sighed. "How about a shower? And maybe a change of clothes?"

"I can wait," I said. "You go ahead."

"Are you sure? Usually I'd argue that you're the guest but…" She stared down at her uniform, stained beyond repair and torn at the hem. "I'd really love to get out of this and burn it."

"Please," I said. "I'm going to have another glass of water and maybe one of your apples?"

"Help yourself. I'll be out in a jiffy."

An hour later, clean and dressed in one of Claire's soft night-gowns, my delicates washed and hung over the shower rod, Claire and I sat on the sofa in the dim light of the sitting room, listening to the news on the radio and trying not to jump out of our skin at any sound outside her four walls.

James called at seven, the ringing of the little black phone cutting through the quiet and causing Claire to knock her glass of water over. Pressing her palm to her breast, she answered and then handed the receiver to me.

James was fine, but Wheeler had been hit as bad if not worse than Hickam. Somehow his barracks had survived though, only victim to a few bullet holes. He sounded shaken up.

"I'll stay here tonight," he said. "There's not a lot left standing. The hangars aren't much more than frames. Most of the pilots' barracks were hit—some are still burning. Only another and mine were spared. And some of the smaller buildings are still intact. If there is another attack, there's no point in hitting here again. I don't think there's a single plane left."

I thought of all the new recruits that had stood at attention in the training hangar that morning, so eager to fly over this beautiful island. And Mae and Bill...what had become of them?

"I have a few of the recruits from this morning bunking on my sofa and sitting room floor tonight," he said as though reading my mind. "Everyone's on edge, as you can imagine. Are you and Claire doing okay? Would you like me to come back? I can get these guys set up and be there in a half hour or so."

"No," I murmured. "Thank you, James. We'll be fine."

I glanced up at the blanket-covered windows. The silence outside was eerie. Normally at this time the streets would be teeming with officers and tourists alike. But not tonight. Tonight thousands were dead, and those left alive were either clinging to life or mourning.

"Did you see Mae or Bill?"

"I didn't," he said. "I figured I'd ask around tomorrow."

We grew quiet, the only sound over the phone line our breath.

"You still there?" he asked.

"Yeah," I said. "I can't stop thinking about Ruby and Catherine. And Jean." I whispered the last part, my eyes filling.

"I know. I'm so sorry. I'll come get you first thing tomorrow and we can inquire around. How does that sound?"

"Don't you have work?"

"There's cleaning to do," he said. "But until we have orders, there's nothing official that needs doing."

We talked for a few minutes more and then said good-night and hung up. I glanced at Claire. She'd nodded off, her glass clutched in her hand. In the distance I heard a faint buzzing sound.

I inhaled and tapped her on the knee, gently at first, and then with more persistence.

"Claire," I whispered.

"Huh?" she said, blinking at me. "What's going on?"

The buzzing seemed to increase in volume and I hit the floor, crawling under the kitchen table.

"They're back! Come on!"

She followed me and we sat knees to knees, huddled together, our hands clasped between us. After a moment she sat back and frowned as she cocked her head.

"Oh, Audrey." Her voice was soft as she gave me a sympathetic smile. "That's the neighbor's radio. It's old and buzzes horribly through these thin walls."

Tears of relief and fear and grief came fast and furious as we hung on to one another beneath the little yellow table. When we'd caught our breath again, we crawled back out and sat on the sofa, hands still clasped.

"Oh gosh," Claire said, sitting up, her eyes wide. "I should call my folks."

I blew out a breath. I'd been so distracted by the horrible events of the day, I hadn't given one thought to what my family must be going through.

"May I use your telephone when you're finished?" I asked. "My parents must be beside themselves with worry."

"Of course. Just give me a few minutes."

After a brief but tearful telephone call, Claire gave me a hug and went off to bed to try to sleep amid the terror of wondering if we'd be attacked again beneath the cover of darkness.

I sat on the sofa, my hands shaking. I couldn't remember ever feeling so alone or so scared.

I pressed the receiver to my ear and dialed the number I knew by heart. My father picked up before the first ring finished.

"Hello?" His voice was hushed. Desperate.

"Dad?"

"Oh thank God, bird."

CHAPTER NINE

For the next two weeks, James came by Claire's apartment every morning. We had breakfast and then went to Wheeler, where we took inventory of the planes and helped haul away debris.

Bill, the crew chief, was found dead beneath part of the roof that had fallen. Mae was shot by strafing bullets at her desk. Out of the twenty new recruits who had reported for training that morning, sixteen were still alive.

It took four days for me to hear any news of Catherine. Every afternoon, James drove me around to the hospitals so I could look for her and Ruby. On that fourth day, moments after we entered the front doors of Hickam's medical center, the woman at the front desk asked us to wait while she went in search of Claire, who then led us downstairs to a large room with a hand-written sign on the door that read Morgue.

I glanced at Claire. Her eyes were full of tears as she opened the door.

James walked in beside me, his arm around my shoulders. It

was cold and smelled of death. Claire walked down a line of bodies covered by sheets. She stopped next to one and took a breath.

"Do you want to see her?" she whispered.

I took a moment and then nodded.

She looked like an angel in her white dress, her dark hair fanned softly around her head. Were it not for the dark red stain spreading up from the wound to her stomach, she would've appeared as though she were sleeping.

I knelt beside her and placed the back of my hand against her cheek. Her skin was smooth and cool, the color drained, the life gone.

Rather than go home alone to Claire's that night, James took me to his barracks, keeping a watchful eye on me as I wandered his small sitting room, reading the titles of the books on his shelves, picking up a carved wood turtle and setting it down, moving the food he made us around my plate, unable to put into words my feelings of grief and loss.

I slept alone in his bed, while he slept on the couch in the living room. When I awoke to the sun peeking through the curtains the next morning, it was with a feeling of comfort, as though arms had held me through the night.

We found Ruby two days later. Alive, thank goodness.

She had left the dance club in the early hours that morning and gone home with two friends to their house on the windward side of the island. When the planes flew in, they ran to a neighbor's and hid in the basement with a radio and a sack of food. They didn't emerge for three days, too afraid there was more to come.

We were two vehicles back at the guard booth at Wheeler when I saw her red hair emerging from a friend's car. She raised her hands and dumped the contents of her handbag on the pavement, digging helplessly for her ID. But when she held it up, the guard shook his head. After shouting at him, she broke down in tears. I jumped out of the passenger seat of the jeep and ran to her, calling her name. When she saw me, she whimpered and reached out her arms.

"The house," she croaked.

"I know," I whispered.

She looked like a small child later that afternoon as she slept, fresh from a shower, curled on Claire's sofa. Gone were the perfectly drawn eyebrows and red lips normally adorning her face. In the evening she called her parents. As soon as she was able, she'd be going home to Kansas.

"What about you, Audrey?" she asked as we sat at Claire's kitchen table. "Will you stay? Or will you go home too?"

She looked younger than her twenty-one years, her blue eyes wide above her pale cheeks.

"I'm going home as well. James got his orders yesterday. He's to report to a base in Texas. He leaves next Friday. I'll get a ride with him."

"I wish I could go with you," she said. "I'm terrified to get on that boat."

Anyone wanting to leave the island was being permitted to do so by boat to the US mainland. The windows would be blacked out and they'd be escorted by a destroyer. James had already secured Ruby a spot on the SS *Lurline*. She was to be packed and ready to go at a moment's notice.

Claire had the following day off and the three of us women went into downtown Honolulu to buy Ruby some clothes, something I'd finally done for myself two days before, and an activity sure to keep Ruby's mind occupied. She'd had horrible nightmares and woke crying for our lost roommates. But she wandered from rack to rack, barely looking at anything until Claire and I started grabbing things and helping her try them on.

The day before James and I left, he drove me to Haleiwa. Roxy and the B-17 still sat where we'd left them, dusted with sand, salt water crystalized along their wings and bodies.

I ran my hand along the holes that had dug deep into Roxy's

sunshine-yellow body, my pulse quickening as I recalled the sound the bullets had made upon impact.

"Can I take a couple pictures?" James asked.

I turned to see him with a camera in hand.

"Where did that come from?" I asked.

"I brought it along in case you wanted some photos."

I gave him a small smile before turning back to the plane and pressing my cheek against her body, warm from the ever-present sun.

I heard the camera click a few more times and then one of the guards from the guard booth came over.

"Sorry," he said. "My boss said you have to leave."

"No problem," James said. "I think we're done here." He glanced at me and I nodded. "Can you take one picture of us before we go though?"

"Sure thing."

James and I stood in front of the little Fairchild, my arm around his waist, his around my shoulder. There was a click and then, as we looked up at one another, a second click.

We drove to Aiea next and parked on the street outside Erma and Ken's house.

"Audrey!" Annie yelled, running out the front door and toward me.

"Hello there," I said, kneeling and taking her in my arms.

We sat with Erma and Ken in their tiny sitting room, Annie on my lap, the other three kids at the dining table finishing up their breakfast. Ken, like me, had seen his duties at the airfield dwindle since he was not military. Thankfully Erma's brother-in-law had offered him a job doing construction, but he wouldn't start until the week after Christmas.

James took my picture with the family, and then another with just Annie, who insisted. I promised to stay in touch with Ken and Erma and then we hugged each other goodbye.

As we left, I bypassed the jeep and walked to the end of the street where my house once stood. My breath was lost as I stared at what was left. The front half and most of the west side where our bedrooms had been were gone. The bathroom and kitchen had caved in, a pile of rubble that was barely discernable as once being part of a home. I treaded lightly around the edge, lifting pieces of broken wall, looking for something, anything, to take with me. James followed me, helping as he shoved aside the fragments of my home.

I found only a few undamaged items: a jadeite pitcher for cream, a bottle of one of Catherine's favorite perfumes I'd give to Ruby, a baby blue scarf that had belonged to Jean and a black-and-white photo of the four of us. The glass in the frame was broken, but the picture unscathed. James loaded the objects in the jeep as I crouched one last time before the wreckage, sifting my fingers through the soft overturned dirt, remembering my life here with Jean, Catherine and Ruby.

There had been so much laughter in this space. Joking, thoughtful conversation, pranks and love. Catherine's gentleness, Ruby's flirtatious nature and Jean's spirit. I closed my eyes, picturing Jean on the tarmac of Wheeler.

"Let's take to the wind!" She'd yell and raise her fist as we climbed inside the cockpits of our planes. "Fly 'em high, girls!"

I reached down and wrote her and Catherine's names in the dirt.

"Rest in peace, Fly Girls," I whispered.

Saying goodbye to Ruby wasn't easy. The sassy, carefree girl I'd come to know and love was changed after the attack, constantly on edge, her hair undone, clothes subdued, no lipstick to be seen.

She'd held on to the bottle of perfume I'd given her and cried when she'd pulled off the lid, the familiar scent reminding us of the sweet friend we'd lost.

"You take care of yourself, you hear?" I said, hugging her

tight. "Call me when you get home. My telephone number and address are in your wallet. Don't forget."

She nodded and held me tighter.

"Be careful," she whispered.

I hugged Claire next. "Thank you for everything," I said. "Don't forget Christmas, okay?"

"Of course not," she said.

After hearing about Ken's job issues, James and I had run downtown and bought Christmas gifts for the family. I'd entrusted them to Claire who had promised to deliver them Christmas Eve.

Claire, who was originally from Oregon, had decided to stay on the island, despite—and because of—the destruction. "I'm needed here," she'd said with a shrug when I'd asked if she would leave and go to the mainland like so many others. "And I love it. This is my home. My community."

I couldn't argue with that.

"Don't forget to write," she said now.

"I won't. Same to you."

I hugged her and Ruby both one last time and then drove with James back to his barracks where we'd spend a final night, me in his bed and him on the sofa, before our flight out the next morning.

We ate steaks that James had ordered from Kemo'o Farms by the light of a single lamp. The curtains were closed with blankets hung over them to keep any light from escaping. The fear that we may be attacked again had kept the island in a state of perpetual terror. Any buzz of a plane engine, the slam of a door, sirens of an ambulance going by, and everyone stopped what they were doing, staring wide-eyed at one another...waiting.

"Are you nervous?" His voice was low in the small room.

"About which part?"

"The flight tomorrow. Going home. Whatever comes after."

"Yes," I said. "And no. I'm a little worried about being in the air again. I wish it were going to be me in the cockpit. It's hard not being in control. But I trust you. And I think being home now will be different than it was before I left. At least I hope so. But my mother…she's a bit of a planner. I have a feeling I'm going to get there and she'll already have every day scheduled for me. She'll say it's for my own good, to 'keep my mind off things,' but really it's for her. She doesn't like to look bad. Can't have me come back a war hero, as she called me on the phone, and shirk my duties. I'll admit I'm dreading it a tad. As far as what comes next in my career, I have some ideas."

"Care to share them with me?"

I told him about the program Mae had spoken of. How I hadn't been interested before, but now, with the country being at war, it was my opportunity to help.

"They won't let me fight, but maybe they'll let me get soldiers in the air."

"Sounds like a perfect fit for you."

"If Ms. Love can get the program going. She still didn't have approval the last time Mae and I spoke about it. I'll have to look into it as soon as I get home."

"Well, I can't wait to hear about it."

We fell silent as we ate and then, "Audrey?"

"Yes?" I met his gaze across the table and my heart pounded.

"Will you write to me?" he asked. "I know we're not— That neither of us wants—"

"I will," I said.

"Good."

I said good-night and went to his room as he made his bed on the sofa. But I couldn't sleep, thoughts of getting on a plane the next morning troubling me. I listened to the clock on the bedside table tick away the seconds until I could take it no more and swung my legs over the side of the bed and padded out to the living area.

"James?" I whispered.

He didn't answer.

He was lying on his back on the too-small sofa, his ankles hanging over the armrest, arm flung overhead, shirt off and folded on the end table.

I walked back to the bedroom and pulled the quilt and a pillow off the bed, then went to lie down on the floor beside him.

When I woke in the morning, he was lying beside me. Our eyes met and held in the dim light and my chest tightened, my eyes brimming with tears. This was it. After today, who knew when or if we'd see one another again.

Without a word he pulled me close and I clung to him, our breath becoming one, our hearts beating in sync.

We folded the bedding together, our eyes meeting time and time again, and then ate a quick breakfast, gathered our things, took a last look around and headed for the airfield where we boarded a plane for Texas.

PART TWO

AUGUST 1943

CHAPTER TEN

"Are you finished packing?" Mama asked, coming into my room.

"Just about," I said, tucking a pair of tan heels and a new matching cloche with a wide burgundy ribbon into my suitcase.

"Are you taking the new navy-and-white dress as well?"

"I am. And the yellow and the gray."

Despite much of the country buckling down, the future uncertain, my mother had insisted on buying me a few new things before I left for Sweetwater.

"I hope you have opportunities to wear them," she said, running her hand over a pale blue-and-cream houndstooth skirt. "It won't be much fun if it's all work and no play."

The fear of losing her eldest daughter had changed my mother in subtle but noticeable ways. The clothes she wore were more casual, and her hair worn in a looser style. But she also now kept us to strict schedules, wanting to know where we were at all times.

The preciousness of life had been revealed when Pearl Harbor was attacked and, despite the threat to our country, she now saw that we needed to embrace it, rather than keep it so tightly tethered. Which was why, after her initial fury over my invitation and acceptance to the new Women Airforce Service Pilots program, headed by aviatrixes Jacqueline Cochran and Nancy Harkness Love, she'd backed down.

The ferrying program Mae had originally told me and the girls about in Hawaii, led by Ms. Love, was put into action in September of 1942, nine months after I'd arrived back home in Dallas. Only twenty-eight women had been accepted and immediately put to work flying military aircraft across the country. But, like Jean, Ruby and Catherine, I'd never sent a letter of interest. I'd loved the little life I'd created on Oahu and hadn't been keen to leave it just then. And after the attack on Pearl Harbor, my only goal was to get home safely.

Upon returning home, my mother had lined up a multitude of activities for me to try to keep the overwhelming sadness I'd felt at bay. Activities that included crop dusting for several of the local farms that had lost their pilots to the war effort, driving around town with Evie collecting items from our neighbors for scrap metal and rubber drives, putting together care packages at our old high school for the boys overseas and doing deliveries out of my old instructor Hal Hudson's airfield. Three of the men in Hal's employment had left to go fight in the war, including Tom Barrows, an old schoolmate of mine who had begun working for Hal straight out of high school. Tom was like a brother to me, and not having him around to tease was strange. Knowing my gangly old friend was risking his life overseas also made me want to work extra hard to do his job well. And so I'd stayed, and flying military planes became the last thing on my mind.

Until the letter came.

The military decided to combine Ms. Love's program with an idea Ms. Cochran had. The new program included months of training and even more opportunity. We wouldn't just be delivering old patched-up aircraft at bases across the country—we'd be testing new warplanes as well.

My excitement at the opportunity was only slightly dampened by the thought of telling my mother, who responded as I'd expected. The arguing between us had ensued for a full week until she finally broke down in tears.

"Why?" she'd cried. "Why must you always put yourself at risk?"

"It's flying, Mama. I do that now. I do it here."

But that was a lie. Whereas Ms. Love's former program had been only flying, the new combined program included ground school training as well as flight school. We'd be jettisoning across the skies in anything from old warplanes on their last leg, to new planes fresh off the production lines. Per the letter I'd received, we'd be learning "the army way." I wasn't sure what that entailed, but it didn't sound like just a bit of flying to me.

"Yes, but those are warplanes, not Jennies. And you'd be flying all over the country. What if you crash?"

"I could just as easily crash here."

"But crop dusting is done low. Close to the ground. And if you crash here we'd be nearby."

There was no point, I could tell, in recounting the facts. Crash landing was crash landing. If I died, I died. The distance to her wouldn't make a difference. Instead, I'd taken her hand.

"Where are we going?" she'd asked as I'd pulled her through the house and out onto the front porch. I invited her to have a seat on the porch swing, and then settled next to her.

This was my spot with my dad. To bring her here was strange and sweet all at once and I'd smiled, seeing her uncertainty.

I never spoke of the horrors I'd seen in Pearl Harbor. Never told them what and whom I'd lost. Never even my father, with whom I shared everything. And they didn't ask. They looked in on me. They watched me more carefully than they ever had before. But they treaded lightly when it came to the subject of the attack, as though afraid talking about it would break something inside me. And I'd cherished the little cocoon they'd allowed me—until that moment on the porch with my mother.

I told her about how Jean had decided to sleep in that morning. The first hit Roxy took, the crash landing in Haleiwa, my beautiful island up in smoke. And death—how it was everywhere. You could smell it, taste it, feel it. She cried as I told her about finding Jean, and then Catherine. How people, like Ruby, changed before my very eyes. And then she held me as I let go of the pain and guilt I hadn't known I was holding on to.

And she gave me her blessing to go.

We were all doing our part for the war effort, and even though I knew she was frightened to have me flying military planes again, she also took great pride in the fact that her daughter was doing just that. And made no bones about telling anyone and everyone, "My Audrey, have you heard? Taking a job with the army. Such a smart girl, that one. Christian and I couldn't be more proud."

I glanced at her now, standing in front of my bureau, trying to decide which sun hat made more sense to take.

"I'm sure I'll have some fun," I said and kissed her cheek. "But not too much. It is the army, you know." I gave her a salute and clicked my heels together and she laughed.

"The bus leaves in less than two hours."

"I know, Mama."

"Any word from James?" Her voice was conversational, but the undercurrent serious.

"No," I murmured.

Another thing she'd been good at since I'd returned home was reading my mind. And James had been on it a lot in the past few months. Ever since his letters had begun coming once every few weeks, rather than every week.

Friends. That's what we'd agreed on again and again. But my mother hadn't believed it. Not after meeting him in the entryway of Fort Sam Houston in San Antonio where we'd flown in. She'd eyed him like I'd seen her do a hundred times to a roast of lamb, the heel of a shoe or the fabric for a new set of chairs.

Was it large enough to feed eight? Sturdy but high enough to show off the slenderness of her calf? Expensive but durable to last the season?

Was he good enough for her daughter? Was there something more between us?

I saw her take in everything. The pressure of his handshake, the way he held himself when he walked, how he'd smiled kindly down at Evie but hadn't seemed overly curious, his esteem for both her and my father. But mostly, how careful he was with me and how I—the one woman she knew who cared not to be in the arms of a man—acted around him. She missed nothing, no matter how careful I was.

"Friends?" She'd sniffed delicately on the drive home. "Mmm."

She wrapped an arm around my shoulders now and kissed my cheek.

"I'm sure he's fine," she said. "It can't be easy to have regular mail service to and from Europe when there's a war going on. For all you know, three letters from him will arrive tomorrow. And if they do, we'll forward them on to you at Avenger Field."

"Thanks, Mama."

She disappeared into my closet and I sat on the edge of my bed, remembering my last moment with James. My parents had thanked him again for bringing me home safe and sound, and then dragged Evie to the car so we could say our goodbyes in private. I'd stared up at his handsome face, trying not to cry while memorizing every lash, the exact color of green in his eyes and the one freckle on his right cheekbone. It wasn't fair to have him pulled so abruptly out of my life. But there were less fair things in life, and I had a feeling I'd only seen the beginning of them.

He'd pulled me close so that my head rested on his chest, his heart beating beneath my cheek.

"You'll write?" he'd murmured into my hair.

"Every chance I get."

"You won't forget me?"

I'd pulled back then and wiped a tear from my cheek.

"What's that?" he asked, the damn crooked grin inching up. "Well, now I'm honored. Audrey Fitzgerald Coltrane has interest in no man. Certainly she wouldn't shed a tear for me."

"You damn well better be careful over there, Lieutenant Hart."

"I wouldn't want to face your wrath if I'm not, Miss Coltrane," he said, gazing down at me with such tenderness I wanted to beg him not to go. To stay. To forget all the things I'd said.

But I couldn't say the words. It wasn't me. And it wouldn't have been him to stay. And it was because of that that I liked him more than any other man I'd ever met.

"I adore you, you know," he'd said and I'd nodded. I did know. Because I felt the same.

He'd held me fiercely to him then and I'd dug my fingers into his shoulders, my face tucked into his chest, taking in for the last time the scent of his soap, the salt water and island air still on his skin.

He'd pulled back, holding me at arms' length, and looked me over, memorizing me as I'd done him. And then he shook his head, his eyes damp, and let go, snapping to attention and giving me a last salute.

"It was a pleasure serving with you, ma'am," he said.

"The pleasure was all mine, sir."

He dropped his hand. "I will miss you terribly, little bird."

I'd nodded, my eyes feeling too big in my face. We stood facing one another, unwilling to be the first to turn away. And then, choking on a sob, I hurled myself into his arms.

He kissed me something fierce, his lips pressed to mine, stealing my breath as he crushed me to him. When he at last tore his mouth from mine, we both took a step back.

"Goodbye, my friend," I'd said.

"Goodbye, my friend."

With a heavy heart I'd turned and walked out of the building. When I'd looked back, he was gone.

My bedroom door swung open now. Evie barged in and headed straight for my closet, nearly crashing into our mother, who was emerging with another dress in hand.

"You're not taking the red shoes are you?" Evie called from inside.

For the past week Evie had been overbearing with her questions about what items I'd be taking to Sweetwater with me. The navy shoes? The red hat? What about the brooch with the pink stones? The little yellow belt? The shiny one with the daisy clasp? I'd been annoyed at first, but then Father made a comment that made me stop.

"This is how she expresses herself," he'd said. "It's all a fuss. Fuss over this, whine over that. She doesn't know how to just come out and say 'I will miss you. I am scared to lose you. Please come back.'"

He'd lowered his paper then and given me a sad smile.

"*I* will miss you," he'd said, his voice soft. "*I* am scared. Please come back, bird."

My mother swung the dress in front of me, capturing my attention once more. I shook my head and she returned to the closet.

"I am not taking my red shoes," I said to Evie. "You may borrow them, but only for something important."

"Fine." She emerged pouting.

"Goodness, Evie," Mother said. "You have a job now, go buy your own red shoes."

Evie sat on my bed with a huff. I watched her carefully as I packed the rest of the items I'd chosen to take. She'd started waitressing two months before after a soldier she'd taken a liking to had been shipped out—and promptly killed on the front lines. After hearing the news, she'd gone out and found a job because "Times are changing. I think it's time I learn how to take care of myself."

Though she was still exuberant and childish at times, a stillness had fallen over her. Oftentimes we found her staring blindly into space, a troubled look in her eyes, her heart-shaped lips downturned. The easy, happy bubble she'd always known had been pierced—the needle significant. Father was right in his assessment. Evie just couldn't find the words to express herself. Pouting and acting out was the only way she knew how. But I could see it now. The fear. It lurked behind the baby blue eyes, beneath the fluff of strawberry blonde hair and pretty dresses.

I went to the closet and came out holding the red shoes.

"Here," I said.

She looked up at me, her big blue eyes as wide as saucers.

"Really?" She reached for them and then retreated. "Why?" A cloud passed over her face. "You said you're coming back."

I tousled her hair and she swatted me away.

"I am coming back, you goon. But what's the point in having them if I hardly wear them? You should have them. But you have to promise to let me borrow them sometimes."

She took them, though hesitantly, and placed them on her lap as though they were precious and might break.

An hour later Father carried my suitcase to the car while I stood on the front porch with Mama and Evie.

"Well," Mama said, wrapping her arms around me. "I guess this is it. You stay safe, you hear? No fancy tricks or stupid stunts."

"I'll fly smart, Mama. I promise."

I hugged Evie then, who was in better spirits now, her new red shoes safely in her own closet.

"Call the girls and go dancing," I said. "You need to go out. Have some fun. Show those red shoes a thing or two."

She looked up at me with something fearful in her eyes.

"I'll be careful," I whispered into her soft curls. "Be good for Mama. Don't let Dad sit alone for too long. He gets sad."

She nodded and I stepped back.

"Well," I said, looking from my mother to my sister. "See you in a few months for my graduation."

"We'll be there. In the front row if we can reserve it." My mother frowned and I laughed, knowing she was mentally making a note to call ahead to Avenger Field to see if she could indeed reserve seats.

I waved one last time as my father and I drove down the gravel driveway, then turned to face forward in my seat.

"Ready?" he asked.

I sighed and looked over at him. As much as I'd wanted to leave home, coming back had been necessary for my broken heart and damaged soul. The nightmares that had plagued me would've seemed endless without Evie tiptoeing into my room and crawling into bed beside me. Without my mother's expert scheduling, I'd have spent so much of my time wallowing in a misery that would've been hard to recover from without the constant tasks that kept my mind busy. And if my father hadn't encouraged me to take the crop-dusting jobs, getting me over that initial fear of being in the sky alone again after being shot at in Hawaii, I might not have had the courage to answer the call to serve my country in the best way I could—flying.

I'd learned a lot about myself in the past year and a half. I was stronger than I'd known. And more resilient. But it was time to let go of the ghosts of my recent past and find a new life for myself. Starting with training at Avenger Field.

"Yes," I said to my father. "I'm ready."

At the end of the block my father continued straight through the intersection toward town.

I glanced at my watch. "Wait," I said, placing my hand on his arm.

"Did you forget something?" he asked.

I nodded.

Ten minutes later he stopped on the hill where the sign for Hudson Airfield stood.

"I'll be back in a minute," I said.

I stepped up to the old sign as I had so many times before, placing my hands along the wood smoothed by age and the elements, solid beneath my fingertips.

Stretched out before me was the airfield's lone runway. I knew its every bump, dent and crack from years of takeoffs and landings. There were three hangars, but it was in front of number two that an imprint of my seven-year-old self's hand was set in the pavement Hal had had to pour that year to fix a spot that had crumbled.

Off to the left was Hal's office. The sign above the door had long since blown away in a thunderstorm and all that was left were the rings it used to hang on. The white paint was chipped in several places, despite his yearly slopping on of a coat to freshen it up. As I watched, the red door leading inside swung open and in my mind I could hear its telltale creak.

Before the office building stood the general store, a pale blue structure where Mrs. Markison sat on a green-padded swiveling stool manning the counter; her little dog, Henry, in his bed on the floor beside her. From 2:00 to 9:00 p.m., the hours of the airfield, Jerry ran the till. If you were lucky, he'd give you a lollipop. If you were really lucky, his wife sent him to work with a box of fresh-made cookies.

Behind the main office and the general store was an empty stretch of grass that I now thought of as the hotel James had suggested. It would be two stories high, painted pale blue like the general store with white shutters. And it would have a clever name. The Fly Inn or The Hangar Hotel.

I took in a deep breath and smiled. I remembered the first time my father had taken me up. I'd been five years old and couldn't see over the side of the plane. But I'd sat in my seat, too-big goggles and a grin the size of Texas on my face. I was in love. And then when I was twelve I took the Jenny down the runway for the first time with me at the helm. The utter joy of lifting that little plane into the air and circling above our home had lit a fire in me. A fire that had led me to this moment.

One day soon this would all be mine. Just mine. No one to tell me how or when or what. I'd make the decisions. I'd unlock the gate in the morning, draw up the contracts for new clients, choose the furnishings for the hotel, hire the new staff, check pilots in and out and lock up at night. And at the end of hangar three, next to the spot where Hal kept the Jenny I'd learned to fly in, would be a space for my very own plane—once I could afford one.

"Bird?" Dad yelled from the car. "We're going to be late if we don't get a move on."

I gave the airfield one long last look.

"I'll be back," I whispered. "Wait for me."

CHAPTER ELEVEN

The bus ride from Dallas to Sweetwater was long, hot and full of unpleasant smells from body odor and food. My window wouldn't open so I was forced to either exert energy fanning myself with my book, or lift myself up to catch a breeze from the window of the seat in front of me, a feat that made me acutely aware of sweat pooling in places I didn't care to think about.

I read for a while and then stared out at the countryside flying by and the farms we passed, each one marked with its own distinct brand. Double D Ranch. Olson's. W. W. Trees. They were rustic and simple, and at times run-down, as though perhaps no longer inhabited. At least not by humans. They were very unlike the elegant white gate and iron sign at the front of our home.

Though our home itself had felt foreign upon my return after months in Hawaii. And too much. Too much opulence. Too much stuff. I longed for my simple wardrobe and even simpler routine. Not having to worry about putting down a coaster before plunking down my water glass in my own room, or having someone cleaning up after me. I missed the scent of the air and the sight of the water. I missed my friends. Here, no one understood. They'd heard. They'd read the newspapers and seen it on their television sets or on the newsreels at the theater, but they didn't know what it was like. They didn't understand how little all their things meant. How they could be gone in an instant. But I knew. And I knew that many of them would soon learn what it was like to be in war. Maybe not on the front lines, but certainly as the ones who stayed behind. The ones who had to wait for the news. News that would rock them—and break them.

I'd done my best in my early days at home. I replied to the basic questions people asked and evaded the ones that would break my heart to answer. After a few days' rest, I approved my mother's schedule for me and got to work. And every evening I came home and glanced first thing at the little silver tray that sat on the entryway table. If there was mail, I sifted through it, my heart in my throat. Had James written? Where was he? Still stateside? Overseas already? If there was no mail, I'd trod to my room and lie very still on my bed, eyes closed, until someone called me for dinner.

He wrote often that first year...

Little Bird,
How are you? How is it being home again? Has your mother entered you in a beauty pageant yet? Are you wearing pearls? I'm trying to envision you dressed like a proper lady having lunch on a veranda. Please send a picture of this. I will frame it and title it Lady Bird.

We are still training. Long hours, but that is to be expected. I'm not allowed to give out dates, but we will be leaving for overseas soon. I have a good squadron under me and, while apprehensive about what will greet us, I am also enthusiastic to get into this war.

Along with the letters came small gifts, articles he cut from the newspaper he thought I'd find interesting and photographs. The first gift he sent was a new pair of gloves for flying, since he knew I'd lost mine. The second gift was a necklace.

"You sure he's just a friend, dear?" Mama had asked when she'd spied the little gold hummingbird hanging from a delicate chain around my neck.

The photographs were the ones taken at Haleiwa, and I stared at them every night before bed. Me and Roxy. Another of me standing and looking out at the ocean, my hand raised to shield my eyes from the sun. And two of him and me. In the first we were standing side by side, but the officer who had taken it had sneaked another as we began to separate, our arms hesitantly sliding from one another, the look in our eyes saying more than we ever had. I'd tucked that last picture inside my journal in the drawer of my bedside table. It was for my eyes only.

After he flew overseas, the letters still came with regularity.

Little Bird,
Jolly old England is cold. And rainy. Have you been? I believe it's
a requirement to earn your string of pearls...

Oh, but he wouldn't let me live down the string of pearls I'd told him I'd received for my sixteenth birthday. I'd recited the story over dinner our last night together and his eyes had nearly fallen out of his head.

"Pearls?" he'd asked. "For a sixteen-year-old girl?"

"A society girl," I'd said, sitting tall in my wobbly seat.

"A society girl with sauce on her chin," he'd responded.

But a year later the letters began to change, a hint of melancholy lacing the edges and permeating each short paragraph. I pulled his last letter from my handbag. It had arrived a month before, crinkled and dirty.

Dear Audrey,

Please excuse my delay in writing to you. You are always so prompt and I feel like a horrible friend to not reply immediately, but as you can probably imagine, life here is quite busy and stressful. More often than not, when I retire for the day I go straight to my cot and try to sleep. If only sleep would erase the awful images I have seen, but no. They will most likely be forevermore branded on my mind.

How is Dallas—or have you left for Sweetwater already? By the time you receive this, I imagine you will be well on your way, if not already there making waves in the air with your spectacular flying.

I hope this letter finds you well and keeping busy. I think of you often and fondly. Please know that even if I don't write nearly as often these days, it is not because I am not interested in knowing how you are, but rather, I wish to forget myself for a while. Just until this war has ended and I am once again at home where I belong.

All my best,

James

With a sigh, I tucked the letter away and glanced out the window as the bus slowed. We stopped in Ranger to refuel and were allowed thirty minutes to disembark and stretch our legs. I wandered down the tiny main street and bought an apple at the general store, and then ambled back, anxious to get going again.

We arrived in Sweetwater around four in the afternoon. It was small but bustling and I had to dodge a couple walking their dog as the bus driver unloaded my suitcase onto the sidewalk.

I walked down the street to the six-story Bluebonnet Hotel where all classes of trainees were to stay before being bussed to Avenger Field the following day. For such a small town, the hotel was well kept, the blue-and-white lobby clean and fresh smelling, with several women of all shapes and sizes milling about. They eyed me with curiosity and smiled or nodded as I came in.

"Coltrane," I told the man at the front desk.

I took the key he proffered and climbed the stairs in search of my room, passing several more women chatting on the stairs and in the hall on my way.

I unlocked the door to my room, swung it open and set my valise down in the entryway.

"Hiya," a young woman said.

"Oh," I said, my hand over my heart. "You startled me. Hello. I hadn't realized we'd be sharing rooms."

"Nice of them to tell us, huh?" she said, her low, warm voice a blanket of Southern charm. She bounced up from the bed she'd been sitting on and came toward me, hand outstretched. "I'm Carol Ann Bixby. From Alabama."

"Audrey Coltrane," I said, shaking her hand. "Dallas."

"Nice to meet you."

Carol Ann was full of information about the other women she'd met already and had an infectious laugh. Her mousy hair was styled in one sleek victory roll, her sweet round face dusted with pale freckles, making her look younger than her twenty-four years, and her big, warm brown eyes were fringed with the longest lashes I'd ever seen. She talked almost nonstop, pausing only to ask if I was hungry.

"I already walked around town," she said, grabbing a small tan handbag that complemented a belt in the same shade cinching in the waist of her navy dress. "There's a place down the street called McKay's that looks decent."

"Swell," I said, picking up my own clutch. "Should we ask any of the other girls?"

"Sure."

Five of us ended up going together to the restaurant, Carol Ann inquiring about everything from what towns everyone was from to when we all began flying.

"What's your story, Audrey?" she asked as she slid in next to me in a booth with high-backed, green-tufted vinyl benches. "How'd you end up here?"

I contemplated my response, glancing from one face to the next.

"I needed something to do besides organizing scrap metal drives and crop dusting," I said. "How about you?"

She peered at me. "Darlin'," she said, leaning closer, her voice soft so the girls across the table discussing the menu options wouldn't hear. "The brand name on your suitcase is clearly the real deal. That clutch of yours costs five times what my little handbag does—and it's half the size. And I don't even want to guess at the price of your shoes because the answer might just make me cry. You clearly aren't here trying to make ends meet. Did you make your dad mad? Get knocked up and the guy ran out? Come on. Tell me."

Had it been said with any less of her look of innocent suspense, I might've been offended. But Carol Ann had a way about her. She said what she was thinking, but in the curious way a child might. You couldn't possibly be mad at a child for asking what was decidedly an inappropriate question, just because they were inquisitive. And I couldn't get angry with Carol Ann either.

I leaned toward her and dropped my voice as well. "I shamed my family by running off with the maid's son, who then left me for the butcher's granddaughter. Flying is all I have left."

Carol Ann laughed so hard the entire restaurant strained to see what was happening.

"We're gonna get along real well," she said, nudging me with her elbow. "I can tell."

More women arrived at the restaurant throughout the evening, waving hello on the way to the surrounding tables, sometimes stopping to chat. Our other tablemates hailed from Ohio, Oregon and Tennessee respectively, and our stories about joining the Women Airforce Service Pilots program sounded a lot alike. We'd all taken part in our communities to help with the war effort. Three of the women, including Carol Ann, had taken jobs vacated by men; one as a fry cook, another as a store clerk selling shoes, and Carol Ann had taken up welding at a plant that manufactured tools. And while all that was amazing, it was what each had been doing before we entered the war that I found most fascinating.

One woman had been busy planning her wedding when she got the letter. With her fiancé off to war and their nuptials on hold, she'd said yes right away. Another woman came from a family of horse breeders. She'd been showing horses since she was old enough to ride, but flying was her real passion. And a third had been in college, studying to be a nurse.

"I'll go back one day," she said. "But this seemed like an opportunity I couldn't pass up."

Carol Ann had worked for a company crop dusting farms, something she would've kept doing but the airfield she worked out of was taken over by the military and the few men left were given her job.

"What about you, Audrey?" Carol Ann asked, raising her bottle of Coca-Cola. "What were you doing in Dallas?"

"The same as you all. Crop dusting, collecting scrap metal and rubber, putting together care boxes to be sent overseas." I took a sip from my cola, keeping my eyes averted from Carol Ann, who already showed a knack for seeing right through me.

"That's it?" she asked.

I caught her eye and looked away. "That's all," I said, my voice firm.

Her eyes widened and I felt terrible. It was an innocent question as we all tried to get to know one another, and I had closed her out.

"Okay," she said and changed the subject.

On our way back to the hotel, Carol Ann was uncharacteristically quiet. The others walked ahead, chattering about this and that.

"We're gonna walk around for a bit," one said, glancing back at us. "You ladies interested?"

"Nah," Carol Ann said. "I'm tired."

I smiled and shook my head and followed Carol Ann into the hotel.

"I'm sorry," I said, putting my hand on her arm as we walked up the stairs to our room.

"For what?" she asked, her eyes on the floor.

"For being so terse back there. It's just... I don't like to say what I did before. People always have so many questions and it's hard to think about. Much less talk about."

The questions I'd gotten in Dallas after returning home, sometimes from mere strangers, had felt intrusive. I knew people were curious because they'd never seen war and I'd been in the midst of it. But people I'd known and respected had perished while sitting at their desks or fixing the planes they looked after. And my friends had died. I could still clearly see Catherine's angelic face as she lay there in her white dress, the red stain spreading across her abdomen. And Jean...

There had been moments since the attack when I hadn't wanted to get out of bed. Times when the sound of a car backfiring had sent me scurrying beneath a table. Talking about it now still didn't come easily. But I could see that, while some people had a morbid curiosity about it, most were simply scared and wanted all the information they could get—as if that would prepare them. As for Carol Ann—she had no idea what I'd been through. She just wanted a friend.

"That's fine," she said. "I understand."

I squeezed her arm and she met my gaze finally.

"I was in Hawaii," I said. "When it was attacked."

Her lips formed a little O.

"Come on," I said, taking her hand and pulling her back down the staircase.

We walked to the ice-cream shop I'd spied on our way back from dinner and I ordered two double cones. We meandered along the town's streets, racing our melting dessert with our tongues to keep it from dripping onto our hands, and talking.

I told her the things I'd only told James in my letters to him. I told her about the guilt I felt for leaving Jean behind. If I'd only insisted she come to work that day. If I'd dragged her from her bed...

"It's not your fault, Audrey," Carol Ann said, stopping in the middle of the sidewalk. "No one knew what was coming. There was no way you were to know that day would be any different than the one before."

I sighed and nodded. It's what I'd told myself a million times. It's what James had insisted as well. And yet, it never helped.

"I wish I could go back," I said. "I wish I could change it. I'd make the girls come home with me. I'd make them come to work the next morning."

"But who's to say they wouldn't have died in the attack anyway?"

I stared at my new friend, my ice cream running in a little rivulet down the back of my hand. It was something I'd never considered—but she was right. There was no controlling our destiny. There was only what we did in the moment. All we could ever hope for was the best outcome. But it wasn't guaranteed.

As we circled back to the hotel, Carol Ann asked about the planes I'd flown—an easier subject I was only too happy to indulge in.

"If we get to pick our bunk mates, do you want to pair up?" she asked as we settled in for the night.

"I'd love to."

She flopped on her bed and kicked her shoes off. "You got a beau?" she asked.

I shook my head slowly, an image of James flashing in my mind. "No," I said. "I don't."

"Really?" She looked me up and down.

I shrugged. "I have better things to do with my time than fawn all over some silly man."

Carol Ann grinned. "You're the silly one," she said. "You've got it all backward. They're supposed to fawn over *you*. And then, as a thank-you, you let them buy you things."

I laughed.

She was Jean and Ruby and Catherine all in one. Sass and smarts and silliness. And heart. A whole lot of it.

"What do you think it's going to be like?" Carol Ann said later, after we'd gotten in bed and turned off the lights.

"Training?" I asked as the sound of warplanes buzzed in the distance. "It's going to be fantastic."

CHAPTER TWELVE

The buses arrived at the Bluebonnet Hotel promptly at 9:00 a.m. There were one hundred and five of us, standing on the sidewalk, waiting for our turn to board. It was loud and crowded, the humid air ripe with perfumes, powders and nervous sweat.

We drove through the tiny town, waving at kids in their Sunday best, eager to reach the airfield.

"Look!" someone shouted and we watched as a plane lifted off and flew over us.

"What is it?" someone else asked.

"Curtiss P-40 Warhawk," I said, watching the dark green plane with its painted-on shark teeth and nose fly overhead.

"You ever fly one?" Carol Ann asked.

I nodded, remembering the one I'd parked at Haleiwa Airfield almost two years ago. I wondered what stood on the airstrip now. The letters I'd received from Claire told of beaches fenced off with barbed wire and more soldiers than ever. The Royal Hawaiian, where Jean, Catherine and Ruby had loved to go, was now all military personnel. How different the little island had become. I was glad not to be there to see it.

"Look!" Carol Ann breathed, her arm flying past my nose to point out the window at the edge of a runway where another plane had just taken flight.

The road curved and the bus drove beneath a sign reading Aviation Enterprises LTD. We passed a small guard building and pulled up to the front of a low-standing brick structure marked Administration and stopped. A burst of excited energy filled the space as everyone got to their feet and began gathering their things before filing out one by one.

This airfield was smaller than Wheeler, but much bigger than Hudson. There were several long buildings to the right and left of us and patches of manicured grass just beyond. Farther out I could see three large hangars. Past them were the runways. Overhead, the familiar buzz of engines made me smile. I closed my eyes, feeling the hum fill the air, vibrating my entire being, making me part of it.

"Hot dog!" Carol Ann said, squeezing my arm. "Look at 'em all, Audrey!"

We were brought to one of the three hangars, where we were instructed to seat ourselves for orientation. Ms. Cochran, Ms. Love and General Henry "Hap" Arnold led the meeting, welcoming us and letting us know our presence at Avenger Field was needed, appreciated and would not go unnoticed should they have anything to say about it.

"The army is grateful for your service and commitment to your country," the general said. "Your flying experience is invaluable, and the knowledge you gain here will hopefully be put to use long after you've left Sweetwater."

The list of classes we'd be taking seemed endless—and to some, pointless, as was evidenced by a smattering of under-the-breath muttering.

"I wouldn't have my license if I couldn't navigate," someone mumbled.

A passing grade in navigation, mathematics, physics, maps, weather, the science of flying, Morse code, among others, was required to be successful in the program. We would wake every day at 6:00 a.m., eat breakfast, do calisthenics and change into our flight suits for either ground school or flight line, depending on what schedule we were on. We would learn to use a .45mm pistol, and take swimming lessons in our flight suits. After dinner at 7:00 p.m., we'd adjourn to our bays to study. Lights out at 10:00 p.m. The army expected us to excel. Any floundering, arguing or outright failing and we'd be asked to leave the program. Fail a flight checkout twice with an officer and we'd be out. Unwillingness to follow rules? Out. The army had no time to deal with insubordinates. We were here to serve our country by freeing up the male pilots to fight.

"You are an elite group of women," Ms. Cochran told us. "But not all of you will make it through the program. Some of you will wash out long before graduation. Some of you will be asked to leave for failing to comply with the army's way. If you fall behind in your classes, you will be expected to adjourn to the study area after supper for additional tutoring. If that still doesn't help, you will be notified and sent home at your own expense. Let me leave no doubt in your mind—you are in the army now."

My head was full of information and my body was buzzing with excitement as I moved to the back of the building after the meeting with everyone else to find the duffel bag with my name on it. Inside were a trainee handbook, the obligatory GI coveralls, exercise apparel, goggles and helmet, tan slacks and white button-down they'd recommended, and shoes, as well as any extra items we ordered—like my leather jacket and gloves for flying at high altitudes in cooler temperatures. Everything was at our expense. If you couldn't afford the basics, you weren't here.

"Look at this," Carol Ann said, flipping through the hand-book as we walked toward the barracks to find our assigned room. "Look at the simulations we'll take part in. Bomb drop-ping, strafing, rescue missions— Audrey." She stopped walking. "Reveille? What's that? I don't know how to do that. And taps?"

I chuckled. "Reveille is when we get up. Taps is when we go to sleep."

"Oh. How do you know that?"

"I worked on a base, remember?"

I stopped in front of bay number five. "This is us," I said, looking at the plain white door with its screened-in window.

"Looks cozy," Carol Ann said. "What did they use it for be-fore? Livestock?"

"I believe soldiers lived here until recently."

"I hope they hosed it down."

The barracks were long and simple with four bays to a build-ing. They looked to have been freshly painted and were tidy and unfussy in the military way I'd come to appreciate during my time in Hawaii.

We hurried through the door to see who else we'd be room-ing with, taking a quick look around at our new home for the next few months. White walls, brown laminate floor and six no-frills cots with tall white lockers beside each made up the perimeter of the room. In the center was a long table with small wooden partitions making six individual desks, each with its own chair.

"Found the bathroom," Carol Ann said, disappearing through a doorway at the back of the room.

I followed her in and we took in the two showers, two sinks and two toilets. Across from our door was another door lead-ing to the next bay over. I looked at her with raised eyebrows.

"It's going to get cozy."

We returned to the main room. One of the beds had already been claimed, a trunk sitting atop it. We chose two on the other side of the room. As we unpacked, the other women assigned to our bay trickled in. Sharon, Maxine, Geraldine and Tanya arrived one at a time, each selecting her bed as she came in by dropping her duffel on top, except Geraldine who was the owner of the trunk already there, and Tanya, who was last to arrive and subsequently got the last available spot.

Carol Ann, Geraldine and I made idle chitchat while the other women walked around getting their bearings.

"That bathroom is gonna be a problem, I can tell you now," Tanya said. She was a deceptively delicate-looking blue-eyed gal with flaxen hair and a gravelly voice, a cigarette tucked behind her ear. "Not for me, mind you. I grew up the youngest of seven. Six older brothers always fighting to get to the bathroom first. I can wait hours. But I have a feeling some of you aren't gonna do well with waiting to get your hair done up and your lipstick on before it's time to go."

Carol Ann snorted as Tanya's gaze shot straight to Sharon, a peroxide blonde with light brown drawn-on brows, carefully painted lips and a figure that could only be described as lush. She was practically bursting out of her white blouse with its navy sailor collar, the buttons straining to contain the large bosom underneath. Her skirt was navy-inspired as well, fitted over the hips before flaring at the knees with four white buttons running down the front of each hip. On top of her bleached hair perched a little navy beret.

"Don't you worry about me, hon," Sharon said. "I'll be up way before the rest of you gals." She slid her hands over her hips. "All this takes work."

We made introductions then, going around the room, each woman stating her name, where she came from and what she used to do before she got her letter from Ms. Cochran.

Geraldine, the eldest of us all, was the mother of two boys. Her husband owned their town's only grocery store and she stayed home. She patted the curls of her short ash-brown hair the entire time she spoke, when she wasn't fidgeting with the bow tied at her neck, her ankles crossing and recrossing.

"Two boys, huh?" Carol Ann said.

"Well, three if you count their father," Geraldine said. "And I often do." She mumbled the last part and the rest of us laughed.

"All men are boys," Tanya said, chewing the end of a pencil she'd pulled from behind her other ear. "So long as you go in knowing that though, it ain't so bad. I'm used to it, with six brothers and all. I actually prefer their company. They only have about one thought in their head at a time. Not like women. I almost didn't come here 'cause of all the women. I mean, y'all seem great but clearly I ain't into fashion or hairstyles." She waved a hand to indicate the scarf covering her hair, the men's button-down shirt she wore knotted at the waist and her dark blue trousers with a stain on one thigh. "And I ain't big into sharing my feelings neither. I was a mechanic back home in Wyoming. Not a lot of women in that field. I like to go in, get my work done, have a meal and get some shut-eye."

"I prefer being in the company of men too," Sharon said in a breathy voice. "I'm an actress. From New York. Originally Pennsylvania."

"How did you get into flying?" Geraldine asked.

"A boy." She smiled. "Why else?"

"I can think of lots of reasons," Tanya grumbled under her breath and began to chew her nails. She glanced back at Geraldine. "What's your name again? Geri?"

"Geraldine," she said, a rash of color spreading up from her neck. "I hate Geri."

"Sorry, Ger. What kind of flying did you do?"

She pursed her lips, her hands twisting so much I feared they'd end up in a knot. "I was a barnstormer," she said in a soft voice.

"A what?" Sharon asked. "What's a barnstormer?"

"We entertained people. We did shows and fancy flying tricks."

"What kind of tricks?" Maxine asked, her eyes wide.

"Ever hear of the hat trick?"

My mouth dropped open. "You did that?" I asked in a hushed voice.

"What is it?" Carol Ann asked.

"The plane comes in low and upside down," Geraldine said, "and someone stands on the ground with a hat on. When we flew over, I'd remove it with my hand."

The room went silent for a moment as we all stared at the older, slightly frumpy woman hunched on her cot as though trying to disappear from sight.

"I've seen barnstormers," I finally said. "I'm impressed. It's a dangerous job."

"That's why it's illegal now. Since nineteen thirty-eight. But I'd stopped before that. I got married and he didn't want me doing it anymore. It didn't pay much anyhow, and then I got pregnant so..." She shrugged.

"What about you?" Tanya said, tapping the frame of my cot with her foot. "Where you from?"

"Dallas. I did some crop dusting and deliveries for local companies, scrap metal drives, rubber drives...same as most these days I suppose."

Carol Ann gave me a look but I shook my head and turned my attention to Maxine, a doll-like dark-eyed young woman with shiny black hair twisted into two plaits on either side of her head. She wore a prim white short-sleeved blouse with a lace collar, a green-and-white-checked skirt and little lace-up white oxfords.

Maxine hailed from Michigan. Born into a wealthy family, she was in her first year of college when she heard of the Civilian Pilot Training Program. She signed up and started logging miles almost immediately. But during her second year of school the circus came to town. They were hiring and she had a specific skill set they desired.

"They called you what?" Carol Ann asked, her eyes nearly popping out of her head.

"The Rubber Girl," Maxine said. "I can contort my body."

There were several blank stares so Maxine stood and swung one leg backward, catching it by the ankle above her head. She bent her knees so that her toes rested on top of her head.

"Oh dear," Carol Ann said. "Stop it. Please. Something's gonna snap off."

Maxine laughed and released her leg.

"Okay, well, I can't top that. I'm Carol Ann from Tuscumbia, Alabama. Same place Helen Keller was born. I was a crop duster until my job was given to a couple of men whose jobs elsewhere dried up. Lived with my aunt and uncle until now. Parents are dead. I got engaged Saturday, December 6, 1941. I'm sure you all know where this story is going. He's overseas and I'm worried as heck for him, but I'm glad to be here 'cause if he were home I probably wouldn't be doing anything as exciting as all this or making so many new friends."

"Cheers to that," I said and she grinned.

We broke for lunch, where more introductions were made and stories shared as we got to know the women of class 43-W-2. Carol Ann struck up a conversation with a woman who reminded me so much of Catherine I gasped when I saw her sable-colored waves and warm brown eyes.

"Audrey, this is Nola," Carol Ann said.

We shook hands and exchanged pleasantries. Nola was born and raised in Savannah, Georgia. At eighteen she'd rejected her mother's constant badgering about getting married and settling down and instead applied to college at Sarah Lawrence in New York. Like Maxine, that's where she'd found out about a Civilian Pilot Training course and fell in love with flying.

"I love to take pictures from up there," she said. "I have quite a collection. I brought some with me—I can show you both if you'd like. They're pretty spectacular if I do say so myself."

"I'd love that," I said.

She looked around the room then, her dark waves swishing over her shoulders. I looked away for a moment to catch my breath. Even the small gestures she made were similar to Catherine's. They could've been sisters. When she turned back though she looked worried.

"Do you think many of the women here have flown military planes? I'm afraid I won't be able to keep up. I only started flying three years ago and only in a Jenny. Some of those planes out there look downright evil."

I felt Carol Ann's eyes on me.

"Well, I haven't," Tanya said, joining the conversation. "Geri? You were a daredevil. You ever fly any of those planes out there?"

"No," Geraldine said, setting down her fork with a pointed look. "And it's Geraldine, Tanya."

"Yeah, yeah. Max! Rubber Girl!"

Maxine looked up, her cheeks flushing pink. "Yes?" she choked out.

"You ever fly military planes?"

She shook her head and glanced over at Sharon, who was busy staring into the mirror of her pink enamel compact and powdering her nose.

"I'm gonna guess that one hasn't either," Tanya said and Carol Ann snorted.

"I sure wish someone could shed a little light on them before we take them up," Carol Ann said. "With us being so nervous and all."

"Mercy's sake," I muttered, throwing an elbow into her rib cage. I sighed and looked around the group. "Fine. I have. I've flown nearly every one of those planes out there."

All eyes were on me.

"You?" Tanya asked, her pale gaze wide with skepticism.

"Yeah, me," I said. "I was a civilian contractor in Hawaii.

Didn't you girls have those flyers posted around your towns a couple years ago? See the islands! Fly for the army! There was a man that went around to the airfields and airports too."

"Oh yeah," Geraldine said. "I remember that. I didn't pay attention to it though. Not with a husband and two boys. Plus, I thought it was only for men."

"I'll bet a lot of women did. But four of us didn't," I said. "And it was glorious."

"Wow," Maxine said. "There are some big planes out there. With two engines even."

I grinned. "I've flown one with four."

Carol Ann's eyes bugged.

"So…" Nola furrowed her pretty brow. "Were you there when…"

Our eyes met, and damned if mine didn't fill with tears.

"When what?" Tanya asked.

"The attack," Geraldine said, her voice soft. "You were there, Audrey? You saw it happen?"

"I did." I nodded, staring down at the table.

"What was it like?" Sharon asked, her compact forgotten, her hand held aloft mid-puff.

I sighed. "Imagine the most beautiful place you've ever seen. And then imagine it obscured in the blackest smoke, reeking of the worst smells, and instead of hearing the waves lapping on the shore, happy music and voices on every street, screams and sirens and the wailing of those hurt and dying. And all the while, planes are strafing everything in sight and battleships and buildings are exploding from bombs. It was the worst thing I've ever seen."

"Where were you when it happened?" Maxine asked, her dark eyes huge in her small face.

"In the air with a young airman. We landed as soon as we could on an unpaved airstrip and then hopped in a jeep and drove to one of the bases to help out. It was…chaos."

For the thousandth time, I pictured the island that morning, the plumes of acrid black smoke billowing toward the sky as James and I raced toward Wheeler, my heart beating hard in my chest as I stared in disbelief at the sight.

"You must have been so scared," Carol Ann said. I met her gaze. I'd already told her the whole story, but I imagined hearing it again made it a little more real in her mind.

"I was terrified," I said. "I lost several people I cared about and—" My voice caught and I pursed my lips.

A hand reached out. Then another, and another after that.

"I don't know if I could get back in a plane after having that happen to me," Sharon said, her compact now closed as she turned it over and over in her hands.

"There were moments of hesitation," I said. "But flying is the one thing I know with certainty I am meant to do."

"Well, thank goodness for that," Carol Ann said. "Or you wouldn't be here now."

The door to the mess hall slammed and we all jumped in our seats. Ms. Cochran crossed the room, grabbed a tray and made her way down the buffet.

"Ladies," she said with a nod as she passed by on her way back out.

"Ma'am," we said.

We stacked our trays and filed out into the hot and humid air. Some of the women headed back to their bays to finish unpacking. Carol Ann, Tanya, Nola and I decided to take a walk around the airfield to get our bearings.

We passed a large fountain and peeked in classroom windows as we made our way to the runway where plane after plane was lined up.

"Tomorrow morning, gals," Tanya said. "This will be our playground."

"Is it anything like Hawaii?" Nola asked.

I glanced around at the hangars and runway. "In some ways,"

I said, remembering the sweet humid air and the sound of men around the base calling out cadence as they marched here and there. "The planes. The hangars. That's all very similar. But Wheeler Airfield was in the middle of paradise. This…" I stared out at our brown surroundings as a gust of wind picked up, carrying with it a cloud of dust. "Is no paradise."

Carol Ann put an arm around my shoulder and squeezed.

"But we'll have fun," I said, looking at each of the ladies standing with me. "So much it won't even matter about the dust."

Our room had transformed since we'd left, personal items having been placed all over, making it look lived in. Maxine, Sharon and Geraldine had put items they'd brought from home on their desks. Sharon's had several small framed photos of men and a stack of flowery stationery. Geraldine had placed one framed family photo on hers, as well as a notebook and pencil. Maxine's desk had a small pink vase, two notebooks, five pencils and a feather.

Carol Ann plunked a framed photograph on her desk.

"Is that your fiancé?" I asked, glancing at the picture of a dark-haired man with thin lips and a kind smile.

"Yes, that's Gus. We've been going steady since the tenth grade. He's not the best looking, but he is the sweetest. How 'bout you?" She glanced at the open suitcase on my bed. "Any pictures of the family?"

I placed a framed photo of Evie and me with our parents on my own desk, as well as what seemed to be the required notebook and pencil.

We convened in the mess hall once more for dinner and then took turns using the showers with the girls in the bay across from ours. Taps was at ten so we still had a little over two hours before bedtime to chat or go through the handbook.

Most of us moved outside so we could socialize with the other women. Chatter and smoke from cigarettes drifted back and forth as we sat around exchanging information in the evening heat.

"What time is it?" Carol Ann asked through a yawn after a while.

I checked my watch. "Twenty till."

"I'm gonna head in. I'm beat."

We said good-night to the others and I followed her inside and pulled off my slippers, stowing them beneath my bed.

"What's your family like, Audrey?" Carol Ann asked as she climbed under her blanket.

I rolled onto my side and propped my head up on my hand. I told her about my father, an intelligent and handsome man who had grown up poor and on a farm. Rather than doing as his father had done, and his father before him, he'd decided not to go into farming as a way of putting food on the table, but instead got into the oil business in the twenties. He bought a huge plot of land a year later, built a house and met and married my mother—a society darling who planned every second of every day down to the most minute detail.

"She'd have planned my entire life had I let her," I said. "But I was too much to bother with and she finally gave up and concentrated on my younger sister, who is much more amenable to things like society parties and dating the right men."

"Do you and your sister get along? You sound like you're very different from one another."

"We're not really, she's just better at doing what she's told than I am. I adore her. She has a naughty sense of humor. She always knows how to cheer me up. Had she not been around when I got home from Hawaii, I'd have been lost." I smiled, remembering her being my constant shadow in those first weeks, and played with the little gold bird charm at my throat.

"Did she give you that?" Carol Ann pointed to the necklace.

"No," I said, dropping my hand to the bed. I hesitated to mention James, but found I wanted to share everything with the honest and open woman across from me. Including the man who had made me question things about myself I'd thought decided long ago.

I reached down and pulled my suitcase out from under my bed and opened it. Carol Ann sat up, eyes wide in anticipation. I lifted the frame I'd left inside and looked down at the photo behind the glass. After a moment, I passed it across the aisle into her outstretched hand.

"Holy Lord," she said, her eyes practically falling out of her head. "Is he famous?"

I laughed softly. "No. He's Lieutenant James Hart. We met in Hawaii."

"Wow," Carol Ann whispered. "I'll bet that was steamy. You and him on that island oasis… But wait, I thought you didn't have a beau."

I took the photo from her and stared down at it, my chest rising and falling, remembering the day the photograph was taken. How we'd stood there on the beach with the sun going down, the warmth of his hand on my shoulder.

"We're just friends."

"He doesn't look as though he thinks you're just a friend," she said, taking the picture back. "He looks proud to be standing next to you. He looks in love, Audrey."

I shook my head. "Even if he were, we have different goals for our lives. He wants to move up in ranks and go wherever the army sends him. I want to live in Dallas and own an airfield."

"And he gave you that necklace?"

I touched the little bird again. "He did."

"Why a bird?"

"It's what he calls me."

Carol Ann smiled and sat up.

"What are you up to?" I asked, peering at her.

She rose from the bed and set the framed photo on my desk beside the one of my family.

"He should be there," she said. "If he's your friend, he belongs on that desk."

"I suppose."

"And just wait until Sharon sees him!" She giggled. "She's gonna spit nails she'll be so jealous."

I laughed and hit her over the head with my pillow just as a flurry of activity burst in the door from outside. Sharon hurried to the bathroom while Geraldine patted the curlers beneath her scarf and removed a demure rose-colored nightgown from her locker. Maxine rushed in, slamming the door behind her, the smell of smoke clinging to her tiny body. Outside we could hear the stomps of women putting out their cigarettes in the dirt.

Sharon returned to the room in a waft of freshly sprayed perfume and a negligee that covered just the essentials as Tanya entered the bay from outside.

"Dear Lord," Tanya muttered. "Where does she think she is?"

"What's that?" Sharon asked from where she sat perched on the edge of her bed wrapping a bright pink scarf around her curlers.

Taps sounded out across the little base.

"Lights out," Tanya said, her hand on the switch. "See you ladies in the morning."

CHAPTER THIRTEEN

The army way was no small thing. Our first official day brought heat exhaustion for several of the women during morning calisthenics. Geraldine and two other women were helped off the field to the infirmary to get water and cool down while the rest of us did exercises I hadn't done since grade school.

A stout woman with a vicious whistle stood at the front of the group shouting instructions. We did push-ups, sit-ups, jumping jacks and more as we groaned and moaned and wiped the sweat and dust from our eyes and mouths. By the end of it, we were soaked, our T-shirts clinging to our bodies, our shorts hiked up in unflattering ways.

We staggered back to our barracks to shower and change into our new flight suits.

"Whom is this supposed to be for?" I asked, holding up my arms, my hands hidden by the extra length of fabric. "Did they realize they were ordering for women? Not men? I'm going to drown in this thing."

"It's awful," Sharon said, lowering her zipper so it hit mid-bosom. "So unflattering."

"I could care less about flattering," Tanya said. "I can't even walk in this thing." She took a step and tripped, making her case.

Ten minutes later, still overheated, the arms and legs of our suits rolled and pinned up the best we could get them, belts wrapped twice around some of our waists, we hobbled to breakfast, where most of us hungrily ate the scrambled eggs, bacon and toast waiting for us while others labored over the meal after the intense exercise.

We were almost finished when Sharon slammed her water cup on the table.

"Who is that?" she said, causing us all to turn to see who she was looking at.

The gentleman in question was tall, blond, wearing military "tans" and walking with a cane. He spoke to an older man as they headed for the food line, and seemed oblivious to the fact that he was on display, over two-dozen pairs of eyes glued to his every move. Including mine, I noticed, and looked away.

"That is Officer Wilson," a woman sitting at the next table over said, tossing a lock of bleached blond hair over her shoulder, her beady eyes taking us in from beneath overplucked eyebrows. "He teaches navigation. I got into town early and by some stroke of luck ran into him. He's a doll. Smart too. And single. I'm Hildie, by the way. I'm in the bay attached to yours."

"We're not supposed to fraternize with the men," Tanya said.

Hildie rolled her eyes. "Well, what Ms. Cochran doesn't know..." She winked and turned around in her seat.

"Yuck," Maxine said and the rest of us snickered.

"She's trouble, that one," Geraldine said. "Mark my words."

We finished eating and delivered our trays and dirty dishes to the bins on the other side of the room. As we headed for the doors, Sharon whispered to Maxine, the two of them staring at the table where Officer Wilson sat with three other men.

"Stop staring," Tanya said under her breath.

As she spoke, Officer Wilson looked up. His gaze took in each of us in turn, landing on me last as I brought up the rear. His eyes widened and I looked away, my skin warming as I quickened my step.

"Anyone else see that?" Carol Ann asked as we pushed out the doors into the heat of the morning. "Someone has a new admirer."

I swatted her on the arm as Tanya muttered, "Don't go telling Hildie," and everyone laughed.

Everyone but me.

Our first class of the day was geography. We studied the west coast of the country, focusing on landforms and climate changes. After that we moved on to mathematics, where we began learning how to calculate routes. In our maps course we sat, stood and sprawled on the floor, getting familiar with maps of counties, cities and states.

When it was time to break for lunch, we went gladly, our minds reeling from the amount of information thrown at us.

"You okay?" I asked Carol Ann as she walked beside me, her brow furrowed.

"They teach so fast," she said. "I don't know if I can keep up."

"We'll study every night. You'll be fine. We'll help each other."

After we ate we got on flight line, the most anticipated part of the day. We were divided up by experience, four trainees to one instructor, which meant long wait times as each girl got her hour in the sky.

Since everyone knew how to fly, we got to skip basic flying instruction, but most of the women had never flown an aircraft built for the military and would need to start in my favorite model, the Fairchild PT-19, with an instructor.

My breath caught when I saw the five Fairchilds lined up on the tarmac. I thought of Roxy and remembered the last time I'd seen her, her wheels dug deep into the Haleiwa sand. I wondered if she was still there, or if she'd been taken back to Wheeler to get patched up once again. Without Bill's loving and patient hands, I feared she'd been hauled off to wherever the rest of the ruined planes had gone.

Those who had experience in the PT-19 got to fly the BT-13 Valiant or AT-6 Texan. Since I'd flown all three, I took up the double-engine AT-17 Cessna Bobcat.

"What the hell is that thing?" Tanya asked when she saw the plywood and canvas aircraft.

"The men call her the 'Bamboo Bomber,'" I said, slipping on my parachute.

"Good luck," she said and made the sign of the cross.

After we had a turn, we went to the back of the line and waited to go up again. At any one time, ten of us would be in the air simultaneously, each at a different altitude to avoid crashing.

After dinner we retired to our bays, where we studied, showered and lounged around talking until taps.

The entire first week was the same. Calisthenics, breakfast, geography, math, maps, lunch, flight line and dinner. We studied every evening, taking small breaks on the grassy common areas between the barracks, chatting with the other women, sharing tips and information about the different classes we'd been sorted into.

On our first Sunday off, we followed the example of the class before us and dragged our chairs outside to sunbathe. We tipped the chairs upside down, throwing a shirt or sheet over the back of them to recline on, and someone put a radio in the window so we could listen to Count Basie while we browned our skin.

"Whose turn is it?" I asked, shielding my eyes from the sun and squinting at the bodies lying limp around me.

"Mine," Carol Ann mumbled. "But I can't get up."

"I can't believe you fools are out here," Tanya said, walking by on her way inside.

"Oh! Tanya!" Carol Ann called, waving her hand. "Can you please, please, please fill that bucket with ice from the mess hall for me?"

I peeked at Tanya and stifled a laugh. She'd used the afternoon as an opportunity to log more hours and was still in her flight suit, which was drenched with sweat, her pale hair plastered to her scalp making her look almost bald.

"No," she said and walked inside the barracks, slamming the screen door behind her.

"I just thought since she was up…" Carol Ann said.

"I'll go," I said. "I think I'm done out here anyhow." I glanced at Carol Ann. "You might want to come in yourself. You look like a lobster."

She shielded her eyes with her hand and peeked up at me.

"So do you."

We staggered to our feet, grabbing our bedding, chairs and the bits of clothing we'd strewn about. I caught a glimpse of myself in the mirror as I headed for the showers and stopped. The parts of my skin that had previously been white were now bright red.

"Oh dear," I said. "That's going to hurt."

"Be careful," Carol Ann said as I stepped into the shower. "The water feels like needles."

"The bottoms of my feet are burned!" Maxine said, hurrying in behind us. "Can you make room for one more?"

"Dear Lord. I don't know how I'm going to be able to fly tomorrow," Sharon said, stumbling in. She held out her bright pink arms. "I was just hoping for a little color. This is ridiculous."

"At least your backside isn't burned," Carol Ann said, turning to give us all a view of the bright red skin where her swimsuit hadn't covered.

"Ouch," I said, glad I'd had the forethought to throw a shirt over my own behind.

"Oh dear," Geraldine said when she got an eyeful of us after an afternoon in town. "You girls look…bright."

"We know," Carol Ann moaned, tossing a piece of ice at her.

She batted it away and it landed on Maxine, who threw it at Tanya who had just walked into the room from the bathroom.

Tanya yelped, grabbing a handful of ice from the bucket on the floor.

After that, ice and ice water went flying, our burns forgotten as we screamed and ran around the room slipping and laughing.

By the third week we knew every state and major city in the entire United States, and most of us could do twenty army-worthy push-ups without once falling to our knees. We'd flown at least a half dozen different planes and had begun testing new ones that had come straight off the assembly line, and old ones that had been repaired and needed flight-ready status again before being ferried out to bases all over the country.

There had been a few moments of terror when some of the patched-up planes experienced engine failure or the landing gear got stuck. Or the time one of the new planes began to drop parts onto the ground below. But for the most part, the flights were safe and so far no one had gotten hurt.

Our evenings were still consumed by studying, when we weren't sitting outside with the other women from our class, exchanging stories and cigarettes and sodas. I often kept to the area in front of our bay since Hildie, our neighbor with the crush on our navigation teacher, Officer Wilson, had apparently heard from other sources how he'd looked at me that first morning—and several subsequent mornings, afternoons and evenings as well. She hadn't taken kindly to his attentions going elsewhere, and had made it her unofficial task to pester me at any given moment.

"Why don't you just tell her off?" Tanya asked. "Or tell her you're with that guy in the picture on your desk. Unless of course you do like him."

"I don't," I snapped. "But even if I did, it wouldn't be her business. I've been surrounded by women like her my whole life. Women who like to create drama for no reason at all. I'm not about to fall into her pit of self-loathing just to satisfy some crazy need she has."

"Amen to that," Geraldine said.

But I wasn't being entirely honest. There was something about the officer that had piqued my interest. It wasn't his looks. It took more than a handsome face to get my attention. Maybe it was the unexplained cane, or his ability to shift the focus off himself every time one of the women tried to strike up a conversation if they caught him on his way to the mess hall. All anyone could say about him, besides the fact that he was dreamy to look at, was that he was kind and funny, and sure knew a lot about maps.

I felt guilty any time I found myself wondering about him rather than thinking of James, whom I still hadn't heard from. Which then led me to silently admonish myself for thinking of either of them when I should've been doing something else—like studying or making a new list for my airfield.

We worked most Saturdays, but Sundays were ours. Sometimes we took the bus to town, or caught a ride with one of the women who had cars at the base. We'd see a movie, get a soda or just walk around town poking into shops. Sometimes we swam at the town pool, other times we went to the lake where we'd run into some of the officers we saw on base. Tanya and I made bets about who'd sneak off with whom. So far I was ahead.

"How do you always know?" Carol Ann asked one day. "I'd never have put that girl with that guy."

"It's all about confidence. See how he acted like he didn't care about her? It drove her nuts and made him that much more attractive. It's all about the chase."

"Hmm… Now I think maybe I should've made Gus work harder to get me," she said and I laughed.

We also went dancing on the rare Saturday night. The restaurant we'd had dinner at our first night in Sweetwater hosted live bands on the weekends. We'd put on dresses and do our hair, pile into buses and head to town, where we'd drink and dance with strangers and come home tipsy and whispering loudly as we tiptoed to our bays.

On the rare occasion, the army brought male cadets over for a Saturday night dance. Music and food was provided in the mess hall and we all went since there wasn't much else to do. Mostly we hung around in groups gabbing until one of the men got up the guts to ask us to dance. I usually hung near the back to avoid it all. Tanya feigned an ankle injury, which I'd found ingenious but caused Sharon to ask why she'd come at all.

"For the desserts, of course," was her answer.

On one such Saturday night, Officer Wilson made an appearance, creating such a stir, one would have thought Cary Grant had entered the room.

"Hildie's got her eyes on you," Carol Ann whispered to me.

Tanya stepped forward as though to guard me from her stare.

"Old Hildie can blow it out her—"

"Tanya!" Geraldine said, causing us to laugh.

We watched in amusement as Hildie approached the officer, gesturing to the dance floor. But he smiled and shook his head, proffering his cane as his excuse.

"Ha!" Tanya said as Hildie ducked her head and hurried to rejoin her group of friends. "That'll teach her. Of course he can't dance. He has a cane."

As I sipped my punch I watched him move about the perimeter of the room, stopping to talk to other teachers in attendance and some of the cadets. After an hour or so he took leave, smiling as he passed by us on his way to the door.

"Ladies," he said, nodding his head, his eyes locked on me.

My stomach did a little flip in response and, without thinking, I smiled.

CHAPTER FOURTEEN

In September, the Allies invaded Italy, leading to the country's surrender, the people rising up against German occupiers. Still more Jews were captured and sent to camps. And we, the Women Airforce Service Pilots, began a new set of classes— our service to our country never more necessary as it pushed to win the war.

Firearms training, navigation and swimming were our lessons for the month, and we approached each with a newfound determination and excitement.

Firearms was taught by Sergeant J. R. Woodley, a tough-talking retired marine with a buzz cut and wad of chewing tobacco so large we were in constant fear of it tumbling from his mouth and landing somewhere near us. A stern woman appropriately called Ms. Poole, who reminded me of Mae with her short gray hair, was in charge of the swimming lessons. And Officer Wilson taught navigation.

I was at once eager to learn something new, and uneasy, as I would now be subject to scrutiny from those who knew of Officer Wilson's constant glances my way—and Hildie's subsequent hatred of me, which she'd made painfully obvious.

"I feel like I'm back in high school," I'd muttered to Carol Ann one day after Hildie had purposefully bumped into me, nearly taking off my shoulder.

"Maybe we can tell the principal on her," she replied.

I was also anxious. Shooting a gun was not something I'd considered a necessity in my life, but the army deemed it a skill of utmost importance and required us to learn it in case we were captured while working for Ferry Command, the group responsible for delivering planes to bases all over the United States. Besides transporting planes, sometimes we'd also be flying personnel, as well as sensitive information. Should we be captured while in possession of such material, we would need to know how to use a .45mm pistol to shoot the fuel tank.

Swimming lessons were also for dire situations. Crash landing in water or ejecting and landing in water in a flight suit could prove to be perilous. Learning to quickly remove our gear would be a matter of life and death.

As we marched to the gunnery first thing after breakfast, I whispered to Carol Ann, "What if we accidentally shoot someone?"

"I suppose that depends on if they die or not," she said, making Tanya snicker.

"That is not helpful, Carol Ann," I said in my mother's disapproving tone.

"Just aim for the target," Tanya said.

"Maybe they can make her target look like Hildie," Geraldine offered and we all laughed.

An hour later, our first class in weapons training in the books, we headed to navigation class.

"You nervous?" Carol Ann whispered from behind me.

"No," I said, my voice firm. But I was. Not for the class itself, but because of the man teaching it.

I was tired of hearing about Officer Wilson, even from Carol Ann, who I knew was only kidding around. And I was angry. Angry with my body for responding to his looks and my mind for conjuring images of him when I was supposed to be concentrating on my training. It was only going to get worse now that I had a class with him. I knew all eyes would be on the two of us to see if those looks he was always giving me would happen during our lessons and if they'd eventually turn into something more. And more important to everyone—would I finally respond in kind. As an added bonus, it would all be witnessed by Hildie, who unfortunately was in all my classes.

In truth, what really bothered me the most about Officer Wilson was, if I was going to think about any man—I wanted that man to be James. But I hadn't been receiving letters from him nearly as frequently lately, and his figurative distance had left me feeling as though maybe our friendship had come to a close without my knowing, and I was beginning to feel hurt by his silence.

Most of our instructors at Avenger Field were civilian men or women. Older civilian men who could only be described as curmudgeons, and tough women who didn't take kindly to whispers during class, tardiness or even the need to be excused to use the restroom.

Officer Carter Wilson was not old. Nor was he a woman. He'd been a soldier. A navigator, we learned, for aircraft serving in the Pacific Theater. But that's where his introduction of himself ended. There was no explanation about his cane. No story of his time in the war. He was there to teach. He hoped we would learn too.

On each of the four walls were maps of the world. As we entered the classroom, we were all given small maps of the United States. Each state was left blank.

"Please fill in every state you know," Officer Wilson said, walking across the room. "Just coming from a maps course, this should be easy. That being said, it's not a contest, it's a starting point. How can you map a course if you don't know what state you're in?"

We sat quietly for the next twenty minutes, the only sound the frustrated breaths of students unable to identify a state and the soft thud of Officer Wilson's cane on the floor as he checked our progress. As he neared my desk the room stilled, several heads turning in my direction.

"Nice work, Miss...?"

"Coltrane," I said, my voice low.

"Miss Coltrane," he murmured and kept moving.

I glanced across the row at Tanya, who raised her eyebrows. I rolled my eyes and stared down at my paper. I'd already finished and was now doodling around the state lines to make it look as though I was still working. I did not want to be the first to rise and walk to the officer's desk, all eyes on me as I went. Including those of our teacher.

The chatter about Officer Wilson didn't stop for the rest of the day, no matter how many times I tried to change the subject. Even Geraldine couldn't help herself.

"You too?" I asked as we sat down to dinner.

"Audrey, dear," she said with no modesty to be found. "When you're a married woman with children, you too will find any form of entertainment will suffice. I apologize that it's at your expense, but, dear, watching that man struggle to look at anything or anyone but you is quite sweet." She sighed. "Oh, to be young and in love."

"I'm not— He's not..." I gave up and shoved a forkful of potatoes in my mouth. There was no point in trying to get them to stop. It was as if they were watching a movie play out right before their eyes, and I was the unfortunate leading lady.

I glanced at Carol Ann, who shook with laughter.

"Stop it," I muttered. But it only made her laugh harder.

The following morning Hildie sat lurking in the bathroom waiting to ambush me.

"So," she said. "Still going to deny your little fling with Officer Wilson? Seems to me the cat's out of the bag now."

"There is no cat to let out, Hildie," I said, letting myself into one of the stalls and locking the door. "He's all yours if you want him."

"Gee, thanks. How kind of you to offer him up when you've clearly put your hooks in him so far he can't see no one else. I don't even understand the attraction. It's not like you're beautiful."

"You're right," I said. "So go get him and leave me alone please."

"I should really just report you to Ms. Cochran."

That made me mad. I swung open the door, startling Hildie, who got to her feet, and stepped so close my nose was practically in her eye.

"If you feel the need to report me for things I haven't done, you go right ahead," I fumed. "But I will let you know that if you do, I will be forced to give a report of my own."

"Oh yeah?" she said. "Saying what?"

I narrowed my eyes and leaned in another centimeter. "That you and that cadet—Carlson was it—were found in the men's room outside the mess hall during the last dance, and his trousers were around his ankles."

She gasped and tried to step away, but the bench behind her made it impossible and she landed back on her rear.

"I wasn't the only one," she said, her voice faltering.

"You're the only one I'll tattle on though."

With a huff she got to her feet and scooted from between me and the bench.

"Fine," she said and disappeared through the door to her bay.

I washed and dried my hands and then stood for a moment trying to calm my nerves. Because of a man, that woman wanted to get me kicked out of the program. A man I wasn't remotely interested in no less.

I glanced at my reflection in the mirror.

Liar.

With a sigh I returned to my bay. As I entered, someone began to clap. Then another and another.

So they'd overheard. I grinned and ducked my head.

"I'm proud of you," Carol Ann said. "And of Tanya for keeping her composure."

I glanced at the small blonde whose fists were clenched at her sides.

"I was this close to coming in there and punching that gal right in the mouth," she said.

"We all were," Geraldine said.

"Thank you," I said, my voice soft as I looked around the room.

I couldn't help smiling as I hurried into my clothes for calisthenics. They might tease me, but they had proved to be good friends. For the first time since returning home from Oahu, I felt part of a true kinship again.

Throughout our next lesson on visual navigation aids, Officer Wilson pointed to aeronautical charts as everyone but Tanya and me sat like pert little statues hanging on his every word. I kept my head down whenever possible and made sure never to meet his gaze no matter how many times I felt it on me.

"I don't think your plan is working," Carol Ann said as we left class and headed to the pool for swimming.

"What plan?"

"The plan where you ignore him. It'll just make him crazy."

"I don't know what you're talking about," I said.

"Didn't you hear him lose his place in the lesson? It happened about four times. Every time he looked at you and you wouldn't look back he got flustered."

"Well, I never heard him sound flustered."

"That's because you were too busy ignoring him."

The women never stopped talking about him. As we stood outside, waiting for our turn to swim laps and participate in timed treading exercises, on and on they went about the fit of his clothing, the way his hair shimmered in the sunlight pouring through the windows, and his soft, sweet voice. A voice I was beginning to find rather annoying as a matter of fact.

At lunch I wrapped a sandwich in a napkin and headed for the door.

"Where are you going?" Carol Ann asked, her brows furrowed as she grabbed a tray and headed for the buffet line.

"I'm going to eat in our room. I'll see you after lunch."

I let the door to the bay slam closed behind me as I kicked off my shoes and sat on my bunk with a loud sigh. So far the only good part of my day had been not having Hildie trail me muttering rude things to her pals as we went from class to class. But hearing from Carol Ann that my concerted effort to dissuade Officer Wilson from looking at me hadn't worked and, in fact, might have made it worse, frustrated me to no end.

I stared at the framed photo of James and me on my desk. With a huff I got up and grabbed it.

"Where *are* you?" I whispered, the fury leaving my body as I peered down at his handsome face.

As mad as I was about not hearing from him, I knew I had no right. I also knew my anger was a cover for what I truly felt. Sadness. Worry. And fear.

My body ached with misery at not knowing if he was okay. And no matter what I did to keep busy, to keep my mind engaged and focused on my training, I couldn't dispel the desolation not hearing from him caused.

I sank down on my chair and closed my eyes. Maybe, though I'd claimed otherwise, I did have feelings for James that stretched beyond friendship. Maybe I had let expectations for our future arise. Maybe I'd misconstrued things he'd said by imagining they meant more than they had. And sure we'd kissed but maybe it hadn't meant anything either. Maybe it had just been a moment. A moment he'd moved on from.

My eyes filled with tears, blurring the picture of the two of us. Perhaps the lengthening time between each letter's arrival had been his way of retreating. Had I missed his goodbye completely?

The door slammed open and Carol Ann stood on the threshold, her eyes wide. "Are you okay?"

"Well, no, Carol Ann. You've just startled me to death."

"Sorry. You had me worried."

"Not so worried you didn't eat lunch first though."

"Of course not, silly. They had chicken salad!"

I laughed. I could always count on Carol Ann to lighten my mood. Pointing to the sandwich still sitting uneaten on my bed, I said, "I know."

She plunked down in her chair beside me and searched my face before glancing at the photograph on the desk.

"You wanna talk about it?"

"What is there to say? I still haven't heard from James and am worried every day that he's dead and no one's bothered to tell me. Either that or I'm blind and I've completely missed something in his letters that was meant to indicate our friendship was coming to a close. In all honestly, I feel a little stupid—and I'm not used to the sensation. That combined with everyone making such a fuss about Officer Wilson, whom I've no interest in whatsoever…it's enough to make a girl crazy."

"Well, I don't know what to tell you about James. I pray to God he's not dead. I can't imagine what that will do to you. Not that his ending your friendship would be much better—but probably easier to get over. And I may be wrong but, you don't seem like the kind of gal to get all worked up about what people are saying unless there's something to get worked up about. Like my auntie always says, deniers wear blinders."

"I can see just fine," I snapped.

"Okay." She held up her hands in surrender.

I sat back in my chair contemplating if there was truth to what she said.

"So you think I like him too?" I asked. "Officer Wilson, I mean."

She shrugged. "What I do know is, if you didn't, you'd ignore everyone giving you a hard time about him. Just like you've always done with your school friends or your mama any time they took issue with your flying."

"He's not even my type."

Carol Ann snorted. "You have a type?" she asked.

I looked down at the picture of James and my heartbeat quickened. Yes. I did. But if he only considered me a friend, and maybe not even that anymore…

"Audrey," Carol Ann said. "You are the smartest woman I know. You made it clear from day one you're here to fly and when you're through with all this, you're gonna go home and buy yourself that airfield you won't shut up about. So, whether you and James are just friends, or if you like Officer Wilson or you don't, it's your life. You're allowed to like one, none or both. Ignore all those silly women. They're just bored without a bunch of men around."

"I know you're right. I just don't like being the center of attention. Especially this kind of attention. Even if I did like him, he's off-limits. And…" I looked at the photograph of James again.

"He is divine." Carol Ann sighed. "But, hon, if he ain't giving you the time a day…maybe it's time to stop waiting on him."

Tanya burst in the door then, followed by the others. I gave Carol Ann's hand a squeeze and mouthed a thank-you as we rose to change into our flight suits with everyone else.

I ate my sandwich while standing in flight line, thinking about our conversation and listening with half an ear to the conversations around me that ranged from insects to fear about the plane we were flying that afternoon.

"Just pray Fifi keeps us safe," Carol Ann said.

Fifinella, the official mascot of the WASP, was a happy little fairy-tale gremlin with horns and wings that supposedly kept the bad gremlins out of the engines. I wasn't sure I believed in gremlins, but I did believe every plane had a gender, so maybe gremlins weren't so strange after all. And I'd never speak ill of the idea out loud. Pilots could be suspicious folk.

"Here it comes!" Geraldine shouted, pointing to the sky.

The B-17 Flying Fortress was a four-engine bomber that in war had a crew of ten to man all its working parts. We'd be going up four at a time though, taking turns in the pilot's and copilot's seats. Since I was the only one in our bay who had ever flown one, I'd had to answer multiple questions about the heavy plane on the way to flight line from some of my more nervous roommates.

"How does it even get off the ground?" Sharon asked.

"Is it hard to manage?" Geraldine asked.

"It's just a plane, ladies!" Tanya said, rolling her eyes.

Geraldine, Carol Ann, Maxine and I were the first group to take the large bomber up. When we disembarked an hour after a successful test flight, Nola shouted to us.

"Smile, ladies!"

Standing beside the mammoth warplane, we slung our arms around one another and she took our picture.

"Take that, boys!" she said.

Sunday I went into town with Carol Ann and Nola for lunch at the soda shop. After our meal I used the restroom, exiting into the narrow hallway only to find myself face-to-face with none other than Officer Wilson.

"Miss Coltrane," he said, his eyes widening as a shy smile spread across his face.

I inhaled. He was certainly as handsome as everyone said, and had a boyish charm that was endearing. He seemed young though, and naive, even for someone who had been in war. Or maybe it was just that I was always comparing him to James, and the two couldn't be more different than night and day.

"Sir," I said, my face warming as I sidestepped to go around him. But he stepped in the same direction, accidentally blocking me.

"Pardon me," he said, moving out of the way so I could get by. But for some reason my feet wouldn't go.

"Is there— Can I—" He stumbled for words before shoving his hands in his pockets and waiting for me to say something.

I wanted to ask why he was always looking at me. Did he know how it made the other women act? Was there something he needed to say? Was I doing something wrong in class?

But I didn't.

"Excuse me," I murmured and finally maneuvered my body around his.

His fingertips grazed mine as I passed and I hesitated for a brief second before hurrying back to my table.

"Are you ready to go?" Carol Ann asked as I approached.

"Yes," I said, grabbing my handbag and heading for the door.

"What's the rush? Wait up!"

I pushed out the door onto the sidewalk, the cool autumn air a welcome relief, and took a deep breath.

"Audrey?" Nola said from behind me. "Are you alright?"

I nodded, plastering on a reassuring smile. "I'm swell. Should we head back now?"

"I suppose so," Carol Ann said, her eyebrows drawn in concern. "Did you happen to see Officer Wilson?"

"No," I said, looking away.

I wasn't sure why I lied, except that I could still feel the touch of his fingers on mine—and I was upset about the butterflies it made flutter in my stomach.

The following day in navigation class I was charting a course to California with three other women on a map we'd spread out on the floor. It wasn't rare for Officer Wilson to get down on the floor and help us—but when he sat beside me, the whole room stilled regardless. The warmth of his body so near mine was disconcerting, the scent of his citrusy cologne, so different from James's more subtle and earthy scent, almost distracting. At one point I got so flustered at his nearness, I shoved the pencil at Sharon and told her to finish writing down the route.

Two days later we were changing for dinner when Sharon rushed in waving a stack of mail she'd picked up from the main office.

"Someone has a letter," she said, wagging her drawn-on brows.

I didn't understand at first, distracted from a conversation I was having with Geraldine.

"Audrey," Carol Ann said, grabbing my wrist and pointing to Sharon, who held the letter aloft. "You have a letter."

The room went quiet as I walked slowly to Sharon and took the letter from her outstretched hand. At the sight of his familiar handwriting my heart skipped a beat and my eyes blurred with tears.

"Is it from him?" Carol Ann asked.

"Yes," I whispered.

The envelope, like the one I'd received two months ago, was wrinkled and dirty and I chewed my lip as I looked around the little room, longing to be alone as I read this precious letter I'd waited so long to receive.

"I'll be back," I said, putting my jacket back on over my flight suit and stepping out into the cool evening.

I walked toward the hangars, turning his letter over and over in my hands, brushing my fingertips over his handwriting.

"Miss Coltrane," a voice said.

I jumped and turned to see Officer Wilson smoking under the eave of one of the administration buildings.

"Sir," I said, clutching the letter to my chest.

"Out for an evening walk?"

"I just needed some space," I said, gesturing toward the barracks. "It gets a little crowded in there sometimes."

"I remember all too well what it was like sharing a room with a bunch of men. Gets pretty loud. Smells bad too."

I smiled and he laughed before sobering, a look of uncertainty settling over his face, reminding me once again of a young boy with his soft features and slightly goofy demeanor.

"May I join you?" he asked.

"It wouldn't be prudent," I said. "If someone saw... Well, there's already so much talk."

"Talk? Of what?"

"Us," I said softly. "You. The way you're always looking at me." I was glad for the dark as I blushed furiously.

"And here I thought I was hiding it so well," he said. "My apologies if I've caused you any trouble."

"It's fine. Truly."

"I will admit, it is hard not to look at you. It's not often I run across a woman who knows her stuff and looks like an angel to boot."

We stared at one another in the dim light, the airfield so quiet around us I was sure he could hear my heart pounding in my chest.

"Oh, Officer Wilson, there you are," someone said, causing us both to jump.

I turned to see Hildie, her beady eyes flicking from me to our teacher, her friend Agatha right behind her.

"Ladies," Officer Wilson said. "Good evening. On your way to dinner?"

"We were, but first we wanted to stop by and ask you a few questions about the Link testing today. I suppose Audrey had a few questions of her own?" She crossed her arms over her chest and peered at me as though in challenge.

"How can I help you ladies?" he asked, avoiding her question about me and turning his attention squarely on her and Agatha.

"Why don't I walk you two to the mess hall and you can ask me anything you like." He turned back to me with a nod and a wink. "Miss Coltrane, have a good night."

"You too, sir," I said and did an about-face.

As I hurried to the tarmac, I remembered why I was out there and glanced down at the envelope clutched in my fist. It was crumpled worse than before and my heart ached that I'd forgotten it in my hand at the first sight of Officer Wilson.

With a heavy sigh I sat beneath the wing of one of the PT-19s lined up and waiting for flight. Resting my back against its tire, I took a breath, readying myself for whatever was inside as a mixture of emotions whirled through my body. Happiness that he was alive and had written. Fear that the reasons he hadn't written earlier had nothing to do with the war, and everything to do with me.

With each letter I'd received over the past couple of years, it was as though he was with me. I heard his voice in the written words, smelled his woodsy, clean scent, felt his palm against mine, his thumb rubbing the soft skin between my own thumb and forefinger. But tonight the sentiment was bittersweet. One I hesitated to feel, and yet longed for.

I slid my finger beneath the flap of the envelope and held my breath as I unfolded his letter.

Little Bird,

I suppose by now, per the marking I made on my calendar, you are off on your new adventure, trying out those stellar wings of yours, and making new friends once again. How does it feel to leave everything behind again? Bittersweet? Exciting? If anything, I imagine you are having the time of your life. Different from life on Oahu (during the good times), but wonderful all the same.

We are flying missions often. Not much changes over here, except my bunk mates. I can't remember the last time I had one that stayed longer than a few months. It's hard to think of all the personal items I've had to pack up, all the new faces I welcome, each time with more dread, as I wonder how long they will last. It's hard to form bonds—and yet, it's all we have here. That and the hope that one day soon we'll get home and see the faces of the ones we left behind.

Have you heard from Ruby or Claire? How about Erma and Ken? Little Annie and her stuffed dog? If you do, please tell them that I hope they are well.

As for you, my dear, dear friend. I think of you often and I wish you so much happiness in your life. I dream of this war ending and being stationed somewhere quiet and warm, with friendly people to chat with and good books at the ready. I dream of you at your little airfield, working on plans for your hotel and making plane-shaped cookies. I dream of flying into Dallas and surprising you. I'll buy you a cup of coffee or a beer—maybe a steak?—and we will walk the length of your runway, talking about life and the future and what ideas we have for the next twenty years.

But as I sit here writing this, the bunk across from me empty once more, I wonder if I will ever get that chance. My hopes are dwindling.

Stay safe, my dear little bird. Never stop using those wings. They are stronger and more beautiful than you know.
Your friend,
James

The feeling of despair was overwhelming, his distance from me now so stark and obvious. And his presence, ever felt as I read his words, weakened. He had disappeared.

It was everything I'd feared and hoped against. In not so many words, he had said goodbye.

I didn't realize I was crying until a sob escaped my lips and echoed across the airfield.

CHAPTER FIFTEEN

October came and with it more news of the war, including the horrifying report of ninety-eight American civilians being executed by the Japanese on Wake Island. But with every story, with every report, we were only that much more invigorated to do our part and get back to work.

A new crop of trainees arrived the second week of the month, and along with them cooler weather. Instead of the breath-stealing ninety degrees, it was a mere seventy-five, which seemed frigid in comparison, but was just enough to keep us sweating in our flight suits.

The wind still blew in an almost constant gust, coating everything in dust, including the floor of our bay, causing us to sweep the room at least three times a day.

I had just put the broom away for the second time that day and sat at my desk to begin working on my map when I saw Carol Ann look up from her navigation book.

"You okay?" she asked. "That was a big sigh."

I'd been so preoccupied by my task I hadn't realized I'd made a sound.

I hadn't written James back yet after his last letter. When I didn't make it to dinner, Carol Ann had come looking for me, finding me crying beneath the wing of the Fairchild. We'd sat for a long while, talking about what it must be like for him over there. How losing so many friends and bunk mates must take a toll, and how being constantly in fear of getting bombed on base or shot down from the sky could make a person sink into a hope-lessness that might be hard to recover from. It made me wonder where all of us would be when this war was over. Those of us who had seen it—our bodies may survive, but would our souls?

I stared at the picture of us on my desk.

"You sure you don't want to write to him?" Carol Ann asked, her voice soft.

"What's the point?"

"Because he's miserable and I bet he could use some news from home. Especially from you."

"He doesn't want to hear from me. He made that clear."

"Did he? I think you're reading something that isn't there."

"It's his tone. His 'I wish you so much happiness in your life.' That's a goodbye."

"You know, sometimes I get a letter from Gus that makes me want to fly to wherever he is and smack him upside the head. I understand it's horrible over there, but I don't need no maud-lin letter to make me worry more than I already do! Write him back. Tell him what you've been doing here. Tell him about your great new friend, Carol Ann. How she's the prettiest, funniest, smartest girl you've ever known."

I snorted and she pretended to look offended before burst-ing into laughter.

"I don't know," I said. "It feels pointless. And if he doesn't respond..."

"Honestly, Audrey—it doesn't matter what you say. Gus always tells me how separated he feels. How he feels like he's missing out on so much and it makes him sad. I'm sure it's the same for James. It probably feels like the war is never going to end. He's seen a lot of death. A lot of terrible things. Give him something to smile about. Tell him about all of us. Tell him about Sharon and her eyebrows and Tanya with her cigarettes behind her ears even when she sleeps. It's bound to make him feel better, and maybe even write back quicker."

"What if he really was saying goodbye though?"

Carol Ann pushed away from her desk and faced me, putting one palm on each of my cheeks so that I looked at her as tears hovered on my lower lashes.

"Maybe he is," she said. "Maybe he feels more for you than he'll ever admit so he has to say goodbye, because it's killing him inside. Maybe he's scared and sad and has to let go of you so he can keep doing this terrible job he has to do. Maybe he loves you, but it hurts too bad to know he could die any minute. He sees it every day with his men. Maybe it makes him a little bit happy to think of you living life, going on…even if it's without him. Maybe you do have to say goodbye. But all you can really do is what's in your heart, Audrey. And you're the only one who knows what's happening in there."

The tears fell from my lashes and streamed down my cheeks.

"I don't know if I can say goodbye."

"Then don't. Send him a happy, funny note filled with stories of the scorpion you killed the other day. Boy, did that thing crack loud when you stomped on it. Or the engine that caught on fire last week right before Tanya took it up. Or how fun swimming lessons in our flight suits are."

I smiled. The swimming was awful.

"I'll think about it," I said and returned to my map.

Carol Ann did her best to distract me as we made our way through October. I trudged along beside her as we moved from firearm training to navigation to swimming each day, watching her delight in my progress with a gun and her own in the water.

Some of the women in our class had begun to complain about the rigorous training schedule. Three had washed out already, unable to keep up with the classes and failing several of the tests despite lots of after-hours studying. Carol Ann, who had initially worried she wouldn't make it through the coursework, was doing better than expected, but Maxine was floundering as of late and we'd all committed to helping her, determined that the entirety of our bay graduate at the end of the training period.

"I just don't understand why I have to know all this stuff!" she'd yelled one day, throwing her pencil across the room and narrowly missing Sharon. "We aren't actually in the army. We just fly for them."

I understood her argument. I felt the same way at times. But the truth was, even though we were civilian pilots, we were flying the army's planes. And they weren't going to let us do that unless they knew we'd been trained the army way. Which included being able to shoot out a fuel tank should we be captured while delivering confidential information, swimming in our flight suits, towing targets and using a map, a compass and the geography of the land to assert ourselves in the air. Our jobs as civilian trainees were to take all the same courses the army's male aviation cadets had, as well as test patched-up and new right-off-the-line planes so they could then be flown to bases around the country where they'd be taken overseas to fight in the war. Our presence freed up more men to fight. And we took that responsibility seriously.

The last week of our second month of training came quickly and we were put to the test in each class to make sure we knew our stuff.

In gun training our instructor surprised us with some fun assessments that included daily contests with a prize of a blue ribbon and a plate of homemade cookies for the winner. Carol Ann won twice and shared her winnings with our bay.

In swim class we were timed in laps, treading water and getting out of our gear while submerged. We'd drag ourselves out of the frigid water at the end of our hour each day, exhausted and starving.

For navigation we practiced in a flight simulator called a Link Trainer—also fondly known as the "dreaded blue box." The Link was a small blue contraption that looked like a cartoon version of a plane with its round fuselage and tiny wings, and replicated flying blind, as one might do when flying at night or when clouds of smoke were likely to obscure vision. The pilot of the Link was closed inside the apparatus and had to rely solely on the gauges in front of them to navigate simulated flying conditions. This exercise prepared us for the next phase of training— flying "under the hood." The hood was a view-limiting device placed over our helmets during a daytime flight. Once airborne, it was lowered so that we could see only the gauges before us. Once we mastered flying under the hood, we were allowed to move on to night flights. But before we got to any of it, we had more classroom work to do. Which meant more time for the women to stare at Officer Wilson, and more time for me to pretend to not see his glances.

"VFR," Officer Wilson stated, pacing at the front of the room. "What does it stand for?"

I placed my hands beneath my legs and my eyes on the back of Maxine's head.

Nola raised her hand.

"Yes, Miss Jenner?"

"Visual Flight Rules," she said. "Meaning the weather is good enough that you can navigate by sight. You must be able to see outside the cockpit, control the altitude and avoid obstacles. Especially other aircraft."

"Good," he said. "And if the weather is below visual meteo-
rological conditions, you will fly using…what?"

Sharon raised her hand and waved it eagerly, but Officer Wilson called on me.

"Miss Coltrane?" he said.

Sharon dropped her hand to her lap, her lower lip protruding in a pretty pout as several heads turned to where I sat with
my hand decidedly not in the air.

"IFR," I said, avoiding his stare. "Instrument Flight Rules.
Operating the aircraft primarily through referencing the in-
struments."

"Correct," he said, turning to the blackboard.

"Or," I continued, "I Fly by the Railroad."

There were several snickers and he turned back around. A
hush fell over the classroom as the corners of his mouth rose in
a small, almost intimate smile.

"Very good, Miss Coltrane," he said, his eyes lingering before he turned to the rest of the class. "If you find yourself lost,
look for railroad tracks."

"I know I'm engaged," Carol Ann said when we left class,
"but I think I'm actually jealous."

That Friday we had our final exams for each of the three
classes we'd been taking that month. For gun training we had
a two-part test. For the first half, at least fifteen of our twenty
shots had to hit an immobile target. The second part was harder,
the target moving in a jagged line as though simulating a moving plane.

For navigation we were given a slip of paper that had written on it a destination, a weather report and a particular model
of plane. Based on plane speeds and weather conditions, we
each had to plot a course. Afterward, we stood in line for one
last go-round in the Link, where we were given two tries to
successfully navigate without anything but the gauges in front
of us.

"You ready?" Martha, the woman running the drills, asked.

"Yes, ma'am."

I lowered myself in and put on the earphones. Martha closed the hatch and I was all alone in the tiny simulator. I took a breath, keeping my eyes on the dashboard.

"Can you hear me?" Martha asked through the earphones.

"Yes, ma'am."

"Here we go."

It took me one try to successfully fly and land my pretend plane. I exited with a triumphant smile on my face, thrilled not to have to do it again and happy to be done with both navigation class and the eyes of Officer Wilson.

Our last test of the day was in swimming. We treaded, swam laps, escaped from our harnesses and held our breath all to the ticking of a stopwatch.

"If I land in water," Sharon said breathlessly as she dragged herself from the pool and lay on the pavement, "just let me drown."

Somehow, we all made it through, passing the class and, if not confident we'd survive if we went down in water, at least sure we had a fighting chance.

"Unless there's crocs," Tanya said. "Then we're doomed."

We trudged back to our bay to shower and dress for lunch. As we headed for the mess hall, Sharon and Maxine went to the main office to check for mail.

"Save us a seat," Sharon shouted.

"Ooh!" Carol Ann said when they delivered a small stack of mail a few minutes later to the center of our table.

We took turns passing the pile around, removing the letters for ourselves before handing what was left to the next girl. I received three letters; one from my father, one from Claire and the last from Ruby.

I read my father's letter first, smiling as he recounted a story of Evie up in arms after she'd ruined her last pair of stockings.

He also wrote of Tom Barrows, who had been a schoolmate of mine. Tall and wiry, his curly black hair had seemed to have a mind of its own, driving his mother to distraction every morning as she ran after him to class with a comb while he batted her away.

He's home from the war. Took two bullets to the thigh three months ago and they thought for sure he wouldn't make it from the blood loss alone. But he's alive and well and took up his old job at Hudson Airfield again. I ran into him last week and told him you'd be running the place soon enough. He was proud to hear you're at Avenger. Said he always knew you'd do great things. Also asked me to put in a good word for him to keep his job. He said it in jest of course, but I could tell he was a little worried...

I read Claire's letter as we walked back to our bay to wash up before flight training. Claire and I exchanged letters once or twice a month. She kept me abreast of the news on the island, knowing I was both interested and worried for the people I'd come to know there. Most especially Erma and Ken's family.

She'd made good on her promise to check in on them for me, and sometimes sent pictures she'd taken. Annie was seven now and clearly going to be taller than her mama. She drew pictures of animals and flowers and wrote little notes with big loopy letters to send along to me with Claire's, since Erma didn't write as often.

Claire also sent pictures of the island, noting its beauty, but also how it had changed under the shadow of war. The barbed wire lining the beaches, sidewalks and shops crowded with officers, and tanks and jeeps lining the streets.

The Hawaiian spirit never falters, she wrote. *But, oh, does it carry a weight on its shoulders these days.*

I saved Ruby's letter for after dinner. She'd had a hard time recovering from the attack on Pearl Harbor. It had shaken her to the core, which was not helped by the crossing she'd taken to the US mainland on a ship with blacked-out windows. The long trip had been filled with terror, even though a destroyer escorted them. She'd barely left her room the entire time, too afraid she'd see death coming.

I kept waiting for us to be swallowed by the darkness, she'd written afterward. *Never to be heard from again.*

After disembarking, she'd gone straight to a train station and boarded for Kansas. She hadn't flown a plane since and didn't seem to miss it one bit. She was happy to work her family's farm these days, herding cows, gathering eggs and running after the dogs.

I like my feet on the ground now. I am reconnecting to the aina, as Erma would say. I like to run barefoot in the grass with the kids after church, playing tag and hearing them squeal and giggle. I've started teaching Sunday school and am thinking about going to college, can you believe that? I think I might be a good primary school teacher. I do love to wander around our farm though, and wonder if maybe the life I'd run from is actually the life for me.

There are four cows that like to gather together. They remind me of the four of us. There's one with a dark patch around her eye—that's Catherine. And one that's always running around rounding up the others—Jean. The roundest one that is hard to get moving is me, and the slender one always looking off in the distance is you.

Lord, but sometimes it's hard to breathe without you all near.

I sat for a long while on my bed after I'd returned her letter to its envelope, wondering about life and the way we each react to a set of circumstances. How some of us stay the path, others remain tormented, letting the pain devour them, and still others find a new route—different from the original—but somehow just as satisfying.

I swung my legs over the side of my bunk and took a piece of stationery from my desk.

"How is Ruby?" Carol Ann asked.

"She sounds like she's finally starting to move on from what happened."

"That's great, Audrey." She smiled and glanced at the paper in my hand. "Are you going to write her back?"

I nodded.

She grabbed a couple sheets of her own stationery and sat on her bed beside me.

"Well, I suppose I should write to Gus. He's probably up to no good and needs to be reminded not to get killed because he has a fiancée waiting for him on the other side of the world."

I sat with my pencil poised above the paper, but instead of writing Ruby's name, it was James's that appeared.

My heart thudded in my chest as I stared down at the familiar letters.

For weeks since receiving his letter I'd tried to put words to paper, but could never find the right ones to express what I was feeling. Did I ignore his melancholy tone as Carol Ann had suggested, or did I acknowledge his distance and gracefully exit the friendship I'd come to appreciate and count on?

My confusion brought anger that led to horrible words, railing at him for his insensitivity. How dare he dismiss me after what we'd been through together? How dare he wish me well and push me away? How dare he give up?

But I didn't send those letters. I tore them up and threw them away.

After that came despair, sad paragraphs of anguish and sorrow and desperation. Had we learned nothing on that little island? How precious life and friendship were? How lucky we were to be alive and still be friends?

I tore those up as well.

My head was clearer now as I sat on my bunk, space and time giving me a clarity I'd struggled to find before.

Our friendship, like so many other relationships, was a victim of this war. And if he needed to let it go, I wouldn't fight him. But I wouldn't make it easy either.

My Dear Friend,

Avenger Field is lovely. The work is hard, the studying harder, the flying fantastic. There is something about the buzz of a warplane that makes a girl rush out of bed in the morning.

There have been some close calls. My roommate Sharon became part of the Caterpillar Club during our second week here, having forgotten to buckle into her harness and falling out when the instructor did a slow roll. I hate to say she wasn't the only one that happened to. It was frightening to witness, but funny nonetheless. And I have a new appreciation for how you handled that B-17 on Oahu that morning, now having flown a previously damaged one myself. Picture that if you will, little me behind the controls of that monster.

I cannot imagine how heartsick you must be daily, wondering if you will have to pack up another friend's belongings, or if this time it will be yours. The fear you must feel. The surrender you must give to the circumstance. And even the anger for having to be in it at all.

I too dream of the day this war ends. I dream of handing my money over to Hal and him giving me the keys to my new airfield. Of fixing and refurbishing the older buildings and planning my new hotel. And I dream of you, flying into my town. We talk about that time we escaped the Japanese over a beer and dinner, and you stay a night, marveling again at my baking skills, and leaving the next morning with a hug and a wave.

Please know that I think of you every day. And every day I think you brave, and kind, and an example of what people

should be. You are an amazing man, James Hart. I am honored
to be your friend.
Forever your bird,
Audrey

I slipped the picture Nola had taken of a few of the women and me in front of a B-17 bomber after a test flight into the envelope with my letter. In the morning with a trembling hand, I dropped it in the mailbox near the main office.

CHAPTER SIXTEEN

To celebrate another successful completion of lessons, on Saturday night we went to town for dinner and to listen to live music at McKay's.

It was busy, music and bodies pouring in and out the front door every time it opened.

"Is the whole town out tonight?" Carol Ann asked as we squeezed our way inside.

"The cadets are here," I said, noting the familiar uniforms.

"I think I see some people leaving over there," Nola shouted and pointed to a booth not far from where we stood.

We weaved through the crowd, reaching the table seconds before another group. Carol Ann practically shoved me in and then slid next to me, pulling Nola with her.

"Dear Gus," Carol Ann said, her head swiveling back and forth as she took in the crowd. "Please forgive me but Mama has to dance tonight."

Sharon, Maxine and Tanya appeared and we squeezed in to make room.

"No Geraldine?" I asked.

"She decided to stay in," Maxine said. "Said she wanted to take advantage of the peace and quiet."

"Hot damn, there's a lot of handsome men here tonight," Sharon said, her head whipping around. "Someone order me a Sidecar, will ya? I'm gonna find a man to dance with." She disappeared into the sea of moving bodies with Maxine hot on her tail.

A tall young man in uniform stopped at our table.

"Any of you ladies want to dance?" he asked.

"She does," Nola said, pointing to Sharon's retreating back.

He stared after her and then turned back to the table.

"Anyone else?" he asked.

"Not yet, bubs. We just got here." She waved him off and he slunk away as she pointed around the table. "Who wants a drink? Let's celebrate conquering that damn Link trainer."

"And no more swimming," Carol Ann said.

"I'll say cheers to that," Tanya said.

I sipped a Gin Rickey as we chatted over the music about anything but training. Nola passed around a new crop of photographs she'd taken in the air, as well as several she'd taken of us women around the base while Tanya, much to our amusement, got more and more animated the more alcohol she drank.

"And then there was the time I was nine and stole my brother Kipper's truck," she said.

"I don't think I've ever heard her talk so much or seen her be so friendly," Carol Ann said in my ear. "Maybe she should drink more often."

Another gentleman appeared at our table.

"Ladies? Can I interest anyone in a dance?"

Carol Ann looked around. When none of us accepted the invitation, she bounced up, her pale pink dress flouncing out around her.

"Me!" she said and followed him out to the dance floor.

Halfway through my second drink the band started in on a Bing Crosby song and the ladies pulled the men to the already crowded floor.

"Sorry gals," Nola said, sliding out of the booth. "But even I can't resist Bing."

Maxine followed behind her like an eager puppy and I glanced across the table at Tanya, who rolled her eyes. Laughter rumbled through me. I hadn't felt this loose and free outside of a plane since that last night on the beach with James.

The sudden, startling thought sobered me and I sucked in a breath and sank back in my seat. What was I doing giggling like an idiot, free as could be, when he was overseas embattled in a bitter world war for the freedom I was enjoying, and worried he might lose another friend, or worse yet, his own life?

As Tanya prattled on about some story involving a tractor and a bottle of bourbon, my eyes welled as I thought about how inconsiderate I'd been about not hearing from James. How angry I'd been with him. How hurt.

I had no right. How could I have written him a letter barely acknowledging the terrible things he must be feeling? The ache of loneliness and fear. The misery of his circumstances. And the abject horror of what he must be seeing on a daily basis.

"I'm awful," I murmured.

"What's that?" Tanya said.

I shook my head and she shrugged and continued with her story while I stared into my drink in misery.

After a few more songs the other women returned, their dance partners lingering nearby.

"I'm going outside to cool off," I announced, sliding from the booth.

"Do you want me to come with you?" Carol Ann asked, fanning herself with a napkin.

"Nah," I said. "I'll only be a minute."

I inhaled deeply as I stepped into the fresh air, a cool breeze whipping over my shoulders and making me shiver.

"You're a vision in that yellow dress," a male voice said.

I spun and found Officer Wilson leaning against the wall a few feet from where I stood, his cane beside him.

"Hot in there, isn't it?" he said.

I crossed my arms over my chest, as if somehow it would quiet my pounding heart. I just couldn't seem to escape him, no matter where I went, and I was at once irritated by his presence and intrigued by his candor.

"It is," I said.

The door swung open and a couple emerged, the soft strains of a slow song escaping into the night behind them. They smiled at the two of us before walking down the street and out of sight.

"Would you dance with me, Miss Coltrane?" Officer Wilson asked.

"Can you dance with your injury?" I asked, nodding to the cane.

"I can. The cane is just for added support."

"Do you mind if I ask what happened?"

"Not at all. I was wounded in a battle on the Coral Sea. Both the pilot and I were shot and barely made it back to the carrier. Due to the severity of the injury—two bullets and a bit of shrapnel—I lost flight status."

"I'm so sorry," I murmured. "I don't know what I'd do if I were told I couldn't fly."

"Well, it's a little different for me. I was never a pilot. But it was disappointing. They gave me the choice of an office job or instructing. I'm not much for sitting around so…"

I nodded, taking in his solid build and posture. Most people I saw with canes were older, their bodies shrunken by age and disuse. But Officer Wilson's use of a cane diminished none of his masculinity, as evidenced by the way nearly every woman in a room responded to him, whether they were engaged, married or otherwise.

"So?" he said, motioning to the door. "A dance?"

"No, thank you," I said.

"Because I work on base, or because you're not interested?"

He was the kind of man most women made a fool of themselves over. The kind of man mothers dreamed their daughters would end up with.

The kind of man I'd never liked.

He was too sunny. Too forward and sure of himself in a way that led me to believe he'd been doted on and fawned over his whole life—something I found unappealing both for the way it kept a person from working hard to achieve better, and gave them a rose-tinted vision of themselves.

Sure, he'd made my heart pick up the pace. Yes, I felt flattered by his attention. But there was something missing. Intrigue, perhaps. What you saw was what you got. And while some women may appreciate that simple nature—the easiness with which he carried himself—I did not.

I crossed my arms over my chest. "Officer Wilson—"

"It's Carter," he said with a little grin, his sweet demeanor shifting into an amused one that only served to annoy me more.

"Officer Wilson," I said again, my voice firm. "As you well know, fraternizing with men is off-limits to us women."

"That hasn't stopped several of your classmates from flirting shamelessly with me."

"Is boasting about that supposed to get me to change my mind?" I asked.

"I didn't mean to— I wasn't trying—" He stumbled over his words, the smile he'd had a second ago gone.

"What others do is not my business, sir," I said. "I am not willing to jeopardize my spot here."

He watched me for a silent moment. "Is that the only reason you won't dance with me, then?"

"No," I said.

His eyebrows raised in clear surprise that there would be other reasons a woman wouldn't want to be in his arms.

"Why else then?" he asked.

"If you must know, I don't much enjoy dancing. Especially with men I'm not attracted to. Is that all, sir? May we be finished with this conversation now?"

He had riled me and I wasn't sure why. It wasn't the first time a man hadn't taken no for an answer without challenging me. But for some reason, rather than walking away, I was still standing there engaging in the conversation. It was as if I was waiting for something. Perhaps for him to change my mind.

"Do you enjoy much, Miss Coltrane?" he asked, pushing off the wall and stepping closer.

"What do you mean?" I asked.

"You always seem so serious. In class you barely looked up from your work."

"I'm there to learn."

"Of course, but others in the class had no problem making eye contact. It is a natural response to being talked to. But you avoided it at all cost it seemed. I wonder why."

"I told you before—the girls noticed you looking at me. I didn't want to give them more to talk about by looking back."

"Hmm," he said, putting his hands in his pockets and nodding.

I glared up at him. "Hmm, what?" I asked, and then grew angry with myself for asking.

"You're a rule follower."

"Of course I follow the rules. That's what they're there for."

"Do you ever have fun?"

"I fly, Officer Wilson. That's all the fun I need."

"That's it?"

"If you must know, I also enjoy reading." But even as the

words came out of my mouth I felt embarrassed. And then angry again. Why did I care what he thought?

I stared down the street. I could just go inside. I didn't need to be subjected to this. And yet my feet stayed cemented where they were.

"Do you have a boyfriend? Husband?" he continued.

I inhaled, drawing myself up so that I stood to my full five feet six inches, and placed my hands on my hips as I'd seen my mother do many times when she'd had enough of whatever someone was giving her.

"I do not have a boyfriend, Officer Wilson. Nor a husband. I rarely dance. I like to fly and read books and avoid overly flirtatious men."

"Good to know. I'll make sure to guard against any I see coming near."

He stood tall, his hand over his brow, and pretended to scan the area.

"All clear," he said, dropping his hand to his side.

I ducked my head to hide my grin.

"I saw that," he said.

"You're a pest, Officer Wilson."

"So I've been told."

"By your dozens of girlfriends?"

"So interested in my love life. Shame on you, Miss Coltrane. You're a student, for goodness' sake. You could be kicked out of the program." He shook his head. "I'll have you know my mother and older sister are the only ones who called me such things. Might have something to do with bringing frogs home and making houses for them out of their shoes. Who knows?"

I laughed.

"A laugh even? I feel so honored."

The door to the restaurant swung open and two young men I recognized from the couple of Saturday night dances held in the mess hall stepped outside.

"Carter! There you are. We were looking all over for you," one of the men said. "We're heading back. You coming?"

"Not yet. I'll see you boys back on base."

"Sure thing, mate," the man said and gave me a once-over before leaving, the other trailing behind.

I turned toward the door, ready to go back in and join the girls.

"You're leaving me now too?" Officer Wilson asked.

"I am."

"You sure I can't persuade you to take a spin on the dance floor? Just one?"

He held out a hand and I glanced down at it. For one brief, crazy moment, I imagined what it would feel like to dance with him, his hands on my waist, my arms around his neck. I blushed and looked away.

"I can't," I said. "Thank you for asking though."

"Can't or won't?"

I looked up at him, seeing it now, the thing that had the other women all aflutter. The intensity I'd missed before, or had maybe misconstrued for something else. As my father liked to say, he hadn't shown all his cards. No, he'd held one back. And it was powerful. My father would've called it his ace. My mother would've said it was the king of hearts.

I didn't like card games. I took a step backward.

"Have a nice night, Officer Wilson," I murmured and slipped back inside the restaurant.

I hurried to the restroom, afraid he'd follow and try to stop me. Once inside, I splashed cool water on my face and patted it dry, but it wasn't enough to calm my nerves or the quickening of my pulse. I sank onto the little yellow bench, not out of sadness, but to feel something steady beneath me as my legs trembled.

I stared blindly at my reflection, my mind reeling. I was irritated with myself and angry, but also confused for having those feelings at all. Why did he irk me so? Why did I let him bother me? Why couldn't I just ignore him like I'd done so many others before him? And for a moment there, when he'd made me laugh, I'd almost liked him. But I didn't want to and I wasn't sure why. It was okay to like a man. To have a friendship with one. But something about it felt wrong. It felt like...betrayal.

Betrayal to James, whom I hadn't seen in two years. Who only wanted to be my friend. Who'd barely said anything in the few letters he'd sent this past year. Who had given me a sort of permission to go off and live my life without him.

Somehow I felt I was betraying a man who had made me no promises. He wasn't my husband. He wasn't my fiancé or boyfriend. He was a friend. He'd made certain to say it more times than not. As if to make a point. As if to put up a wall. As if to let me know it was okay to find love elsewhere if I so chose.

I was angry—but at whom? Officer Wilson for showing interest in me? Me for having feelings of curiosity about him? Or James for not wanting me?

A single tear made a path down my cheek. I missed him. But he clearly didn't miss me.

"Where did you go?" Tanya asked as I slid back into the booth. "You were gone forever."

"I was outside," I said and took a sip of my drink.

"Are you feeling okay?" Carol Ann asked.

"Just warm," I said, flashing her a smile.

We stayed until midnight and to my relief I didn't see Officer Wilson again. Carol Ann got me out on the dance floor, which prompted Nola to ditch the skinny gentleman she was dancing with and join us. Sharon and Maxine caught sight of us and couldn't resist.

"Tanya!" we all yelled across the room.

To our surprise, she put down her beer and jitterbugged across the floor to complete our circle.

CHAPTER SEVENTEEN

Our third month of the program brought Morse code class, taught by a former ship radio operator. Carol Ann loved Morse code and often left me little messages to decipher under my pillow or tucked inside my books. I hated Morse code—all those dots and dashes, walking around the airfield muttering "dah dit-dit dah dah" under our breath.

"We sound like lunatics," I grumbled to Carol Ann.

"Dit dah," she responded.

For her part, Carol Ann hated meteorology.

"Why do we have to learn this again?" she complained right back to me.

"Atmosphere, climatic changes, precipitation…they're just silly little things that affect flying."

"Know-it-all," she griped.

As we had the two months prior, we studied quietly each night for an hour. You could study more if you wanted after the veil of silence was lifted, but you had to make do in the noise, most of which came from Sharon as she lamented some subject or another while spreading on face cream or plucking her invisible eyebrows.

That hour was the only time, other than when we slept, that the bay was silent. I often looked up and smiled as I watched each of the women in her process. Geraldine made little clucking noises as she wrote notes, Maxine twirled her braid or brushed the ends of it against her cheek, Sharon was full of dramatic sighs and looking off into the distance, Tanya had a permanent furrow between her brows and Carol Ann leaned so close to whatever she was studying, I wondered if she was trying to absorb it by sight alone.

As I'd hoped, along with the change in our class schedule and the cooler weather came fewer opportunities to run into Officer Wilson. Trips to town were rare as no one wanted to walk in the cold, and I found if I hurried out the door a few minutes before our first class started, I'd miss the handsome officer who was wont to stand in the doorway of his classroom, greeting his students and scanning the grounds—presumably for me. I even left the Thanksgiving feast early, passing on the dance they threw for us in favor of eating pie in my room—all to keep from having him talk to me.

I hadn't heard back from James after my last letter and my hopes were dwindling with each day there was no word from him. I could feel Carol Ann's eyes on me each evening during mail call. But I avoided her by busying myself with studying or burying my nose in a book. And when she asked, I told her it was fine. I was fine. Everything was fine, fine, fine.

But it was a lie, and we both knew it.

We were a week into December when we woke in the middle of the night to the sound of a high-pitched siren sounding throughout the base.

"What's going on?" Sharon asked as Tanya leaped from her cot to look out the window. "Are we being attacked?"

It was a natural fear being on base, even a small one such as ours.

"I don't know," she answered, her raspy voice groggy with sleep. "Maybe a drill or—"

She was interrupted by a high-pitched scream, and the sound of an explosion and the subsequent shaking of the bay got us all out of bed.

We grabbed robes and blankets, draping ourselves and running out the door, joining the women from the other barracks, our bare feet pounding the frozen ground as we raced toward the runway where, at the far end, orange flames engulfed a plane.

"Oh God," Maxine whispered as instructors and mechanics rushed toward the aircraft.

Someone started sobbing. Then another. Carol Ann grabbed my hand.

"Ladies." Ms. Mayburn, one of the instructors, hurried in our direction, her arms outspread. "Back to your rooms, please."

"Do you know who—" someone started to ask.

"Please," she said, her voice low. "Go back to bed. There's nothing you can do here."

There was no way we could sleep though. One of our own was either injured—or dead. We stood out on the lawn talking quietly until the fire was out, waiting to hear the fate of whoever was in the aircraft. At long last, someone came to share the news with us, head hung, a cane in his hand.

"Ladies," Officer Wilson said, his voice thick with emotion, eyes red, soot and ash smeared across his face and staining his pajamas. "I am very sorry to tell you that Ms. Walters did not make it."

His eyes met mine through the crowd for a brief moment, and then he turned on his heel and disappeared into the darkness.

Peggy Walters. Twenty-five and married to a navy man. Before coming to Avenger Field she'd worked as a hairdresser in San Diego, California. Funny and smart with a penchant for extravagant hairdos and the romance novels she carried with her everywhere, she was well liked and her absence would mark us all.

The plane Peggy had flown caught fire while she was coming in for a landing. There was a note on file that the latch on the canopy sometimes stuck. Had she been able to open it, Peggy would've been able to lift the hood and jump from the plane. Instead, she burned to death in her seat.

What started as a whimper grew to a wail as the pain of losing one of our own hit home. Her roommates, who had been waiting for their own night flight, returned after a while, clinging to one another, their faces masks of disbelief and pain.

We sat with them until the crying waned, and then one by one we returned to our rooms to lie in our beds and mourn for the woman whose life was lost, and pray we wouldn't be next.

We held a service for Peggy in one of the hangars, her bunk mates each saying a few words before the simple wooden coffin we'd all chipped in for was loaded on a truck to her parents' home.

"We're up next," Tanya murmured as we walked to our bay after the service.

We were in line to train for night flying, something we'd all looked forward to, but were now wary of.

"Those preflight checks are important, ladies," Geraldine said. "I'm not ready to lose any one of you, so make sure you're thorough."

I sat on my bed and removed my shoes, glancing at the women sitting around me, who all had much to lose. Geraldine had a family, Carol Ann a fiancé, I had the airfield and the other three were just trying to figure out what they wanted to do with their lives. Dying wasn't an option we'd counted on. And Peggy most likely wouldn't be the only woman lost to the cause.

"If I die here," Carol Ann whispered, "promise me you won't let them talk about me like I did something brave. 'Cause I'm only here for the great pay and glory. And I'll be cursing my choices the whole way down." She grinned then. "But what better way to go, right?"

I pulled her into a hug. If this was where I was meant to perish, I'd be honored it happened around women I loved and respected, in a plane, while working for my country.

Despite our newfound reservations for flying in the dark, we couldn't help but love it. Even Sharon, who almost quit the program from fear, her bags half-packed when we stopped her, found she loved the serenity flying at night brought. There was something almost magical about floating through the navy sky, the stars twinkling above, and the cool air caressing your face while the moon guided the way. And even though it meant sleeping and waking at odd hours and sometimes missing meals and fun, we all thought it worth the sacrifice.

For the week we were on the night flight shift, we ate breakfast for dinner, dinner for breakfast, missed lunch altogether, slept through the day with blankets covering the windows, and then waited around entertaining ourselves and studying until ten o'clock at night when we got back on flight line. And when we finished, unscathed but exhausted, we were exhilarated. Not only had we survived, putting our worries to rest, we'd exceeded our own expectations with some of the highest marks in our class.

The following week brought cross-country flying. We flew for two hours using a flight map of our own creation, calculating the altitude, and factoring in air currents and wind speed. We checked weather reports for anything unwieldy, and then we set off, landing in an unfamiliar field, and flew back.

As Christmas approached we grew restless and were constantly reprimanded by our instructors for talking in class, dawdling and daydreaming. The trips into town were more frequent again as everyone shopped for gifts to send home or overseas. Many of us planned to spend the holiday on base since we were given only two days off.

"Is anyone going home for Christmas?" Sharon asked during lunch one day.

"The boys would never forgive me if I didn't," Geraldine said. "But we only live one town over so it's easy for me. What about the rest of you?"

"Not me," Carol Ann said.

"Me neither," Maxine said.

Sharon, Tanya and I all shook our heads. Some of the women had family or friends coming to town. They'd stay at the Bluebonnet and get to tour the base. My mother had offered to do the same, but I couldn't imagine her canceling the Christmas Eve party she began planning in July.

"It's fine, Mama," I'd told her over the phone. "It's only one Christmas. I'm sure I'll be home next year."

"But what about gifts?" she'd asked. My mother was a connoisseur in gift giving.

"I don't need anything, and truly, there's no room. But if you must send something, maybe a warm hat and I'd love your help ordering a pair of monogrammed gloves for each of the girls in my bay. The temperatures here are not like in Dallas and we could all use an extra layer or two when we're flying."

The following Sunday Carol Ann and I ventured into town again. She still needed a gift for her uncle, and I was looking for a little something for Evie.

"Shall we split up and meet at McKay's for lunch?" she asked. "Say, in an hour?"

"Perfect," I said.

I scanned the list my mother had sent with her last letter, detailing the latest items Evie desired but that my mother had refused to purchase.

What in heaven's name does a respectable young lady need a pale pink negligee for? she'd written. *Never mind. I do not want to know.*

Also on the list were perfume, rouge, nail polish and jewelry. Why my mother thought I was the woman for this job was beyond me, but I set about finding at least a couple of the items, knowing Evie would be thrilled that I hadn't once again bought her a book or a sensible cardigan.

An hour later, dizzy from smelling perfumes, carrying a bag with three wrapped gifts inside, I hurried down the sidewalk through the snow to McKay's.

"Holy Moses," I said to the hostess as I stomped my feet to get warm. "When did that little bit of snow become a blizzard?"

I glanced around for Carol Ann but she was nowhere to be found, so I ordered a cup of coffee to warm up with and waited. As I removed my white fur-trimmed gloves and hat, someone was seated at the table next to mine.

"You're a vision as always in all that pale blue and white fur," a now-familiar deep voice said. "Like a snow angel. All you need is a pair of wings."

I stared over at Officer Wilson, handsome as ever, his blond hair sticking up all over, making him look like a little boy just in from playing outside.

I smiled. "Officer Wilson, I hate to tell you, but your hair is a mess."

"And in such fine company too," he said, sweeping his fingers through the cropped strands. "Are you eating alone?"

"No," I said and hoped he wouldn't ask to join me.

He pointed to the empty chair across from me. "Do you mean to tell me someone is sitting there now?"

"I do. And she doesn't like the way you're pointing at her."

He snatched his hand back and I chuckled.

"I'm waiting for Carol Ann," I said. "Are you dining alone?"

"I am. I come here nearly every Saturday for lunch, and most Sundays too."

"That explains why we rarely see you in the mess hall on weekends."

"You've noticed my absence?"

"Many of the other women enjoy gossiping about your where-

abouts. I believe there's a wager going around about you having a girl in town."

"And are you in on it?" he asked.

"I don't place bets, Officer Wilson."

He peered at me so long I grew uncomfortable and shifted in
my seat. "Where are you from, if you don't mind my asking?"

"I don't. I grew up in Dallas."

"And what did you do in Dallas, before you came to Sweetwater?"

I could tell he was trying to figure me out as he noted the
fine gold necklace at my throat.

"I volunteered and worked on my flying."

"And when this program one day wraps up, what will you
do then?"

I shifted in my seat again. "I plan on buying an airfield."

His eyebrows rose. "A whole airfield? Not, say, a plane or a
space to stow a plane?"

"It's a small airfield. I've been saving for it my whole life."

"That's not very long, Miss Coltrane. Unless, of course, you're
much older than you look."

I smiled and took a sip of my coffee.

"What did you do before we entered the war? When there
was no volunteering to be done?"

I set my cup down harder than I meant to.

"Am I under investigation, Officer Wilson?"

"It's Carter. And no. My apologies," he said, a little grin
bouncing around his lips, soft and pink and full. I frowned and
met his eyes once more. "I merely want to know more about
you. You're interesting."

"How do you figure?"

"You're quiet, reserved and incredibly smart. But one might call
you a daredevil since you fly warplanes. I find that intriguing."

"All the women at Avenger fly warplanes. Do you find them
intriguing as well?"

"Not as much as you," he said. "Tell me what you did before the war began."

"Why?"

"I'm interested. Did you go to college?"

"I did."

"And then what?"

I sighed. "After college I was a flight instructor. See? No intrigue there."

"Where?"

I peered at him. "I get the feeling you already know the answer to that question."

"I've heard rumblings. Some of the other instructors caught wind of something and I'm curious."

"I taught airmen recruits in Hawaii." I shrugged as if it weren't a big deal.

"And you were there?" His voice dropped. "When it happened?"

There was something about the way he asked. A knowledge gleaned from having experienced war for himself. An empathy for what he knew I must have seen and felt and feared.

"I was," I murmured.

"But you're okay now?"

I looked across the aisle at him, staring deep into his baby blue eyes, seeing that there was more to him than I'd ever given credit or had ever paused to consider.

"Mostly," I said.

He nodded. "I'm glad to hear that." He was silent for only a moment before he asked, "Maybe next week I could take you out somewhere else for dinner. Abilene, perhaps?"

"You are relentless, Officer Wilson," I said.

"What can I say? I can't help myself."

"Why is that, do you think?"

"Brains, beauty and wit. My three downfalls."

"My mother would love you. She'd call you a charmer."

"Please call me Carter. And I can't wait to meet her."

I laughed. "You are brash, brazen and—"

"Handsome?"

"Full of yourself."

"Damn." He snapped his fingers. "Tell me something, Miss Coltrane."

I peered warily at him. "What?"

"What was your favorite toy as a child?"

"Why?"

"Just curious."

"A model airplane," I said without thinking twice. "It was a Marx pressed-steel biplane."

He nodded and smiled. "I'll bet you played with it so much the paint wore off."

"In fact I did."

"If you weren't in this program of flying daredevils, would you go on a date with me?"

"Why isn't this hypothetical situation you're describing one in which you aren't an instructor? Why would I have to give up what I like?"

"Touché. And an interesting response."

"How so?"

"Well, you didn't immediately say no, which leads me to believe you would."

"I didn't mean—"

"Nope. I heard it myself." He nodded toward the front of the restaurant where there was a flurry of movement as Carol Ann appeared, blustering about the snow and the wind.

"Right in the face, I tell you," she said, dropping her bags to the floor and slipping out of her coat. "Oh! Officer Wilson. How are you?"

"I'm well. And you, Miss Bixby?"

"Wet," she said and gave me an apologetic smile as she sat.

"Sorry I'm late. Looks like you weren't wanting for company though."

"Miss Coltrane was kind to tolerate me while she waited," he said.

"You should join us," Carol Ann said and I could've kicked her.

"You are kind to offer," he said. "But I've eaten already, and I still have lessons to prepare for the week. It was lovely to see you both. Have a nice afternoon."

"Bye," Carol Ann said.

I smiled as he took leave, shaking my head as he exchanged a laugh with the waiter, tipped his cap at the hostess and swept out the door into the snow.

We shopped more after lunch, and then hopped on the bus back to base in time for dinner, rustling in with our bags, our noses red from the cold. When we returned to our bay after eating, I found a plain brown box on my bed with my name written across the top.

"Who's that from?" Carol Ann asked.

"Someone left it on the doorstep earlier," Maxine said.

Inside the box was a folded piece of paper. I pulled it free and opened it.

This one's a beauty. Just like her new owner.

*C

Beneath the note was a small bundle wrapped in newsprint. I took it out and unfurled the wrapping. Inside was a model plane.

CHAPTER EIGHTEEN

I'd hoped to hear from James by Christmas. It was a holiday after all. A time to wish those you care about goodwill, to reflect on days past with fondness and cherish family and friends. But as the day neared, I'd still received nothing. No card. No letter. No small gift like he'd sent the past two years.

My disappointment and distraction was evident in the way I lost interest in nearly everything but flying, so much so that I got my first B on a test, walked out of our bay one morning without my boots and almost missed my last chance to send off the Christmas gifts I'd bought, too preoccupied by thoughts of being unimportant and forgotten. I'd even forgotten to thank Officer Wilson for the model plane when I ran into him the day after he'd left it for me.

I hadn't realized how morose I'd gotten until Tanya commented on it. The last straw, however, was when I'd voluntarily called my mother.

"You haven't received a reply since when?" she asked.

"Since you forwarded the last letter I received at the house."

"That was quite a while ago. And you wrote him back promptly? You didn't berate him for taking so long, did you? Men hate to be bothered by such things."

"Of course not, Mama."

"Did you send him anything?"

"I did. A card and a leather-bound notebook."

"Well, darling. I suppose at this point, it's all you can do."

I sighed. "Thank you, Mama. Is Dad home?"

"He's not. I swear, ever since you left for training that man has decided he can work all hours of the day and night. As if he can't possibly tolerate dinner conversation without you. I know I'm not as well-informed about the news as you always are, but I do have top-notch conversational skills."

"I'm sure it's not you, Mama. Everyone is in a state these days. Who's to say at this late stage the war doesn't end up getting brought to our shores after all?"

"If it does we'll handle it. We made it through the Depression. We'll make it through this damn war."

Christmas Eve fell on a Friday. The army set up a dinner and dance in the mess hall, bussing in cadets for the event and serving food that made me wonder if others were going without so we could be fed in what seemed like abundance.

As I was watching gravy swirl and slide down the small pile of mashed potatoes into a dam of turkey on my plate, Carol Ann elbowed me. "I think someone is looking for you," she murmured.

I glanced up to see Officer Wilson who stood talking with a couple of the other instructors, his eyes wandering every few seconds to me.

"Swell," I said, staring back down at my food. "He found me. What now?"

"Audrey, are you okay? I know you still haven't heard from James but…I'm starting to worry about you."

I put my fork down with a little slam and took a breath, my shoulders slumping. "I don't understand, that's all. We were supposed to be friends."

She put her arm around me. "Well, he doesn't know what he's missing out on. You're the best friend I've ever had."

I turned to her with tears in my eyes and hugged her.

"Thank you, Carol Ann. You're the best friend I've ever had too."

I sat up and took a breath, determining I needed to make a decision here and now. Let James go, or keep waiting and hoping… and being let down.

I looked around the room at the faces so familiar to me now I could hear their voices with my eyes closed and know who was speaking. These women had left their homes to be here. To help the war effort. To be part of something that felt special.

If James didn't want to be part of my life anymore, then I would accept that and stop waiting. Maybe it was for the best. I'd never wanted to be sidetracked by a man and here I was, being exactly that. No, he hadn't stopped me from doing what I wanted—but he had consumed my thoughts for far too long.

It was time to let go.

We stayed long enough for Sharon and Maxine to dance a few times and have dessert, and then we hurried out the door with a pie Carol Ann smuggled under her coat and a jug of milk Maxine had somehow pilfered from the kitchen. She was always stealing treats. We never knew how and no one asked. "She must bend herself around corners," Carol Ann had once mused.

After putting on our pajamas, we made a nest of blankets and pillows at one end of the room and snuggled in, passing the pie around as we told stories of Christmases past and sang carols.

"It's too bad Geraldine couldn't be here," I said.

"I'll bet her boys are so happy to have her home though," Carol Ann said.

Maxine fell asleep with her head on Sharon's shoulder and we all lifted her onto her bunk before getting into our own beds and turning out the lights.

In the morning after a pancake breakfast, we opened the gifts we'd bought for one another. Sharon had gotten everyone lip gloss in shades she felt complemented our complexions. Maxine gifted us with exotic-smelling soaps she'd found in town. Tanya bought warm socks in different colors. And Geraldine had knitted us each a hat, which she'd wrapped and left on our desks with instructions not to open until Christmas morning.

With the help of my mother, I'd ordered each of the women a pair of monogrammed leather gloves like the ones James had given me two years before. Everyone always commented on them and so I'd thought it the perfect gift.

"They even have our initials!" Sharon exclaimed, holding up her gloved hands and flipping them back and forth for all to see.

Afterward, we showered and dressed and visited our friends in the other bays before going to the mess hall for lunch. As we returned to our room later, Carol Ann pointed to something on my desk—something that hadn't been there before we left.

A small box wrapped in brown paper and a green ribbon, an envelope beside it.

I trembled, my heartbeat quickening as I walked over to it.

"Is it…from him?" Carol Ann asked.

But there were no markings on the box other than my name in a nondescript handwriting. No return address. No stamps.

"It can't be," I said, picking it up and taking a seat on my bed. I held up the envelope so she could see. "No return address."

It wasn't much bigger than a shoebox and weighed hardly anything at all. I pulled the plain brown paper off and lifted the lid.

Beneath a sheath of white satin laid the most delicate ornament I'd ever seen. I put my finger through the white ribbon at the top and lifted it. We watched it twirl, the lights above glinting off the intricate mosaic glass that made up a pair of angel wings lined in downy-white feathers.

"Wow," she breathed.

I didn't need to read the letter or card to know the wings were from Officer Wilson.

"Like a snow angel," he'd said that day in McKay's. "All you need is a pair of wings."

I returned the ornament to its box and set it and the card in my locker, ignoring the look I could feel Carol Ann giving me.

I knew it was hard for others to understand, my abject feeling of loss over James's silence. As far as most were concerned, I'd barely known him. We'd spent minimal time together in Hawaii before the bombs fell, and even less after. But to me, the connection had been singular. Unique. And though I stood by my decision not to engage in a deeper relationship, losing his friendship hurt in a way I'd never experienced before. And the idea of disregarding those feelings and replacing them with the attentions of another man felt tawdry to me. And deceitful to the friendship we'd shared. Also, while I didn't know Officer Wilson well, I did think he was kind, thoughtful and undeserving of a woman who would merely be trying to distract herself from the hurt inflicted by another man.

But I would admit, while I'd never been prone to flattery, there was something to Officer Wilson's attention that felt good. He hardly knew me, and yet he had taken the time to pick out a thoughtful and lovely gift. Not once, but twice. And while several of the women fawned over him in a most inappropriate manner, so far as I could tell or had heard, he'd never once taken any of them up on their seductive offers. In fact, to the dismay of all the women vying for his attention, and despite my refusal to fall for his charms, he seemed quite devoted in his pursuit of me. Were I to entertain the idea of something more than friendship, his loyalty and perseverance would certainly be swaying factors. But for now—and most likely for always— it was not to be.

CHAPTER NINETEEN

A week into the New Year, we were in line waiting for our turn to fly patched-up planes needing to be flight-tested before being flown off for battle.

"Why do we have to do it?" Maxine asked in a rare showing of displeasure. We all turned to her with a look of surprise. "What?" She shrugged her diminutive shoulders. "Shouldn't that be a task for the new girls? Haven't we served our time?"

"I believe it's in the job description," Geraldine said without looking up from the book she was reading. "It doesn't necessarily end here either. Depending on where you're assigned, you might have to do more of it at whichever base you end up at."

Maxine sighed as Sharon's name was called.

"Ladies," Sharon said, dipping in a curtsy.

I shivered and jumped up and down while Carol Ann stomped her feet, trying to keep warm. Geraldine gave up on reading, the constant gusts of wind ruffling the pages and making her lose her place, which in turn made her swear and caused Maxine to giggle. Beside us, Tanya sat crouched, using us as a wall to block the wind.

"Shit!" she said and got to her feet.

"What?" Carol Ann said, looking around, one knee suspended in the air.

Tanya pointed and the entirety of flight line looked skyward.

"Oh no," Maxine whispered as Carol Ann grasped my arm, her nails digging through the thick fabric of my flight suit.

Geraldine dropped her book and sprinted inside the hangar to find our instructor.

The Valiant Sharon had taken up was smoking, plumes of gray enveloping the small single-engine plane.

"Come on, Sharon," I murmured. "Bring it down. You can do it."

My heart raced in my chest, the sound of my quickened breath mixing with the sounds of those around me as we stared in horror at the plane plummeting several feet before leveling out again. The smoke cleared a little, and there was a collective sigh of relief followed quickly by a gasp as a loud crack echoed across the miles of sky above us and the Valiant tilted one way before violently rocking the other.

Geraldine raced out of the hangar followed by our instructor plus three others behind him just as the sirens of a fire truck and ambulance screamed toward the base.

Several of the women had turned away, unable to watch. Others were running to the tarmac from classrooms and barracks, their cries of alarm like fingernails on a blackboard, only serving to aggravate my feelings of fear for my friend.

I caught sight of Officer Wilson, his chest expanding as he inhaled and looked around at the women, searching frantically until his gaze landed on me. He closed his eyes briefly, his shoulders sagging.

As mere spectators to the horror above, we were helpless to do anything but watch as Sharon came in blind.

"The landing gear!" someone shouted and we all looked up to where the wheels should be visible but were only partially showing.

"Audrey," Carol Ann whispered.

I met her horrified gaze and put my arm around her waist, drawing her nearer and closing my eyes.

The sound of metal hitting cement was like a small explosion, the screech across the pavement making the hairs on my body stand on end. Carol Ann buried her face in my shoulder as I stared helplessly at the small silver plane careening down the tarmac until it mercifully slowed to a stop.

There was a moment of silence and then thunder on the ground as we ran to the plane.

Tanya reached it first and yelped as a spark shot at her from the fuselage.

"Open the canopy!" she yelled, banging her palm on the wing of the plane.

"Get out!" several women shouted.

Four firemen pushed through the crowd toward the aircraft and Sharon.

"Move back, please," one of them said.

Two of them jumped up on the wings, one on each side, and tapped on the canopy.

"Miss," one said. "Can you unlatch the lid? Miss?"

Sharon sat unmoving, her eyes wide with terror, watching the swirls of smoke rising from the front of the plane.

"What is she doing?" Carol Ann asked.

"She's scared," I murmured, watching our frozen friend through the glass.

"What's that sound?" someone asked and we quieted, listening.

A quiet hiss could be heard coming from the aircraft and several of the women scurried backward, Officer Wilson and two other instructors ushering us away from the warplane.

"Miss!" one of the firemen yelled again, knocking on the glass. He looked down at the crowd below him. "What's her name?"

"Sharon," Tanya said.

"Sharon!" he shouted and she jumped and glanced up, a look of confusion that quickly turned to terror crossing her features. "Unlatch the canopy!"

She nodded and did as he said. A moment later she was being helped out of the Valiant.

There was blood on her face from a gash on her forehead, and she held her arm as the firemen lowered her down and helped her to the waiting ambulance. Maxine shoved her way through the crowd and jumped in beside her as a couple of the base mechanics hurried forward to assess what had gone wrong, the firemen standing by, hoses at the ready.

Other than a broken nose, a concussion and a sprained wrist, Sharon was fine, albeit a bit shaken up. She stayed two nights in the hospital and almost everyone from Avenger came to visit and bring flowers.

"It looks like a florist's shop in here," Geraldine said before putting down the bouquet she'd brought.

"Doesn't even look like you almost died," Tanya said, inspecting Sharon's injuries.

"My nose is swollen," Sharon exclaimed.

"What? Where?"

Sharon sighed and picked up the pink enamel compact on the table beside her and flipped it open, examining her face.

"All around here!" she said, pointing to the bridge that looked exactly as it had prior to the crash.

"I don't see it."

"Well, you don't have to sound so disappointed," Sharon said, clicking the compact shut.

"How's your wrist?" I asked, shooting Tanya a look. She shrugged and sat in the corner with a little grin.

"It hurts terribly," she said, lifting her arm an inch to show us her bandaged and braced appendage. "But I'll survive. No flying for a week though and I have to wear this ugly brace for three. How am I to do my hair with this thing on?"

Maxine sat beside her friend and smoothed her hair from her face.

"I'll do it for you," she said.

"Can I draw on your eyebrows?" Carol Ann asked, which made Tanya snicker.

"You may not," Sharon said, glaring. "I didn't hurt my drawing hand."

"Ah, come on," Carol Ann said. "I want to give you dastardly brows. Or maybe surprised…"

I couldn't help myself, a laugh burst forth. Tanya followed suit, then Geraldine. Carol Ann giggled and, after a moment of desperately trying to hold it in, Maxine joined in.

"I don't like any of you," Sharon said, right before her peal of laughter filled the room.

The feeling around the base in the days that followed Sharon's brush with death was a sobering one. Coming into the program, we'd all read and signed the disclaimers about possible injury and death due to faulty aircraft—but having experienced a death and now a near-death had stirred not only a heightened sense of our mortality, but a tighter bond between us women. We truly were a family. Sisters through the common love of flying. And no matter where we went after the program ended, we would always have this place and these experiences, so different from any other, to reflect back on and cherish.

Unfortunately, Sharon's mishap was the beginning of a string of more like it. Two days later, the engine of a plane a woman in Bay 10 was flying failed and she had to land in a field about ten miles out. Lucky for her, a farmer saw her go down and drove her back. She got away with nary a scratch.

A week after that, a woman in Bay 15 had to bail out, ejecting from a two-engine aircraft whose left engine quit, sending the plane into a spin she couldn't recover from.

But then tragedy struck when Mary, a woman from Bay 11, was killed when her engine blew, sending her careening into a lake.

We had another service, more tears, and a few women quit, too terrified to continue. But the next day the rest of us got back to work. There were planes to be tested and men to get them to.

Our fifth month of training came with overviews and more cross-country tests. Our ability to navigate was of the utmost importance, and we found ourselves once more in the classroom of Officer Wilson as we proved our prowess with a map, a compass and a watch had only improved.

"You're exceptionally good at this," he murmured, stopping beside the desk I was bent over, my eyes moving from map to compass to watch in quick succession.

"Thank you, sir. But you're distracting me."

"And here I thought you couldn't be ruffled. Rather like a determined bird."

I gasped and sat up straight.

"Even birds get ruffled sometimes," I said at length, pushing the route I'd mapped toward him. "Here you go, sir." I gathered my things and hurried out the door.

A while later, as I sat on one of the two benches in the bathroom of our bay, I heard Carol Ann's voice.

"There you are," she said, sinking down beside me. "I've been looking everywhere for you. Are you okay?"

"I think I like him," I mumbled.

"James?"

"No, not James," I said, my voice echoing off the walls. I pulled my knees to my chest and wrapped my arms around them. "Why would I like James? He broke a promise...or something like that. Who would still like someone after they did such a thing?"

"Okay," Carol Ann said. "So you mean Officer Wilson then?"

"Yes," I whispered and looked at my friend with wide eyes. "Carol Ann. What's happening to me? I don't care about men. I never have. And now I've cared about two within two years."

Carol Ann snorted. "Most women I know go through liking twenty times that number in two years," she said. "But I understand you never have and this must be very confusing for you."

I moaned and dropped my forehead to my knees. "He's just so…nice. And happy. Rather like a puppy. It's annoying. He's nothing like—"

"Like what? Like James? James who's so nice he broke a promise or something? Maybe nice is just what you need."

I closed my eyes. "It doesn't matter."

"Apparently it does. A lot. What's so special about James anyway, besides his good looks? I know he was there for you—with you—when Pearl Harbor was bombed. I know you both understood the other's need to be more than just somebody's spouse. But what makes him so special that you compare all other men to him now?"

In some ways it was hard to remember. It had been just over two years since we'd last seen one another. Our only communication since then had been through letters, but the letters had changed throughout his time overseas, and the James I'd said goodbye to in San Antonio—the one I had memories of from Oahu—wasn't the James who'd said goodbye to me a few months ago. The man I'd taken to on the little island where good and bad had collided in spectacular fashion, changing the lives of everyone we knew, had disappeared overseas. And while I understood he was living a life of uncertainty and terror, and that we were merely friends, I didn't understand how he could sever ties with nary another word.

"He was quiet," I said, remembering sitting beside him on the beach in Haleiwa, the sound of the waves crashing to the shore, the sweet Hawaiian trade winds brushing against our limbs and whispering through my hair. "And intelligent. He didn't push, which made me want to share some of myself, and to know more about him. It frightened me." My voice caught. "And excited me. It was all so foreign and...I felt if I allowed myself to fall for him, letting go of my dreams would be next and I'd end up like every other woman, married with a baby on the way. A house in the country, a well-tended yard, a car or two in the driveway."

"That sounds dreamy," Carol Ann said and I nudged her. That was all she'd ever hoped for as a girl.

"Maybe to you," I said. "But to me it was terrifying."

"And so you promised to stay friends."

"Yes."

"But clearly it was more than that."

I shrugged.

"Honey, you can tell yourself that all you want—but you weren't. And deep down, you both know it. That's why it hurts so bad that he hasn't written back. If he were just a friend, you'd be mad, but you'd get over it. Love makes it harder."

"I didn't love him." My voice was stern but I couldn't look her in the eye.

"I'm sure you didn't, little bird," she said and poked a finger to the tiny gold fowl on the delicate chain around my neck.

My eyes filled. "That's why I left class," I whispered.

"Because of the necklace?"

"No. Officer Wilson—he compared me to a bird. I—"

I crumpled and she wrapped her arms around me.

I was exhausted by emotions I'd never experienced before. Tired from holding it all in when it so badly needed to come out. And I was angry with James. Angry he'd let me go—and then in the same breath, mad at myself for being angry at a man who was fighting in a war he didn't start, but was sacrificing himself for regardless. Sacrificing himself for me and everyone else in this country. And I was sad. His friendship, which had come to mean so much, was now gone. The first man, other than my father, that I'd wanted to spend time with, whom I trusted and respected—no longer had anything to say to me. And all of this made me feel weak. I wanted to be able to let go and move on—for both our sakes—but purging him from my mind was a task I continually failed at. And now, to make it all that much worse, another man had my attention, adding fuel to my emotional fire. I didn't want to like Carter. I certainly didn't want him to compare me to a bird. I didn't understand why his focus had gone to me when there were so many other lovely women on base vying for his attention. But maybe that was it—I hadn't been plying him with kindness and flattery. Hadn't I seen it in so many romantic interactions among others? My disinterest had made me mysterious. The intangible intriguing.

I sighed and got to my feet to splash water on my face. Carol Ann stood beside me, turning her head from side to side as she considered her face.

"I know you want that airfield—" she said.

"I will have that airfield," I interrupted.

"Of course." She smiled. "But years down the road, when you've been running it for a decade or so and it's running smooth and you're settled, don't you think you'll want something more? Someone to talk to?"

"I'll have friends. And people who work at the airfield," I said with a shrug.

"That's not the same as having someone to come home to," she said in a soft voice. "Companionship. Someone to tell the events of your day to, and listen to theirs. Being there for someone and having him be there for you. I can remember so many times sitting around the table laughing with my aunt and uncle over something silly. Or doing the dishes, or just listening to music. They'd get up and dance and I'd watch until one of them grabbed my hand and pulled me in with them. Are you telling me you'd rather sit alone in your kitchen every night, rather than have that?"

I stared at her and then at myself in the mirror. No, I couldn't tell her that. Because I'd never thought of it that way. But now I was.

And it scared me more than ever.

CHAPTER TWENTY

Three weeks before graduation Carol Ann, Nola and I were shopping for scarves when I ran into Officer Wilson again.

"Afternoon, Miss," he said.

"Sir," I said, my heartbeat quickening as I tried to hide a smile.

"Audrey," Nola said, coming up behind me. "Oh. Officer Wilson. Good afternoon. Audrey, honey, we're hungry. Are you done here?"

"She's not," Carter said. "She just offered to help me find the perfect gift for my mother."

I opened my mouth to protest but instead shrugged with a smile.

"I won't be long," I said to Nola, who raised her eyebrows and walked away.

"Do you mind?" he asked.

"I suppose not, since I didn't tell her you're a liar."

He laughed and waved for me to follow him.

"Thank you for your help," he said a half hour later as he paid for the items I'd picked out for his mother, sister and great-aunt

Edna. "Now I understand why a man gets married. It's for the shopping."

The woman behind the counter giggled and I resisted the urge to roll my eyes.

"I'm glad I could be of service," I said. "Have a lovely evening, Officer."

"Audrey!" he said as I left the store and headed up the block.

I glanced around. "Did you need something else?"

"Can I take you to lunch? As a thank-you?"

"That's not necessary," I said.

He shoved his one free hand in his pocket and peered down at me.

"I have to thank you properly for your time today. My mother would be horrified if I didn't." He flashed me a smile that would've had half the women of Avenger fainting and, if I were being honest, made my own pulse quicken.

"I'm having lunch with the girls."

"Dinner?"

"You certainly are pushy."

"I know what I want," he said, looking like an overgrown kid, mischievous and unapologetic.

I shook my head. "If I were caught…"

He grinned. "So you're considering it. We'll go somewhere no one else will be. I promise. I wouldn't risk getting you in trouble. What good would it do me to have you kicked out?"

There were so many reasons to say no—I'd gone over them ad nauseam. But there was one reason to say yes—the excited pull in my gut every time I caught him looking my way.

"Fine," I said.

His eyes widened. "Yes?"

"Yes. But just dinner. Nothing else. And when I say I need to get back, you'll have to bring me back."

"Of course."

"Where do I meet you?" I asked, my heart galloping in my

chest as I tried to shut my brain up, its never-ending reprimands for saying yes almost deafening.

"I'll park down the street from McKay's. Say about six?"

"Six it is."

Six hours later I paced the floor of our bay in a panic. In my determination to not get caught, I'd asked Carol Ann to pretend we were staying in together for the night, rather than go out with the rest of the women. She was happy to lie for me, so long as I provided details afterward.

"All details," she said, wagging a finger at me. "Don't you even think of leaving anything out."

I rolled my eyes and kept pacing. "What will you tell people in the mess hall if they ask where I am?"

"That you don't feel well and are sleeping. I'll even bring some food back with me to make it look real."

"Okay." I stopped at the foot of her bed. "How do I look?"

"I mean, you could show a little more skin. That collar is buttoned almost to your nose."

"Carol Ann." I glared at her.

"You look great. Prim and proper. Like a lady. Your mother would be proud."

"I'll be back before nine," I said. "If anyone comes back early…" I twisted my hands.

"They won't. Now go before you miss the bus."

The bus dropped me a block from McKay's at 5:56. I stared at the restaurant for a moment and then turned on my heel and walked down the street and around the corner, choosing to take the extra time to go around the backside, rather than pass by the windows and be seen.

I spied Officer Wilson through the darkening night leaning against a car, tapping his cane against the curb, and staring toward McKay's. He turned at the sound of my footsteps, his eyes widening in surprise.

"There you are." He smiled almost nervously. "I thought maybe you'd changed your mind."

"I went around the block. Seemed a bad idea to walk right in front of the restaurant filled with my friends."

"You are a smart woman, Miss Coltrane—I mean Audrey." He opened the passenger side door. "Shall we?"

He drove us about thirty minutes away to Abilene and parked in front of a small white house.

I looked at him questioningly, but he just smiled, got out and opened the door for me.

"Where are we?" I asked, stepping onto the driveway.

"Somewhere we won't be seen," he said, leading me up the path to the front door. "This is my great-aunt Edna's house. It's the other reason I took the job here, so I can look in on her. I also mow her lawn and get her groceries."

"That's sweet of you. Is she home?"

He laughed. "No. Can you imagine?"

I chuckled. "It would certainly be interesting."

"Hmm...trying to have a conversation and impress a woman with my old auntie wandering in and out of the dining room in her purple robe... I'd never live that down." He grinned. "She plays cards every Saturday night with a group of women four houses down."

"She sounds fun."

"She's a riot."

Dinner was a pasta dish and salad he'd picked up before meeting me, as well as a bottle of wine.

"I don't cook," he said, setting his cane aside and pulling out the boxes of food. "And figured you deserve to not have to tolerate my attempt our first time out."

"First time?" I asked, watching him scoop the food onto plates.

"I'm hoping if this goes well you'll say yes to another evening with me. Wine?"

"Please," I said. Anything to help calm my nerves.

It was strange being in his aunt's home, but endearing as well. Clearly she hadn't redecorated in the past couple of decades, the furnishings clean but shabby and faded, the decor outdated. On the mantle of the fireplace were family pictures, a blond boy I recognized as a young Carter making an appearance in several. And above the sofa was a large photograph of a handsome couple.

"Is this your aunt?" I asked, pointing to the image.

"Yes. And my uncle Frederick. He died seven years ago. He grew up in Abilene, met my great-aunt on a business trip to Seattle. She followed him back here and never left."

"Any children?" I asked, noticing the only pictures of them with small children were the ones with Carter and some others who looked so much like him I assumed they were his siblings.

"No. They liked to travel and she was always busy volunteering for this society or that one. She sure doted on us though. Still does." He smiled and gestured to the plates he'd set out on the little dining table. "Dinner is served."

He was stiff as he asked the basic getting-to-know-you questions during dinner; what did my parents do, how old was my sister, where did I go to college. I gave simplified answers before turning the tables on him, in hopes of avoiding any uncomfortable silences. But Carter was a skilled conversationalist once he stopped trying to be the perfect date, and by the time we finished our meal, I knew he grew up in Seattle with a professor father and a homemaker mother, and had two older siblings, Winston and Adelaide.

"Would you like dessert?" he asked as he cleared the plates.

"I'd love some."

He disappeared into the kitchen and I sat listening to the clink of dishes, my heart once more picking up speed. What would happen after dessert? We were all alone here. Would he try to kiss me? Would I have to fight him off? How long could his great-aunt play cards? I clasped my hands in my lap, praying she'd come home early so Carter would be forced to drive me back to Sweetwater.

"I hope you like chocolate cake," he said, returning to the dining room.

"I love it," I said, picking up my fork while my stomach did somersaults.

"My mother makes a fantastic chocolate cake," he said. "Three layers. The richest icing you've ever tasted. It's decadent and award worthy. One year my sister decided she was going to make the cake. It was her first time and it was for a big family celebration. She was so proud as she carried it in on this tray she'd decorated with flowers from the garden. My father did the honors of cutting it while my sister passed it around. No one took a bite until everyone was served." He chuckled and I grinned, waiting. "Unfortunately, she'd mistaken the salt for sugar. She was devastated."

He laughed, shaking his head as he remembered, and I stared across the table at him with new eyes. This was not a man to be frightened of by any means. He was kind and sweet and had an outlook on life that was uplifting. Maybe Carol Ann was right. Were I to need a man at all, maybe a nice one was the kind to attach myself to.

"So," I said, pointing my fork at the cake before me, "who made this cake? Your mom or your sister?"

"Neither," he said. "I made it last night."

"For…" I frowned. He couldn't have known we'd run into one another in town today and I'd say yes to a date.

"It was supposed to be for my aunt's card game. I drove straight over after you said yes and made another. It was slightly lopsided and not nearly as well frosted. She took that one to save me the embarrassment."

"She is a good woman," I said. "I'm excited to taste it."

He watched as I cut a small piece and lifted it to my lips.

"Sugar, not salt, right?" I asked.

"Right."

The cake was as delicious as promised, the conversation over a second glass of wine relaxed and entertaining. Carter was the perfect host, a lovely date and every mother's dream for a son-in-law. But no matter how enticing he was, in the back of my mind were two thoughts—he was a distraction I didn't need, and what would James think. The former made me upset I'd agreed to the date, the latter furious that I should care. And it was the latter that kept me longer than I'd intended.

We'd moved to the floral sofa in the tiny sitting room where he regaled me with stories of his childhood in Seattle. His upbringing sounded magical, his mother very hands-on and available, his siblings inclusive—bringing their little brother everywhere with them, his father a great big presence and full of mirth and generosity.

"It sounds like a fairy-tale existence," I said.

"It was good," he said. "We didn't have a lot of money, but my mother is creative. There were always things to color and paint, and stories to be whispered from beneath a blanket. We camped out in our backyard in the summers. And in the winters we built snowmen and hung our socks by the fire to dry. Was it very different in Dallas?"

I bit my lip. I didn't like to discuss my parents' wealth, and certain details easily gave away how fortunate we'd been.

"Not very different," I said. "We had campfires at night in the summertime and my sister and I would catch fireflies in mason jars. We'd leave them out on the little porch that attached our rooms and watch them blink until we fell asleep. It doesn't snow much in Dallas, but there were plenty of fun things to do in the winter as well. To be honest, once flying became part of my life, I didn't care for much else."

"I have a feeling a lot of the women over there at Avenger feel the same way."

At the mention of the airfield I glanced at my watch and gasped, shooting up from the sofa and spilling wine down my front.

"Oh dear," I said as Carter ran to the kitchen and came back with a wet cloth.

"Here," he said, dabbing at the spot on my abdomen.

I sucked in a breath and took a step back.

"I'm sorry," he said. "I shouldn't have— Here." He shoved the cloth at me and our hands touched.

Later I would reflect back on that moment. Had I not spilled my wine, had our hands not touched, had our eyes not met… would we have kissed? But in that instant, there were no thoughts, only the wish to be held and touched. Wanting to be wanted.

His lips were soft on mine, his hands on my waist firm. He stepped forward and I stepped back until I was against a wall and there was nowhere else to go unless I wanted to stop what was happening. And I wasn't sure I did.

"You're so beautiful," he whispered, his one hand rising to bury itself in my hair as he pulled me closer still.

I tried to lose myself in the moment, to not think about how strange his mouth felt on mine, how foreign his hands, how almost overwhelming his cologne. His lips were persistent and I parted mine, pleasuring a little in his groan while wondering if he'd try to touch me—and if I'd let him.

I tried to shut off my mind and get lost in him. Because I could. Because James was gone. Because…

I pulled back, slipping from Carter's grasp and putting several feet between us.

"Too fast?" Carter rasped.

I shook my head and then nodded.

"I'm sorry," he said, taking a step toward me.

"It's fine," I said.

I moved to the entryway of the house, picking up my coat from where he'd laid it so carefully hours before on the back of a chair, and standing near the front door, my arms crossed protectively around my waist.

"I should really get back to the base now though."

"Of course," he said. "Let me just get my keys."

The drive back to base took forty minutes. Forty minutes of minimal conversation broken up by awkward silences.

He parked a little ways away from the front gate and we sat for a moment not speaking, a heavy blanket of discomfort over us.

"I'm sorry if I overstepped or misunderstood," he said, his voice low, the look on his face pained.

"It's not your fault," I said. "I should never have said yes to dinner. Not that it wasn't lovely. It was. It's just—I don't date."

"Why not?"

"I have no interest in what it normally leads to."

"Sex?"

I blushed and looked out the window. "Marriage," I said. "Babies."

"Of course," he said hurriedly. And then—"You don't?"

I shook my head. "It's never been part of my plan."

"And what is your plan?" he asked, leaning against the door and turning in his seat to face me.

"It used to be to buy the little airfield I learned at, just as soon as I had saved enough. But then this program was created so now the plan is to do well here, work in Ferry Command for as long as they need me, and then go home and buy my airfield."

"That's it?" he asked.

"That's it."

"The whole plan?"

I sighed. "Yes. The whole plan."

"What about the rest of it? Where's the fun?"

"That is the fun, Carter."

I smiled. No one ever seemed to understand it. Even my father had some reservations, but he at least accepted it. And then of course James. James had understood completely, because his vision for his own life was so similar. Neither of us feared a mostly solitary existence. Rather, we thrived on it. The idea of doing what we wanted when we wanted was exhilarating. But most people, I'd come to find, couldn't comprehend that way of life. It wasn't the norm, and thus deemed strange.

"That's all I want," I said. "To fly and make a living doing it."

"But life isn't just about work."

"I don't consider getting to run my own airfield work," I said, raising my chin a tick. "It will be a privilege."

"And when you go home at the end of the day? What will you do? Who will you share your day with? Who will you laugh with?" he asked, repeating the same argument Carol Ann had. "When you go to bed at night, who will whisper they love you and brush your hair from your face and kiss you good-night? Who will make you coffee and pick you flowers and chase you around the kitchen? Who will you make memories with?"

"Not everyone needs a relationship to feel fulfilled," I said.

"Maybe not," he said. "But everyone does need companion-ship."

There was that word again. "Friends will do."

"Friends are swell. But friends won't do this."

He leaned forward and lowered his mouth onto mine. For a split second I wanted to push him away, but then a flood of emotions washed over me and rather than pull back, I sought solace in his embrace. Maybe he was the answer to what pained me. To the wound James had inflicted. Maybe if I got lost in Carter, I could finally let go of this tiny idea that had found a home in the back of my mind. A fantasy of James flying into my little airfield one day—and never leaving.

I wrapped my arms around Carter's neck and pulled him closer still, parting my lips as his hand made a path down my neck, over my breast and waist and hips, to the hemline of my dress. His fingers slid beneath the fabric and I gasped as his cool,

smooth palm glided up my thigh and gripped my flesh as though
to stop himself from going any farther.

"Audrey," he whispered against my mouth.

There was no latch on the seat to make it lie back. With a
grunt, Carter pulled away, swung open his door and got out of
the car. He walked around to the passenger side, opened the door
and took my hand, drawing me out and pressing me against the
side of the borrowed military truck.

I could feel his urgency, the tightening of his body as he
brought me closer with one hand on the small of my back while
the other made its way back beneath my dress, over my thighs,
to the hem of my undergarment. Part of me wanted to stop him,
but my body, so unfamiliar with the sensations driving through
it, laid waste to my brain's protests.

"Come with me," he whispered.

"Where?" I asked, assuming he meant to wherever his living quarters were. I hadn't anticipated such an offer, and was
surprised to find I wasn't entirely against the idea. So I was surprised by the next word out of his mouth.

"Seattle."

I frowned and pulled back, my hand on his chest as I stared
up at him in confusion.

"Pardon?" I said.

"I like you. I think you like me, even though you've been
resistant to it...until now." He grinned, a hint of cockiness
shining through. "Move to Seattle with me. We can wait until
you graduate if you like, or go sooner. I'll find a job teaching
navigation somewhere, and you can find an airfield to fly at,
maybe give lessons? We'll get a little house, have babies... It'll
be great. I promise."

My mind reeled. What was he talking about? We were just
kissing, not making plans for a life together. Not changing the
entire blueprint of my future.

I slid out from between him and the vehicle, trying to get space. Air. A clear thought.

"No, don't," Carter said, his hand on my arm as he spoke quickly. "Audrey. Think about it. You and me in Seattle. It's a great city. Have you been? There's so much to do and it's beautiful. So green and surrounded by mountains on every side. You would love seeing them from the sky."

"I can't leave." My voice was so soft I wasn't sure he heard me.

"After you graduate then."

"But the program," I said, frowning in puzzlement. Was he serious?

"You want to ferry planes. I understand. So I'll stay and teach while you work the program. And then, maybe in a year?"

"I don't understand." I stared out at the base beyond. "What are you saying, Carter?"

"I'm saying, come with me. We'll build a life together. We'll get married and find a house you love."

"But...we hardly know one another. And I live in Dallas."

I couldn't think. I didn't understand. How could he be thinking these things when we'd only gone on one date? I'd told him my plans. How had he come to the conclusion I'd change my mind and move to Seattle with him? And marriage? I'd said I'd never considered that for myself, and he was putting it on the table as part of the bargain?

"I need to get back," I said.

"Are you upset?" he asked.

"I'm confused. I told you how I imagine my life. That didn't change in the matter of some chocolate cake, a car ride and a kiss."

"I just thought... You said you don't date. And you're not interested in being more than friends with anyone. But then you kissed me."

"A kiss isn't going to change my mind," I said. "It's just a kiss."

"I know it's fast. I must seem crazy to you right now. But

I'm not. I just know what I want—and that's you. I knew it the minute I saw you and every day since. It's why I can never stop looking at you when we're in the same place. I know what you said about how you've always imagined your life…but sometimes what we imagine is different than what ends up making us happy. You can still fly. As long as you want. Until there are kids, of course. And then—"

I held up a hand and took in a long, slow breath. "Thank you for dinner, Carter," I said. "Good night."

I spun on my heel and walked toward the front gate of the base.

"Will you think about it?" he called.

I paused. I understood why girls went crazy for him—there was a lot to Carter that was likable. He exuded joy. Even his kisses were a lesson in happy surrender. And I had surrendered. But he thought he could change a woman's mind with a simple kiss. And maybe he could. I'm sure there was a woman out there who would be only too happy to exchange whatever her life had served up so far for a kiss and a promise from a man like Carter. But I wasn't sure I was that woman. Or could ever become her. No matter how tempting he was.

I turned to face him. Was there a future I could imagine with this man? Would being loved by him make me not regret setting aside my goals for something I'd never considered? Would I find satisfaction in holding his hand while we walked to the park, our children running ahead of us? Or cooking him dinner, or folding his clothes? Would I glory in being introduced as his wife and throwing dinner parties for his friends and their wives? Would I lie in bed at night, happy with the choices I'd made?

Or would I sit at my kitchen table in the brief moments of silence after everyone else had gone to bed, and dream of flying, my eyes closed as I imagined the cool wind in my face and the feeling of freedom I'd always sought. Would I go to my grave

wondering if James had ever flown into that little airfield, looking for me and not finding me where I'd said I'd be?

I'd never considered other options for my life because there'd
only ever been one I wanted. But here was this lovely man offering me something that in my wildest dreams I'd never anticipated wanting. And I didn't know if it would be as awful as I'd
always dreaded—or as exciting as he said it would be.

"I will," I said, and turned and walked to my bay.

As I slept that night, Carol Ann snoring softly beside me, I
dreamed I lived in a little house. I sat at the kitchen table, Carter
across from me, a child's highchair beside him. Outside the window was a view of a mountain. There was a knock on the door
and I got up to answer. I opened it and looked up. I didn't see
his face, just the dark head of hair. And I heard his voice.

"Hi there, little bird."

CHAPTER TWENTY-ONE

The letter from James arrived that Monday. It lay on my desk where someone had left it as though it was just any letter. As though it was nothing.

I stared down at it, my body shuddering with each beat of my heart, the silence in my head deafening.

The door to the bay swung open and the girls tromped noisily inside, shedding layers as they talked and hurrying to change into their suits before we left for flight line.

"I thought you had to use the restroom," Carol Ann said as she kicked off her shoes and pulled down her slacks.

It was why I'd hurried ahead of them to get to our bay. But then I'd seen the letter and forgotten my need to go.

My eyes were cemented to the return address in the upper left-hand corner. North Africa. He was in North Africa.

"What's—" Carol Ann said, coming up beside me. "Oh. Oh my. That's…"

"Five minutes, ladies!" Geraldine shouted.

"Are you going to open it?" Carol Ann asked.

I stared at her, blind with incomprehension.

"I don't have time," I said and placed it on my desk where Carol Ann and I stared down at it as if it were some sort of strange and magical object.

"Ladies, you coming?" Tanya said, rushing past on her way to her locker. "I hear we get to take up a pursuit today. You don't wanna miss that."

I stared at Carol Ann and she stared back. I looked down again at the name in the upper left-hand corner of the envelope. J. Hart. I wasn't imagining it.

"What do you think it says?" Carol Ann asked as we marched to flight line after I used the facilities.

I had no idea. All I knew was, I was terrified to open it. What could he possibly say after so much time? Was it an apology for his silence? Or an affirmation of his previous sentiments?

"Why do we have to do this again?" Maxine groaned, cutting through my thoughts.

Rather than flying a pursuit plane, the fastest aircraft the military built, we were flying a Curtiss Helldiver, a carrier-based bomber, and towing targets.

"To make sure we know what we're doing," Tanya grumbled. "Some of us will be sent to Tow Target programs, you know."

"I hope it's not me," Sharon said, wrinkling her nose.

"They wouldn't send you," Tanya said. "You'd distract the fellas too much. They'd wind up shooting down planes instead of targets if you were in the air."

"You sweet thing," Sharon said.

I glanced at the two women. Since Sharon's near-death experience, Tanya had softened her attitude toward her, marveling instead at the way she'd returned to flying quicker than anyone had expected. She'd been nervous, visibly shaking upon boarding her first plane since the accident, but brave and unyielding in spirit, which had impressed all of us, Tanya included. Also, since that fateful day, Sharon's strict beauty routine had been

reduced, giving way to a much more natural and approachable
look even she admitted looked nicer. Gone were the platinum
strands and red lipstick, replaced instead with warmer golden
hair and a rose gloss my mother would approve of. The eyebrows were still drawn on, but without them she looked to be
in a permanent state of surprise.

So distracted was I by the sight of James's letter, I hadn't noticed the other women hanging back, making me first in flight
line.

"Coltrane, you're up!" the instructor hollered.

I looked around in surprise and saw Tanya snickering. I glared
at Carol Ann, who I hadn't noticed slide out from her spot beside me to move three spaces back.

"I hate towing targets," she whined.

I shook my head and climbed up to the aircraft.

"This one has a patched-up wing," the instructor said. "See
if you can take it off."

"Swell," I said.

I strapped myself in. As the engine roared to life I pictured
again the envelope sitting and waiting for me back at our bay.

"Damn you, James Hart," I said and sped the plane down
the runway.

Angry that just when I'd begun to loosen the ties that bound
me to him he should reappear, I flew the Helldiver like I really
wanted the wing to come off.

I hit my altitude and dove toward the soldiers in wait, simulating strafing runs and bomb drops, whipping in the wind, the
sound of antiaircraft weapons unloading below as they tried to
hit my target. Time and time again I dove, buzzed and climbed,
rolling across the sky before taking another turn. I pictured the
envelope again and let out a frustrated shriek, driving the plane
so low that this time, rather than shoot, the men scattered, dust
roiling up and outward, the smell of dirt and fuel filling my
nostrils. I laughed and pulled up, going again.

When my time was up I put the plane down without so much as a bump and jumped down onto the tarmac.

"Well," the instructor said, scratching his chin. "That was impressive."

"I think the wing is good," I said and marched to the end of the flight line.

When we returned to the bay to wash up and change for dinner, I entered last, as if by delaying entry I could postpone the inevitable. I knew I could choose not to open it—to instead toss it in the bin and try never to wonder about what words lay inside for me, and had considered that option all afternoon while twisting the chain where the hummingbird hung around my neck. But I knew I would regret not knowing—and would never be able to erase it from my mind—an idea more dreadful than the potential of opening it to find miserable words that might scar me.

The others hurried out of their flight suits and into sweaters and trousers and skirts while I picked up the letter and sat on my bed, turning it over and over in my hands.

Carol Ann settled herself across from me, her knees nearly touching mine. "Do you want company while you read it?"

I chewed my lip and then shook my head. As always, to read James's words, I needed to hear his voice. And though it had faded with time, the only way I could do so was if I was alone.

"Do you want me to bring you some dinner back?"

"That would be great," I said with a small smile for my friend. "Thank you, Carol Ann."

She squeezed my hand and disappeared out the front door with the others. I grabbed a scarf, pulled on a hat and a pair of gloves, and walked out into the cool evening air once more.

I went to the place I always went for sanctuary—the tarmac. I sat with my back against the wheel of an AT-6, the closest aircraft to the glow of Hangar Three's outside light.

I stared down at James's handwriting and brushed my fingertips over his name. My body trembled with anticipation and my eyes welled. The fear I felt over a single letter was overwhelming. It had been months since I'd last heard from him, and still I'd told myself he'd write. He had to. He couldn't just go. And yet, with each passing day, each night lying in bed staring through the dark at the ceiling while I prayed to hear from him again, a part of me felt I never would. Faith gave way to hopelessness, creating a hollowing dread that scraped away at my innermost parts, excavating the emotions I'd reserved for him, and leaving me empty.

I'd tried to reason with my feelings. I'd argued with both heart and head. We had both spoken of our dreams and goals, how we'd never let anything or anyone interfere—and he had stuck to his word. I had to understand now, just as I had then. No matter how hard it was. No matter how much it hurt.

I assumed this letter would be the long-awaited response of thanks for the gift I'd sent. Maybe a few words about life on base, and some tender but firm parting words wishing me well and encouraging my future endeavors.

I sucked in a breath and tore the envelope open.

My Darling Bird,

In my darkest hours, it is always you that I hear. When the nightmares find me, your voice awakens me, pulling me out, bringing clarity once more. And, oh, the nightmares...they come every night now. Mercilessly and without care for the damage they will do upon waking. Thank goodness for thoughts of you. They are the happiest I possess. I cannot imagine how other men survive the horrors of war.

The last six months have been rife with fear and despair. How can I apologize for my distance? My lack of communication? My utter failure as a friend? If only you were here to see it—but thank God you are not. This is not something I would wish on anyone.

Not my worst enemy, and certainly not the woman I care for most in this world.

My dear Audrey, how I miss you. I offer you the utmost of apologies and can only hope you can forgive me. The feeling of not being able to do anything, of losing so many men, of defeat and sadness, has made me retreat from everyone I care for—too bereft to form sentences that make sense or even express the sadness I feel.

Christmas. Your gift and card were lovely, and lovingly received. I am ashamed to say I purchased no gift this year. Not for you. Not for my sister. Not for any one friend. I hid in my room, shut down, shut out by choice. Willing it to go by, my pillow pressed over my head to muffle any sounds of holiday cheer.

I fear to know the truth of what you think of me now. But please know, my distance and inability to write had nothing to do with how I feel for you—which, if I am to be honest, is so much more than I ever allowed myself to speak aloud. But I see it clear as day now and ask myself why at least a dozen times a day. Why didn't I just tell you how I cared? But I know the answer. I was too afraid you'd run. Too afraid to be like all the other men you turned away. And so I had to be satisfied with being your friend. And I will be just that until the day I die, if you allow it. But if not—if too much time has gone by, if you are too angry at my silence these past months—I will make myself understand and I will let you go.

It is hard to find the words to ask what I must next—I am terrified of the answer. Maybe there will be no answer—which would be the worst answer of all. But I have prepared myself for that.

In a month's time, I am coming stateside along with several others under my command to retrieve a small fleet of planes. I will be staying at Fort Myers in Florida. It is my hope that you might find a way to join me there. I will make sure you have a hotel room of your own and anything else you might need, including a flight in and out. Even if it's only for an hour, I wish to see you again. Even if you've moved on and it is only for one last goodbye.

I am heading back to base in England tomorrow. If you write, and I hope you will, please send your letter to the same address as before.

I hope to hear from you soon, little bird.
All my love,
James

I read the letter at least a dozen more times sitting there in the cold, the ice-like cement below me chilling my bones and causing me to shiver. I read it until the words ran together and my tears began to smear the ink.

He hadn't gone. He was still with me. And he was coming stateside.

I touched the little gold pendant at my throat and inhaled a shaky breath. I was still his bird.

"I don't understand why he couldn't write," Carol Ann said later after reading the letter. "At least to say he's okay. He has to know you were worried and waiting."

We were standing outside the bay, huddled together and talking in hushed tones so the other women smoking and chatting on their stoops wouldn't hear. Most especially Hildie, whose ears always seemed to perk up whenever I was near.

"He didn't write because he was lost."

"He was lost?" Carol Ann said with a frown.

"Not literally."

"But if he really cares for you…"

I gave my friend a soft smile. It was hard for some people to understand the need to be alone, wanting instead to always be near another body—sometimes anybody. But I understood too well the necessity of quiet and solitude. It was why I'd always known, despite everyone else's fears, that I would be okay living a life by myself. It wasn't as if I'd never see another soul. I'd have my family, my friends, my employees and the many people flying in and out of the airfield. It needn't be the lonely existence my mother assumed—and likely wouldn't be. It would be full and satisfying. Just because I wouldn't go home to another person, or have someone to speak to when I climbed in bed at night, didn't mean I would be lonely. It just meant I'd be on my own.

"He and I are built to do things on our own," I said to Carol Ann. "We've always known it. We don't fear it. We prefer it."

She hugged me to her. "I worry for you," she said. "You say all this now, but what if you change your mind one day and Carter is long gone and James still hasn't changed his mind, and you're all by yourself on that airfield with no one who cares for you?"

"Then I'll get a dog."

She grinned and gave me a little shove.

"Forget a dog. I'll drive down and come drag you home with me."

"I'm sure Gus will love that."

"By that time, he'll be so tired of me talking his ear off, he'll be thankful to have someone else take the brunt of it." She rested her head on my shoulder and sighed. "What about Carter then? Is he just…not a thought in your mind anymore after reading James's letter?"

"Who's James?"

We both jumped and turned to find Hildie had crept up on us.

"None of your—" I began, but Carol Ann interrupted me, her hands on her hips.

"James is Audrey's boyfriend. See? All the grief you've been giving her over Officer Wilson was for nothing because she's already taken."

I sucked in a breath and Carol Ann turned to me, her mouth forming a little O.

"Well." Hildie sniffed. "Just because she has a beau doesn't mean she wasn't making a play for our instructor to pass the time while she's here."

"Have a good night, Hildie," I said and pulled Carol Ann inside the bay behind me.

"I'm so sorry," she whispered. "I don't know what I was thinking. She makes me so mad."

"I'm sure it's fine," I said. "Maybe she won't say anything."

But Carol Ann shook her head. "It's Hildie. She's sure to tell him first thing. Oh, Audrey..." Her eyes filled with tears. "Will you ever forgive me?"

"Of course," I said. "I just need to figure out what to do—and what to say when he asks me why I never told him about the boyfriend I don't really have."

I slept fitfully, tossing and turning as thoughts churned over and over in my mind. My future, once so decided, now seemed up in the air—and not in the sense I liked.

I could still have what I'd always envisioned. But was that what I still wanted? Carter wanted me to move to Seattle and marry him, buy a house and have babies. All things I'd never considered, but was now, surprisingly, giving some thought to. And James...

James was the biggest question. What was the purpose of going to Florida to see him? A friendly reunion? More? What was to be gained from our meeting again? Would we confirm our friendship and part ways once more, only to spend the next however many years exchanging letters? Or was there more to it and we'd finally find ourselves in a place where we were ready to admit it?

I flipped onto my back and stared at the ceiling. I wanted to scream out, "What do I want?" But it was the middle of the night and I knew the others wouldn't be appreciative. Instead, my eyes welled and tears slid down the sides of my face, dampening my hair and pillow.

"What do I want?" I whispered.

I fell asleep finally, no answer to be found.

★ ★ ★

I woke early and ventured with the others to the mess hall, Maxine and I watching for Carter while Carol Ann and Sharon kept a lookout for Hildie. When neither had been spotted by the time we sat with our food, I knew I was in trouble.

"Maybe she just left," Carol Ann said. "She never misses a meal."

Nola sat down across from us. "Who are you looking for?"

"Hildie," I said, my voice lowered.

"She was headed for the classrooms about ten minutes ago," she said.

I closed my eyes.

"You sure?" Carol Ann asked in a strangled voice.

"I am. I was shocked actually. She's usually one of the first here. Maybe she's flunking a class though and hoping to beg her way to a better grade."

"Not likely," I muttered.

I was almost done with my meal when I heard Carol Ann swear and looked in the direction she was staring.

The far door to the mess hall swung closed behind Officer Wilson. Behind him stood Hildie, a victorious smile as she stared directly at me while Carter scanned the crowd, still looking for my face.

"Damn," I muttered.

"Oh, Audrey," Carol Ann said. "I'm so, so sorry."

I drank the last of my water and stood.

"Might as well get this over with," I said. "See you ladies in class."

I felt his eyes on me as I bussed my dirty tray.

"Can I have a word?" he asked from behind me.

"Of course, Officer Wilson," I said with a pleasant smile pasted on my face. "How can I help you?"

"Outside," he said and turned on his heel.

I took in a deep breath and, after a beat, followed.

"Who is James?" he asked through clenched teeth as soon as the door swung shut behind me.

I looked around, noting three women heading for the mess hall.

"Maybe we can talk somewhere less likely to get me in trouble?" I said, crossing my arms over my chest.

"Fine." He walked around the corner to the narrow corridor between the mess hall and one of the administration buildings. "Better?"

"Not really but it will do."

"Who is James?" he asked again.

"James is my friend," I said.

"I heard he's your boyfriend."

"And did you hear this information from Hildie?"

"She said Carol Ann told her this information about this… James person."

"Carol Ann did say that, I will admit," I said. "But merely to get Hildie to leave me alone. She was covering up for me and my uh…relationship with you."

"Oh," he said, standing down, his shoulders releasing. "I see. So he really is just a friend?"

"Well… Yes. That's what he always has been. It's what we decided we would be."

"But?" His defenses were back up.

I sighed and dropped my hands to my sides, staring at the ground between us. "But."

"It's more than that, isn't it?" he said in a low voice.

It was time to be honest. With myself more than anyone. But for now, Carter deserved at least some version of the truth, even though I wasn't entirely sure what it was.

"I don't know," I said. "But I think so. At least for me."

"I don't understand."

"I think I feel more than friendship for him."

"You think?" he said. "That doesn't sound very promising. Has he said he feels more for you?"

"No," I whispered.

"Audrey. Not to sound crass, but I've known a lot of women in my life, and I've never been remotely interested in settling down with any of them. I knew I wanted to get married one day. I knew I wanted to be a father. And I knew that must mean eventually I'd meet the woman meant for me. And as far as I'm concerned, I have. And you're telling me, what? You maybe have feelings for a man who has never said he wanted anything more than friendship with you?" He scratched his head. "But standing in front of you right now is a man who does love you. You may not feel the same for me yet, but I believe you would if you give me a chance."

"Carter," I said, "you can't possibly love me."

"Why not? Why do you get to decide what I do and do not feel? And what do you know about love anyway?" He stood tall, his arms crossed over his chest. "From what you've told me, not much."

"I understand you're mad—"

"I'm not mad, I'm confused. It doesn't make any sense. You don't know if this man has any interest in being more to you than just a friend. And regardless of that, not to be completely insensitive, but who knows when or if you'll ever see him again? Who knows if he even makes it home? I'm here *now*, Audrey. I'm offering you a life with a home and a family and security. He can't offer you anything. He can't even tell you he loves you. I can. I *do*. I love you."

Tears clouded my eyes. He wasn't wrong. In fact, all of what he said was right. But despite it all, I couldn't help what I sensed in my gut. I had feelings for James—and I wanted to see what that meant. If it was nothing, if he didn't feel the same, my heart might get broken and my ego bruised, but it would only be a further sign that what I'd intended to do with my life from the beginning was my true path. And, I realized here and now, losing Carter in the process of figuring it all out was okay with me.

"You're right," I said, my voice hoarse. "I can't deny what you're saying. He may not have feelings for me. I may never see him again. But there is something between us—something that began in Hawaii that I can't forget. No matter how hard I try or how much time goes by. And I need to know if it means the same to him as it does to me."

"And if it doesn't?" he asked.

"Then I buy my airfield and have the life I always dreamed of."

"What about me?"

"Carter, what you want—it's not for me. I've tried imagining it. The house, the kids, the happy little home life. It's a sweet ideal. But I need freedom. I need airplanes. And I need something of my own. I'm not afraid of sitting at the dinner table alone or lying in bed at night with only a good book by my side. I am, however, afraid of doing something for someone just because I think he's a sweet man."

"I suppose it's better finding this out now rather than later, when there are kids involved," he said and looked up with a sad smile. "I understand. Truly, I do. He's a lucky man. I hope he knows that. And if he doesn't, you make damn sure you tell him. I don't take kindly to losing, but for you... I'll lose for you, Audrey."

He walked away from me down the narrow corridor and disappeared around the corner. The tears I'd been holding back tumbled down my face.

I stared after him. I didn't believe he loved me, even if he felt he did. I think he felt displaced. Uncertain. Carter's feelings of insecurity had made him cling to the one thing he felt might bring him the stability he was searching for. And that thing was me. In me he saw a future again—a life beyond this terrible war. Unfortunately for him, I was the wrong woman for the job. I hoped he found the right one.

Rather than go back to the mess hall and the prying eyes of Hildie and everyone else who had seen me leave with the handsome officer, I went to my bay.

I couldn't deny that I felt relieved. What I'd said to Carter had finally been the truth. My truth.

I sat at my desk and placed a piece of stationery before me.

Dear James, I wrote.

CHAPTER TWENTY-TWO

The class of 43-W-2 graduated on a frigid Saturday in February. We wore white blouses and tan slacks, our hair brushed, our faces filled with pride. An army band played as we marched to Hangar Three for the last time.

I scanned the audience as I made my way to my seat, smiling when I spotted my parents and Evie, then turned back as General Arnold addressed the group.

"You came here as fine pilots," he said. "Women looking for a way to serve your country. You leave here as extraordinary aviatrixes—as good as, and in some cases better than, your male counterparts. The army and the United States of America thank you. Congratulations to you all on a job well done. We applaud your hard work, determination and, most of all, your bravery."

Ms. Cochran stood and smoothed a hand over her impeccable hair. "It is with great pride that I stand here," she said. "You have triumphed over what others deemed impossible. And you have shown not only the army, but also yourselves, that you are

notable and fearless pilots. You are, in fact, military-grade pilots. Congratulations, ladies."

They called our names and one by one we stood, stepping
onto the stage where General Arnold shook our hands and gave
us our certificates, and Ms. Cochran gave us a pair of silver wings
with a diamond shape in the middle.

"You think the army paid for these?" Carol Ann asked as she
checked out the pin on her lapel.

"Fat chance," Tanya said.

When it was over, as was tradition set by the class before us,
we jumped in the fountain by the main office and then ran
freezing and laughing to our barracks to change.

Food was provided in the mess hall, as well as a huge cake
with the army insignia in one corner, an American flag in another and Congratulations Class 43-W-2 in the middle.

"Congratulations, bird," Dad said, putting an arm around my
shoulders and kissing my head.

"Thanks, Dad," I said, looking up at the strong man who had
always supported me.

"You look so grown," Mama said, kissing my cheek.

Evie threw her arms around me next.

"Are you really not coming home?" she whined.

"I've missed you too," I said and hugged her tighter.

I introduced my family to my roommates and in turn was
introduced to their friends and families.

Geraldine's husband and sons had come, all three looking uncomfortable in their button-down shirts and ties as she hugged
them repeatedly and told them how handsome they looked.

One of Tanya's brothers had come.

"They look like twins," Carol Ann whispered as we watched
them chat off to the side.

He was small-boned like his sister, with the same fair hair and
light darting eyes, tough demeanor and gruff voice.

Carol Ann had invited her aunt and uncle, but they couldn't afford to get away.

"It's okay," she'd said after she'd called to invite them. "I didn't expect them to. I know they're proud whether they're here or not."

As I moved about the room, talking to the other women in our graduating class, I noticed I had a shadow.

"I think someone is trying to get your attention," Nola murmured in my ear. "Poor guy. I don't think I've ever seen someone look so forlorn."

"I don't believe that for a minute." I laughed. "I'm sure you've left plenty of men pining for you."

"True," she said and moved away.

I glanced across the room and Carter's eyes locked on mine. I'd known we'd likely cross paths today. All instructors were invited to attend the graduation. I'd wrongly assumed he'd keep his distance though, as he'd done since my refusal of his offer. Since that day, I'd seen him only twice in the mess hall, and never in town or around base. I was at once glad and disappointed we wouldn't have a last moment to speak in private. I'd have liked to have at least thanked him, both for his instruction and his kindness.

"Who is that?" a voice said beside me.

I glanced down at Evie, her cornflower blue eyes wide, her heart-shaped lips parted.

"Officer Wilson," I said. "Our navigation instructor."

"I'd be happy to have him show me how to navigate a few things," she said.

"Evie!" I said and she walked away laughing.

I looked across the room again, but he was talking with one of the graduates and her parents.

"Just as well," I murmured. But as I began to turn away, he looked up as though he was about to say something.

I gave him a small wave before rejoining my family.

"Well," Dad said. "I think we'll be off. Your mother has an early morning tomorrow. Do you have everything you need?"

"I do."

"Do you all go to the same place?" Evie asked.

"No. Some of us join Ferry Command, others go on to more specialized training and some go to programs like target towing or bombing simulation."

"Where are you going?"

"San Antonio with Carol Ann and Nola. Ferry Command."

I had originally been selected for additional training in pursuit aircraft in Long Beach, California, but had requested to be in Ferry Command instead. While testing and flying pursuits would've been exhilarating, Carol Ann and I had hoped to continue on this journey together as long as possible. My request to join Ferry Command hadn't been popular with Ms. Cochran, but she'd approved it regardless. Instead of testing the maneuverability and speed of fighter planes straight off the production line, I'd be delivering and picking up planes across the country for the men involved in the war to then fly overseas for battle. And I couldn't be more excited to do so.

"Good," Evie said. "I don't want anyone shooting at you again."

I smiled and patted her back. Ever since my return from Oahu, she'd been plagued with nightmares about me being shot out of the air. I didn't bother to tell her about all the target towing I'd done here at Avenger, or how some of the planes lost parts in the air. And I never told her about the women we'd lost. No use in adding fuel to the imaginative fire burning in her mind.

I gave my parents another hug, waved goodbye and walked back to our bay with the others to gather our things and say a last goodbye.

Tanya was headed to Moore Field in Mission, Texas, to tow targets, something she actually enjoyed. Sharon had been stationed in Newark, New Jersey, as part of Ferry Command,

Maxine in Romulus Air Base in Michigan. And Geraldine, as she'd hoped, was stationed in her hometown of Abilene. It was a newer airfield with no barracks for the lone female pilot based there, so she got to live at home.

"My own bed," she'd said when she found out. "I can hardly wait."

"I can't believe this is it," Geraldine said now, sitting on the edge of her cot with tears in her eyes. "You girls... I'm sure gonna miss you. I was so worried when I came here. I thought I wouldn't fit in. That I'd feel old and out of place. But you all made me feel like I belonged. This was the best time I've ever had."

Maxine sat beside her and took her hand. "Me too."

"Me too," Sharon said.

Tanya grumbled something under her breath as she shoved a flight suit into her bag.

"What was that, Tanya?" Carol Ann asked with a smirk.

"It wasn't the worst thing I ever did," Tanya said. "You happy?"

We all burst out laughing as Carol Ann hopped up and gave a squirming Tanya a hug.

After we'd checked and double-checked our room and the bathroom for any items we'd forgotten, exchanged addresses and promised to keep in touch, we hugged one another one last time.

"You girls stay safe," Geraldine said. "And behave!" She pointed to Sharon who feigned innocence.

Carol Ann and I waved goodbye as they filed out one by one, staying behind to wait for Nola. The three of us would then take the bus to town where we'd stay the night and catch the train to San Antonio the following day.

"Have you heard anything back about your request?" Carol Ann asked, lying on her bed, her hands behind her head.

I shook my head. "I'll ask as soon as we arrive."

I'd put in a request for leave for the third weekend in March so I could go see James in Florida. When I wrote him back, I said I'd come if I could get the time off approved. I wasn't hopeful. As a new employee of Ferry Command, I was sure they'd deny my request. But, as Carol Ann had pointed out, we were in a war. Maybe they'd understand.

I wasn't so sure. I was to send James word as soon as I found out.

"You gals ready?" Nola said, swinging the door to the bay open.

As I walked out the door I turned and gave the room one last look, taking in the six beds and the long table in the middle.

"It was fun, wasn't it?" Carol Ann said.

I wrapped an arm around her shoulders.

"The best time I've ever had," I said and closed the door.

CHAPTER TWENTY-THREE

We checked in at the main office at Fort Sam the following afternoon. While Carol Ann and Nola received instructions to our room, I inquired with the officer in charge about my leave request.

"Normally a request like this so early in someone's service would be denied," he said, staring over the top of his glasses at me. "But I'm allowing it. This time. Please don't abuse the privilege."

"Yes, sir. I won't, sir."

"One condition. You must finish up whatever job you're on Thursday, even if that brings you back late Friday. And you must be back by Sunday."

"Yes, sir."

"If you do not report to work Monday morning at o-seven hundred hours, there will be consequences, including but not restricted to grounding and possible termination."

"Yes, sir."

"You've received directions to your barracks?"

"My roommates are receiving those now."

"Good. There are two women already stationed here. I believe one is out on a job. The other should be able to show you gals around. We have a barbecue every Friday evening over at the recreation center. It's a fun time." He was so straight-faced in his delivery, I wasn't sure if he was being sarcastic or not.

"Thank you, sir," I said and backed out of the room.

"How much farther?" Carol Ann whined as we lugged our suitcases across the base.

"Almost there," Nola said breathlessly.

The barracks was a three-story brick building with each room meant to house four men—or women in our case. Unfortunately, there were five of us so they'd shoved a single cot beneath the room's lone window and a fifth locker near the door to the bathroom, making moving around a bit like being on an obstacle course.

As we entered, a woman sitting on a bottom bunk stared up at us with brown eyes, her frizzy caramel-colored hair floating around her round face.

"Hello," the woman said, removing a cat from her lap and getting to her feet. "I'm Beatrice."

"You have a cat," Nola said, her voice flat as she stared at the orange feline.

"Do you not like cats?" Beatrice asked, putting a protective hand on her pet.

"So long as it understands my things are not his things, we will get along just fine."

"Well, I love cats," Carol Ann said, sitting on the bed and giving the animal a long stroke down his back. "I'm Carol Ann, by the way. And that's Audrey and Nola." She pointed to each of us and went back to giving the cat her full attention. "What's his name?"

"His name is Captain, and it's nice to meet you all. The top bunks are open, as is the bed by the window."

Carol Ann and I chose the top bunks while Nola took the one by the window, and then Beatrice gave us the full tour and the rundown of how things operated.

"We work around the clock. Each time you get back you check in at the office to find out when your next flight out is. If you return in the afternoon, you may have another flight immediately. If you come in at night, you get some food, have a shower and go to bed. If there is nothing scheduled for the following day after you get in, you still get up and check in first thing in case something came in while you were sleeping."

"Do we get days off?" Carol Ann asked.

"Yes. Unscheduled. Like I said, we work around the clock. If you get a day off, take advantage. Go shopping, go swimming at the pool, get your hair done—whatever you need. Because you won't be able to schedule those things like you normally would."

"Who's our fifth roommate?" Nola asked.

"Name's Anna. She's been gone almost a week."

"A week?" Carol Ann's eyes bulged.

"It happens." Beatrice shrugged. "You ferry one and they have another for you to take, but not back to your home base. So you fly in somewhere else and now *they* have a plane that needs ferrying. You just keep going until you end up home or there's nothing to fly back here so you get on a commercial flight or hop on a train."

"What about clothes?" I asked.

"Not a lot of room in the planes for extra luggage. I'll show you how we pack anything extra, but you won't be bringing much. If you find yourself gone more than a day, wash what you need in a sink and throw it over the radiator to dry. Iron it in the morning if need be."

"Oh dear," Nola said.

We ate in the mess hall, talking among ourselves as officers came and went, eyeing the new blood with interest.

"Hello, Bea," a young man with jet-black hair said, leaning against the table. "Who are your new friends?"

"Buzz off, Bradley."

"Prickly thing, aren't you?"

She rolled her eyes.

"Fine, fine. Well, welcome ladies. I'm Officer Bradley. It is nice to make your acquaintance. I'm sure I'll be seeing you around." He leaned in with a wink. "Don't listen to anything Miss Bea here tells you about me. I'm much nicer than she says."

"I forgot to mention," Beatrice said in a soft voice after he left. "Beside the phone in our room there's a list. Who to date and who not to. You'll find Bradley's name at the very top of who not to. Underlined twice."

"I cannot wait to see this list!" Carol Ann said.

"You're not even single," I said, laughing.

"Who cares! I wanna see who makes the who-not-to list."

The bathroom was bigger than the one in Sweetwater, but not by much.

"Where does this lead?" I pointed to a door on the other side of the bathroom.

"That's the room for visiting female pilots," Beatrice explained. "So far we haven't had many though. At least none that needed to stay the night."

Beatrice was sweet, if a little quirky. She wore what looked like waders during the day, and her pajamas were men's long johns that were two sizes too big for her small albeit chunky frame, pooling at her wrists and ankles.

"My dad's a fisherman," she explained when Carol Ann sized her up. "So's my uncle, my brothers, my grandpa and pretty much every boy I've ever known. Since my ma had all boys before me, she forgets I might like something more feminine."

"Does she wear women's clothing?" Nola asked.

Beatrice frowned. "Come to think of it, not really," she said and we laughed. "She works with the men. I think shopping is a chore for her so when the men need clothes, she just throws a couple more items in for the two of us. I've never complained. I'm used to it. But having gone through training and seeing some of the women the men bring to the barbecues and dances… A dress or two might be nice to own. And maybe some footwear other than boots."

"I'm almost afraid to ask what you swim in?" Carol Ann said. Beatrice had mentioned she liked to go to the pool in the evenings.

"Shirt and shorts," she said.

"Oh dear," Nola said. "Honey, first chance we get we're taking you shopping."

But that chance would have to wait. After breakfast the following day we headed to the main office to get our orders.

"Where you going?" Carol Ann asked, peeking at my slip of paper.

"Newark, you?"

"Michigan. Nola?"

"Ugh," she said, holding up her slip of paper like it was infectious. "Nevada."

And Beatrice was headed to Oklahoma.

"Bet I beat you all back," she said with a glint in her eye.

"Oh," Carol Ann said, hurrying to the door. "I'll take that bet."

Beatrice showed us how to pack our things, folding items so they were flat and could be slipped into our flight books.

"Some of the planes have room for storing more. Pursuits do not. Since you never know if you'll be picking up another plane when you land and what it will be, always pack light."

"So long as I have a pocket for lipstick and a comb," Nola said. "I'm set."

We locked up and walked to the airfield.

"Well," Carol Ann said, her eyes wide with excitement. "Here we go!"

The three of us hugged while Beatrice looked on, and then we climbed into our planes and got in line to take off.

I checked the map I'd strapped to my thigh and glanced at my watch. I was flying a Grumman F6F Hellcat. Its gleaming silver body practically glowed in the early morning light and I raced down the runway like a shot and lifted into the air seamlessly, the smell of fuel filling my nose.

In Newark I checked in and was given another plane to ferry, but rather than taking it back to Fort Sam, I headed for South Carolina, where my welcome was less than enthusiastic. In fact, it was downright unnerving.

We'd all been warned. Ms. Cochran had spoken to us about the discriminatory nature of some men.

"Not all, mind you," she'd said. "But those who find you a threat will seek you out and try to make your lives hell. Be polite. Be professional. Do your job. You have every right to be on those bases. The army has authorized it."

And we'd heard stories from some of the women in the class before us of men they'd encountered that had confronted, harassed, demoralized and criticized them for doing a "man's job." For taking jobs from them, no matter that we were freeing them up to fight in the war. As far as some were concerned, we too were a kind of enemy. A threat against a way of life.

"The commanding officer sneered at me and then cornered me in his office," one woman had said when she'd flown a plane in for delivery to the base. "Had his hand on my backside when another officer walked in. I hurried out fast as I could, found the nurse's quarters where I was staying, and made sure to keep a good six feet between us at all times when I went in the following day to retrieve the next plane."

Another woman told of one base where the men made her so uneasy with their hostile looks that she decided to stay in town rather than on base.

But other women in the program had nothing but nice things

to say. Thankfully, the bad reports seemed few and far between. At least, that's what we hoped.

But as I disembarked the aircraft I'd flown into South Carolina, I overheard one man on the ground speaking to another.

"Did you see that?" he said. "Another damn girl."

"Goddamn women," the other man said. "Who do they think they are, flying our planes? Mark my words, one of them is gonna go down putting on her lipstick. That'll put a stop to this."

"So long as they don't get it in their pretty little heads that things is gonna stay this way after the war is over..."

I was instantly on guard, gathering my things and walking at a clipped pace to the main office.

"Yes?" a young man at the desk said, his brow furrowed.

"My name is Coltrane. I'm with the Ferry Command," I said, keeping the pleasant smile I usually reserved for such encounters off my face. This base required a force of character I wasn't sure I could muster in such a tense atmosphere.

"I'm sorry," the officer said with a smirk, his eyes lowering to my chest before meeting mine again. "What is Ferry Command? Never heard of it."

I pulled my paperwork and pilot's license from my bag and slid it across the countertop.

"I'm a pilot," I said. "With the Women Airforce Service Pilots. Perhaps you've heard of it? General Arnold approved its inception. Maybe you would like to call him."

"Um. No, Miss," he said, barely glancing at my paperwork before sliding it back.

"Fine," I said. "I've just delivered a P-51 Mustang to your base. Do you have something for me to fly out?"

"*You* flew a Mustang?" he asked. This time he looked impressed.

I pasted on the smile I'd withheld a moment ago. "I did. Your superior is expecting it so it can be used in the war we're fighting. But if you don't want it, I'm happy to fly it back to Texas."

I turned on my heel and headed for the door.

"Wait!"

I stopped.

"Coltrane?" he said.

"That's me." I turned back to face him.

"Here you are," he said.

There was a sheepish smile on his face as he pointed to an open notebook in front of him.

I walked to the desk and looked down. Next to his finger was the model of plane and my name. At the top of the page were the words *Ferry Command*.

"Never heard of it, huh?" I said and he went red. "Do you have another plane for me or not?"

"We do."

I stalked to the waiting P-40 Warhawk, glancing at the two men who had been talking about me when I'd landed. One stood frowning at the back end of a little Stinson Reliant training aircraft while the other climbed aboard.

"Nice ride, boys," I said. "Maybe, if you can master that, they'll let you fly the girl planes."

They glared as I strode past, but neither said a word.

From South Carolina I flew back to my home base in San Antonio. I landed and checked in at the front desk at 11:00 p.m. with a yawn and a smile.

"Evening," the officer at the desk said. "How can I help you?"

"Do you have my assignment for tomorrow?"

He checked a large logbook and then slid a paper across the desk.

"Thank you," I said and walked to the barracks, my body aching and tired, my mind excited. Tomorrow I flew to Long Beach.

Beatrice was asleep when I let myself in. Nola's bed was empty. By the sound of the shower and the mess on Carol Ann's bed, I knew she was still up. I grabbed my pajamas and toiletries and joined her in the bathroom.

"You were gone forever!" she said when she saw me. "Did something bad happen?"

I told her about my busy day. She'd had only the one stop where she'd picked up another plane and come right back.

"Took no time at all. And I beat Beatrice back." She grinned. "The men sure were surprised to see me get out of the plane. The looks on their faces...you woulda thought I was naked!"

I laughed and nodded. I'd felt the same way.

"Where you headed tomorrow?" I asked.

"California. Long Beach."

"Me too!"

We whispered excitedly in bed until midnight when we fell asleep.

Nola still hadn't returned when we woke the next morning.

"Either she got sent all over the place, or they didn't have a plane for her and she had to catch a ride back by train," Beatrice said over breakfast. "Like I said, Anna's been gone over a week now. It's happened to me before. When you finally get back you eat, shower and get up the next day and start all over again."

Carol Ann and I flew a pair of SBD Dauntlesses to Long Beach. From there they would head to the Pacific Theater. The trip over was uneventful, until I noticed what I thought was a military base below us.

"What base is that?" I radioed to Carol Ann. "I don't see it on my map."

"It's not on mine either," she said.

"Oh God," I breathed, my mouth falling open, the hairs on my arms rising.

"What is it?" Carol Ann's panicked voice echoed in my ears.

"I think that's..."

I peered down at the long buildings lined up one after another. There was no runway. No planes lined up. No hangars or barracks or buildings to house an administration.

"It's a camp," I murmured.

We'd seen images of the internment camps in the newspaper, but flying overhead one was something entirely different. It made them real. Below me were hundreds of Japanese Americans who had been ripped from their homes to live in who knows what kind of conditions out of our government's fear that there might be a spy among them. And while this war had taught me our worst fears could come to light, I found the decision to imprison thousands of innocents to be no better than what Hitler was doing on the other side of the world. And it sickened me.

"It's a prison," Carol Ann said, mirroring my thoughts.

Sobered, we landed forty-five minutes later and were informed upon check-in that we'd be flying a pair of pursuit planes—P-51 Mustangs—out the following day, delivering them to Langley Airfield in Virginia so they could be taken overseas to Europe. Until we were due to fly out though, our time was our own. We spent it at the beach.

As we flew into Langley the following day with me in the lead, I radioed into the tower that I was inbound to land, but was denied.

I grabbed the handheld. "Carol Ann, they're not letting me land."

"What?" Her voice was like a shot in my ears. "Let me try."

A moment later she was back in my ear. "I don't understand," she said. "This is the correct base, right?"

"Of course," I said. "I'll try again."

But once more I was denied.

We flew in a wide arc, each quiet with our own thoughts. When I'd done deliveries at Hudson Airfield, there had been a few instances where they hadn't let me land right away due to traffic on the runway. Perhaps this was the same. If not, we didn't have enough fuel to go much farther and would have to find another airfield nearby, or a field to land in. We couldn't stay in the air forever.

I recalled my treatment in South Carolina. Maybe this wasn't about a crowded tarmac. Maybe it was about something else entirely.

"Carol Ann," I said. "Do you know of any other airbases nearby?"

"No. Why? Do you think we'll have to land these things somewhere else?"

"Maybe," I said. "Let me try again. Hold on."

I took a breath, my hand shaking as I pressed the button once more.

"Tower, this is—"

"Ma'am!" a man's voice shouted at me. "Get off the line! We have two Mustangs circling the airfield and are unable to make contact. If you do not keep off this frequency—"

I frowned as I processed what he'd said. Two Mustangs. I glanced out the window at the nose of my plane, then looked over my shoulder at Carol Ann's.

I pursed my lips and took a breath and then pressed the button again.

"Tower," I said in a loud and firm voice. "*We* are in the Mustangs."

"What?"

Ten minutes later, after an exchange with the tower that would have been hilarious if it hadn't been so frustrating, we were on the ground.

"Holy hell," an officer said as we jumped down from the pursuits. "Those were girls flying those planes?"

I wondered, as we walked to the office to check in, if we would ever not be underestimated. If men would ever look at us and not blink an eye or find themselves surprised by our presence doing jobs they'd only ever thought they could do. If we'd ever get the credit and acknowledgment for both our skill and our bravery. Or if we'd always be "just girls" in their eyes. Playing at something they didn't deem us hardy enough for.

The next two weeks went off without a hitch, every plane

in good condition, every base happy to receive me and every scheduled pickup and drop-off running on time.

In between jobs, if I was home at Fort Sam, I enjoyed the rare meal with one or two but rarely more of the women in our barracks. Nola was back when we'd returned from Virginia, full of stories about the lively nurses she'd bunked with in Nevada, and we finally met our fifth roommate, Anna, a serious-looking young woman with glossy brown hair and striking blue, almost lavender, eyes who hadn't been a part of the WASP program, but rather a part of Nancy Harkness Love's WAFS program— the Women's Auxiliary Ferrying Squadron. They called them- selves the "Originals" and had been ferrying planes for nearly two years now without having to go through any of the ground school training we'd had, due to Ms. Love's gathering a group of already military-aircraft-trained women, rather than the many women who entered the WASP program with no knowledge at all of military planes.

"Do you ever get tired of it?" Carol Ann asked one night during dinner.

"Sure," Anna said. "If I have to go too many days without a day off in between. But I love it. And I won't be here much longer."

"Are you quitting the program?" I asked.

"No. They're sending us to officer training school."

"For the military?" Carol Ann's eyes bulged.

"Yes."

"We're going to be militarized?"

While the army had taken us under its protective wing, we weren't officially part of the military. We'd been trained in the army way; we followed army rules and protocols and were rec- ognized as part of the army program—but we were not mili- tarized. We took no oath. We received no benefits. We were unrecognized by our country as part of the armed forces, even though they allowed us to fly their planes onto military bases around the country, test military aircraft and transport military personnel.

"That's the hope. It hasn't been approved yet, but Nancy and Jackie are both pushing for it, and General Arnold is putting in the request."

"Wow," Carol Ann said and looked across the table at me. "You gonna do it?"

I pushed my potatoes around my plate. It seemed as though everything I did these days took me further away from my little airfield. If I joined the military, what then? I'd be stationed somewhere and my job would be to serve my country.

I shook my head. "No. It's not for me."

"Because of your airfield?" she asked and I nodded. "That must be some airfield."

I laughed. "It's a tiny thing. But I love it. It's all I've ever wanted."

"Well, I can't wait to see it one day. Do I get a free room at your hotel?"

"I'll give you a discount."

As the women talked more about officer training school, my mind remained on Hudson Airfield. I knew from a recent conversation with my father that Hal was getting antsy. Was I ever coming back? Did I still intend to buy it? To calm his fears, my father had given him a down payment.

"I know what you're going to say, bird," he'd said over the phone. "But the man is getting old and he wants to retire in the next couple of years. It was the only way to keep him from putting up a For Sale sign. You can pay me back later. For now, I've reserved your spot."

"Thank you, Dad," I'd said. "I will pay you back. I promise."

"I'm not worried about the money, bird. You know that. Now you can relax and do your job without the stress of wondering if it will be here for you when you're done. You'll be home soon enough, fixing up that decrepit hunk of rickety hangars and happy as can be. And if Hal decides he's done sooner than we all thought, I'll hire someone to run it until you're ready."

But I didn't want someone else running my airfield. The thought worried me and made me question if I wanted to stay with the Ferry Command or give it up and return home now. But as I looked from Carol Ann to Anna, the sound of military aircraft overhead, I knew I wouldn't. It wasn't time yet. I still had so much more to do.

CHAPTER TWENTY-FOUR

"You've got everything you need?" Carol Ann asked, standing beside me as I checked and rechecked my valise.

I nodded as I reluctantly zipped it up and set it on the floor beside me.

I'd received a telegram from James a week and a half after sending him the letter saying I would meet him. He'd sounded so grateful I'd nearly cried. How had I ever thought him indifferent?

"Where are you staying again?" Carol Ann asked.

"In a hotel near the base. There's no women's barracks at Buckingham Army Airfield where I'm flying in, and since I'm not military, I can't stay on his base. He said he'd take care of it."

"Will you tell him about Carter?" she asked in a low voice.

"I don't know."

"Don't," she said. "There's no point and it's a distraction he doesn't need."

"I feel awful though."

I'd spent a good amount of time since leaving Avenger Field

haranguing myself over the kisses I exchanged with Carter. Carol Ann and Nola wouldn't hear it though.

"He didn't write, Audrey," Carol Ann had said. "What were you supposed to do? Never kiss a man again?"

I smiled ruefully. "That was always my plan."

"Men ruin all our plans. Don't you know that by now?"

"That's why I always stayed away."

"I know," she said. "But that's also why you weren't having any fun."

I smacked her on the arm playfully. "I had fun."

"Okay, Grandma. You had fun. I believe you. Next thing you know you were gonna start knitting scarves for all your friends and inviting them over to play cards."

We dissolved in a fit of laughter.

In the morning I took extra care with my hair, rolling it tighter than usual in hopes that when I removed my helmet it would still look good. My hands shook as I placed each pin and I shouted out when I poked my ear by accident.

"You'll have the entire bus ride after your flight in to tidy yourself," Carol Ann said, entering the bathroom on stealthy feet. "Here." She took the last few bobby pins from me and slid them into my hair.

"Thanks," I whispered. "I'm so nervous. I didn't think I would be."

"How could you not be? It's been a long time," she said. "But he's going to be so happy to see you. Remember, he's been in a war. You're going to seem like a dream to him. The best dream he's ever had."

"What if all the things I think I feel are gone?"

"Maybe neither of you will feel what you did in Hawaii. And if you don't, then you'll be what you both always said you were—friends. And if you do feel more, then just allow your-self this brief moment of bliss while you get to be together. It's only a couple days. Enjoy it. Who knows how long it will be before you get the chance again."

I grabbed her in a hug and she held me tight.

"You're the best friend I've ever had, you know that?" I said when I pulled away.

"Of course I do," she said with a grin. "You're mine too, if you couldn't tell. I don't know how I'd get through the day without you to complain to. Speaking of which, did I show you Gus's latest letter?"

I followed her back to our room where she handed over the wrinkled piece of paper that had arrived the day before. I scanned the page and handed it back.

"A summer wedding?" she railed quietly. Nola had the day off and was enjoying a rare morning sleeping in. Anna and Beatrice hadn't returned yet from the last jobs they'd gone on. "Who wants a summer wedding in Alabama? Not me, I'll tell you that. All those bugs and the humidity? I'll look like a drowned rat. What are they feeding those boys over there? I swear. He knows it has to be a winter wedding. I already have my dress picked out—it has sleeves, for God's sake!"

She complained the entire way to the tarmac, stopping only when I was standing beside my plane, helmet and goggles on, staring at her.

"So," I said. "I'm going to go now."

"What?" she said. "Oh. Right." She pulled her own helmet on and gave me another quick hug. "Have *fun*, Audrey. I can't wait to hear all about it."

With a last wave, I climbed aboard the Warhawk I was ferrying and got in line for takeoff.

I brought the plane into Buckingham Army Airfield several hours later and hurried to the office to check in and ask about the nearest bus station.

I was nervous, my hands sweating. It had been over two years

since I'd seen James. Would we still get along? Would the undercurrent of something more than friendship still be there? Or
would we now, as Carol Ann had said, be the friends we'd always said we'd be? Either way, I was excited to see him—but
also anxious.

A little bell hanging on the handle jangled as I pushed through
the door and went to the front desk. I tapped my fingertips on
the counter while I waited for the officer manning the front
desk to get off the phone.

"Yes?" he said as he hung up. "Can I help you?"

"I'm Audrey Coltrane from Ferry Command. I just brought
in a Curtiss P-40 Warhawk from Fort Sam Houston."

He pulled out a ledger and ran a slow finger down the page,
after which he looked around me to peer out the window.

"Swell," he said and made a note.

"Do you have a schedule for the bus?" I asked as the bell on
the door rang behind me.

"I do." He opened a drawer. "Somewhere."

"I'm in a hurry. Maybe you can just point me in the direction of the nearest stop?"

"Hang on," he said, shuffling some papers.

I sighed and closed my eyes, trying to refrain from getting
angry, but I was anxious. I was finally in the same state as James
and this man couldn't find a damn bus schedule.

As I inhaled to keep calm, I noted a familiar earthy scent. I
exhaled, trying to place it—and then everything seemed to stop
as I turned around.

He was leaner than the last time I'd seen him, and splendid
in his uniform, his green eyes filled with something I knew he
could see reflected in my own.

I'd been right to come.

"James," I whispered and flew into his arms.

He said nothing as he pulled me to him and buried his face
in my neck, his whiskered jaw scratching deliciously against my

skin, his heart pounding as he breathed me in and melted further into me.

We stayed that way for a long moment, ignoring the young
officer behind the desk still rifling through papers, absorbing
one another, taking each other in…remembering.

He pulled back and searched my face, as if looking for the
anger he was sure would meet him on this trip. But any mis-
givings I'd had about his silence had left my body the moment
I decided to come.

"God," he said. "I didn't realize just how much I missed you
until this minute." He ducked his head. "I'm so sorry, Audrey.
I never should have— There was so much—"

"You don't have to apologize," I said, resting my cheek against
his chest. "I understand."

He brushed a stray strand of hair from my face and tucked it
behind my ear, reminding me of another time and another place.

His gaze met mine again.

"Hi there, little bird," he whispered and I smiled as my eyes
filled with tears.

"Um…" the officer at the desk said, holding up a crumpled
piece of paper. "Do you still need directions to the bus stop?"

I grinned up at James.

"I think we're okay," he said and slid the bag from my shoulder.

"Thank you anyway," I said and took the hand James held out.

We couldn't take our eyes off one another as we walked to
his borrowed jeep.

"This feels familiar," I said, climbing in the passenger seat.

He looked around at the palm trees and blue sky, the humid
air embracing us. "It does, doesn't it?" he said and got in beside me.

We sat staring from our respective seats, drinking in each
other's presence, our eyes wandering as we rediscovered one
another.

War had aged him. Any of the boyishness I'd seen in Hawaii had been chased away by the horrors he'd witnessed, and in its place was a wiser and worn version. Still young, but shrewder. His gaze missed nothing. His lean body on alert at all times. There was a quickness and no-nonsense preciseness to his movements, as though he had no time for the unnecessary or indulgent.

I heard his sharp intake of breath and found him staring at my throat.

"You're wearing the necklace," he said, his voice husky as his eyes grew wet.

I touched the little bird hanging from the delicate chain around my neck. "I've never taken it off," I said.

"I wasn't sure you'd like it," he said, a momentary look of insecurity flitting across his handsome features. "I saw it in a shop as I was walking by. I wanted you to have a piece of me to have with you always. That probably sounds silly..."

I placed my hand on his knee. "I love it. It's perfect."

He took me to dinner and we picked at our food, too busy staring across the table at each other to be bothered with eating. He told me about the men he led, how some had left high school to serve and others were new fathers, their first children born while they were away. He spoke of the places he'd been and the destruction he'd seen. How even Hawaii couldn't compare to the war-torn countries he'd flown over.

"Entire towns are gone," he said. "Not just the buildings, the people too."

I watched him as he spoke, his eyes darting about the room, his back and shoulders rigid. He was different, thinner, a touch of gray in his hair that hadn't been there before, new lines around his eyes—but so handsome still. And charismatic without trying.

"I'm sorry," he said suddenly. "I'm finally seeing you for the first time in years and all I can talk about is— Tell me about you, about your training. What was Sweetwater like? Tell me about Carol Ann."

"It's okay," I said, reaching for his hand. "I want to hear it. I want to know everything."

"I can tell you all that in letters—which I promise to write more of." He smiled sheepishly. "I want to hear about you. I can't believe I'm sitting here with you," he said, putting down his fork and sitting back. "You are more beautiful than I remember. When I saw you in the office earlier…that hair and your figure—almost regal. So stunning. I've dodged bullets and bombs, but your affection…your willingness to bother with me at all—that's what nearly stopped my heart."

This time when he looked at me, I blushed, his stare so intense and filled with such emotion—an emotion I knew too well and had kept hidden for too long.

"I'm almost afraid to move or breathe," he said. "For fear that if I do, I'll wake from this dream as I've done so many times before—and you'll be gone."

"I'm not going anywhere. But please, James, promise me you won't disappear again. I can't—" I shook my head and stared down at my lap. "I couldn't bear it. I didn't know if you were dead and I had no way of finding out. No one I could ask. Every day was miserable not knowing if you had disappeared from my life—or disappeared from all life. One of which I could learn to heal from, the other…"

He took my hand and held tight.

"It would take my leaving this earth completely to get me to ever leave you again. I'm so sorry, little bird. I never meant to hurt you."

I stared down at my lap, blinking back tears and taking in several shuddering breaths, my fingers grasping at his. When I met his gaze again, a single tear traced a sad path down my cheek.

"I didn't realize how much I cared until I didn't hear from

you," I said. "I didn't know how bad a broken heart would hurt."
My voice faltered.

He moved his chair so it was beside mine and leaned in so
that his forehead pressed against my temple, his lips brushing
my cheek.

"I promise you, Audrey Fitzgerald Coltrane. I will never leave
you again. Not ever."

After dinner, he bought ice-cream cones and we walked with
our hands clasped down a little promenade near the water as
the sun went down.

"Tired?" he asked, catching me yawning.

I nodded and moved closer, placing my head on his shoulder.

"Do you want to go to your hotel?" he asked. "It's not far
from here. I can grab some beer or wine and we can talk for
a while more. Unless you'd rather go to sleep. In which case,
I'll be back first thing to take you to breakfast. Whatever you
want to do."

"Beer and more talking," I said.

His shoulders rose and fell in a heavy sigh. "I was hoping
you'd say that."

We stopped at a store for beer and snacks, giggling like a couple of kids who'd sneaked out of the house against their parents'
wishes. Afterward, he drove to a small three-story hotel with
grounds covered in palm trees and tropical-looking flowers,
and a pool surrounded by blue-and-white-striped deck chairs
around the back.

"This is lovely," I said as we walked to my room, which was
on the first floor with a sliding door that led to the patio and
pool.

I slid open the door as James handed me a bottle of beer, and
we took off our shoes and sat on two of the deck chairs.

"I may never go back," James murmured, taking a sip and
closing his eyes.

"Me neither. Think they allow people to move in permanently?"

"I'll offer to clean the pool as a trade."

"I'll sweep the patio," I said.

"You should make those shortbread cookies with the chocolate," he said. "That will convince them."

I smiled. "You remember those?"

He opened his eyes and peered at me. "I remember everything about you."

As the sun dipped lower in the sky, we talked about our families, the WASP program and my new job with Ferry Command.

"I flew a Mustang," I said. "A couple of them actually."

"What did you think?"

"I think Roxy has competition."

"Roxy," he mused. "I wonder if that poor plane is still stuck in the sand or if someone dug her out and is flying her around the island."

"I hope so," I said, smiling as I pictured the little yellow-and-blue plane.

"What else," James asked, adjusting his chair so it lay flat, and turning on his side, his head propped on his hand. "What about the airfield? Still the plan?"

"It is. Why? You want a job?"

"I might. You hiring?"

"I'm sure there are a lot of positions I'll need filled. Janitor... handyman..."

He flicked his bottle cap at me and I laughed and swatted it away.

"There's only one position I'll accept," he said.

"Oh yeah?" I asked, my voice husky as I raised one eyebrow.

The tiny gesture made him suck in a breath. "I do believe bunking with a group of sassy, forward-thinking Rosies has rubbed off on you, Miss Coltrane. Are you flirting with me?"

I ducked my head, blushing furiously.

"Don't be embarrassed," he said, sitting up and setting down his beer. "Please."

I sat up too, swinging my legs over the side of the chair and preparing to stand—or run if need be.

"I'm not—" I looked around the little patio area, avoiding his eyes. "I didn't know what to think coming here. It was never my intention, when we met, I mean…" The words stumbled from my lips and I was unable to stop them. I felt stupid. Naive. Why were we here? I thought I knew but maybe… "But now I don't know. I can't be sure I know why you wanted to see me. Is it just to apologize? To solidify our friendship? Or is it something more? And if so, what? I don't know what to think. The hand-holding. The kisses." I was flustered and still couldn't look at him. "I just want…" I sighed and closed my eyes for a moment and then looked up at him. "You."

The silence was like a vacuum and I stood, sick with embarrassment and wanting nothing more than to jump in the pool and sink to the bottom. I set my bottle down on the table harder than I meant to and went inside and sat on the bed.

"Audrey," James said, following me. He stood in the doorway, the light of the setting sun casting a halo around him, making him look otherworldly as the filmy white curtains swayed in the breeze. "I know what we said. But you were never just a friend to me."

We fell asleep fully clothed, my head on his chest, his hand gripping mine. When I woke in the morning, we hadn't moved. I looked up at him and sighed, convinced I'd never felt more content, and then rolled onto my back.

"Don't," he said, grasping my hand and pulling me back to him. "Don't go."

I grinned against his chest. But when I met his eyes, I froze. He wasn't kidding.

I remembered the dreams he'd told me about as we'd lain

side by side the night before. Nightmares he'd had about me. Terrible images embedded in his mind, of bombs falling and me beneath them. I'd wrapped myself around him, my one leg tucked between his, his heart beating beneath my cheek as I tried to comfort him while he recounted the horrors his mind had imagined nearly every night.

I pushed myself up and kissed him lightly on the lips. "I'm here. But I do have to use the restroom."

He rolled me over and kissed me hard. "I suppose I can be brave enough to let you do that," he said and released me.

"You're the bravest man I know, James Hart," I said as I sat up. But a cloud passed over his eyes.

"Maybe once," he murmured, turning away. "I'm not so sure anymore."

I laced my fingers through his.

"Even if you don't feel it," I said, "your sense of duty to your country makes it so. As does the fact that you stay and fight, regardless of the terrible things you've seen."

"And done," he whispered.

This was the other side of war. The guilt for taking lives, sometimes innocent ones, all for the cause. All for saving the ones who couldn't fight for themselves. It was a noble deed, but taxing on the souls of the men with their finger on the trigger.

He lifted my chin so I was looking into his eyes. "I want you to know—I will carry these few days with me for the rest of the war."

"James—"

"It means the world to me that you came," he said. "No matter what happens, I need you to know that I've never felt for any woman what I feel for you. I love you, Audrey. I have since the first day I saw you."

In my lifetime, the only thing I could equate this moment to was taking flight for the first time. I was breathless, my heartbeat speeding in my chest, my extremities weightless, my mind clear. There was only one emotion. The same one I'd felt upon that first lift into the air.

"I love you too," I whispered.

I'd never seen a man look at me the way he did when I returned those words.

We spent the day sharing things we never had before. Thoughts and dreams and memories previously kept to ourselves. We couldn't stop staring, touching, blushing and smiling.

Our meals went almost completely untouched. We forgot to drink our water, our coffee, the beer we ordered. We walked for miles, never at a loss for words, until we found we had no idea where we were and James got us a taxi back to the hotel. And once there, we realized we were starving and ordered room service and sat cross-legged on the bed, still staring, smiling and blushing.

When we were finished, we cleared the trays of food from the bed and went outside to watch the sun set.

"Sit with me," he said, sliding over to make room on his deck chair.

I snuggled beside him, my head resting in the crook of his neck. We were quiet now, lost in our own thoughts, a heaviness blanketing the fun we'd had all day. It was our last night together. Who knew when or if we'd see one another again.

"Do you want me to stay?" James asked.

I nodded and we both held on tighter to the other.

Not knowing what we'd be doing all day, he'd packed a bag with a few personal items and a change of clothes and tossed it in the back of the jeep earlier in the morning before we'd had breakfast. He retrieved it while I changed into a nightgown Carol Ann had insisted I buy and bring with me. It wasn't fancy. Nothing like the lacy numbers my sister liked to sleep in. It was a simple navy cotton slip of a garment, with delicate straps, satin trim and a little slit up one leg.

"It says a lot without saying too much," Carol Ann had said, to which I'd frowned.

"What does that mean?" I'd asked.

"Just trust me and pack it."

And so I had, now frowning at my reflection while I waited for James to return. It really was quite simple. Disappointingly so. But before I had a chance to scour my bag for other options, he'd returned.

"Wow," he said when he entered the room. "That is… You are…lovely."

I looked down at the modest neckline. Carol Ann was right. It apparently said a lot.

The ease of the day was erased the moment he emerged from the bathroom. A tension unlike any I'd felt before charged the room, and we both became suddenly shy.

"Are you sure you want me to stay?" he asked.

I waited to feel a hesitation. A sign that his staying was a bad idea. But there was no reluctance. No second thoughts. With my entire being I wanted him here.

"I'm sure," I said.

He sat on the edge of the bed and ran a hand through his hair, a gesture I remembered well. I sat beside him and twisted the diamond stud in my ear. He chuckled and nudged my arm, making me laugh.

It was funny how well we knew one another after so little time spent together. How small movements, smells or just the sight of palm trees brought me back to another time. A moment later though, all levity was forgotten as my leg brushed against his, sending an electric charge shooting through me as he sucked in a breath.

We turned to face each other, like magnets drawn together. I knew what I'd said to Carter was the absolute truth—it didn't matter that James might never be able to offer me anything tangible. What I wanted from him was this feeling right now.

I didn't need promises. I didn't need the security of marriage or a house with a garden. I didn't need to have his children to tie me to him. I was tied to him regardless. Maybe because of what we'd experienced in Hawaii. Maybe only because of who he was and who I was. And together we made sense—even if this weekend was all we had. Even if we met only occasionally throughout our lives, to laugh and hold hands and tell the other we loved them. All I needed was to know he loved me and thought of me. And years from now, while he flew around the country and I ran my little airfield, I would remember this weekend. This moment as we stared at one another with so much love I thought my heart might burst. It would carry me. It would be the air my wings floated on.

We reached for each other at the same time, his mouth meeting mine as his hands buried in my hair and I pulled him closer still.

His lips were at once soft and hard, giving and taking, his tongue teasing mine. Overcome, I slid my hands beneath his shirt and over the surface of his skin. My experience with men was limited, and my brief involvement with Carter had felt foreign and strange. But there was nothing strange about being with James, the headiness of his sexuality intoxicating and overwhelming. For the first time in my life, I felt womanly, and the walls I'd protected at great length came tumbling down. The fear that I knew next to nothing of pleasuring a man disappeared. I was concerned only with getting lost in this moment. I was safe here. And I wanted him.

He groaned and pulled his shirt off and tossed it to the floor before pulling me to him again, his skin hot against mine, his hands roaming down my body and raising the hem of my nightgown. In an instant it was off, joining his shirt in a pile on the floor.

"Jesus, Audrey," he breathed, his green eyes devouring me.

Feeling a touch of modesty, I leaned into him, wanting to

hide in the safety of his arms. But then I stopped, instead getting to my feet and standing to my full height, staring him in
the eye. If I were to be his, I didn't want to hide or shy away. I
wanted to see him, and for him to see me, and for us to experience every second together.

He stood up as well, and I reached out and unbuttoned his
shorts, sliding them down over his narrow hips.

"Audrey," he whispered.

"I love you," I said.

I woke in the morning with James curled around me, his
breath warm against my shoulder. I belonged to him now. And
he was mine.

I stretched, smiling at his sleeping face and gasping a moment
later when he pulled me to him, his whiskers scratching against
the tender skin of my neck.

"Good morning," he said, his voice deep with sleep.

"Good morning."

He trailed a path of kisses down the center of me, pausing
every so often, taking pleasure in making me squirm, before
making his way back up, where he stopped at my lips and kissed
me with such passion he left me breathless, the tightening in
my belly returning.

"I love you," he said.

My eyes filled with tears.

"Audrey?" he said, frowning. "Are you okay?"

"I'm—" I gulped in air. "I think I'm overwhelmed."

I laughed at the absurdity, which made me cry more and he
looked at me with such love, his own eyes watering as he chuckled and rolled onto his back, pulling me against him.

"I should've run," he whispered.

I quieted and stared up at him. "What?" I said.

"I knew it the minute I saw you," he said. "I should've stolen a plane and flown away as fast as I could. Because how am I ever going to leave you now?"

Tears slid down the sides of his face, soaking the pillow beneath him.

"James," I whispered and climbed on top of him. "It's going to be okay. I promise."

He placed his hands on either side of my face.

"No matter what happens, I will never forget a second of this," he said. "I will take it with me all the way to England and back again."

And with that we made love again, giving ourselves over to all the fear, all the worry, all the love we had for now, for each other and for our future.

We ate breakfast on the patio, exchanging glances and trying to distract ourselves from the fact that this was our last day together and tonight we would both be asleep in different beds.

After we ate, we packed our things and James drove us to the beach. We walked barefoot in the sand, holding hands, splashing in the surf and staring into one another's eyes.

Lunch was at a small café and we lingered over our last meal together. Afterward we poked in some of the shops the area had to offer. He bought me an ornamental blue-feathered bird he saw in a window, and I bought him a men's stationery set, giving him a stern look as I handed him the purchase.

As evening fell, he drove us to the base. We were quiet as he pulled into a parking spot and turned off the engine.

"We could make a run for the border," he said with a sad smile.

"You'd never forgive yourself," I said.

"Damn pride," he said and slid from the jeep.

I followed him to the office and hung back while he spoke with another officer.

"Miss Coltrane," a voice said from behind me and I turned.

I frowned, not recognizing the young man standing before me.

"It's Hurst, Miss. From Wheeler Airfield."

"Officer Hurst," I said as I took note of the insignia on his flight suit. "My goodness. How are you? It's good to see you."

I remembered him as the haughty young man I'd taken up that fateful December morning. But time and war had changed and shaped him. Gone was the roundness of his youth, in its place a square jaw and formidable physique. He was no longer a boy, but a soldier and a man.

"It's good to see you again too, Miss Coltrane. I always hoped I'd get to one day. So I could thank you."

"Thank me? For what?"

"You saved my life."

"I didn't," I said, shaking my head.

"You're being modest, but it's true. December 7, 1941 was the day I truly learned to fly, and what it is to be a military pilot. And that is thanks to you. I owe you. And if I can ever return the favor, I hope you'll let me know."

"You are very kind, Officer Hurst. I did nothing but try to get us out of the way."

"You saved more than one life that day. I remember." He looked over his shoulder to where James was still talking with another officer. "I tell everyone who will listen about the woman who saved my life and taught me to fly. I'm honored to get to fly you back to your base tonight. I hope I'll do you proud."

I raised my eyebrows. "You're taking me home?"

"I am. And you have nothing to worry about. Like I said, I learned from the best."

"I see you've met your pilot," James said, joining us.

"I have," I said.

"Officer Hurst is part of my squadron. He's been with me since we left Hawaii. He flies the bombers while I fend off the bullets for him."

The two exchanged a smile.

"It's been a long road," Hurst said.

"And a vast, smoke-filled sky," James said.

Officer Hurst checked his watch. "We take off in thirty," he said to me. "I'll see you out on the tarmac, Miss Coltrane?"

"I'll be there."

He saluted James and turned smartly before walking off. We followed behind at a slower pace, biding our time and our last moments together.

"What time do you leave?" I asked. I knew already, but was having trouble finding things to say, my emotions running high.

"Nineteen hundred hours. Just an hour after you."

We stood staring at the plane that would take me home, a silver B-26 Marauder with black stripes across the wings and a crew of five from my count of the men standing nearby waiting.

"I'll write as soon as I land," James said, taking my hand. "And the next day. And the one after that."

I smiled. "You have no excuses now. You have supplies to last you a year."

"I'll put them to good use."

"Ready?" Officer Hurst asked.

My hand tightened around James's, panic tightening my stomach like a vice.

"Give us a minute," James said and Hurst nodded and waved to the others to get on board.

James tipped my head up so that my gaze met his.

"I love you, Audrey Fitzgerald Coltrane," he said. "I've never loved anyone but you—and don't plan to. I will be back for you when this horrid war is over. No matter how long it takes. And our dreams... We'll figure it out somehow. So we'll both be happy."

"I love you, James," I whispered. "If you don't come for me, I will find you and drag you home."

We grinned at one another and then kissed one long, last time.

"Fly safe," I said.

"You too, little bird."

"He's a good man," Officer Hurst said as I buckled into my harness.

"He's my man," I whispered.

Moments later we tore down the runway and the Marauder lifted us up and away.

CHAPTER TWENTY-FIVE

"Golly, it's warm," Carol Ann said as we stood at the desk waiting for our assignments, our blouses sticking to our backs and underarms beneath the new Santiago Blue suits Ms. Cochran had made for us. We now looked like we belonged, but we were also swimming in pools of sweat beneath our "blues."

"Coltrane. Bixby." The officer handed us each a slip of paper.

"What'd you get?" Carol Ann asked.

"Seattle. You?"

"Lucky. It's always raining there. I got North Dakota. They're probably having a heat wave *and* a tornado."

I slung my arm through hers and dragged her out the door.

Seattle wasn't rainy, it was warm and green, and I found myself not minding I didn't have a plane to ferry back until the following day.

It was strange being in the city Carter had said he wanted to take me to. I wondered, as I walked around downtown, if he was still in Sweetwater or if he was here. The thought that I may run into him opened a pit of dread every time I saw a tall blond man.

Sometimes at night I thought of him with bewilderment. How had he managed to get under my skin so quickly? How had he almost convinced me to go with him?

I looked up at the buildings around me. What if I had chosen a life with him? Would I have liked to live here? Would we have had a nice life? I imagined it would have been full of sweetness and kind gestures—and little blond children who would love him but eye me suspiciously.

Would we have had fun? Would he have been able to make my heart race years later? Would I have ever stopped comparing him to James?

I stepped inside The Bon Marché, a department store I'd never heard of, and wandered through the aisles, eyeing the beautiful scarves and hats until the smell of food wafted in off the street.

I dined alone while looking out over the waterfront, watching officers go to and fro. As I ate, I received several curious looks from people not used to seeing a woman in uniform, and declined an invitation to join a table of rowdy sailors.

I was given a room to myself back at the airfield and the constant buzz of aircraft coming and going lulled me to sleep.

In the morning I learned the plane I was to fly back to San Antonio had never arrived. I was instead given one to ferry down to Long Beach, where I enjoyed an afternoon with some of the women I'd met previously when I'd gone with Carol Ann.

It was a full week later before I returned to San Antonio, my uniform heavily wrinkled, my luggage twice what it was when I'd left from needing to buy several more personal items, as well as another pair of trousers and a blouse since the items I'd flown out with began to smell after my not being able to properly launder them.

"There you are!" Carol Ann said when I came in the door

to our room. "I thought you met a handsome sailor and ran off to Canada."

"I thought about it," I said. "Who else is here?"

Beatrice and Anna had returned from officer training while I was gone, their rumpled beds a sure sign they were in town. They were full of information and excited about the possibility of officially joining the armed services. General Arnold was positive we'd be allowed in, and both Ms. Cochran and Ms. Love had made sure we'd all get the opportunity to enter officer training if we were interested.

In early June it seemed as though life was on an upswing. The largest attack by sea, land and water had been executed by the Allies on the beaches of Normandy, France. Many were injured and thousands more killed as we pushed the Germans back substantially, giving us a major advantage.

Nola, Beatrice and I went to church to light candles for those who had fought so bravely. When we returned an officer was waiting at the door to deliver letters addressed to each of us.

"Well, this feels daunting," Nola said as she ripped hers open.

The letter informed us that the army officer training some of the women had already undergone, and that others were waiting to begin, was all for naught—we were not to be militarized. The army wouldn't have us after all.

"Goddamn army," Nola fumed. "We're risking our lives for our country and they can't give us benefits? Job security? I'm of a mind to pack up and leave this instant!"

"At least you didn't waste your time going through the training program," Beatrice said, throwing herself onto her bed. Captain catapulted off and scurried to the bathroom to hide.

"Ladies," Carol Ann said. "I know this is terrible news, especially for the three of you." She looked to Beatrice, Anna and Nola, all of whom had been counting on becoming militarized as a next step in their careers. "But rather than cry about things we can't change, why don't we go out to dinner instead. Focus on the good. We still have jobs. We're still flying planes."

"I'm not in the mood," Anna grumbled.

"Well, get in the mood. We're all here for once. Let's go out. Audrey? Dinner and dancing?"

"I'll say yes to dinner," I said, glancing around at the down-turned faces of the others. "Drinks are on me."

"Fine." Anna pulled Beatrice off her bunk. "Get out of that damn uniform."

It was nice to be out together for once. I was especially happy to spend time with Nola. Oftentimes with our schedules we missed one another or only got to say hello in passing as we hurried to bed, to the airfield, to the bathroom... It had been at least a month since we'd been able to sit and have a conversation.

"I met someone," she said as soon as our drinks were served. "He's a bombardier. He's skinny as a stick and hilarious."

Carol Ann turned wide eyes on me and I kicked her under the table. She always commented when no one was around to hear that she thought Nola's taste in men was mind-boggling.

"Most women go for large men with big muscles. You know, the quarterback," she'd said once as we'd watched her turn down such a man to dance with a gangly fellow with a large nose. "But she always goes for the jester."

"Where's he based?" I asked Nola, avoiding Carol Ann's insistent gaze.

"He's in California now. I'm trying to get another flight out there. If anyone gets a plane there, I'll swap you. Throw in five bucks on the deal too."

"I'll take that swap," I said.

"I don't know," Carol Ann said. "If I get California and you get some godforsaken place like no-man's-land, hotter-than-Hades Nevada, I don't know if I could do it."

"Ten bucks?"

"I'm in."

We decided not to go dancing, everyone so tired we could barely keep our eyes open during the ride home. It wasn't even seven o'clock.

We climbed the stairs to our room slowly, Nola and Anna in front, Carol Ann and me bringing up the rear.

"Can I help you?" Nola's voice carried down the outdoor passageway to us.

"Looking for a Miss Coltrane. Miss Audrey Coltrane."

I reached the top of the staircase and stopped, grabbing Carol Ann's arm. We stared at the young man, his plain brown uniform hanging on his lanky frame. Nola, Beatrice and Anna turned, unsure what to say.

"Is that a telegram for me?" I asked, finding my voice.

"Not a telegram, no," he said. "A certified letter."

I swallowed. Everyone knew the bad news came in telegrams. Not that I would receive one for James. His sister was listed as his next of kin. So what was this? Maybe something from my parents?

The young man held out the clipboard.

"Please sign here," he said.

I glanced at Carol Ann and then did as he said and handed it back. He held out the letter. I stared at it for a moment and then took it.

"Ladies," he said, taking leave.

I stared down at the name on the return address.

Ava Hart. James's sister.

I looked up at Carol Ann with wide, fearful eyes.

"Let's go inside," Nola murmured and Anna opened the door.

The women milled about the room, quietly putting away their things as I sank down on Nola's bed near the door, unable to walk any farther into the room.

Nola sat beside me; Carol Ann sank down on the other side and put her hand on my shoulder.

"It might be nothing, you know," Carol Ann said. "I'm sure

James has told her all about you. Maybe she just wants to get to know the woman her brother has fallen in love with."

It was possible, but I was doubtful. There was an invisible weight to the letter. I handed it to Carol Ann.

"You want me to read it first?" she asked, her eyes wide. I nodded.

She sat silently beside me, her eyes flying back and forth over the page while Nola rubbed small circles on my back. After a few minutes, she took a breath and set the letter on her lap.

"Audrey," she whispered.

My heart racing, a feeling of sickness in my stomach, I snatched the letter from her lap.

Dearest Audrey,
It is with great sorrow that our first correspondence is one of such terrible news. James has been listed as missing in action. I was told by telegram in no uncertain terms that his plane was shot during a mission over Germany. Per the report, he seemed to think he'd be able to make it back to base. He experienced trouble though and went down near Luxembourg. They have not recovered him or his plane, nor have they attempted to. It is too dangerous. If he was not killed on impact, it is likely he was taken prisoner.

The rest was a blur as my eyes filled, a shuddering sob rocking my body. Carol Ann and Nola wrapped their arms around me while Anna knelt before me and placed her hand on my knee, Beatrice beside her.

After a while I stood to shaky legs and went to the shower, letting the hot water blast my skin until it was red and as raw as I felt inside.

I climbed up to my bunk and lay staring at the ceiling. Movement in the bed next to me caught my eye and I glanced over at Carol Ann. She reached across the divide and I grasped her hand, not letting go until the sun rose the following day.

★ ★ ★

I spent the next month moving from bed, to shower, to whatever plane I was scheduled to ferry as though in slow motion. My mind wandered as conversations happened around me, and I ate only as an afterthought. At night I stared wide-eyed through the dark at the ceiling, replaying that last weekend with James. The sweetness of his words, the sensation of his skin on mine, the feelings he'd confessed, and the ones I'd felt comfortable enough to finally express.

I prayed for sleep to take me, but when it did the nightmares, worse than the ones I'd had after Pearl Harbor, came to find me.

Every part of me hurt. My chest ached as though I were carrying a fifty-pound weight on it. My stomach was on the constant verge of returning anything I ate, which wasn't much. The shortness of breath I'd felt when reading Ava's letter hadn't gone away. At any moment I felt I'd crumble. If I could just keep focused, fly when I was scheduled and not fall apart—maybe, just maybe, I'd make it through.

"Any news?" Nola asked as she came in from a job one evening in late August.

I shook my head. Ava had promised to write as soon as she'd heard anything. But so far there was nothing.

"I'm so sorry, Audrey." She hugged me and I patted her back listlessly.

Carol Ann entered the room behind her. "Oh God. Audrey—"

I pulled away from Nola and shook my head. "No news," I said.

"I thought— You were hugging…" She looked from me to Nola. "Did something happen to Stu?" Stu was Nola's bombardier beau.

"No," Nola said. "Stu is fine."

"Oh. Okay," she said, her hand on her heart. "Golly, don't scare me like that. No hugging!"

I laughed and both women startled. Guilt swept over me.

"You are allowed to laugh," Nola said. "I know it doesn't feel like it, but you are. And you should. It might help get you through the agony of all this waiting."

But I didn't want to laugh. So I started to cry instead.

"I wish I didn't have to go," Carol Ann said the next morning.

"I'll be fine," I murmured.

I was dressed in my blues and lying on my bunk. The plane I was supposed to ferry out had broken down and so I had the day off, something I normally would thrill at, but these days it meant more time to sit and think about James, possibly lost, possibly captured, possibly dead.

"If I don't get back too late, let's go out to eat," she said, slinging a small bag over her shoulder.

"Okay."

"You going to be alright?" She stepped up on Anna's bunk below and popped her head next to mine.

I pulled gently on a lock of her hair. "I will survive until you get back," I said. "I promise. I might still be lying here in these clothes, but I'll survive."

"I worry about you."

"I know. And thank you. But I'll be okay." I rolled onto my back. "I just wish there was a way to turn my mind off. What if he was captured? Or is lost? Or…" I closed my eyes. I couldn't fathom the third option.

A tear ran down the side of my face to my pillow.

"I pray for him every night," Carol Ann said. "Before I pray Gus will stop asking me about a summer wedding and, please God, a relief tube for women in these damn planes. Can someone create that already? Girls have to pee too!"

My grin turned into a giggle and I took a swipe at her as she jumped out of the way.

"I love you, Audrey Coltrane," she shouted as she swung open the door. "You're the best friend a girl could ask for. Get up off your ass and enjoy your day off. That's an order!"

"Love you too. Fly safe, you maniac."

"Will you two shut up?" Beatrice shouted from her bunk, where she'd been sleeping after flying in late the night before.

The door slammed shut on Carol Ann's hysterical laughter.

CHAPTER TWENTY-SIX

Exhaustion seeped from every fiber of my being as I showed my ID to the guard at the gate. My delivery run had turned into a nightmare when the second plane I was to ferry out of Arizona didn't come in and threw off all my other deliveries. Unable to catch a flight back via commercial airline until the next day, I'd had to take the train, which had taken two days and was packed the entire ride. I sat on my B-4 bag and parachute the whole way back to San Antonio, nodding off with my head resting against someone else's suitcase.

I checked in at the main office and waited to hear what my assignment was for the following day.

"Can you tell me if any of my roommates are around?" I asked the officer manning the desk.

As happy as I was to be back and to see their friendly faces, it was just after seven in the evening and all I wanted was to fall into bed and sleep until morning.

He checked the book. "Looks like everyone is out on assignment for the night, though Miss Bixby should be flying in sometime this evening. As far as your schedule," he added, "you have tomorrow off."

"Wonderful," I said.

As I turned toward the door a loud boom shook the building, a window bursting, shards of glass spraying the room.

"Get down!" the officer yelled, knocking me to the floor.

I lay flat, my arms over my head, the young man thrown over my back. Outside we heard shouting and another small explosion and then sirens.

"A plane went down!" someone elsewhere in the office yelled.

The officer stood and helped me up as several others ran past and out the door. My earlier exhaustion forgotten, I followed after them, my heart pounding as I glanced at the sky. Had the plane crashed? Or had it been shot down? But the only other plane above was one of ours and I turned my attention to the smoking and charred fuselage of a P-47 Thunderbolt that had skidded upon landing and crashed into an army truck parked to the side of the tarmac.

Flames rose and the engine sparked, plumes of thick black smoke billowing out and obscuring the canopy of the plane that firefighters were trying desperately to reach in hopes of saving the pilot inside. Water from two fire hoses doused the wreckage as a crowd gathered, talking in hushed voices for what could only be concluded was a fallen comrade.

We'd been there a half hour when I noticed several of the men looking at me and then glancing away. I caught the eye of the young officer who had used his body to cover mine when the crash happened and he winced and looked away.

A pit opened in my stomach, dread spreading from its depths to my outermost extremities.

I took a step forward. Then another. The men parted like the sea, quietly in small waves.

"Miss," one of the firemen said as I stepped toward the wreckage. "Stand back, please. I can't guarantee it won't blow again."

"Who's inside?" I asked.

He frowned and glanced at one of the other firemen. "I'm not sure," he said.

I looked behind me. The officer from the front desk where I'd checked in stood staring at the ground only a few feet from where I was rooted. I was about to ask him when the sound of another plane landing caught my attention.

I watched as the plane rolled to the end of the runway, turned and drove to a nearby hangar. My eyes were glued to the aircraft as it came to a stop and the canopy opened. The pilot disembarked and removed his helmet. I trembled and turned back to the burning mass in front of me, then again to the young man from the office.

"Who was flying this plane?" I asked.

Several of the men around me ducked their heads. I stepped closer to the officer.

"Do you know?" I asked, pointing to the burning and smoking mass of metal.

"I can't be sure," he murmured. "But I believe... I heard a Thunderbolt was coming in from Savannah."

"And who flew to Savannah?"

"Miss Bixby," he whispered.

My knees trembled.

"Are you sure?" I asked.

"Yes but—you women are always having schedule changes. That could be anyone in there."

But it wasn't. I knew it. I could feel it in my bones.

I took a step closer to the burning plane.

"Miss," someone said, warning in his voice. But I ignored him. If Carol Ann was inside that tangled mass, I had to get her out. I had to save her.

I ran forward.

"Carol Ann!" I screamed, choking on smoke, the spray from the waters soaking me.

I reached the canopy and placed my palm on the glass, shouting as it burned my skin but reaching still with the other hand as if I alone could open it. Two arms wrapped around my waist and hauled me back, several others holding me as I fought to be free. There was still time. She could still be saved. But a moment later the canopy glass splintered and shattered, more smoke rising into the sky.

No one could survive that.

I don't remember going back to my room. Don't recall walking to the bathroom and sitting on the floor of the shower fully clothed, the water off but dripping from one of the faucets. At some point I became aware of the light changing as I stared blindly at the tiled wall across from me.

I was numb from head to toe, my mind unable or unwilling to process what had happened. Every so often an image of the burning wreckage would fight its way through the fog of my shocked state and I'd gasp for air, having been unconsciously holding my breath. In those moments my eyes would dart around the room, taking in my red and blistered palms, my clothing covered in black ash, stinking of smoke and wet from the hoses. And then I'd close my eyes again, thankful for the darkness that overtook me once more.

Anna found me sometime later, slumped over, my face pressed to the floor.

"Audrey?" she said, her hand hesitant on my leg. "Are you...?"

I stared at her with blank eyes and then closed them again.

"Audrey? Hon?" I opened my eyes again, but now Nola sat before me, tears running down her face. Anna was nowhere to be seen.

The light that had poured through the bathroom window had dimmed, the sky dark beyond.

I pushed myself up, wincing at the pain in my hands as my face peeled off the tile.

"Audrey," she said again, her voice catching. "I can't— I don't—"

I met her sorrowful gaze and we wrapped our arms around one another, at once heartbroken and numb.

When I woke again Nola was asleep beside me, her pretty brow furrowed as she slumbered. She had a smattering of pale freckles across her nose that I'd never noticed before, and there were strands of red among the long, dark tresses.

"Hey."

I carefully turned over and met Beatrice's concerned gaze.

"Anna had to fly out a few hours ago. She told me—" Her eyes filled and she sniffled and swiped an arm across her face. then held up a paper bag. "Your poor hands. I got some salve and bandages from the doctor. If you want, I can apply it for you. Maybe after we get you cleaned up?"

I nodded and together we woke Nola, who stumbled to her bed and resumed sleeping. I returned to the shower where I stood beneath the spray, my tears mixing with the water, my sobs echoing off the tile walls. When I was done, Beatrice was waiting to dress my wounds.

I slept in Anna's bed that night, unable to bear staring across the space from mine to Carol Ann's empty bunk. Nola rose once to use the restroom, and then promptly climbed back in her bunk, still fully clothed. Beatrice moved about quietly, checking on us both once before turning out the lights, and as the room fell silent, I lay reliving the nightmare of my best friend's death.

There had been no screaming, not like the terrifying minutes before Peggy Walters had perished at Avenger Field. There had been only the sound of the burning aircraft as it encased my friend inside, consuming her in smoke and burying her alive while I stood outside helplessly watching.

As the sun rose again several hours later, I lay in the same spot, the pillow soaked beneath my face. The numbness that had gotten me through the night had passed and the raw pain of loss ripped through me, the agony taking my breath from me.

Carol Ann was gone.

James was missing.

Jean.

Catherine...

Bill and Mae.

How many more loved ones would I lose to this war?

I clenched my bandaged hands and yelled, the sound like a wounded animal crying out in agony.

"Audrey!" Nola rushed across the room to me.

My howl of despair filled the room as she and Beatrice held me, rocking me as I cried.

I requested, at Nola's insistence, and received a week's leave from service. Seven days. No more, no less. The military needed me.

"Soldiers don't get time off to grieve," my boss said, his voice soft to lessen the blow of his words.

Most of the time was spent lying on my bunk, facing Carol Ann's bed across from mine and picturing her face. Sometimes, when no one else was around, I had quiet conversations with her, whispering to her empty bed how I missed her, how I wasn't sure I could fly anymore, and how I was so, so sorry I hadn't been able to save her.

Two days after the accident we had heard an unofficial report that the crash was being blamed on Carol Ann.

"What did they say?" I asked in a hushed voice as Anna delivered the news.

"Just that she couldn't control the Jug," she said, referring to the nickname for the large plane. "She was too small."

"That's a lie," Nola said. "She could handle planes bigger than that even!"

"It's a bum rap," Anna said. "They don't have answers so they blame the girl."

I rolled over on my bed, turning my back to the conversation. There was no way that plane crashed because Carol Ann couldn't handle it. Something had to have malfunctioned.

As it turned out, something had. Wires in the ignition system came loose and found themselves some metal to rub against. Scorching metal and loose wires makes for kindling in an engine sweltering with heat. Add to that a jammed canopy, a well-known issue of the Thunderbolt, and Carol Ann never stood a chance.

The next morning, I stared at Carol Ann's bed, my eyes blurred by tears. I couldn't care less if I never flew another plane. Once the thing that kept my hopes alive, now, in the wake of James going missing and my best friend dying, it was something I dreaded. Not for fear, but for what it had taken from me. I was angry, desolate, my heart shattered. For all my good intentions, I kept getting knocked down. What was the point of going on? Why did I bother to dream when all it led to was nightmares?

"I give up," I whispered to Carol Ann's pillow.

What will you do instead? I imagined her saying.

"It doesn't matter," I said, and rolled away from her ghost.

I hadn't left my room in three days. The girls often returned after a job with plates of food from the mess hall, where they stopped after disembarking from their flight, no matter what time of day. They also tended to my hands and reminded me to shower.

It was on that third day that Nola walked me to the main office to call home.

"You need to let them know what happened," she said.

"Why?" I asked in a flat voice, not really caring about her reasoning.

"Because they're your family. And because you can help get her home."

Since we weren't technically a part of the army, we, and our families, were responsible if an injury or death occurred. Carol Ann's aunt and uncle, as we knew, were poor. She'd told stories about birthdays and Christmases where the only gifts were for her, her aunt and uncle sacrificing presents for one another to spoil their only niece. There was no way they could afford the cost of transporting her remains home, as well as pay for a funeral. But my parents could. And would.

"Mama?" I said, my voice catching when I heard her voice across the line.

"Audrey?" my mother said. "Honey, is everything okay?"

That was all it took for the tears to fall again. "Oh, Mama."

As I knew she would, my mother took care of everything; calling Carol Ann's aunt to offer her condolences, sending flowers and making sure my friend's remains were taken care of. She picked out the urn for her ashes, scheduled my transportation to and from Tuscumbia, Alabama, and found a local caterer for the reception and florist for the service.

She offered to come with me, but I wanted to go alone. Carol Ann was my friend and I needed to say my goodbye standing on my own two feet.

Six days after the tragedy that took her life, I flew on a commercial flight holding Carol Ann's ashes in a blue-and-white ceramic urn with the image of a dove flying across it. A car picked me up at the airport and took me to her aunt and uncle's home.

I stood at the end of the gravel walkway and stared at the little blue house. The paint had peeled off in strips in different sections, and half a dozen wind chimes hung from the eave. I walked up the front steps and smiled when the top one creaked, just like Carol Ann had told me it did.

"Sure made sneaking in and out a pain in the neck," she'd said with a laugh.

Beside the front door was a sign that said, "Bless this house and all who enter."

I knocked and waited, staring out over the vast front yard where wildflowers had sprung up, their little pink and yellow and orange faces gazing at the sun.

"Well, you must be Audrey," a woman said, opening the screen door.

"Yes, ma'am," I said, stepping out of the way.

"I'm Nan, Carol Ann's aunt. But you probably guessed that, huh?"

"Yes, ma'am."

"Well, come on in. The service isn't for another couple of hours. Can I get you a glass of sweet tea?"

"That would be lovely."

I followed her through a dark sitting room, taking in the well-loved furniture and many plants, some flowering, others climbing whatever they could grab hold of.

I entered the kitchen, which faced the east and was bathed in sunlight, and got my first good look at the woman who had raised my friend. Nan was a sturdy woman with rough hands and a gentle voice. Her thin, pale red hair had thick streaks of gray but looked pretty pulled back in a tidy knot. She wore a simple black dress, no jewelry, and her feet were bare.

I held on to the urn, unsure where to put it, and not wanting to let it go just yet.

"Is that our girl?" she asked, her back turned to me as she poured the tea from an etched glass pitcher.

"It is," I murmured.

"That urn sure is something special. Did you choose it?"

"My mother did."

"She's a kind woman, your mother," she said and handed me a green glass filled nearly to the brim. "She called to extend her condolences, one mother to another." She sniffed, her eyes glassy as she looked past me. "I told her Carol Ann was my niece, but she knew better. 'If you raise them, they're yours,' she said. She's a fine lady. You're a lucky girl."

I nodded and took a sip of tea.

"May I?" Nan asked, pointing to the urn.

I took a breath. "Of course."

She took it carefully and held it to her breast and closed her eyes.

"She was a feisty one, wasn't she?" she asked.

"She was."

"She talked about you every time she called home. Said you were beautiful and tough. I was so sorry to hear about your beau. James, is it?"

I nodded, my eyes welling.

She reached out to me and I placed my hand in hers.

"God doesn't give us more than we can handle." She raised the urn an inch. "It's what I keep telling myself. But I know you've lost a lot in so little time. For such a young woman, what you've been through is particularly difficult. But I can see what Carol Ann saw in you. You're made of something stronger than most. You'll get through this, no matter how hard it is now. And whatever happens with that soldier of yours, well, you'll get through that too."

She set the urn down and gave it a pat, then pulled me to her. I stayed still for a long moment, neither of us wanting to let go.

I was on my second glass of tea when Kurt, Nan's husband, finally made an appearance.

"This look okay?" he asked Nan before catching sight of me. "Oh. Excuse me. I didn't realize we had a guest. You must be Audrey. Carol Ann sure thought you were the bee's knees."

"Cat's pajamas," Nan said.

"Bees. Cats." He shook his head. "I can never keep the lingo straight. She liked you, that's all I know. Thank you for coming." He glanced at the urn. "And thank you for bringing our girl home."

The memorial service for Carol Ann Bixby was held in a little church perched on a hill. I sat behind her aunt and uncle, listening to their quiet sniffling, the hard wooden pews creaking under the weight of their grief, and staring at a framed photo of one more friend lost to the war.

Afterward, at her aunt's urging, I sat in her childhood bedroom, staring at walls covered in pictures of planes and wind chimes with little birds swaying from the ceiling.

I picked up a model plane and turned it over, smiling at Carol Ann's handwriting on the underside of the wing. *Carol Ann, Age 11*, it read.

"You should take something," Nan said from the doorway. "To remember her by. She would've wanted that."

I looked around, unsure what would be okay to take.

"Here," she said, entering the room. She opened a wooden box on top of the bureau and took out a white hairpin. When I looked closer, I saw it was a bird.

"It's beautiful," I whispered, holding it in my palm.

"She was going to wear it for her wedding to Gus."

I shook my head. "You should keep it then. Or give it to him."

"Oh, honey." Nan's eyes filled. "Augustus was killed in action two days before Carol Ann. She never knew. His folks found out the same day we heard the news about her."

I sank to her bed and stared down at the handmade quilt with squares of pink and yellow and individually sewn airplanes.

This war had taken so many. Young, old, guilty...and so many innocent. The span of the death toll reached several oceans and six continents. No one had been spared, the far-reaching fingers of destruction and sorrow touching nearly everyone in some form, whether it be a family member, friend or neighbor. Grief had blanketed our world, darkening our days and smothering hope.

But of course my own losses struck me the most. The deaths of the lovely, strong and brave young women who had become my friends...my sisters in the sky, had been soul crushing. The news of James missing in action heartbreakingly stark, the loss of the one man I'd ever loved singular in its pain.

During the nights, as I lay in bed, the quiet closing around me, I saw their faces and heard their voices. I fell asleep to the memory of their laughter. It was there that I found solace, my dreams keeping them alive in my mind. We played in the Hawaiian surf and raced across the great big Texas sky in the army's warplanes. I lay beside James as he traced his fingertip across my collarbone to the little bird resting against my throat. He whispered that he loved me as I held tightly to his hand. And it was there in those dreams that Carol Ann found me, whispering to me across the space between our beds until something woke me and I realized with a start that she was gone.

At night was also when the nightmares found me. When fire and smoke and gunfire stole them from me again and again. On those mornings I woke to my pillow soaked with sweat and tears.

And beneath all the torment was anger and fear. Anger that anyone had to die. That so many had to give their lives. And fear. Who else would be taken from me? Could I be next?

I now looked upon the planes lining the tarmac at Fort Sam Houston with unease rather than excitement. Had my love for being among the clouds marked me? Was I destined to die the way I lived?

But if I didn't fly...what did I have?

I remembered one of the last conversations I'd had with Carol Ann. As usual, we were lying in our bunks, whispering back and forth as the others slept below us.

"Do you think one day when we're old biddies," she had said, "we'll sit on our front porches, rocking away while our grandkids run around our yards, drinking sweet tea and talking about the old days? How we were just girls in planes doing a job like it were any other? Back in the days when the men were gone. When the world was finally forced to give us a chance? Back when we had wings?"

I'd smiled, picturing it. And then she'd continued.

"On second thought, I don't think I'll ever stop flying. They're going to have to pry me out of a plane."

I glanced around Carol Ann's childhood room now. How terribly poetic that in the end, she had been pried from a plane. But I knew without a doubt that while it had happened far too soon, it was how she had wanted to go.

I gave Aunt Nan a small smile.

"She was a great friend to me. Like a sister. We had a lot of fun together." I stared down at the little white bird hairpin, blinking through my tears. "I'm so sorry she's gone."

"She sure loved you," Nan said. "She never had a friend as close to her as you were. Please, take the bird. She'd want you to have it. You can wear it when you marry your beau one day. It will be like she's there with you." She gave me a sad smile and turned to leave the room. At the door she stopped. "And don't stop flying."

"Excuse me?" I said.

"She told me you were there in Pearl Harbor and that you had a hard time afterward. She knew if anything happened to her during training—or after—you would question whether or not to fly again. She made me promise if anything happened to her to tell you to keep flying." She hesitated. "Have you thought of quitting?"

I nodded, unable to meet her eyes.

"What would you do instead?"

I shrugged. I'd never considered an alternative to flying.

"Do you love it?"

I met her gaze. "More than anything."

"Then, honey, don't stop now. As I told Carol Ann, even though I was afraid every time she went up, if you don't do what you love, why be alive?"

I said goodbye with a long hug an hour later, the bird and one of Carol Ann's wind chimes inside a paper bag, along with a slice of pie "for the ride home," Nan said. I promised to stay in touch, and then walked down the long driveway to the waiting car.

We slowed at the end of the road to wait for a tractor to pass and I looked out the window. Beside the car in a flowering shrub, a hummingbird flitted about. I thought of James and the ornamental bird he bought me in the shop in Florida.

"They're a reminder to seek out the good in life," he'd said.

I sighed and leaned my head back, staring up at the bright afternoon sky. It had been an awful week and I'd dreaded coming. But somehow there'd been a lightness to the day. An easiness in the flow of the words, the passing of the food and the glances shared. And it was because of Carol Ann, who had fluttered in and out of my life like the hummingbird outside my window that had just disappeared from sight.

PART THREE

OCTOBER 1944

CHAPTER TWENTY-SEVEN

I lay on my bunk with a stack of letters on the pillow next to me. I'd been gone for three days, flying from Texas to New Jersey, Michigan, North Carolina, Nevada and back to Texas. My neck and back ached, my backside was numb and my legs were stiff. It was only six o'clock, but I was done for the day. I didn't even care if I ate dinner.

"Rough few days?" Anna asked when she returned to the room and found me dressed in my pajamas, my hair wrapped in a towel.

"It was nonstop," I said, sifting through the letters and noting with relief there was nothing from James's sister, Ava.

Every time a letter came for me my stomach tightened. I knew if there was good news about James, it would most likely come from him by way of telephone, a telegram or a letter. But if I received mail from Ava, it would be bad news. News I couldn't fathom. So every day I prayed not to hear from her. So far it had worked.

"You want anything from the mess hall?" Anna asked.

Despite the rationing, the cooks in the mess hall had a way of turning the most mundane ingredients into something delicious, making you feel like you were eating a meal your mother had made. There weren't a lot of extras or treats, but occasionally we were blessed with homemade oatmeal raisin cookies or sweet potato pie, depending on what they could get their hands on. But since Carol Ann's death, my appetite had waned dangerously, my clothes hanging off my slender frame more than ever. Despite that, I couldn't bring myself to stomach much more than a few bites here and there.

"Maybe a roll," I said.

"What if they have pie?"

The women I roomed with hadn't been shy in their concern for me and were always trying to tempt me with more food, oftentimes bringing back a napkin with an extra piece of chicken or a small helping of roasted potatoes tucked inside, acting as if they'd brought it for themselves but now didn't want it.

I sighed. "If there's pie, I'll have a slice," I said, more to appease her than because I wanted it.

"You got it."

I looked again at the return addresses of the letters. Claire, Erma and my father had each written. The last envelope had the official stamp of Ms. Jacqueline Cochran. It was probably an updated list of our duties. I left it for last and opened Claire's letter.

She was well. Work had slowed down some, freeing her up to travel to one of the other islands for a mini vacation. She'd gotten a raise and was contemplating moving to a nice apartment in the New Year.

The letter from Erma was filled with news of the children. Everyone was doing well in school despite losing several classmates and friends to the internment camps. Annie still asked about me and wanted to know if I'd ever come back. Erma had included a picture she'd drawn for me. It was the two of us under a palm tree, me with yellow hair, her with black, and a big yel-

low sun in the sky above us. I wiped away a tear as I remembered my little friend and her stuffed doggie, always clinging to
my legs, waving goodbye as I'd left that last day.

My father's letter was, as usual, full of thoughts on the war,
comments about the household and words of comfort. Mama
had extended the garden again. It now took up half an acre. Evie
was busy with work and friends. She'd been dating an officer
for a few months now and it seemed to be going well. He spent
every moment he could with her and when they weren't together
he was all she could talk about. But he was shipping out soon
and she was nervous, *as one has every right to be*, Father wrote.

As always, he ended on a bolstering note, writing of the hard-
ships one must endure not only in war, but also in life. And how
we cannot honor those who go before us if we allow ourselves
to go numb.

*I hope you are grieving, my dear. Not because I wish you pain,
but because it is through pain that you will find healing.*

I stared at Carol Ann's empty bunk and remembered how
she'd whisper stories across the space between our beds, making
me laugh quietly into my pillow as the others slept. Her lack of
modesty, sunny disposition and innate honesty had inspired me
to be more open, not only with others, but with myself.

My heart ached and I forced myself to turn back to the last
letter in my stack, the one from Ms. Cochran.

I skimmed over the words and then read them again, this
time more carefully. I shot up, my head brushing the ceiling in
my haste as the front door swung open.

"They had cake!" Anna said as she came through the door.
"I brought you two pieces."

"Have you read this?" I asked, waving the letter at her.

She put the dessert down and frowned. "What is it?"

"A letter from Jackie Cochran."

She sifted through a pile of unopened mail in her locker, pulled an envelope out and held it up.

"Read it," I said.

I slid from my bed as she scanned the letter and then read it again more slowly before looking up at me, her brow furrowed.

The letter informed us that on December 20, 1944, the WASP program would be disbanded.

It is with deep regret that I found it necessary to recommend inactivation of the entire program, Ms. Cochran wrote. *How very sorry you girls will be to divorce yourselves from army flying. How grateful we can be to know our disbandment is the result of unexpectedly low combat losses.*

"I don't understand," Anna said in a small voice. "It's over? What will we do?"

"It's not over yet," I said. "We have until December."

"But—"

"I guess we just go back to whatever we were doing before we were accepted into the program," I said.

I linked my arm through Anna's and she sagged against me. Even though I was sad to see the program end, it would be easier for me to go than many of the others. While I'd miss learning the different aircraft, talking to my roommates and seeing the country, I had an airfield back home waiting for me to take it over. I had plans to set forth, people to hire and ground to break. It was nearly time. It was finally going to happen. For others, though...

Anna stared back down at the letter. "I don't want to go home. There's nothing for me there."

Nola returned a few hours later and read her letter with a scowl. As Captain, Beatrice's cat, roamed from lap to lap, we listlessly petted him and discussed the news and our options going forward.

"So we can get a commission, but no more flying?" Nola said. "At all?"

Upon further investigation into the disbandment of the program, we were able to find out that we could have jobs within the sanctuary of the military, but we still weren't considered military and the jobs available to us would be desk jobs, factory-type jobs and the like. The bottom line was, after December 20, we would no longer be allowed to fly the army's planes. All pilots returning from war would have dibs on our jobs and we would either be sent home on the army's dime, or left to fend for ourselves. Transportation was decided by each individual base.

"No more flying," I said. "I suppose on the one hand it's good news for the country. It means they're anticipating the war ending soon. But on the other hand…"

"We're out of jobs." Nola frowned. "Which is just plain stupid. Who's going to ferry the planes when we leave? They can't fly themselves! And half the new recruits barely know a wingtip from a tailfin. The army wants them to be responsible for their precious cargo and personnel?"

"Don't we deserve to stay?" Anna asked. "We've proven we're just as qualified to fly those planes. In some cases more so."

"Not in the army's eyes," Nola grumbled. "Or the country's. To the men who run the world, we're second-class citizens."

She got to her feet and peered down at me. "You hiring?"

"I will be."

"Let me know when I can apply for a job," she said and slammed out the front door.

I looked at Anna, who stared back at me with tears in her eyes. "I'll work for cheap," she said and I smiled softly.

"It won't be for a while," I said.

"That's okay. I'll wait."

CHAPTER TWENTY-EIGHT

The next two months went by quick, with us savoring each flight, each plane, each touchdown in another city. We shared with the women we encountered from the program the same sad smile and little shrug. We'd been a part of something special, and even if no one ever knew it but the military, our families and us, we were proud. And we'd do it all again. The training, the long work hours, the heartache—just to get to fly those planes.

In November I had received mail from James's sister, a card wishing me a lovely holiday.

I apologize for not writing sooner. I was afraid the sight of a letter from me would be worrisome. But the holidays are here. James and I do so love the holidays, and so I felt impelled to reach out to you. To let you know I am thinking of you and hope you are well and in good spirits despite it all.

I've received no word about him and, it may be silly, but our father always said no news is good news. More than anything I want to believe that to be true now.

I pray every day James is somewhere safe, biding his time, making his way home to the both of us.

We didn't work on Thanksgiving so the girls and I went into town before the feast the base provided to pop into any of the shops that might be open and see a movie.

We settled in the back row and I opened my box of M&M's, smiling as I thought of James that night in Hawaii.

We spent the evening eating until we couldn't take another bite and playing games while chatting with some of the soldiers and their guests. At ten we made our way back to our room, our arms slung around one another.

"Can't believe this will be our last holiday together," Nola said.

"Seems strange, doesn't it?" I said.

"Remember last year at Avenger? How Carol Ann sneaked that pie back to your room? I'll never forget watching her slip that thing under her skirt."

"Surprisingly, it was still intact when she got to the room," I said. "Oh God." I pressed my hand to my heart. "I miss her so much."

Nola wrapped her arms around me. "I shouldn't have said anything."

"No. It's good to remember her. It makes me sad, but happy too. Thank you for reminding me of that moment. It truly was ridiculous to behold, but the pie was good."

The following morning it was back to business as I boarded a patched-up Grumman that had seen some action in the Pacific.

I flew to Virginia, and from there I picked up another plane and flew cross-country to California with a woman from two classes behind me who went by the name Mac, smoked like a chimney and had skin like leather.

"Hope they aren't loaded," she said in a gravelly voice, nodding toward the back of the plane where cases of weapons going to the Pacific Theater were stacked. "Wouldn't want one to accidentally go off."

I shuddered at the thought.

I stayed the night in Long Beach and in the morning piloted my first personnel flight for two officers expected in Houston.

"You're our pilot?" asked the taller of the two men. He had a bulbous nose that was hard not to stare at and looked worriedly at his comrade.

"Yes, sir," I said. "I assure you I am an excellent pilot."

"But—you're a girl," he said.

I blinked and kept my smile in place. "That is correct, sir."

"I've heard of this," the shorter man said, eyeing me from below bushy black eyebrows. "Freeing up the men, am I right?"

"Yes, sir," I said and looked to the taller man. "You may check my credentials if you like. I've flown nearly two dozen types of army aircraft."

I held out my flight book and he paused a moment before taking it and flipping through the pages.

"You've flown a B-17?" he asked.

"Several times, sir."

"Pursuits too?"

"Yes, sir."

He sighed and handed the book back. "Let's go."

The flight was flawless and, after the initial nervous silence between the two men, they began to chat.

I set us down gently a couple hours later, parked and unlatched the door. Both men reached out to shake my hand before disembarking.

"You're a fine pilot, Miss."

"Top notch."

"Thank you both," I said.

I chuckled to myself once they'd left. Men, always underestimating us ladies.

★ ★ ★

December 20 came quick and without mercy.

"You see all those planes out there in need of delivery?" Nola asked, stalking around the room. "How the heck are they gonna deliver them without us?"

It was frustrating to all of us. There were to be no more flights given to women pilots, no matter that there were planes to be delivered and not enough men available to do it.

"It's ridiculous," Anna said, shoving a stack of blouses into her suitcase. "How does this help the war effort? Least they could do is let us keep working until there are actual men here to do our jobs."

Beatrice sat on her bed, stroking Captain's head. "I don't know what I'll do now."

"I thought you had a job lined up at the store you used to work at," Nola said.

"I do. But there's nothing exciting about folding women's clothing and cleaning out dressing rooms."

"It's definitely not as exciting as flying military aircraft," Anna said. "But then, neither is being a secretary for some old curmudgeon who barely believes in giving lunch breaks."

"Your grandfather sounds swell," Nola said.

"He's awful," Anna said. "I only took the job to keep my mother off my back. She's afraid he's going to keel over and no one will be there. She doesn't want him to start rotting away before someone notices he hasn't come home."

"Wouldn't your grandmother notice when he's not sitting down for dinner?" Beatrice asked.

"Not necessarily," Anna said, making us laugh.

"It's too bad we all don't have an airfield to fix up," Nola said, giving me a wink.

"Feel free to come by and help rebuild some walls," I said.

"I'll pass. But once you've got a handle on it all, if you need a good pilot…"

"I know three I'll call first," I said.

After double-checking we hadn't left anything behind, we stood staring around the room we'd shared for almost a year. I blinked back tears as my gaze rested on Carol Ann's bunk.

"I can't believe this is it," Beatrice whispered. "Promise you'll write?"

We'd exchanged addresses along with early Christmas gifts the night before while passing a forbidden bottle of wine around.

"I had a good time with you gals," Anna said. "I thought Beatrice and I had it real good, just the two of us. But once you girls came, I realized it had been a little lonely at times. Too often I came home and all I had for company was that grumpy old cat."

"He is not grumpy!" Beatrice said.

"It was fun," Nola said. "I've never been one to have many female friends, but this experience showed me why I should. There's just nothing like a good gab session late at night with a bunch of like-minded women. I'll never forget you girls."

"Me neither," I said.

"You let us know what you hear about James, okay?" Anna said.

"I'll be praying for him every night," Beatrice said. "Same as I have been."

"I appreciate that."

"Well," Nola said. "Shall we, ladies?"

We stopped by the main office one last time to get the bus tickets the base had provided us, and then walked to the station to await our rides home. We sat together on a bench, four women once so happy to have found the place we belonged— now set adrift in a world that didn't seem to understand our drive to be different. To be independent and provide for ourselves.

"You'll be okay?" Nola asked after the other two had left.

"I will. You?"

"What choice do we have but to be okay?"

★ ★ ★

It was dinnertime when I walked up the long gravel drive of my parents' house. The front door swung open as I approached the steps.

"Audrey," Mama said. "Why in heaven's name didn't you call from the bus station? Your father was going to pick you up."

I shrugged. "I felt like taking a walk."

"Well, let me help you with your things." She hurried down the steps, kissed my cheek and took my B-4 bag. "How are you? You look good. Skinny, but good. Maybe a little tired."

I laughed. "I just got off the bus, Mama. I am tired."

"Well, put on a touch of lipstick for dinner, will you? You don't want to scare anyone."

"Who am I gonna scare? It's just us."

"Your grammar has grown appalling in your time away, I see. No doubt from being surrounded by a bunch of unedu-cated women."

I snorted and she rolled her pretty blue eyes and led the way up the stairs.

Father arrived home minutes after I got settled at the kitchen table with a glass of my mother's sweet tea.

"Audrey," he bellowed, his smile lighting up his handsome face. "I'm so happy you're home, bird."

"Hi, Dad," I said, getting out of my seat to hug him. "Me too."

"Was it hard to leave? They didn't stand at the door and es-cort you out, did they?"

"No. It was all very civil. They were good to us at Fort Sam."

"Glad to hear it. So, what's next? Need a ride down to see Hal? He's been chomping at the bit since hearing you were coming home."

"Christian," Mama said. "Let the girl settle in. Get her bear-ings again."

"It's okay, Mama," I said. "It's not as if I've been incapacitated. I'm ready."

"Are you sure it's really what you want to do?" she asked. "Run an airfield?"

Father and I exchanged a grin.

"*Own* an airfield," I clarified. "Yes, it is."

She sighed. "Well, if you need help with anything, I suppose I can make myself available."

"Thank you, Mama."

The following morning, with a grin I couldn't wipe off my face, an extra bounce in my step and a speeding pulse, I drove myself to the airfield.

As the car climbed up onto the rise where the sign for Hudson Airfield stood, I stopped and got out, the gravel crunching beneath the soles of my shoes.

How many times had I stood in this very spot staring out over the buildings, hangars and runway, watching the planes line up at the far end before they flew above my head to destinations unknown? How many times had I watched the sun rise over one side of the lush surrounding green fields, and set behind the other?

I ran my hand over the top of the sign marking the airfield, having memorized every slope and nick a long time ago. Everyone asked if I would change the name but I still didn't know. All my life it had been Hudson Airfield. Changing it to Coltrane seemed almost sacrilegious. As if by changing it, the magic it had always held for me would be tarnished in some way. But maybe one day.

I got back in the car and drove through the gate to the main office. My heart pounded in my chest as I slipped the check I'd written only an hour before from my handbag and slid it into my trouser pocket.

The bell on the door announced my arrival and Hal looked

up with a scowl that quickly transformed into a look of be-
musement.

"Well, there she is," he said. "'Bout damn time. I was about
to give your father his money back and sell this hunk of junk
to the Leary brothers."

I laughed. The Leary brothers were well-known in this town
for buying profitable businesses and running them into the
ground. And yet, their wealthy father handed over money so
they could keep trying, hoping one day an idea of theirs would
stick and they'd finally move out of his house and get places of
their own.

"You'd really punish the fine people of Dallas, and the out-of-
towners who fly in here, by doing something like that?" I said.

"Guy's gotta make a buck," he winked.

"Thank goodness I arrived in time to save the day," I said and
handed him a check for the final payment.

He stared down at it and then back at me. "You sure about
this?" he asked. "It's a lot of work."

"You've been telling me that since the day I said I was going
to buy it," I said. "Hal, I can hardly wait."

"This is a lot of money," he said, still wary and eyeing me like
I might change my mind, and not yet daring to touch the check.

It was a lot of money, and I had it thanks to an inheritance
from my maternal grandparents and all the money I'd been saving for the past several years.

"It's all I've ever wanted," I said.

"Well then," he said, pulling open a desk drawer and proffering a set of keys on a little brass loop.

He stood and finally picked up the check, giving it a careful
once-over before folding it and putting it in his pocket. Coming
around the desk, he held out his hand. As I shook it, he placed
the keys into my other hand.

"Congratulations, Audrey. You are the proud new owner of
Hudson Airfield. Or whatever you decide to call it."

I grinned from ear to ear. "Thank you, Hal. I promise not to ruin everything you've done."

"I trust you," he said. "But even if you do—I don't have to worry about it no more!"

We laughed and walked out the door, strolling toward the runway. *My* runway.

"There's still all the paperwork to do," he said as a red-and-white plane zoomed by and took flight. "But as far as I'm concerned, the place is yours. We'll transition everything over the next couple of months, but don't be shy about coming by anytime to get your bearings."

I grinned up at him and he smiled back.

"There ain't nobody I'd rather pass this on to than you," he said in a gruff voice filled with emotion. "You're the daughter I never had. Never wanted neither—but would have liked regardless."

I laughed and he nudged me with his elbow, his way of showing affection.

He left me standing there for a long while, taking it all in. I'd done it. I'd bought my airfield just like I'd always said I would. Just like I'd told my parents and like I'd sworn to James.

I sighed.

James. I wanted nothing more at this moment than to be able to tell him my news. To sit across from him and talk excitedly about my plans and imagine the possibilities.

My moment of happiness faltered with the realization that I might never get to share this with him. That we might never have the chance to figure out a way to live the lives we always wanted—together.

I looked down the runway with a bittersweet smile. I had everything I'd always wanted but the one thing I'd come to long for—and I could let it tear me apart, or I could keep moving forward.

A metallic clapping caught my attention and I turned to see

a section of the metal hangar nearest me had come loose and was flapping in the wind. I'd have to tell Hal.

I smiled and shook my head. This was my airfield now.

"Guess I'd better get to work," I said.

CHAPTER TWENTY-NINE

A letter from Claire arrived mid-February. She'd gotten engaged to an officer she'd met on the island and they were to marry in June.

I know you would love him, she wrote. *He's kind and funny and makes me so very happy. If you can, I would love for you to come to the wedding. I know it's probably impossible, but think about it.*

They had bought a house, where she now lived. He would move in after the wedding.

It's small, but cozy, Claire wrote. *And has lots of fruit trees and a view of Diamond Head. I still find it hard to believe so much happiness has come from so much suffering—and that if the Japanese hadn't attacked, Carl and I may have never met.*

Two days later I received a letter from Erma. The family was doing well and she still missed having me over for dinner. Included with the letter was a picture of the children. I barely recognized Annie, who I realized was nine now and lovelier than ever.

"Life goes on I guess," I said and placed the picture on my bureau.

The plans for the new buildings were finished and sat on the desk my father had bought for me and put facing his own in the study. Oftentimes in the evenings we'd sit across from one another discussing options for the hangars and what menu items I should add to the café.

"Biscuits and gravy," he said one night.

"They serve that already."

"All day though? Or just for breakfast? Because all day would be better."

I didn't disagree with him there.

In March a letter sat on the silver tray on the foyer table. The return address was for Ava Hart and my heart pounded as I stared at it, afraid to pick it up.

Mama paused as she came down the stairs. "Is everything alright, dear?"

"It's a letter from Ava."

"Oh," she said, hurrying to my side. "Is it..."

"I don't know. I haven't opened it. I'm afraid."

It wasn't a holiday, so the only reason I could fathom her writing for was to pass on news. Bad news.

"Do you want me to leave you alone?" Mother asked.

"Will you sit with me?"

"Of course, Audrey."

We went to the porch swing and sat beside one another, the only sound the quiet squeak of the chains as we rocked.

After a while, I took a breath and tore open the envelope.

James's plane had been found, but he had not been found with it. There was blood, but not enough to suspect he'd died there. There had been rumblings, rumors of soldiers hiding out in barns, in attics, wherever they could as they waited—for word that it was safe to move, to be captured, for the war to end...

No news is good news, was what her father always said. No body was a good sign.

They had men keeping a lookout, but he'd gone down in German territory. The finding of his plane had been purely accidental. They hadn't been able to check the surroundings before having to escape the area.

"Dear God," Mama said, squeezing my hand.

I barely slept for the next month, the radio on constantly as I studied maps of the area James had gone down in and scoured the newspaper for news from overseas. Every so often there was some small mention of a soldier who'd been thought dead being found alive. But not often enough. And never James.

By May I was half-crazed from the lack of sleep. Between staying up late listening to the radio, writing Ava once a week to ask if she'd heard anything more and trying to keep up with the plans for the airfield, I didn't get more than a few hours of sleep a night.

It was after midnight on a Tuesday when my father found me sitting out on my and Evie's shared balcony, the radio holding the door open as I made a list of items each room would need in the hotel.

"Bird?" he called. "You out here?"

He peeked his head out.

"What are you doing?" he asked and bent to turn down the volume on the radio.

"Dad, no!"

"It's late and you had that up so loud I could hear it downstairs."

"Well, sound carries when it's so quiet."

"Yes. Exactly. And your mother and sister are trying to sleep. As are the neighbors down the road."

I chewed my lip.

"You've been wound up pretty tight lately. Is it the airfield? Is it too much?"

"It's not too much."

"Then what?"

"I can't stop thinking about James. Not that I wasn't every day before, it's just...the news of his plane still has me reeling. I can't help wondering every minute of every day if he's hiding somewhere. If he's okay."

"Whoa." He sat beside me and took the notebook I'd been writing in and grasped my hands in his. "Audrey. I understand your fears. It's awful, I know, to be so far away and so helpless. But it's war, my love. It's no good to wind yourself up this tight when there is nothing to be done. At least not now. If— When he comes home...then you can help him with whatever he may need. But until that happens, all we can do is wait."

"It's war," I muttered, pulling my hands from his. "That's all I hear when something bad happens. It's war. So what if it's war? So we just sit by? We wait and see? That's it?"

"What would you have us do? What would you do if you could?"

I bowed my head, tears falling onto my clasped hands. "I don't know. But sitting here on the other side of the world, knowing he might be out there alive, and I'm here just..." I picked up my notebook and tossed it over the rail. "Just making lists of toiletries and towel counts—it's awful. I was so excited to finally have my airfield, and now here I am, a month away, and all I can do is think about leaving it."

"Leaving it?"

"I'd hire someone of course," I said.

"Wait, what do you mean? Leave it for what?"

I turned and stared up at my father. Until James, I'd never loved any man as much as I loved my dad. He was the kindest, funniest, smartest man I knew. I revered him. I looked up to him. I trusted him with my every fear, every question, every hope and dream.

Until now. Because this he wouldn't agree with. This time he wouldn't be on my side. And it would break both our hearts.

"For him," I said.

"Audrey—"

"I don't even know if it's possible. It's probably not. But I have to try. He would for me."

"Honey—"

"Dad." I took his hand.

He sighed and looked out into the night. "I want to treat you like a little girl and put my foot down," he said. "But I know I can't. I could threaten to kick you out, but what good would that do if you're already leaving? And you know I never could anyway. I wouldn't have the heart. But, Audrey...it's dangerous."

"You're right," I said. "It is."

"How would you get there?"

"I'm not sure, but I have an idea. And if that doesn't work, then I really don't know."

"Who would you get to run the airfield? I suppose you could ask Hal to hang around for a while more. Not sure he'd do it though. Every time I see him he seems more and more anxious to be done."

"I wouldn't ask that of Hal," I said. "He'd never forgive me. I do have someone else in mind though."

"God," he said and took a deep breath. "I can't fathom the thought of you going over there while the war is still happening. And your mother—well, this might send her straight around the bend."

"I know," I said. "But, Dad, he's worth it."

"He damn well better be, bird. Because if I lose you over him, I'll never forgive myself."

Until I spoke with my father, I hadn't given much merit to my thoughts of trying to get overseas. But once the words were out, things started falling into place. The first call I made was to Nola. I knew from her last couple of letters that she and Stu had ended things and she was managing a company that manufactured aircraft parts. Was she interested in managing my airfield for me if I went overseas, with the possibility of staying on once I returned? Yes. She offered to drop everything and come that minute if need be.

My next call was to Fort Myers in Florida where I'd last seen Officer Hurst, the young airman I'd trained in Hawaii who had been part of James's squadron when I'd met up with him in March the year before. He was no longer there of course, but that call led me to another base where I left my name and a message for how to get ahold of me. If Officer Hurst was still alive, he'd promised me a favor, and I had a big one to ask.

The last bit to go my way was the biggest and most amazing news. On the morning of May 8, as I drove to the airfield to meet with a contractor, Bing Crosby singing on the radio was interrupted by the announcement of an important news brief. After a few seconds of static, President Truman's voice resonated from the speakers.

"This is a solemn but glorious hour," he began.

My heart pounding, I pulled over, along with two other cars, and sat on the shoulder waiting to hear what came next, which was nothing short of miraculous. Germany had surrendered to the United Nations.

Tears ran down my face and I sat breathless as I listened, my hands clasped around the steering wheel. And when the president finished speaking, I lowered my head and sobbed.

Rather than go to the airfield, I turned around, back toward home. I would apologize to the contractor later. For now, I wanted nothing more than to hug my family.

As I drove through town I smiled through my tears as people stood on the sidewalks hugging one another and waving and shouting to passersby. Horns honked in celebration and people danced in the street.

I pulled up to the house at the same moment as my father, who had also returned after hearing the news. My mother and Evie stood on the front porch, their arms around one another. I don't know how long the four of us stood together crying. All I knew was we were together and the United States was almost out of the war. All we had to do now was come out on top against Japan. And on that day I would truly celebrate. For that would be the end of a terrible chapter that had seen several people I loved and adored killed, and nearly changed the course of my life. But for now...for now I would celebrate for those still alive overseas who would get to come home at long last.

"Let's have a party," Mama said.

"A party?" Dad asked and then nodded. "Sure. Yes. A party is definitely in order. What can I do to help?"

The three of us looked at him in surprise.

"Aren't you going to work, Dad?" Evie asked.

"Not today, honey," he said and kissed my mother's cheek. "I'm taking today off."

While they clamored inside so Mama could make a shopping list and Evie got on the phone to start inviting friends over, I took a seat on the porch swing, the creak of the chains soothing me as I thought of James.

Dad came back out of the house to sit beside me. "You okay?"

"I sure get asked that a lot these days," I said.

"You've sure been through a lot these past few years, and I imagine today's news, while wonderful, also brings up a lot of emotions for you."

I nodded and rested my head on his shoulder.

"I feel like I can barely remember life before the Japanese attacked," I said. "So much has happened since then. I met and got to fly for a program run by one of my idols. I made wonderful new friends, but lost so many of them. I bought an airfield. And..."

"And you fell in love," he finished.

I nodded and stared out across the lawn. Of all the things that had happened, that one surprised me the most. And like I'd always imagined and feared it would—it was the one thing that also altered me the most by making me care about someone else in a way I'd never dared to. I would be forever haunted by the feelings James had stirred in me, and wouldn't be able to rest until I knew his fate.

It was three weeks before I heard anything from Officer Hurst. I'd begun to give up hope and had once again buried myself in work. But this time I also slept, long hours I had trouble waking from most days. It was as though my body and mind wanted no more.

And then I saw it. I came home from the airfield one day, pleased with the way the construction of the new hotel was going, and saw the note my mother left on the tray in the foyer for me. Officer Hurst had called. He was stateside and he'd left a telephone number where I could reach him.

My hands shook and I lowered myself to the bottom step of the staircase.

"Audrey?" Evie said from above me. She wasn't home much these days, between work and spending time with her girlfriends. "Everything okay?"

She hurried down the stairs and sat beside me, looking with her big blue eyes from me to the piece of paper in my hands. I glanced over at her and smiled. The baby fat she'd always complained about, saying it made her look like a child, had all but disappeared, giving way to lovely high cheekbones that made her look like an expensive doll. Her strawberry blonde hair had grown out a touch, and she wore it in a softer style that complemented her delicate features.

I leaned over and kissed her powder-soft cheek. "Everything is great," I said.

"Who's Officer Hurst?"

"An old friend."

"Swell," she said and got to her feet. "Quinton will be here in a jiffy. Let him in, will you? I have to get my sweater."

An hour later, after making polite conversation with Quinton while my sister changed her outfit, her shoes and redid her hair, I sat on my bed with the telephone receiver pressed tight to my ear and dialed the number my mother had written in her perfect penmanship.

Officer Hurst was surprised to have heard from me and we commiserated over James's status. He was even more astonished when I told him why I'd called.

"A flight to Europe?" he asked, his voice crackling over the line. "Gosh, Miss Coltrane, I don't know. I'm not sure how I'd make that happen. You can't get a commercial flight out?"

"They're still not running," I said. "Precautions. It's mostly military from what I've been able to find out. I wouldn't ask if I didn't have to. But if there's anyone who could, or who would understand my reason for going, it's you. All I ask is you try. If it's impossible, I'll accept that and wait."

"I'll get back to you," he said.

"Thank you, Hurst."

Three days went by with no word. I was returning home on the fourth when I heard the phone ringing and ran up the front steps. I flew through the front door and hurried to the sitting room, grabbing the receiver and pressing it to my ear.

"Coltrane residence," I said, breathing heavily into the phone.

"Miss Audrey Coltrane, please." I recognized Hurst's voice immediately.

"It's me," I said.

"I've found you a ride. Or rather, a plane."

"Pardon?"

"I have orders to bring a half dozen planes overseas."

"But the war is over in Europe. Why are more planes needed?"

"They're transport planes. To get the wounded out. The

problem is, one of my pilots has fallen ill." He paused. "I need someone capable to take his place. Know of anyone that fits the description?"

I grinned. "I might."

"How soon can you get to Fort Myers, Miss Coltrane?"

My mind reeled, but there was only one answer to be given. "Tomorrow."

"See you then."

CHAPTER THIRTY

"Nola will be here Friday," I reminded my mother as I threw clothes into a small valise. "I've told her she can stay in the guest room until either I get back or she finds somewhere else. Whichever she prefers."

I glanced at my father who was leaning against the door frame of my room, looking as confused as my mother did shocked.

"Dad, I've told the foreman working on the hotel to contact you should he have any questions. Everything you'll need is on my desk. If something isn't, I trust you to make the right decision." I looked at Evie who sat on my bed with wide eyes, watching me move from my suitcase to my bureau. "Evie, don't go getting married until I get home."

I stopped moving for a moment and took them each in.

"I'm sorry to go like this," I said. "But if I don't, I'll never get another chance. And I couldn't live with myself were that to happen."

"But, Audrey." My mother's voice was a whisper. "It's still so dangerous."

She clasped my father's hand, fear and worry etched on their faces. I sank to my bed.

"Wouldn't you do it?" I asked. "For each other? If there was a chance?"

Mama's eyes filled and my father sighed and leaned his head against hers.

"If it were me," I said, "he'd move heaven and earth. I have to do the same."

The following morning my father found me on the front porch swing before dawn.

"You know, I've never worried about you," he said, sitting beside me. "Not truly. You have a knack for knowing what you can handle. What you're capable of. Sometimes you push yourself. Sometimes you back off. But you always know. You always make the right call."

"Oh, Dad," I said with a rueful chuckle. "I never know."

"You may not here," he said, tapping his finger to my forehead. "But you do there." He pointed to my stomach. "And there." His finger aimed at my heart. "So long as you lead with those two things and let your head cast the deciding vote, you'll be fine."

"I hope you're right."

"Just be safe," he said. "It's all I ask. And come home to us soon."

He and my mother drove me to the airport after I hugged Evie goodbye and she squeezed me until I shouted for mercy.

"Will you ever just stay?" she asked, her blue eyes wet. "I'm tired of saying goodbye to you, Audrey. I'm always afraid it will be the last time."

"I'll be back," I said. "I promise. And next time, I'll stay."

She sighed and shook her head, clearly not believing a word of it. "Send me something nice from Paris?" she asked and I laughed at her predictability.

Father parked and he and Mama walked me to the gate, each with an arm looped through mine.

"I'll check you in," Dad said and went to the desk.

"You'd think I'd be used to this by now," Mama said. She held my cheeks in her palms, her eyes roaming over my face.

She was just as lovely as she'd always been. It seemed unfair to have a mother so pretty. If I were a self-conscious girl, I might develop unhealthy habits trying to live up to her standards. Like so many others though, the past few years had aged her, her face and body diminishing so the bones were more prominent, her hair fading along with the blue of her eyes. But there was a steeliness beneath it all. Power, determination and heart.

The war had taken its toll on everyone. There was a curvature to the older people's spines, a hunching of the shoulders, a slowness to the step. Mothers looked haggard from worry, fathers weary as they wondered about the fates of their sons. Even the younger set, the people my age, looked worn and thin.

But the American spirit had grown twofold since we had entered the war. Our flag waved from every house. "USA" and "Home of the Brave" were painted on shop windows. People believed we'd win. So despite the wear and tear, we were a country united in a way we'd never been before.

I smiled at my mother. "I always thought I got my resolve from Dad," I said. "Watching him go off to work every morning. Fixing things around the house. Working on the car. Mending the fences. But maybe not..."

Her eyes lit up and she held me to her. "In my day," she murmured into my hair, "we learned the subtle art of making them think they did it all by themselves. We just fixed our hair and put on our faces and a nice dress and poured the drinks." She pulled back, a tear in her eye. "It's your day now, Audrey Fitzgerald. Don't hide what you can do. Not for anyone. I've never been prouder of you, sweet girl. Be safe over there. Come home soon."

I hugged her hard and she gasped in surprise and hugged me back.

"Ready, bird?" Dad asked.

I pulled away from my mother and looked from her to him. "I'm ready."

"You call as soon as you get in," Dad said as he hugged me at the gate. "And let us know where you're staying."

"I will. I love you both so much," I whispered.

I got in my seat, buckled myself in and stared out the window, watching the two people who had taught me nearly everything about life and love and respect. Despite their great example of being a couple, I'd never wanted the same. Until I did. And now I was going to fight for it with everything I had.

Officer Hurst picked me up at the airport. He was waiting on the tarmac shifting from one foot to the other when I disembarked, his face a mask.

"Miss Coltrane," he said.

"Officer Hurst."

"May I take your bag?"

"I've got it, thank you."

"This way." He walked at a brisk pace and I struggled to keep up.

"When do we leave?" I asked when we arrived at his jeep.

"O-four hundred hours. I've secured a room for you on base with two nurses."

"Thank you." I shut the door and twisted to face him. "This isn't going to get you in trouble is it?"

"Only if my superior finds out the officer beneath me isn't really ill."

I nodded. "Well, I won't tell. Do they know a woman is taking his place?"

"Not yet," he grumbled.

I woke at three and hurried into my flight suit. Officer Hurst suggested I wear it, as it would make me look less feminine, the heavy fabric hiding any curves I had. I pulled my hair back, left the lipstick in my bag and pulled on my helmet. With a deep breath, I walked out to the airfield.

"Good morning," I said in a low voice to Officer Hurst.

"Morning," he grunted. He pointed across the tarmac. "We're taking those."

I peered across the pavement. "What is it?"

"A Nightingale. We use them as transports and ambulances. You ever flown one?"

I shook my head and he exhaled hard.

"Officer Hurst," I said. "I was trained on nearly two dozen planes so that I could get in any aircraft and fly it at a moment's notice. I promise you, it won't be a problem."

He stared at me for a long moment. "I hope you're right."

"I am."

"Get on with preflight then, Miss Coltrane."

I stalked across the tarmac and went through the checklist one by one. When I was satisfied, I climbed aboard, stowed my bag and buckled my harness.

"You good in here?" Officer Hurst said, poking his head in.

"Yes, sir."

"Keep radio interaction to a minimum." He patted the plane. "See you up there."

I nodded and he disappeared, leaving me alone. I looked over the instrument panel, running my fingertips lightly over each switch, button and light, getting my bearings.

At o-four hundred hours I called up to the tower and waited with my breath held until they gave me permission to take off. Five minutes later I was airborne.

It had been years since I'd flown over an ocean, and the Atlantic at sunrise was spectacular. The curve of the planet, the brilliant tangerine and fuchsia streaking across the horizon, cumulus clouds like puffs of cotton candy dotting the lavender sky…it was breathtaking. Tranquil. A sight no picture could do justice.

It was nearly 8:00 p.m. when we finally landed at Orly Air Base just south of Paris. I grabbed my things, stretched my back and disembarked, looking around for Officer Hurst, who I saw within moments of stepping onto the pavement.

"Miss Coltrane," he said, herding me across the tarmac. "You have your pilot's license and WASP ID on you?"

"I do."

"Good. Get them out. Now, please."

"Did someone find out? Are you in trouble?"

"Yes, and I'm not sure. But we'll find out soon enough."

"I'm so sorry."

He looked down at me and gave me a quick grin. "I owed you."

"I know but—"

"Officer Hurst!" a voice barked.

"Shit," Hurst muttered and stood at attention. "Yes, sir."

His commanding officer was a brute of a man. Tall, stern, with dark hair and eyes that missed nothing.

"This is the pilot you found to replace Miller?"

"Yes, sir."

"This woman doesn't look to be army." He held out a hand to me and I placed my ID and license in it. "Not to mention she's female."

"Yes, sir."

"You're telling me there was no one else qualified to fly that plane over here?"

"That is what I'm telling you, sir."

"You ever fly a Nightingale before Miss…"

"Coltrane, sir. And no, sir. But I've flown nearly two dozen other models of the military's aircraft, including pursuits and bombers, sir. The Nightingale was an easy plane."

"Smart one, are you? Got a flight book on you?"

I pulled it from my bag and handed it over. Hurst was barely breathing as he watched his superior flip through the little book of all the flights I'd flown since my father had first bought the leather-bound book for me thirteen years before. He snapped it shut and handed it back.

"Seems like I shoulda hired you to run my squadron. You look like you might be an even better pilot than Hurst here."

"Hurst is an excellent pilot," I said, ignoring the noise of warning coming from Hurst's throat.

"Oh yeah? Well, that's easy to say when you convinced him to let you fly one of my planes, isn't it?"

"No, sir. It's easy to say because I trained Officer Hurst myself. In Pearl Harbor."

The giant of a man looked from me to Hurst.

"That true, Officer?" he asked.

"Yes, sir," Hurst said.

"Well, shit." He laughed. "You two get out of here. I'll think of something to put in the logbook. Miss Coltrane, it was a pleasure. But stay out of trouble. And, Hurst…" He shook his head. "I'm going to forget this happened—this time."

"Thank you, sir." He saluted.

"Thank you, sir," I said.

"This damn war… It's made everyone crazy," he said as he walked away.

Officer Hurst swore and looked down at me with wide eyes. "That was…"

"Frightening?" I offered.

"Terrifying." He took a breath. "Now—"

"Hurst!" someone called. We turned at the sound of footsteps.

A lanky redheaded man jogged across the tarmac, stopping just short of us. The two men saluted one another and then hugged and exchanged some lighthearted jabs.

"Audrey," Hurst said, finally turning to me. "This is Officer Rooney. You're going to be staying with him."

"I'm what?" I asked. I was not sure I was comfortable staying with a strange man, no matter how harmless he looked, which he did with arms that seemed too long for his body and a freckled face.

"What he means to say," Officer Rooney said, swatting Hurst on the arm, "is that you will be staying in an apartment owned by my fiancée, Marion, and me." He held out a hand. "It's a pleasure to meet you, Audrey. I'm John. Or Johnny if you like, a friend of James's. We grew up together back in Iowa."

My heart skipped a beat as I shook his hand. "He told me about you. About the five of you friends who all signed up together. I'm so happy to meet you, John."

"Well," Officer Hurst said. "This is where I say goodbye. Miss Coltrane, it was an honor and a pleasure."

"I don't know how I'll ever thank you, Officer Hurst," I said.

"You don't have to thank me. I owed you one."

I shook my head and reached up to give him a hug.

"Good luck," he said. "I hope you find good news here."

As he walked away, Rooney took my bag from my hand. "Is that all you have?" he asked.

"This is it."

"You travel light. Marion will fix that for you. She's an expert shopper, not that she's done much of that lately. But the shops are slowly starting to open back up and I know she'll want to do her part to support them." He winked. "Shall we?"

"Yes, please."

He talked the entire way from Orly to Montmartre where they lived, but as we drove through the streets of Paris, I stopped hearing him, my attention taken by the scene outside the window.

This was not the Paris I remembered seeing with my parents seven years before. This city had been ravaged not by bombs—which had been reserved for many other parts of France—but by embarrassment in its surrender, and by the subsequent poverty, starvation and looting after being stripped of life. A city once proud and winking at all others who deigned to try to emulate her magnificence and style, now ducked in humiliation at not being able to stand on her own two independent legs. Her cry for help had been humbling. The peeling away of her confidence chastening. She was a shell of herself, bereft and wanting nothing more than to shine once more and have the world forget the peek they'd gotten beneath her designer skirt.

I stared at buildings older than entire towns in America and was saddened by their crumbling and graying facades. There seemed to be trash everywhere. In the streets, in doorways, in cars that sat dead on the side of the street, and blowing in the wind. There were countless doors covered with boards, darkened windows that stared out in despair and storefronts that looked as if they'd never greet another customer again.

A flower shop on one corner had wood boxes filled with decaying flowers. A small *chocolaterie* I remembered visiting with my mother and Evie displayed empty shelves behind its windows, the white bistro table and chairs a pile of twisted metal on the sidewalk in front of it. There were cars with flat tires sitting curbside all over the city and Nazi signage crumpled and lying in the streets.

"It's awful," I said, turning my eyes from the city to its people. But the sight of them was no better. Old men and women hunched and dressed in what looked like rags. Children being pulled alongside their parents, their little eyes wide in small pinched faces in need of a good meal.

"It is," he agreed. "But don't let her fool you. Paris is still alive and well, she just needs to be reawakened. She's starting to come to. Look more closely. You'll see."

And so I did, and after a while I smiled as I watched a young man and woman saunter down a sidewalk, a fresh baguette under the man's arm. A block down I saw the source of the baguette—

a bakery with a line down the street and around the corner, the smell of fresh-baked bread filling the air.

A man outside a little clothing boutique stood on a ladder brushing off the black-and-white awning above the door. A sign in the window stated they'd be reopening soon. And a few more shops down was a restaurant brimming with young people, music floating out the open windows.

I smiled at John and he grinned back.

"You can't keep Paris down," he said.

The apartment building where Marion and John lived was small and quaint with little wrought-iron balconies and carved details along the roof. A black awning covered the entryway and John parked at the curb and opened the passenger door for me.

"You are here!" a voice exclaimed from the front door, and in a flurry of movement I was suddenly wrapped in arms, lavender-scented red hair and pale green satin. "Bonjour, Audrey. Welcome."

She stood back, holding me at arm's length, and I got my look at the fiancée. Marion Brodeur was the picture of effortless French style with her hair swept up in a messy but elegant twist, her face makeup-free, her satin robe barely hanging on to small, pale shoulders dusted with copper freckles. Her feet were bare, a delicate chain around one ankle, and she seemed lit from within, unaffected by anything, despite the smell of garbage wafting from down the street.

John was clearly delighted by her every movement and laughed as she stood practically naked for all of Paris to see.

"She knows no shame," he said.

"Oh. You *Américains*," she scoffed. "So modest. So embarrassed of your bodies. It is just skin." She let the robe slip from her shoulders, exposing a lacy negligee.

"Let's not frighten our guest away just yet," John said. "She's only just arrived."

Marion laughed, a tinkling sound that was almost musical.

"Fine, fine. *Viens*, Audrey. Let me show you to your *appartement*."

"My…" I frowned and looked to John.

"You have your own apartment," he said, following us inside. "Marion's aunt used to own the building. She sold it to us three months ago and moved in with her sister. We took her much larger apartment and now our old one is empty. Your timing is impeccable. You can stay free of charge as long as you need to."

"Oh no," I said, stopping in the foyer, a lovely room decorated in creams and blues. "I'm happy to pay rent. Please. If it weren't for you both, who knows where I'd be. Most likely somewhere I knew no one and a bit frightened. The peace of mind you've given me…truly. If you don't let me pay you I'll find another way to give you the money."

He laughed. "Okay. We'll talk about it. Now—" He gestured down the hall where Marion was waiting, the door to my new home standing open. "I hope you like it."

It was perfect. The exact thing I'd choose for myself were I a single woman coming to Paris for the first time to live. We entered into a tiny sitting room that looked out onto the street below. To the left was a sunny little kitchen, and to the right a hall that led to a large bedroom with a balcony and a nice-sized bathroom with a claw-foot tub.

"I love it," I said. "I may never leave."

"Oh!" Marion clapped her hands.

"Don't get her hopes up," John said. "We'll let you get settled and get some sleep. I work in the morning but Marion will be home and happy to help you with anything you need. We stocked the fridge and cupboards with a few necessities, but you'll definitely want to go to the market tomorrow."

I followed them back down the hall to the entryway and stood staring at them both. "I don't know how to thank you," I said. "This is…"

John took my hand in his. "I'll do everything I can to help

you find him. Every day off I have is yours. If you need information, a ride somewhere, just let me know. If I'm working, I'll
find someone to help you."

"Thank you, John," I said. "Thank you both. I know this
probably seems crazy, my coming all this way but..."

"He would've done the same for you," he said. "I've never
heard him talk about anyone the way he spoke of you. He
would've moved mountains."

I sighed and said good-night and then shut the door behind
them. I walked around the little apartment, peeking in the cupboards, opening the fridge, until I finally collapsed onto the
cream-colored sofa and fell asleep.

CHAPTER THIRTY-ONE

"Audrey, hurry, *mon amie!*" Marion shouted, banging on my door before unlocking it with the key I'd given her.

"I'm coming, I'm coming," I said, running out of my bed-room.

"John is already in the jeep," she said.

Over the course of the war, thirteen bombs had fallen in the vicinity of Montmartre, all miraculously missing the Sacré-Coeur Basilica, but causing the stained glass windows in it to burst. Nearly every day I walked the eighteenth arrondissement of Paris, sidestepping harried mothers bouncing their babies, old women with scarves over their heads and darting eyes, old men with shaking hands leaning on canes and children grasping their parents' hands who jumped at any little sound as they waited in line for cheese or meat or milk, which were still being rationed despite the war having ended, the country being so depleted by German forces. But somehow, despite the feeling of despair, I felt at home here. I loved the steep hills and cobblestone roads, the little restaurants anxious to serve whatever they had to their

people, altering recipes and menus as needed, and shops putting
their best foot, usually any foot, forward, just to open once more
and provide a sense of pride at moving forward. Before my eyes,
the city was coming alive again, remembering its joie de vivre
slowly, cautiously and moment by moment.

Marion tapped one red fabric wedge as I hurried to the
kitchen and gulped down the rest of my coffee.

"You remind me of my mother when you do that," I said,
shoving a piece of one of the precious scones I'd been fortunate to find at the patisserie down the street two days ago in
my mouth.

"Your mother is a wise woman."

"You don't even know her."

"From what you just say—I know she is wise."

I snorted and she grinned. I grabbed my handbag and we
hurried out the door and outside where John was waiting in a
jeep at the curb.

"I can't believe Marion was ready before you," he said as we
jumped in and he pulled out onto the street.

"You called me twenty minutes ago. I wasn't even out of
bed yet."

Marion reached over and smoothed John's hair. I grinned
watching the two redheads. I commented last week that it would
be a shame if their children were born with something as bor-
ing as blond or brown hair. Marion said she'd blame John if
that happened. "Red hair is strong on my side," she'd said. "His
Américain genes had best not ruin everything."

"Where are we going?" I asked as John sped through the city.

"I got a call about a new group they found."

The rumors I'd heard were true about injured soldiers hiding
out in barns, abandoned buildings, people's attics and wherever
else they could find. As soon as I'd arrived, John had notified
several people about me and why I was there. We had lookouts
all over the country and information coming in almost daily.

So far nothing had led us to James, but many injured soldiers had been found and brought in due to our search and I'd now seen things I never thought possible, or at least hoped weren't.

I'd lost count of the number of limbs I'd seen severed. Lost eyesight, lost *eyes*, noses blown clear off faces, ears missing and gaping abdominal wounds that twice made me run from the site to throw up. Some of the cities we went to were barely standing, mere ghost towns left in their wake, the people having run or been taken away to camps or been killed on the spot. Sometimes a few were left, having hidden in attics or basements, or had ventured back to reclaim what little was left. But most of the time belongings and lives were abandoned, leaving behind homes, automobiles, bicycles, jewelry and, most heartbreakingly, children's toys.

The men we found were often half-crazed, their injuries severe, their brains laying waste to coherent thought. I was glad we were able to help them, but each time we delivered them to nearby hospitals, I left with a deeper feeling of despair than the time before, my hope for finding James dwindling by the day.

We parked and rushed into the hospital, weaving through people until we found the officer who had called John.

"Shit," he said when he saw me standing behind John. "Sorry. It's not him. Looks a lot like him though. My guy was so sure."

"Maybe he's wrong?" Marion said.

"Could be," John said. "Where is he? I'll have a look just in case. You two stay here," he said to us.

We of course didn't listen, following him down a long corridor and another hallway until we all stopped outside a room where a man lay, more than half his body bandaged.

He stared at us with his one visible eye. His one visible brown eye. I sighed and walked slowly back down the hall.

"Dammit," John said as we walked back to the jeep. "I'm sorry, Audrey."

"It's fine. It's one more saved. I can't complain about that. They might die if we don't find them."

Not wanting to go home, Marion and I went back to the hospital. She'd been volunteering there since the war started and got me a job once I'd arrived. I wasn't able to do much besides restock supplies, but I liked being there. It was reminiscent of when I was in Pearl Harbor with James. I felt closer to him here. And I was keeping busy; most days arriving back at the apartment exhausted, which helped me sleep. Sometimes so deeply I didn't have the nightmares that had cropped up again since arriving in Paris. Nightmares of being shot at, crashing planes, James calling out to me... I'd wake in the middle of the night in a panic, my pajamas sticking to my body.

I knew it was because here I could see the war again. It was everywhere. It was tangible still. I saw it on the faces of everyone I met and heard it in their voices. It was in the broken windows and smashed-in doors. The piles of burned furniture and starved, emaciated people.

Back home it was easy to forget just how awful war could be. But here it was in my face every day. Here the people couldn't forget, and thus nor could I. The memories of seeing their neighbors and family members dragged from their homes were still fresh in their minds. Some had been shot in the street, others gathered and pushed onto trains like animals never to return. There was a haunted quality to their eyes. A tremor, a suspiciousness and a desire to hide within themselves. So many of the people I'd encountered looked like they'd seen ghosts. Because they had.

I was reminded of my first days home after the attack on Pearl Harbor. How I'd been furious, stomping from room to immaculate room in our house, railing at the injustices. How they had no idea what it was like. How others had lost everything. How we had too much. I'd wanted to give it all away.

When I wasn't restocking supplies at the hospital, I sat with the wounded. Some days were harder than others, especially when a new crop of soldiers was brought in after having been found hiding out in the countryside of some small town. There were dozens of stories of men getting shot, or their planes going down and finding what cover they could in hopes help would come. Many times it didn't though, and those who were too badly injured usually died, their bodies found in barns or beneath a pile of brush. Others came forward when they thought it safe, the townspeople taking them in and getting them help or caring for them themselves. And still others were too afraid to leave the hiding spots they'd found and were discovered many times by accident, half-mad, their injuries festering, limbs in need of amputation. Those were the ones that broke my heart. They called for their mothers and whimpered in their sleep.

Every day I looked for James among the faces of the wounded and dead. Every day I walked along the beds, searching for his green eyes beneath the bandages. And when I didn't find him, I'd search the morgue. But every time I started to lose hope, a new batch of men came in and I knew that he might still be out there.

All the nurses knew his name in case it came up on a file. All the doctors would meet my gaze as they examined some dark-haired man and shake their heads that no, it wasn't James. And I was on a first-name basis with the group of American soldiers assigned to follow up on rumors of their own still hiding out and unable to get to the hospital themselves.

I'd hold the door open as they carried men in and they'd meet my anxious gaze and shake their heads.

"Not today, Audrey," they'd say.

It was also a possibility that James could be at a different hospital. Especially since his plane had gone down near the France-Germany border, which was miles from where we were. But of course John had thought of that and had put the word out to all surrounding hospitals as well to contact him were a James Hart to be brought in.

Several times I'd asked John if we could drive out to where he'd gone down. But John had heard reports that it was still dangerous in that area.

"They think there are disgruntled Germans hiding out in some of the abandoned houses," he said. "When they found James's plane, shots were fired. They think it was from the homes."

"Why would they still be there now?" I'd asked.

"I don't know. But until it's been cleared, we're not going."

I'd pleaded with him many times, but my pleas were met with deaf ears. If James were found, John would hear about it. Enough people knew to tell him.

It was a hot afternoon in August when Marion came by with a bag of fresh bread.

"Oh my," I said. "That looks divine."

"I wish there were cheese but *pas de chance*… Our rations don't allow for it this week."

I nodded and took a bite of the still-warm bread. I moaned, the pillowy-soft inside of the baguette fresh from the oven practically a delicacy these days in Paris.

"You have many letters today," she said, pointing to the stack.

"They came yesterday," I said. "One from my dad, one from Claire and one from Ruby."

"Ah, Ruby. My *Américaine* sister. How is she?"

I laughed. Marion had wanted to know all about Ruby once I'd told her she reminded me of my old friend, down to the vibrant hair color.

"She is well. Married. Pregnant. Still teaching Sunday school at church."

"Did she send pictures?"

"No pictures."

"Damn," she said. "Do you miss your family?"

"I do," I said and set the letters aside. "But I'll see them soon. Is John off today?"

Marion frowned. "What do you mean you'll see them soon?" she asked.

I sighed and stared out the window. I'd been in Paris almost three months and there'd been no word, no sighting, not even a possible glimpse of James. It was as though he'd disappeared the day his plane went down. And while I wasn't ready to give up just yet, my brain was starting to tell my gut and my heart that what I was searching for no longer existed.

"I just mean that I can't stay forever. Now, what are you two lovebirds doing today?"

She glared at me. "You are changing the subject."

"Yes."

"Fine. We are going to the park for a picnic. Do you want to come?"

"No. Thank you, but I'm pretty sure your fiancé would like his romantic picnic to stay that way."

"What will you do then?" Marion asked.

"I'll probably go to the hospital."

"On your day off?"

I shrugged.

"Oh, Audrey, *non*. Have a picnic with us. It will be fun. No kissing, I promise."

"Next time," I said. "You two should enjoy some kissing."

"*D'accord,*" she said. "But don't stay there too long. You always have the nightmares after."

"I won't," I said.

Four soldiers were being brought in on stretchers when I arrived.

"Where did they come from?" I asked an officer standing nearby.

"Lyon. They left the camp they'd been held in over a month ago and had been hiding in the hills. I found them walking down the street. Filthy, bloody and holding on to one another. When I pulled over they started crying." His own eyes filled with tears. "They couldn't remember where they'd been held, but one day their captors just stopped coming. After several days they left."

I stared at the four men, who were severely emaciated, their skin weathered from exposure. One turned and looked in my direction and I sucked in a breath. His eyes were a vivid green, his hair dark like James's. At this point, after seeing so many soldiers come through in terrible shape, I began to wonder if I didn't hope that James was dead just so that he wouldn't have had to endure what these young men had been through.

The following day Marion had the day off so I took a cab to the hospital, rather than ask John for a lift.

I paid the driver and strode to the front doors, moving out of the way as they suddenly swung open.

"Hello, Audrey," a deep voice said and I looked up.

"Hi, Peter," I said and glanced at the three men behind him. "You guys get another call?"

"Yeah. One of the guys we brought in last night said he'd been in Metz with several others taking cover in some woman's shed. He wasn't as bad off as them though and hitched a ride here. I forgot to ask about James," he said. "But the guy's just inside. Private Wallis. Can't miss him. Big fella. Bandaged head."

"Thanks," I said.

Private Wallis sat on a gurney just outside the emergency area.

"Excuse me," I said. "I heard you were in Metz?"

"Yes, ma'am."

"Where is that, exactly?"

"Near the border. Not far from Luxembourg."

I sucked in a breath. "Do you happen to remember the names of any of the other men you were with? Or remember what they looked like?"

"Honestly, ma'am, it was pretty dark and no one was much in the mood to chat, if you know what I mean. The guy next to me was Willard. I think the guy on the other side was Heard or Hutch—something with an *H* I think, but I can't recall…"

My heart raced. "Hart?"

"Not sure. Maybe." He shrugged.

I rushed down the hall and out the door. "Peter!" I waved.

He and another man had just loaded into two separate jeeps and were headed my way.

"You okay?" Peter asked, slowing to a stop beside me.

"Take me with you," I said, my chest heaving. "Please. Just this once."

He frowned and seemed to think it over. "It's not pretty. I can't promise what we'll find won't make you sick or give you nightmares."

"I already have nightmares."

"Get in," he said. "But don't say I didn't warn you."

It was a two-hour drive to Metz and the hairs rose on my arms when I saw not for the first time how hard some of the smaller towns had been hit, Paris hardly having been touched by the war. We arrived midafternoon and, with the assistance of several locals, found the home of the woman we were looking for on the edge of town. We parked on the side of a dirt road and made our way through a small field of long brown grass to a large run-down barn with a small shed just beyond it.

"Arrêtez!"

We turned to see a stout woman with a blue kerchief over her hair shouting at us. In her hand she waved a wooden spoon.

"What's she saying?" I asked, squinting through the bright afternoon sun at the woman marching toward us.

"She wants us to stop," Peter said.

She was out of breath when she reached us, sweat glistening on her upper lip and forehead. Her hair was greasy beneath the kerchief and she carried with her the overpowering smell of onions.

"You have injured men?" Peter asked in French.

The woman's eyes shifted from Peter to me, then to Stephen.

"We've come from Paris," Peter said. "From the military hospital."

Stephen stepped forward and began pulling his military ID from his pocket. The woman scurried backward and pulled a gun from the pocket of her apron with her free hand.

"Madame," I said, my hands raised in surrender. "*Non.* We are here to help. Please."

She motioned with her gun for Stephen to come closer, then put her spoon in her pocket and grabbed his ID. Her eyes flicked over it and she handed it back. She gestured toward the barn with her gun.

When we reached it the woman clicked her tongue and we turned. She shook her head and pointed at the shed. It couldn't have been more than five feet by five feet; the roof caving in on one side. If there were men hiding inside, there weren't more than a couple. The woman pointed again and Stephen looked at us and shrugged. We passed the barn and tromped through the long grass to the shed.

"*Arrêtez,*" the woman said again and we stopped.

She hurried in front of us then pointed the gun at each of us in turn. Even with my limited knowledge of French I understood every word she said.

"If you hurt any of them, I will kill all of you."

At first glance, the shed appeared to be crammed full of tools and feed for the animals. The woman pressed her back to the wall and slid down a narrow path around the perimeter, moving and shifting items as she went. She stopped at the corner and ducked. Peter held up a hand.

"I'll go," he said. "You two stay here."

I shook my head. He gave me a stern look.

"Fine," he said. "But, if I say run, you run."

We had to turn sideways to descend a narrow staircase that led down to a cavernous room below. My breath caught at the stench, my eyes watering. Peering through the dimly lit room, I glimpsed beds made of straw and covered with tattered blankets, six men in some state of injury lying on top of them.

I examined their gaunt faces, my heart in my stomach as they stared up at me with haunted, hopeful gazes. James was not among them, but this time it didn't matter that I hadn't found him. I'd helped find these men. Men whose families and friends no doubt thought them long dead. These men at least would go home.

I glanced around at what had been their home for who knows how long. In the center on an overturned tin container was a jug of what I assumed was water and some bread and fruit. In the corner was a large bucket I could only imagine was being used as a bathroom from the smell permeating the entirety of the room.

"How did she get them in here?" Stephen asked.

Peter pointed to a door. "I'll bet that leads to the barn."

It took two people to one injured soldier to get them up the stairs and out of the shed, the door to the barn having been barred with equipment from the other side to hide it from prying Nazi eyes.

"What happened to you guys?" Stephen asked as we helped them into the jeeps.

"We were in two vehicles and hit a mine," a blond man named Chuck said. "The neighbors helped drag us into the barn when the gunfire started, and the woman and her husband led us to the shed. Her husband died helping us. Four of our guys were shot and killed as well. They're buried behind the barn. Her son is the town doctor. He's been caring for us."

I grew still and stared at the long grass behind the barn.

"Was…" I couldn't get the words out and stared up in anguish at Stephen, who frowned and then nodded his understanding.

"Lieutenant James Hart," he said. "Was he with you?"

"Lieutenant Hart? No. No Hart. There was Wallis, Willard, Herman and Carpenter. Is this Hart missing in action?"

We nodded and he regarded us sadly. "I wish I could be of more help. Especially since you just saved our lives."

"We didn't do that," I said, pointing to the woman. "She did."

The men loaded, we turned to the woman who grasped each of our hands in turn, her eyes filled with tears. She said something more and I looked to Peter.

"She asked that we please get them home safely," he said.

I patted her hands and nodded. *"Merci,"* I said. "We'll make sure they're taken care of."

She squeezed my hand and I got in the passenger seat next to Peter. The three men in the back were asleep, leaning on one another.

"I wonder how long they were down there," Peter said.

"Awhile," I said, glancing at their injuries. Some of the wounds were obviously infected, and at least one leg would have to be amputated.

Before we drove away, I removed the picture of James I always carried with me from my pocket. I unfolded it and showed it to the woman. It was a long shot, but maybe they'd picked him up somewhere and he'd been in the vehicle with them and was now one of the four buried in her yard. But she gave me a sad little smile and shook her head.

"Merci," I said again and put the photograph back in my pocket.

It was evening when we returned to Paris. We helped check the men in, and then Peter gave me a ride home. I leaned against the door and stared out at the city flying by. With every soldier brought in that wasn't James, my heart grew heavier, my hope waning.

"You okay?" Peter asked as he drove.

I turned to look at him. We'd met my first day volunteering at the hospital. He had a wife and a little girl back home in San

Diego and had taken on the role of big brother to me, fending off the other soldiers who whistled at me from their hospital beds and asked me on dates. He was a nice-looking guy with cropped black hair and warm brown eyes that had instantly put me at ease. I'd told him my story over lunch one day and had breathed a sigh of relief when he didn't look at me with pity.

"Thanks for letting me come along today," I said.

"Sure thing," he said, pulling up to the curb. "Sorry it didn't work out better for you."

I nodded and waved goodbye, then climbed the steps to the apartment and let myself in.

CHAPTER THIRTY-TWO

Late August in Paris was hot and humid and those who could left the city for the coast, where the sea air made the high temperatures bearable.

With fewer soldiers coming into the hospital, Marion's and my presence was hardly needed. She took a job working for a hat maker on the Champs-Élysées, and I worked at a local dress shop and began to think seriously about going home.

I shared my thoughts with Marion and John over dinner one night. John sighed and Marion stared at me with wide eyes.

"He's been gone so long now and no one has seen him or heard a word about him. It's as if he disappeared into thin air. The likelihood he's alive is practically nonexistent. I don't want to give up, but…"

"Maybe it's time," John said, his eyes glistening. "Your coming here gave me so much hope. But maybe we were wrong. We were holding on so tight because he was such a good man, and it's hard to let go."

I nodded and tears spilled from my eyes down my face.

"When will you leave?" Marion asked.

"I don't know. Next week?"

"Then we have a week," she said. "A week to celebrate his life and say goodbye together. He would like that, I think."

She reached across the table and took my hand. John put an arm around her shoulders and smiled through the dim light at me.

"He would love that," he said.

Two days later I woke to pounding on the front door.

"Hang on," I said, hurrying down the hall while tying my robe shut.

I unlocked the door and opened it. John stood on the threshold, his face pale beneath his freckles. I froze, my spine tingling.

"What is it?" I whispered.

"I just got a call," he said. "A group of soldiers brought in from near the German border. There's one... He matches the description of James but he's unconscious and there's no identification on him. None of the men with him know anything about him. I—"

"Hang on," I said, running down the hall to my bedroom, my heart in my throat. I threw on the first set of clothes my hands landed on and ran out to the jeep behind John and Marion.

No one said a word as we sped to the hospital. The tires screeched to a halt as we parked and for a moment none of us moved.

John took a breath. "It might not be him."

"I know," I said.

"Are you ready?"

I nodded but didn't move, my legs numb beneath me. "I can't do it." My voice was shaky.

"What?"

"I can't go in. I just—" Too many times I'd been in this exact situation. Too many times I'd gotten my hopes up only to get them dashed in one excruciating moment as the man matching the description of my beloved turned out to have a different name and a different face. I wasn't sure I could bear it again. And my body was in agreement as it refused to move from the seat.

"Let Marion and me go," John offered. "Or just me, and Marion can stay with you while you wait."

"No," I said, shaking my head like a small child having a tantrum. "Let's just go home. Let's go back. It's not going to be him. It's been too long. And I can't—I just can't."

"We can go home then," John said. "I'll take you now."

"But—" Marion frowned and John shook his head.

He shut the door and started to turn the key but I put my hand out to stop him.

We walked in together. I was in the middle—they both held my hands.

Half the emergency room was in chaos. People rushed about, calling out orders and asking for more morphine.

Teams of nurses and doctors examined soldier after soldier. We stood out of the way, my gaze flitting around the large room, taking in the bruised and broken bodies lined up on gurneys, the worn faces staring listlessly. From where I stood, not one resembled James.

We took a step in, each of us taking in faces, hoping to recognize his.

"I don't see him," I murmured. "There are so many."

"Maybe if we split up," John said.

They let go of my hands, each taking a different side of the room. I stayed in the middle, walking slowly forward, staying out of the way of the nurses rushing to calm fears, bandage wounds, administer sedatives.

At the far end of the room sat a man on a gurney. He was facing the wall and half hidden by a partition. It was hard not to notice him. Up his spine were ugly red swastika brandings some monster had burned into his skin. Some of the marks were only half-formed, as if his torturers couldn't get it right. Until they finally did—time and time again.

I watched a nurse carefully lift the man's dark, scraggly hair, revealing yet another swastika on his shoulder. It looked infected, the skin red and swollen. She tenderly pressed a cotton pad to it and the muscles in his back and arms flexed as he strained against the stinging alcohol. Transfixed, I stepped toward him.

As he moved, the vertebrae of his spine protruded. His shoulders, though severely diminished from malnutrition, were broad and strong.

"James." His name was a prayer on my lips.

I grasped the rail of the bed beside me and moved to the next one, and then the next, pulling myself until I was one bed away. But as he turned my heart sank.

It wasn't him. The frame of his body was similar, but the jaw too narrow, the nose too large and his eyes brown, not green.

With a whimper I turned and hurried from the room.

I heard Marion call my name but I rushed down the long corridor and pushed through the door out into the sunshine. I gulped in huge breaths, my hands on my knees, my body heaving to get air.

"Audrey!" Marion said again, hurrying to me and placing her hand on my back. "Is it— Is he—"

I shook my head.

"Oh no. *Mon dieu. Ma cherie...* I am so sorry."

We sat on the pavement, our arms wrapped around one another as we cried. For James. For me. For a love lost and the stark realization that he was gone...and I had to let him go.

CHAPTER THIRTY-THREE

"I wish you didn't have to leave," Marion said a few days later as she sat watching me pack my things.

"There's no point in staying," I said. "Except for the two of you. But I have an airfield to get back to. And my family of course."

"Of course." She got to her feet. "You will write, yes?"

"Yes. And you will come visit when you and John visit his family, right?"

"Yes. And when we have babies, you will come back to meet them?"

"You couldn't keep me away."

"I will have many then, so you will come often."

I hugged her to me, breathing in the scent of her lavender perfume. So many friends I'd had to say goodbye to in too few years. At least this time the parting wasn't quite as sad as others had been.

"I will miss you dearly, my friend," I whispered.

"Not as much as I."

I left Paris with a heavy heart. Not only for what I was leaving behind, but for what I had not found. I had been so sure I would find James, that we would fly home together, that we would figure out the life that would suit us both and live happily ever after. I had never been so wrong about anything in my life. And still, all was not lost, I'd realized. My journey had led me to other discoveries. To truths about myself I would never have uncovered had I stayed in Texas.

My strength knew no boundaries. When I'd lost all hope, I found a reserve that had carried me onward. I was not alone in this world, there were people who understood me, or who were at least happy to accept me as I was. And I was okay. Despite all that had happened, the loved ones I'd lost, the heartbreak in its many forms, I would be fine. My wings, though bruised and missing a few feathers, were not broken. I would fly again.

"It looks good," Nola said, staring at the sign.

"Why do you sound surprised?" I asked.

"I don't."

"Mmm–hmm." I grinned.

The airfield had been in good hands while I'd been overseas. Nola had left no room for errors in my absence, which was why I hadn't been able to let her go when I returned.

"I need you," I'd said.

"Even if you don't, I'm not leaving," she'd replied.

She'd met someone. But not just anyone. Tom Barrows. Sweet, goofy Tom from my childhood.

"She likes him?" Evie had said, wrinkling her nose.

"She loves him," I'd said. "He's exactly her type."

Tall, gangly and a little bit dopey. Nola was in love, and Tom couldn't believe his luck. They were engaged by the time I arrived home from Paris.

"Coltrane Field," Nola said, running her palm over the new sign that had been installed that morning.

"Don't muck it up with those dirty paws of yours," I said and she stuck her tongue out at me.

"Do you mind if I take the rest of the day off?" she asked. "Tom wants to take me to lunch. I figured as a thank-you I'd give him dessert too." She waggled her eyebrows at me.

"Ew," I said. "Go. Please. And don't tell me about it tomorrow."

"*All* the details," she said with a wink and hopped in her green pickup truck and drove away.

I wasn't sure how I kept getting blessed with such great girlfriends, but I wouldn't trade them for the world.

I stared at the sign with a little grin. I'd done it. There were times I didn't think I'd get here. It had been a hard road, and I was still recovering from a lot of it, but standing in front of this sign made it all seem worth it somehow.

I heard the crunch of tires on gravel and grinned. Nola was always forgetting something. But when I glanced around, I was surprised to find an unfamiliar vehicle pulling up to the airfield.

I raised my hand to block the sun from my eyes as the driver's door opened and the end of a cane touched the ground a split second before a man's shoe. My brow furrowed. I remembered the last time I'd seen a man with a cane. It couldn't be...

But the head that emerged wasn't blond.

It was dark.

For a moment I couldn't move, my eyes glued to his face as my brain tried to make sense of the scene before me. I blinked but he was still there.

"Hi there, little bird," he said, one side of his mouth rising in that gorgeous crooked grin of his.

"James," I whispered.

I took a shaky step forward, and then another, my knees threatening to give beneath me as I broke into a run, stumbling as tears blinded me. I threw myself into his arms and he wrapped himself around me, burying his face in my neck.

"Audrey," he said against my skin.

I pulled back and stared up at him, taking in every inch of his face, searching for something to tell me I was imagining him. That this was a dream. That he wasn't really standing here in my arms staring down at me with a look of such love and wonder.

I exhaled a shuddering breath and let my forehead fall against his chest.

"I couldn't find you," I said, my voice cracking as I shook my head. "I was there. I looked. We went out so many times..." I sank to the ground, my legs finally giving out under the weight of my relief, and he crouched with me.

"I heard," he said. "Rooney told me. Oh, bird." He lifted my chin so that our eyes met. "I'm so sorry it wasn't you who found me. I would've given anything to look up and see you standing there."

"Where were you?"

"Running," he said. "And then hiding. Trying to stay alive." He brushed the hair from my face. "I was shot down over Germany and had a nasty cut on my leg. I had to bail out quick. They had men on the ground with dogs and they were everywhere. I climbed a tree, wrapped my wound and waited until first light before climbing back down. I hid wherever I could. Abandoned homes, gutted automobiles, hollowed logs... I ate bark, rotten fruit—whatever I could get my hands on. It was—" his eyes filled with sorrow "—harrowing, to say the least."

"How did you finally get back to France?"

"After I was captured—"

"You were captured?" My heart nearly stopped as I gripped his hand.

"I was," he said, a shadow crossing over his face.

"Did they hurt you?"

He gave me a gentle smile. "Anything I had to endure was worth it to be here now."

My eyes filled as I sat on the hard ground, not caring about dirtying my trousers. "How did you escape?" I asked.

"I was in no shape to escape. At least not without help, which is what ended up happening. There were four of us—well, three that survived. When our captors left one morning to get food, an old man slipped in and helped us out one at a time and put us in a delivery truck. He'd been watching the house for a couple weeks but hadn't been able to help until he had a vehicle. Then he was forced to wait until both men left at the same time. They didn't do that often so it took a while. Once we were all loaded in though, that was it. He drove for hours, only stopping when he absolutely had to, and took us straight to a military hospital in Paris. First person I saw when I got inside was Rooney. He looked like he'd seen a ghost."

"He probably thought he had," I said, frowning. "But they didn't say anything." Surely Marion would've thought to write to tell me the news.

"I asked them not to," James said, pulling me to my feet. "I was in bad shape. Malnourished, my wounds infected, a few broken bones. The doctors weren't sure I'd make it and I didn't want you to fly back just to see me die. I was pretty vehement about it. So much so the doctor thought I'd burst my stitches."

"But, James," I said, voice broken, "I would have——"

He shook his head. "I couldn't do it, Audrey. No matter how badly I wanted to see you, I couldn't let you watch me die if that's what were to happen."

The thought of him sick and in pain was all it took for me to crumble, and he held me in his arms while I sobbed tears of sorrow for him, for me, for all the lives lost, whether with a hand to hold, or by themselves on the battlefield in a pool of their own blood, their mothers', wives', children's names on their lips. I cried like I hadn't before. In sadness—and relief. It was over. Finally. James was home.

"I love you," I said.

"Dear God, Audrey," he said. "I've never loved anyone more than I love you."

I hadn't wanted to be tied to a man, having always considered it a limiting life. A life of dependency and neediness. I didn't want to need anyone but myself. I didn't want to count on anyone but me. As I looked up at the man before me, however, I knew needing him and depending on him would never limit me—it would only set me free. With James I would fly with wings constructed of trust and dreams for the future, on a breeze of laughter and shared declarations of love. Love that I believed in. Love that I returned.

He stood and reached out his hand to me. "Think the owner will let us take a plane up?" he asked.

I grinned and rose to meet him.

"I hear she's a little testy these days," I said as he wrapped his arms around my waist. "But I'm sure you can convince her."

"Maybe this will help." He lowered his lips to mine and in that instant every awful moment of the past few years disappeared, and laid out before me was a future I'd never imagined, but couldn't wait to explore.

MAY 1980

EPILOGUE

"You ready?" James asked, squeezing my hand.

I leaned into him and he smiled down at me with that crooked grin I never got tired of. Even after thirty-nine years.

"Ready," I said.

A moment later the double doors at the back of the auditorium opened and two by two the small group of women entered the room, marching with proud smiles up the aisle, their dress blues impeccable, the overhead lights glinting off the buttons of their suit jackets.

I peered at each face as they passed, looking for the one I knew so well. And then I saw her—our Caroline.

Her blue gaze caught mine and she grinned the same grin she'd had as a child. Mischievous. Ecstatic. Unfettered. And as lopsided as her father's. She tapped her lapel. I glanced down and smiled. Fifinella, the mascot of the WASP, perched proudly on the jacket my daughter wore, ready to ward off any danger to come her way. I'd often found her digging through my jewelry box as a child, in search of the little gremlin. She'd coveted it from the first moment she'd seen it, and it had been my honor to give it to her this morning, thirty-six years after I'd last worn it on my own lapel.

The first years after the war had been the hardest; the scars James endured deeper than the physical, the nightmares sometimes unbearable.

His dreams of traveling for the army at a moment's notice had waned with his experiences abroad, and he'd readily accepted a permanent position at their base in Dallas. A month after he'd shown up at my little airfield he proposed. I didn't hesitate; there was no point. We both knew we were the only ones for each other and didn't want to waste one more minute arguing that marriage wasn't for us.

We married in a winter ceremony in my parents' backyard. I wore a custom dress my mother had made for me, agonizing for months over the tiniest of details, and in my hair I wore the little white bird Carol Ann's aunt Nan had insisted I take.

Coltrane-Hart Airfield flourished, the hotel full most nights, the runway busy at all hours with aircraft coming and going. The renovations I'd slaved over brought so much new business we had to turn people away. Every so often we discussed expanding, but ultimately agreed it wasn't for us. We enjoyed our simple life. And Nola threatened to leave if we did.

Two years after James and I married I got the biggest fright of my life. I'd been throwing up nonstop for a week before I allowed James to take me to the doctor—only to be told I didn't have the life-threatening disease I swore I had. I didn't even have the flu. I was pregnant.

"A baby?" I'd wailed, much to Dr. Hanson's surprise. "But how?"

He'd turned wide eyes to James who laughed, patted the doctor on the back and promised he'd explain it to me. I pouted the whole way home.

Seven months later, after I'd fretted constantly about the kind of mother I'd be and how my life would most definitely be over once the baby came, James Jr. came into our lives with a shock of dark hair just like his father's and the sweetest disposition.

I stared at him daily in wonder, marveling at how such a small person could make me feel so much just by being. Everyone who met him fell in love with his cherub cheeks and infectious, toothless grin. Not only was my life not over, it bloomed. There was now more love, more laughter and more futures to imagine.

Two years later we brought baby Michael home. Round and blond, he revered his big brother, following him around as soon as he could crawl, and into everything he could get his hands on. Whereas James Jr. made me feel as though I had the parenting skills of a trained professional, Michael made me feel as though I knew nothing at all, his exuberance and clumsiness a recipe for daily disasters. And still, as a family we flourished, taking vacations and running around the yard of our newly built home, our old smaller one quickly outgrown with the addition of a second son.

Despite their parents' jobs, neither of our boys had any interest in planes. They tolerated our excitement as we strapped them in and took them for rides, but flying wasn't in their souls like it was in ours, and eventually we took them up less and less.

It wasn't until a few years later when I was out for a sunrise joyride in the Fairchild PT-19 James had found for me and painted the same colors as Roxy that I felt a familiar stirring in my belly. I brought the little plane down with a heavier hand than usual and struggled out of the harness to hurry to the telephone. But the line I called was busy.

I grabbed my keys and jumped in my car, driving as fast as traffic would allow to the base, only to find James was in a meeting. I paced outside his office until the door opened and I pushed past the men leaving.

"Audrey," James said, getting to his feet, his face filled with worry. "Are the boys okay?"

"The boys are fine. You're the one who's in trouble."

We'd agreed two kids were enough. The boys were happy and healthy and what more could we ask for?

A girl.

Caroline Francesca Genevieve Hart was born on a crisp spring day in May. She arrived with a red scowling face, and a fire neither of her brothers had.

"I don't know what to do with her," I'd cry at night. "Nothing calms her down. I can't make her happy."

But one day on a whim I figured it out.

"What did you do?" James asked when he came down for breakfast and found the baby cooing happily on the floor beside me.

"I gave her an airplane ride," I said with a grin.

"A what?" He glanced outside as though he'd find a plane sitting on the lawn.

"Not a real one, silly. I held her in my arms and flew her around the house making airplane sounds. Look at her! Happy as a clam."

He smiled and shook his head. "That's our girl," he'd said.

"Our little bird," I said.

Now, James gave my hand a squeeze and kissed my cheek before limping to the front of the room to join the other officers as the rest of the audience in the auditorium took their seats.

"She looks so grown up," my mother whispered beside me. "So much like you at that age. I can barely stand it." She pressed a hand to her heart. "You girls make me so proud."

I smiled, taking in all the people who had come today. James Jr. sat with his wife, a sweet girl with wavy blond hair and pale blue eyes. Michael, single for the moment, sat beside them, elbowing his brother every so often. In the next row were Evie with her husband, Paul, and their four kids. Behind them were James's sister, Ava, her husband, Casey, and their twin daughters.

Nola and Tom had come, as had John and Marion, who lived in the South of France now with their brood of three.

At home were gifts from those who couldn't make it, but couldn't stand not to share in our celebration. Cards and packages had arrived from all over for our Caroline. Claire and her husband had sent a box; Ruby had sent something as well. And there were packages from Maxine, Geraldine, Anna, Beatrice and Annie too. I couldn't believe it when I saw the return address with Annie's name on it. She was forty-four now, my little pal from the island, and married. She'd married late though, determined first to go to college and study medicine. She was a family doctor on the island and Claire was one of her regular patients.

No one had heard from Tanya again—which didn't really surprise any of us. And Sharon, we'd learned, had passed away two years ago in a freak skiing accident.

The biggest loss felt today was for my father, who had passed a month ago from an illness he'd fought for years. He was ready to go though, and died quietly in his sleep just hours after learning Caroline's good news.

"Here she goes," Mama said, grabbing my hand.

I sat with tears in my eyes as Caroline stepped up to her father, who had the honor of commissioning her for this momentous occasion in military history, as the first class of women graduating from the Air Force Academy.

I could hear her sweet voice in my head so many years ago as James stood before her and pinned wings on her lapel.

"Here it comes, Mama!" she would exclaim, her little body squirming against mine, her green eyes, the same shade as her father's, staring at the sky with the same delight I felt to this day when watching a plane fly overhead.

Every morning we'd sit on our front porch and wait. Just after seven, the red crop duster would clear the trees in our front yard and she'd jump off my lap and run through the front yard, the dew on her toes, the wind in her hair, her arms outstretched.

My little bird.

★ ★ ★ ★ ★

AUTHOR'S NOTE

Although this is a work of fiction, that doesn't mean each and every one of the characters isn't real to me. I laughed with them, cried with them and ached deeply for them. In each of them is a piece of someone I know and love.

I first heard of the Women Airforce Service Pilots in junior high or high school. I knew nothing more than that they were female pilots during WWII. It wasn't until I found the books about them sitting on my aunt's floor that I learned who they really were—war heroes.

As depicted in the story, the WASP flew every plane the military possessed. Some of the aircraft were fresh off the production line, others beat up from battle and patched up to be tested before being returned to battle...and the men. The women trained "the army way." They were not enlisted. They received no military benefits. If one perished, her family and friends paid for her body to be returned home. And when the program ended, they went back to what they'd been doing before the war and the file on the work they did was sealed. It wasn't until 1976, when the Air Force Academy finally allowed females to attend, stating they would be the first to get to fly the military's planes, that the women of the WASP spoke up. It was they, in fact, who were the first to fly military aircraft. And they wanted the country to know.

Again, while this is fiction, there are moments of truth throughout, borrowed from the archives of these brave women's lives, and from extensive research on the time period. There are moments the timeline may veer a little, and I own that. But my job is to paint a picture and my goal in telling this story isn't to drown the reader in facts. It is not to impress with fancy words or my knowledge of flying (I am not a pilot and won't try to write as if I know how to fly a plane. I'm actually a bit afraid of flying!). What I did set out to do is entertain you. To give you a bit of history. And to hopefully make you fall in love. With a time period. With a young woman trying to find her way in a changing world. With the courageous women of the WASP, who risked their lives and received no recognition for their service until President Jimmy Carter in 1977 granted them full military status for their service. And later, in 2009, President Barack Obama and Congress awarded them the Congressional Gold Medal.

What I have learned from the women of the WASP and this experience writing my first book is that there is always a breeze. We can either hunker down and hide from it, or we can spread our wings and fly.

ACKNOWLEDGMENTS

This book would not exist were it not for the courageous women of the Women Airforce Service Pilots. Over a thousand women risked their lives to serve their country. And when it was over, they asked for nothing in return. Thank you for your service, ladies.

Had I not gone to my aunt Diane's home that fateful afternoon and spied the books that would spark my imagination, this story would not have been born. Thank you, Dakine. Your support of me and your selfless volunteer work for our United States veterans are inspirational.

There are not enough adjectives to describe my fantastic agent, Erin L. Cox, and amazing editor, Emily Ohanjanians. Erin, you held my hand and wouldn't let me stop believing in this book, or myself. Emily, you saw my vision, made it your own and honed it to perfection with your great mind and magical editing wand. To be paired with two fiercely intelligent women has been everything I could have hoped for, and between the three of us, we have shaped a beautiful story. Thank you both for taking a chance on me.

My darling pals, Rebecca O'Brien and Sarah Beyersdorf. Without your early readings of some truly dreadful drafts, and subsequent cheerleading skills, I may not have continued on. I am in debt to you. Please accept payment in the form of another dreadful draft of yet another story.

Jamie Pacton. Peanut. Partner in writing. Thank you for sitting by me that day and becoming my friend. Thank you for being in the trenches with me every step of the way. Your honesty, bravery and aptitude as both a writer and a mother is something to behold. I can't wait to watch you get yours.

Steph and Steve. You came late to this game, but you were game-changers. It is mind-blowing what you did in a matter of hours. Staying up late, drawing maps, schooling me on military terms… What you did for my little book, and me, is nothing short of miraculous. My gratitude runneth over.

No girl is complete without a best pal. Julie, I don't know where I'd be without your constant love, support and belief in me. In my mind we will always be just two little girls from Kent, singing in metals class, making Mr. Werner do the impossible: smile.

My parents, Pete and Sharon. My bonus parents, Al and Margaret Ann. Your support, stories and life experiences continue to guide and inspire me. Thank you. I love you.

My siblings: Sharice, Dianna and Peter. My first friends. My cocoon. You are the reason I love stories. You are my stories. You are my sweetest childhood memories. I'm so blessed to be part of this tribe. The Salazar Kids. I love us.

Last but not least, my own sweet family. My Cowboy Man, Danny. It is your constant encouragement and belief in me, especially when I falter and threaten to give up, that I cannot do without. Also, your love. Also, your guitar playing and beautiful voice. You inspire me daily with your grit and determination.

Thank you for showing me what success looks like. Thank you for always having my back.

Jackson and Sofia. My babies. Who would I be without the two of you? You are my guiding lights. My laughter, my heart. The inspiration that drives every word on every page. No one loves you like I do.

All the time.

Thank you.

THE
FLIGHT
GIRLS

NOELLE SALAZAR

Reader's Guide

QUESTIONS FOR DISCUSSION

1. Women served many important roles during World War II. This book touches on the female pilots who helped train soldiers. What other ways did women contribute to the war effort?

2. Did you know about the Women Airforce Service Pilots program? If so, how did you learn about it? If not, were you surprised to learn of its existence?

3. The story hosts a rich cast of characters, from Audrey's roommates in Hawaii to the girls she trains with in the Women Airforce Service Pilots program. Who was your favorite character and why?

4. The pilots in the story face a lot of discrimination from male officers who don't expect them to have the strength or brains to fly warplanes. Do you think society has come a long way since those days, or do men still discriminate against women in certain lines of work?

5. Audrey feels as if she's very different from her mother, yet they share some similarities. What do you think they have in common?

6. From the very beginning of the story, Audrey expresses her need for freedom. She doesn't want what so many others want—marriage and family—and is okay with being alone. Do you believe she could truly be happy without someone to share her life with, as so many of her friends tell her she must have?

7. Did you feel Audrey made the right choice in holding out for James instead of accepting Carter's proposal?

8. Do you find Audrey hypocritical to her lifelong wish to lead a solitary life when she decides to marry and have children with James in the end?

9. If you were making a movie of this book, which actors would you cast?

10. If you could read this story from another character's point of view, which one would you choose?

A CONVERSATION WITH NOELLE SALAZAR

What inspired you to write *The Flight Girls*?

That era in our history has intrigued me since I watched my first documentary about WWII in junior high school. It was a turning point for our country—and for women. They stepped out of the shadows of men and showed the world how strong they truly were. How much they could endure. And how smart, willing and able. Reading their stories and learning of their bravery moved me, and it became more a question of how could I not write this story? It may be fictional, but there is a lot of truth in these pages, and I can only hope I did this particular group of women justice.

When and how did you learn about the WASP program?

At some point during junior high or high school, probably in one of my much-loved history classes, I learned of the WASP. I didn't know much more than that they were women who flew military planes during the war, and I never looked to find more information about them during that time, but it stuck with me so much so that when I saw a book about them, I immediately knew who they were—and didn't mistake them for a bunch of angry bees.

Did you meet and interview any living WASP women?

Thanks to the wonders of social media and the graciousness of a helpful stranger on Twitter whose grandmother was a WASP, I was given the phone number of one Mrs. (Mildred) Jane Doyle, the last living WASP in Michigan. From the moment she answered the phone, I knew our conversation would be a good one. She was feisty, good-natured and had a mischievous laugh. And she reminded me of my nana. She was happy to answer my questions, which were mostly regarding a day in the life at Avenger, information that was hard to find from websites and books that mostly stuck to facts, rather than anyone's personal day-to-day life. Speaking to an actual WASP was emotional for me—and an honor.

What other kind of research went into writing the book?

Before writing the first draft, I read through a few books and then scoured the internet for more information. As time went on and I found an agent, we did the first big edit of the book, which led me to returning to the internet and finding more facts I hadn't read previously. Upon signing my book deal, my editor and I entered into yet another editing session and again, I unearthed several previously unknown to me details. And then, in October 2017, I went to Sweetwater, Texas, and Avenger Field myself and wandered the WASP museum in absolute awe. To stand where they stood, looking up at the skies they trained in… It was magic.

Is there a character in the story that you identify with? Or a favorite character among the varied cast?

It feels easy to say Audrey—but I admire her gumption, her willingness to evolve and her bravery as she kept moving forward despite the heartbreak, immeasurable losses and fears. There are other characters though that I would love to explore further. Ruby, a bit player, was fun to write. I'd love to see her journey before the war. And Nola seems like a complex woman, another whose eyes I'd love to see through. Carol Ann might steal my heart though. She was the perfect best friend. A little naughty, incredibly loyal and full of life.

What was the most challenging part of writing this book? What was the most enjoyable?

Keeping the dates aligned was the biggest challenge of writing this book. I kept a timeline of the war beside me, picking and choosing events to help guide my story. If anything big in the story was edited out or switched around, I had to scramble to make sure the dates still lined up. I'm not sure I always succeeded. Also, keeping the language true to the time period, but not overdoing it to distract from the story, was sometimes difficult. The most enjoyable parts for me were the character interactions. I love connection. Human desire. To be seen, loved, needed, appreciated. To have that denied. To watch what unfolds. Do they pick themselves up or do they falter? The intricacies of the human condition are intriguing to write.

Is World War II a setting that particularly interests you? If so, why?

I've loved WWII history since childhood. Knowing my papa fought in it made it more personal. Knowing he signed up at the ripe old age of sixteen made him my hero—he's even in a book dedicated to the underage soldiers of WWII—and ignited a fire in me to know more. I wanted all the stories: the good, the bad, the tragic, the unbelievable. On the flip side of that coin was my nana, his tiny, tough-as-nails wife. They wed the same year he enlisted and she stayed home to prepare for the baby girl they were expecting—the same baby girl who many years later in 2011 had a stack of books sitting on her living room floor about a special group of female pilots as she studied to be a docent for the new WASP exhibit at the Museum of Flight in Seattle that opened that year and continues today. My papa never lost his stern master sergeant voice. It echoed down the stairs as he shouted at us to stop running on them. But he also spoiled us with hugs, endured our bad movie choices and homemade plays and let us drive the golf cart. The Second World War shaped him as a man, and because of that, shaped his relationship with his wife, shaped his children and his grandchildren.

Can you describe your writing process? Do you tend to outline first or dive right in and figure out the details as you go along?

I never start a story until I know the ending. Until I can see it and it gives me goose bumps. I like to know where I'm going, but how I'm going to get there is always a mystery—and a fun one at that. I am definitely a pantser—but my left brain likes to butt in at times for a little direction, which I find useful for those moments I begin veering off course. Usually I pick three things I want to happen in a chapter, and then sit back and let my characters get me there. Also, the atmosphere may change depending on the genre of story I'm working on. The first book I ever wrote was dark and moody, so I wrote with the lights off and haunting music playing in the background. For *The Flight Girls*, I wrote at a desk with no music and nearly absolute silence.

I had a serious job to get done and facts to follow. For my newest work in progress, I find myself feeling a bit wistful. I daydream about it often and sometimes write a sentence or two in passing, while other times I sit in bed late at night, the quiet of the house lending a romance to a story that both intrigues me and makes me feel like a young girl again.

Can you tell us anything else about what you're working on next?

The Lightkeeper is another story following the theme of a woman having to not only make tough choices, but also to determine which are the right choices. It is about the bonds of friendship and family, and how they can drive our decisions—but sometimes blind us as well.